INTERSECTIONS

Chance, Fate & Destiny

$$\text{Outcome} = \sum_{e=1}^{n} \binom{n}{e} d^{n-e/2} f^e c^2$$

Where n=Number of Events, e=Event Number,
c=Chance, f=Fate, d=Destiny
Magnitude of c, f & d expressed as integers in range Zero to 100

Event: Past, Present & Future

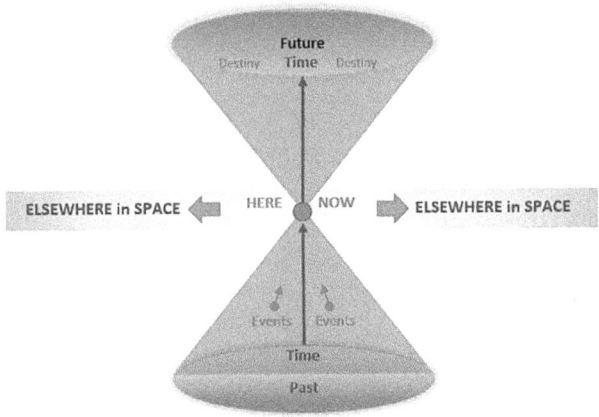

FriesenPress

Suite 300 - 990 Fort St
Victoria, BC, V8V 3K2
Canada

www.friesenpress.com

Copyright © 2020 by Maurice Schmidt
First Edition — 2020

Library of Congress, Cataloging-in-Publication Data
Registration Number TXu 2-134-811
Year of Completion: 2019
Certificate Date: February 07, 2019
Innovation, Science and Economic Development Canada
Canadian Intellectual Property Office (CIPO)
Certificate of Registration for Copyright
Reference Number 1156846 February 11, 2019
Application Reference number: 663257740012035940 Authorization code: 446094

Disclaimer
Events in this book are fictional and the characters and names bear no relationship to actual individuals. Any similarities are purely coincidental and aspersions, if any, against implied nationalities or otherwise are unintended.

https://storylinebooks.com

ISBN
978-1-5255-7206-7 (Hardcover)
978-1-5255-7207-4 (Paperback)
978-1-5255-7208-1 (eBook)

FICTION / SCIENCE FICTION / HARD SCIENCE FICTION
FICTION / SCIENCE FICTION / SPACE EXPLORATION
FICTION / SCIENCE FICTION / ALIEN CONTACT

Distributed to the trade by The Ingram Book Company

INTERSECTIONS

SYNOPSIS

Set in the latter half of the 21st century, the book chronicles the lives of a group of ordinary people from childhood to the brink of events with catastrophic effects in the offing.

Enchanted by Mars as the frontier of human endeavor in its embrace of space, the group enlist on a one-way voyage to the red planet to join the tiny human colony already there. Just as the New World of the Americas promised unlimited opportunities, so too the vanguard stood to open the floodgates to another world.

En route, chance intrudes with fateful consequences. As humanity struggles under dire climate conditions, the harsh reality of the interstellar void, just beyond our protective atmosphere and indifferent to consequences, unleashes a stark reminder of our fragility.

Swept up in events that have far-reaching outcomes on the course of history and the trajectory of human destiny, the group contend with diametrically opposing forces pitted against each other.

Our future stands in balance as the universe gives up one of its secrets.

TRIGGER

Some interstellar objects remain bound to their mother star, their destiny tied to the star around which they coalesced.

Others wonder the galactic void like waifs without a maternal bond and with an uncertain fate. The vagaries of chance steer their course, ever ready to exact retribution for straying from their hosts. Some carry a cargo that stands ready to inflict vengeance on any that cross their path.

There are those that find comfort in the gravitational embrace of stars that offer homage. They bring a perspective borne by the agony of their travels but their motives are sometimes questionable.

Do they adopt the status quo or secure their future by control and subversion?

WHY I WROTE THIS BOOK

The overriding reason is that I had something to say. I wished to delineate contemporary challenges and conceivable responses to them, since these issues, both political and real, will impact our future.

Lived human relationships and strivings in the context of Earth-shattering changes and developments likely lie in humanity's future. How will ordinary individuals respond to exceptional circumstances when they are thrust on them by chance? I don't believe in superheroes but rather that people sometimes rise to the occasion in extraordinary ways when challenged. In the narrative, I in part expresses this belief.

I also wanted to remind us of our place in the cosmos since its boundary is a mere one or two hundred kilometers above the humdrum of life on the surface of this planet.

The license of fiction allows exaggeration to make these points and to this end I wanted to express my perspective, granting that it is just one amongst many. I have no intent to impose mine on anyone but rather to offer the enjoyment that the imagery an alternative invokes.

Finally, the creative process of developing the plot and expressing thoughts in words is a sheer joy. Seeing the finished product in the tangible form of a book and the persistence of this into the future is admittedly another reason for writing the book.

Do enjoy the reading of it.

WHY YOU SHOULD READ THIS BOOK

Firstly to just enjoy the unfolding plot while at the same time immersing yourself in some thought provoking ideas and images.

The wide compass of the novel's vision and my attempts to penetrate and synthesizes a range of insights is hopefully part of the reason to entice you to remain engaged in the unfolding drama.

Although it is set in the latter half of the 21st century it remains grounded in ordinary human responses to circumstances. My hope is that it conjures up imaginary which is parallel to your daily routine. I challenge you to map out alternative paths in the storyline in your mind and enjoy living their fiction and see where they lead you.

INTRODUCTION

The book takes the form of a personal account interspersed with commentary on events that influence the narrative.

I have a special love for plausible science fiction and in an attempt to stay true to this form, have avoided unlikely dramatic effects or technology. That said, the story is set in the future with technological developments extrapolated from their current state.

I have frequently resorted to physics or technological concepts to further the plot, and make no excuse for using considerable amateur license to build the fiction. At best, I hope there is a grain of truth in the ideas but realize that an expert might disagree even with that.

Parts of the story are autobiographical and some people will probably recognize this. Actual places and events that left an indelible imprint on me have unavoidably crept into the book. Some of the better experiences will be obvious and I hope I have not given away too many of my negative attributes.

The book is dedicated to Karyn.

FROM THE EDITOR'S DESK

This is an ambitious and searching novel, which synthesizes a wide range of penetrating insights within a plot that demonstrates deep humanity in both its conception and execution. In terms of the themes and outlooks of the work, these include the wide compass of its vision, and the deep insight and knowledge informing this. Its presentation is of lived human relationships and strivings in the context of Earth-shattering changes and developments. It is able to delineate contemporary challenges and conceivable responses to them with precision. In terms of the execution and form of the work, the management of a plot of this scope and scale is a significant technical feat, and the techniques and devices adopted to achieve it are employed with great skill using variations in perspective and tone.

The perspective introduces many significant developments, often of a cosmic, astronomical order which helps conveys a sense of vast, impersonal forces that happen in a kind of cosmic, mythological timeless, agent-less space. This has a bearing on the themes of book, tied up as these are with the place of human agency in the universe.

Dr. Michael with Book Editing Services

TABLE OF CONTENTS

INTERSECTIONS

1

INITIATION

First, there was a ubiquitous density, bound by the power of gravity, a grip from which nothing could escape. Time itself stood still. Light denied its universal speed, the finite and the infinite, eternity, the past and the present, compressed into a singularity. The laws of physics as we know them were overruled by a higher court.

Then, with one stroke, a stronger force denied the hold of gravity, releasing a power that rent the density. Time began its march. A sequence of events unfolded that set new parameters for the laws of physics that would rule henceforth. The time was 13.7 billion years before the present.

A rapid expansion of superheated plasma followed. Small eddies in the plasma aggregated into gas clouds, where short-lived hydrogen-based stars formed, only to explode soon after. The force of the explosions produced heavier elements, which coagulated, only to explode again. Each iteration forged ever-more complex metals as subsequent generations of stars seeded the fledgling galaxies with a mix of heavier constituents.

In the present time minus 13.6 billion years, the Milky Way took form from this primordial mix, with frenetic star development in the inner reaches of the galaxy and less activity further out. Maturation into the form we know today took billions of years. As it rotated in its stately spiral, the galaxy's form differentiated. Zones of deadly cosmic activity sterilized some neighborhoods while the benign regions toler-ated a diversity of conditions, some less inimical to the formation of complex compounds.

The spiral arms of the galaxy flexed both with the momentum of the centrifugal force of the spin and in a north–south motion. Many individual stars stayed bound to their positions, under the impetus of gravity and the circular forces in their passage around the nucleus. Others moved to different arms of the galaxy. Belying the smooth majesty of the spiral, powerless to resist the ladle of time stirring the broth of fortune, eddies and swirls swept stars radially, displacing them closer to or further out from the center, up or down from the plane of the galaxy. These motions brought stars into proximity with each other, perturbing the orderly passage of the planets as they circled the stars that bound them.

Ejected from the gravitational bond with their mother stars, rogue planets entered interstellar space. Left to the vagaries of fate, they wandered like waifs in a dark vastness. The majestic progression of the galaxy obscures the regional chaos in its midst – and yet it provides stability that fosters living beings, as we can attest.

The explosive force of supernovae continued to enrich the elemen-tal properties of the carousel. After eons, rare combinations and circumstances conspired to allow the conditions for life to emerge in the circumstellar habitable zone, the less egregious mid-reaches of the galaxy. Five billion years before the present time, conditions were ripe for a paradigm shift from the inorganic to the organic, from inanimate to animate. Natal conditions for metabolism, reproduction, growth and death emerged, conforming to a cycle that controls all life with a certainty paralleled by the laws of physics and the evolution of stars and galaxies. The birth pains of archaic life forged in the extremes of supernovae or submerged volcanic vents, with time, dispersed to other habitats by force or extrapolation.

Quietly, unobtrusively, in the deepest region of the Orion Arm, an event, a spark, labor pains gave rise to just such an animation. First *in one locale, then in another, it was the fullness of time for this shift in template. Life from non-life, molded in a harsh chemical habitat, shaped and reshaped, the fittest form surviving to carry forward a prototype to the next iteration until a formula for reproduction emerged. Success, rewarded with exponential replication and diversification, pulsing with vibrant energy differentiating into rich variety, occupied every niche of a few, young worlds. Earth was just one.*

On a planet, distant from Earth, constrained by the proximity of a glaring sun and its binary partner, life struggled to occupy the beckoning lands, impoverished growth its legacy on this insecure footing. Insistent, resilient on the shores of its many seas, life adapted to the hostile emissions from above. It learned to build structures by harnessing the flow of organic and inorganic materials for its needs. Aquatic, beetle-like creatures no larger than ants combined algae spores, phosphates and silicon in the sea bottom to produce castles of coral-like habitats to guard against the elements and as launch-sites for seeding the environment.

Archaic cellular subdivision persisted for reproduction, spawning bloated globules encapsulating a cargo of micro offspring, algae and air for release into the atmosphere from the apex of the coral castles. Lighter than air, these aerosols rose to populate the surroundings. Settling on land, the discarded shells germinated moss from algae spores while the juveniles emerged from pupae as miniatures of their parents to feed on the moss, completing a triangular relationship: symbiotic collaboration between moss, algae and the little creatures.

The fruition of 4 billion years produced an extensive network of structures and moss fields along the shores of this our Exoplanet-**X** *where streams enter the oceans. Evolution labored to branch out beyond the limited number of actors under the onslaught of radiation from the duality of suns in the sky.*

As we know, misfortune guards its intentions, bides it's time then unfolds its dastardly plan with callous indifference. The cultivated laid waste, the constructed razed, all that was, becomes naught. The world of these small beetles whose struggles produced so much from so little bore the brunt of misfortune. Through the millennia, the star-pair inched closer to each other while harboring a giant planet in the inner reaches of their domain. Unstable in its proximity, the planet failed to stave off the attraction of the two stars, migrating ever inwards. Unsustainable in the end, its protective role of sweeping up stray debris expired. It plunged into the furnace of the nearest star, in its wake disturbing the orbital resonance of the remaining planets, the catastrophe localized but the consequential instability profound.

With the centrifugal forces that had held the outer planets loosened, by degrees they wandered from the warmth of the stars until their interplay with each other pushed our Exoplanet-**X** to a new equilibrium in the distant orbiting cloud of comets. By degrees, the warmth was sapped from the planet. It froze over and, layer by layer, snow buried all. Ice and glaciers held sway.

Meanwhile, the accrued weight of the giant planet with that of the smaller star sped the merger of the two stars. The beta sun streamed its atmosphere into the dominant alpha star until critical mass achieved an untenable union. The shockwave of the resulting supernovae cataclysm ejected all its remaining coterie of planets into the interstellar void.

Exoplanet-**X**, in its more distant location, escaped complete annihilation. Scarred but intact, it too entered the void, a rogue with an uncertain future and the inner warmth of nuclei decay it once enjoyed dimmed to an ember. The magnetic dynamo of molten iron at its core became sluggish as its protective shield weakened, its surface scorched, the promise of life all but extinguished.

Debris radiated from the annulled star system at impossible speeds, spreading from the plane of the solar system that once was, a carousel unhinged from its axis.

For eons, the march of time continued, relentlessly, with no sympathy for its actions. An eternity transiting the barrenness of space brought the rogue planet and the debris of meteors to their first encounter with

4

a coherent group of objects, the triple star system of Alpha Centauri. Orbiting each other around a common center of gravity every 80 years and with multiple planets in tow, the stars reeled in the rogue.

Striking at an oblique angle at the nearest pair in the triumvirate, lurched this way then that, first by the pull of the larger Alpha Centauri A (Rigil Kentaurus), then Alpha Centauri B with its Earth-sized planet in the habitable zone, the rogue narrowly escaped the gauntlet, only to be faced with the third star.

The faint red dwarf, Alpha Centauri C, loosely bound to the other two, presented the final obstacle in the planet's path back to the void. The red dwarf loomed large in the planet's sights, inexorably clutching at it to consume it in its inferno. Headlong it rushed.

Scorched by the fiery breath, helpless in its grip, its angle of entry was its only salvation. Slung loose by the impetus, it escaped, its direction bent to a new course.

The planet's target was now our solar system, 4.24 light years distant. Time, now a mere tenth of a billion years before the present, continued its remorseless stride.

* * *

The years have not been kind to Earth. Events conspired to alternatively devastate life and then stimulate its return. While the rogue transited the dark regions en route to Alpha Centauri and subsequently, half a billion years wrought five mass extinctions[1] to planet Earth, bringing life to its knees only for the remnant to recover with an alter-ego. Only the Holocene Anthropocene extinction event of the present stands incomplete but with an uncertain outcome.

Sixty-five million years ago, dinosaurs exploited the rich flora. Gigantism ruled until obliterated by a firestorm radiating from

---

1 Five mass extinctions in the last half a billion years: The Ordovician–Silurian events 439 million years ago, the Late Devonian extinction 364 million years ago, the Permian–Triassic event 251 million years ago, the Triassic–Jurassic event 200 million years ago and the Cretaceous–Paleogene event 65 million years ago.

Chicxulub, the site of a meteor strike. The event left an indelible iridium mark across the continents. Freed from the tyranny of Tyrannosaurs, mammals held sway, oblivious as the rogue drew nearer.

Earth shrugged its tectonic muscles and the mighty Pangaea super-continent spawned new continents, flotsam on a sea of magma, home to the dinosaurs until the comet visited from the clouds. Underfoot, through the eons, the magma roiled around its iron core, creating a magnetic dynamo that shielded the planet from the excesses of radiation from outer space.

Three million years ago, with Earth gripped by a series of ice ages, its oceans delivered vast tracts of snow to the landmasses, covering them with kilometers of ice. The ocean levels fell, revealing a bridge across the Bering Strait that allowed the migration of animals across this frigid wasteland. The fortress of ice eventually loosened its grip and the oceans rose. The English Channel, flooded by the rising waters, severed England's link to Europe; while the land bridge between Africa and the Rock of Gibraltar, holding back the ocean, spilt the Atlantic over its rim, forming the Mediterranean Sea.

Our mammal ancestor homo arose, holding sway in the trees. As the savannahs took root, the trees huddled in protective groups. Homo, shy of the open spaces, darted on all fours to traverse the gaps until, erect, they stood, the better to perceive their enemies. With their new stance, they expanded their range out of the cradle of their birth into the broad unknown. Speciation diversified their offspring to better endure the ravages of the wild as they settled the wide expanse.

Ages of ice waxed and waned; the forests alternatively expanded and contracted from Sahara to Siberia, with the mammals doing so in concert; the currency, warmth for cold. Some of their genus struggled when arctic tundra replaced woodland while others braved the cold with novel tactics to find prey. They succeeded where others failed.

A dominant variety emerged, leaving its footprints on every corner of the globe as it followed a nomadic lifestyle. Those less ingenious, or by chance, cornered in pockets, dwindled under the relentless cold.

Those of the Neanderthal stock, driven back by the ice, made a last stand at Gibraltar but finally succumbed to disease and lack of genetic diversity. Curiously they wondered what lay across the strait in the distant land, little knowing that their ancestors had first emerged there.

As the glaciers finally retreated, sapiens, the invasive species, occupied every niche from the tropics to the poles across continents and islands, overwhelming all that resisted. When the land finally gave up all to the hunter-gatherer, they turned to cultivation for nourishment.

The time is 10,000 years before the present. The rogue planet continues its approach, unseen and indifferent.

The sapiens, ingenious but without wisdom, fashioned a world to their liking while decimating the natural order. Beasts, subverted to their will, lent muscle to their endeavors, swiftness of foot to their explorations, or food to the larder. The inanimate wheel provided tireless motion for some when harnessed to sapiens' animate dominions. Distances shrank and the speed of communication increased. Knowledge was passed on; combined and enlarged, civilization was established. Villages and cities grew from congregations of peoples.

The intellect expanded the frontiers of understanding; resourcefulness fueled skills and versatility furthered the intellect to complete the circle of learning and advancement.

Galileo turned his eye on Jupiter and saw the moons. Kepler overturned Aristotle, explaining away epicycles, and Newton's apple elucidated the attractions of the spheres. Our imaginings saw channels on Mars and we wondered what Eden lay beneath the clouds of Venus. Emissaries roved the surfaces of moons and planets in search of water to find the essence; but evidence of life, the originating spark, eluded us. Turning the scope inwards we saw the orbits of micro worlds and creatures so small they infest our beings.

We wirelessly listened from a distance and spoke over mountains and seas. Observing the birds, we flew; we launched ourselves at Luna and visited Selene while in parallel the means of self-destruction mounted. We pointed barrels at each another and ignited the powder,

7

split the atom and sowed destruction, proliferating the means to engulf the world in deathly winter.

We look back and see history unfolding from the very beginning, time and events so distant, apparently without purpose; a universe chaotic, lethal at every turn, yet our existence stands as evidence to the contrary.

In recent times, the intellectual output of the human collective has grown exponentially. Devoid of empathy or concern for the individual, advances in technology dispassionately dole out their consequences with little regard for the participants, disguising their comforts under the rise of self while suppressing long-established norms of community and faith.

The march of innovation moved below the radar of consciousness, demanded a reaction that required corrective measures, or provided a lever for opportunity. While humankind busied itself with life's daily demands, progress unrelentingly built a considerable edifice. In its wake missteps abounded with catastrophic consequences. Medical science prolonged life expectancy yet offset this with overpopulation. Industry satisfied material needs but in return devastated the environment, spewing its excesses, threatening our very existence. Mineral extraction fed our insatiable needs while global warming continued unabated, raising sea levels and devastating vast areas, leaving uncountable climate refugees in its wake, flora and fauna not excluded. The age of the Anthropocene was upon us: the sixth extinction, Gaia shattered, a dubious distinction wrought by our own hands.

Nevertheless, the inexorable advance continued. Building on the successes of Hubble, Kepler, K2 and TESS, missions searched for exoplanets. The James Webb telescope plumbed the depth of space, identifying numerous new exoplanets, and confirming many Earth-sized worlds in the habitable zones of their stars. Excitingly, atmospheric oxygen detected in significant quantities on planets of two nearby star systems strongly raised the prospect that biological life might exist beyond the bounds of Earth.

Rovers roamed the surface of Titan in search of raw materials or traces of life. An international conglomerate established a permanently inhabited base in a lava cave on the moon that increasingly served up economic benefits. Supplies regularly ferried to Luna in exchange for rare minerals continued as robots tirelessly labored to exploit the wealth of the new frontier.

An historic first: a consignment from a mined asteroid made the first voyage back to Earth, opening the floodgates to follow-on missions.

Remarkably, the first 100 individuals established a colony on Mars in a one-way venture, followed by 1000 more in subsequent journeys. Humankind was no longer Earth-bound.

2

INTERSECTIONS

There is truth in the claim that destiny derives from a combination of will and circumstance, by control and by the whims of variable winds that blow first this way, then that.

Accordingly, I inherit the consequences of events that precede me. These may arise out of the callousness of random chance just as I also contend with the coincidental intersections of my life with the lives of others.

The will that I exert is limited to influencing a near horizon. I may cultivate relationships with specific people to build a future circumscribed by events that interject unexpectedly, but these efforts too may fray or dissipate if conditions dictate.

As you have seen, this tale arises out of a distant past. It overwhelms in scale and leads to a future that we cannot predict. In my brief history, chance has conspired to insert five individuals on a common path: Jabulani, Robin, Julia, Dmitry and I. We five are central to the destiny that unfolds before us. To understand the dynamics of these relationships I must introduce you, dear reader, to the background of each who contributed to what drew us together and then carried us forward.

3

EDEN

I cast my mind back. First, there is a void, a blackness, nothing. Then meaningless shapes and patterns emerge, punctuated with flashes of light at increasing intervals but with no concept of time between occurrences. Splashes of green form. Familiar outlines take shape, still without import. Then leaves, the sky, a tree, and trusted faces. Always reverting to nothing before the curtain sweeps aside for another glimpse. Place has no concept. The touch of objects, some soft, others rough, always gentle.

Suddenly the stark reality of a swing hanging from a tree pierces the foreignness. Grass below on a slight incline and the blue sky above. The first sense of place, but place without name. Again nothing. The sentient stirrings of a child take shape, solidify and gain meaning. The name "Miles" burns into my being, indivisible from my consciousness, and stands uncontested as synonymous with self. How old was I, less than two? How early in life can we remember things, recall from memory's store?

The place: Windy Hill, a village of fewer than forty people. A trading post, a refueling station and a logging transit point en route to a mill – it offers little else. It is here that my father worked in the trading store, gaining valuable experience for his later foray into entrepreneurship.

In my world, limited to the warmth of a devoted family and the back yard of our home, little penetrated my understanding or disturbed my contentment. The formative years of my life carried me through ever-widening circles of understanding as I began to glimpse an abstract picture of the universe from its inception to its present day. This was stimulated, in part, from living through a breathtaking period of human ingenuity that few experienced in past generations.

From this naïve start, people's lives crossed mine, some only briefly yet with lasting effect. Others traveled a parallel path from the point of meeting and then diverged. But my fellow travelers, the four, remained constant.

My parents, without compromise, provided for me during my period of dependency and growth. They nurtured me in my struggle for self-reliance before maturity and the shouldering of the burden of existence. Superimpose on this the rich variety of animal and plant life that Mother Nature shared with me – but which I initially abused through my innate ignorance before I realized the error of my ways – and you have a portrait of my adolescence leading to adulthood.

Windy Hill was my home until I was two. I have no recollection of the excitement that arose when my father and my uncle purchased a trading store of their own at Mount Elias, in a remote territory of southern Africa. The acquisition included two homesteads and many acres of farmland surrounded by virgin bush that stretched as far as the eye could see, interrupted only by scattered mud huts with traditional thatch roofs. The owners of the huts, our neighbors, frequented the store as customers, attended the medical clinic, collected mail and gathered for social interaction.

A road led from civilization through manicured agriculture, on until the terrain refused taming. Wild and remote, strewn with boulders, rivers and streams that dictated intrusion, held sway over progress preventing encroachment except by a determined few. The further you follow it, the worse the road becomes, degrading to a rutted rite of passage to a vast Eden where humanity gives over its dominance.

Forging its way into the pristine heart of Mother Nature, down, down the track descends into an extensive valley system, before rising to a knoll where a dry tree starkly stands vigil at its top. A short distance below and along a spur of land, our farm revels in a commanding panorama of the realm we borrow from the natural order.

The road continues past the farm to a school for natives of the area some ten kilometers beyond. There it ends in a cul-de-sac, where the land drops off to a sheer gorge, the course of the Mvoti River, which denies further access.

Buying the trading post precipitated the move from Windy Hill to Mount Elias, home to our two growing families for the next twenty-five years.

From all accounts, the property was in desperate need of maintenance, but the enthusiasm of the new adventure into ownership carried the adults, who quickly established order from chaos. My recollections pick up where routine has taken hold and all participants have their niches in the daily routine of life in this far-flung corner of the world.

A gap separated my eldest brother from the four siblings who followed in three-year intervals, with me being the middle child of five brothers. This may have contributed to my negotiating skills and independence, as I had to learn to contend with both older and younger siblings. My father's business partner, my uncle, added with his wife five sons of their own, closely spaced in age, with the eldest the same age as my younger brother.

Imagine a world where ten healthy boys share a playground of virgin bush and grassland that stretches to the horizon in all directions, interrupted only by ravines, fast-flowing streams, cascading waterfalls, rock pools and sandstone cliffs. The Mvoti carved its tortuous course through this landscape, producing a deep valley of a thousand hills from which tributaries fed the river. Birds and other animals shared our existence, and at times bore the impact of our amateurish hunting expeditions with sticks, stones and catapults.

The farmstead was located on an elevated spur overlooking the valley, hence the name Mount Elias. At times temperature inversions would flood the valley with a cold morning mist to produce a sea of clouds below, further enchanting the view from on high. As the mist dispersed in the warmth of the morning sunshine, it would reveal verdant, forest-clad hills and a distant escarpment.

A three-hour's drive led to the nearest supply depot and settlement for weekly attendance at the residential boarding school. It served to distract from the boisterous weekends and provided an education for later life.

The remoteness of the trading post imposed a need for self-sufficiency that tested the ingenuity of the residents. Milk, cheese, butter, vegetables, fruit, meat, clothing, water on tap and electricity had to be cultivated, tended or generated to meet needs. The need to experiment and invent instilled in each of us the ability to think from first principles. We learned to apply skills that we did not know we had and to develop capabilities that otherwise would have remained dormant. Basic needs and raw materials came in from the supply depot, along with tradeable commodities to supply the store, or to rework for sale or for own consumption.

Water pumped from a distant spring supplied a raised reservoir to meet our daily needs.

A petroleum driven motor, alternatively coupled to a generator for electricity or to a mill to grind meal from corn for us and for sale or trade with the locals, brought a measure of civilization to our rural existence. Electricity lit up the evenings for the two farmsteads and the mill provided a staple diet of meal for the breakfast table. The motor to generate electricity, with its incessant noise, ran from sunset to ten o'clock at night, disturbing the peace that otherwise would have reigned.

On one particular warm evening, I lingered beyond ten o'clock when the motor turned off and darkness flooded the moonless night. I lay on the lawn, feeling the warmth of the grass on my back, and gazed up at the spread of the Milky Way before me as fireflies flitted back and forth across the vegetation. The profusion of stars was staggering to behold. Away from light pollution, rural life frequently allows visibility of the stars, but on this occasion, the majesty of the spectacle struck home with such force that it inspired a life-long quest to understand our place in the universe. It spawned an insatiable appetite to learn more.

Books soon scattered my bedroom, showing long-exposure photographs of distant galaxies and illustrations of a wide variety of stars, and a range of planets and models of their orbits. Creatures of many alien forms and strange plants inhabited these worlds, driven by a juvenile imagination that knew no bounds. Yet a plausible version of these imaginings that may exist on these distant worlds was more intriguing than the fictional variety. The limitations – of distance and of technology – to observing the vista in more detail were a frustrating barrier even in an era of an explosive rate of scientific discoveries.

Back to Earth, schooling, a more tangible reality, took priority over dreaming. My weekly stint at the boarding school and its rigors challenged a burgeoning defiance of anything resembling discipline.

This was fertile ground for striking up a relationship with a suitable opposite. I befriended Robin, a fulltime boarder from a dysfunctional family that found it convenient to lodge him at this establishment and so distance themselves from the responsibilities of his upbringing. His father, tempted by greed, built an empire on the shoulders of the disregard for his family. His mother, cast aside, sought solace in the false promises that affairs offered, some resulting in short-lived marriages. Her salvation was a board and lodging stipend for Robin to ensure his separation. Despite this, Robin developed an easy-going character that belied the internal struggles that no doubt plagued him.

Our mathematics teacher established a rapport with Robin, built on the logic of algebra, calculus, trigonometry and equations that developed confidence that served Robin well going forward. Such was his interest that he spent his spare time solving puzzles of theoretical physics of a complexity beyond what most at his age could comprehend.

Unfortunately, one of the masters never missed an opportunity to scapegoat him for minor offenses. The master, mistaking his newfound confidence for arrogance, never gave him the benefit of the doubt or a chance to prove himself as something other than a rootless dissident – a baseless judgment stemming from the master's perception of his mother's character.

For my part, Robin's big city bearing, suave good looks and nonchalant attitude enthralled me. Compared to my low self-image and the limitations of my secluded country lifestyle, he represented all that I thought I could not be. This was fertile ground for me to act out my frustrations and for him to lead me down a path of defiance against adult conservatism in general.

For his part, he enjoyed spending holidays and long weekends as a guest at our farm, in counterpoint to his city background. We spent many hours hiking down ravines, swimming in rock pools and exploring the bird and animal wildlife under the canopy of trees besides rising cliffs.

In gathering our kit to set off on these excursions, we would often pass a single-roomed cement-block outbuilding with a flat corrugated-iron roof and two small, pokey windows staring out from the gloom inside. Framed by the door, a wizened old man, Mkize would greet us. As caretaker appointed by my father, he watched over the store of grain and commodities in a shed alongside the shop. He exuded an innate decency that, by his presence alone, deterred would-be pilferers from taking from the shed. His temperate bearing drew respect and deference from all who crossed his path. His countenance would light up with a glow of belief in the deeply embedded best within each person he encountered, a compliment uniquely reserved and eliciting a concomitant response, whether immediate or belated.

"Sawubona ibhungu, good morning, young masters," Mkize would say with a mischievous twinkle in his eyes. Then, stabbing the sky with his knob-stick to indicate his archenemy the hawk, he challenged, "You bring for pot. Yebo! Hmm, must taste good."

His self-appointed duties included feeding the free-ranging chickens, geese and ducks, and guarding them against the constant threat of the hawk snatching one of their brood. Without a timepiece to his name, he marked each sunrise and sunset with a precision that confounded logic. Even the sun seemed to obey his command. At these exact times, he loudly repeated his "Pik Pik Pikoook" calls, in response to which the fowls would cease foraging to gather at his doorstep and feed on the grain that he scattered in a haphazard line on the bare ground in front of his home. Inevitably, the hawk circled overhead, waiting for him to be distracted so it could sweep down and snatch a duckling, gosling or chick, to the raucous alarm of the birds and Mkize's frenzied gesticulations. He would angrily wave his ever-handy staff at the enemy as it calmly rose out of reach.

We would bow deeply in acknowledgment of his challenge, unlikely as meeting it would be. The hawk was too astute for us to approach close enough to do it harm.

The first time Mkize set this challenge, Robin, responding to the unaccustomed respect shown by an adult and not wanting to leave him with the wrong impression, said in broken English, "Sir! The hawk – too quick. How can we catch him?"

"Robin, come! He is just teasing," I said.

Mkize said, "You clever man. Tonight I have pot ready. You think of plan."

Robin frequently mulled over this challenge as, on our outings, we pressed on to our favorite river, the Makeni, a tributary of the Mvoti.

En route, we would pass a kraal. One day, a tattily dressed youth of our age started to follow at a distance to see what we were doing. He tagged along cautiously for many outings, until he discarded any reticence to become one of our group, despite his shyness. Jabulani (which means 'Be Happy' or 'Rejoice') – or more informally Jabu – proved a valuable addition, leading us through paths that we otherwise would have missed.

As the three of us expanded our pidgin language, he would point out geological formations evident as strata in the sandstone cliffs or lead us to overhangs where we could shelter from a passing storm. He was familiar with the location of different birds and their preferred nesting habits. Swallows and swifts in their abundance would build their mud nests high up and swoop down with high-pitched whistles to catch insects on the fly, or simply circle with the sheer exuberance of flight. The secretive purple-crested loerie would flash their exotic crimson underwing feathers as they darted across open spaces to traverse from one thicket to another.

Jabu explained, "Our king, he wear the feathers. Only he. When we have big meeting then he wear them. We protect the birds that they be not harmed."

"I guess it must have protected status. The colors of the wings are really beautiful," I said.

"Yes, yes. Very important bird to us," Jabu said. Then, "Look the hawk on the cliff!"

A pair of hawks guarded their nest on a ledge, lazily taking to the thermals that rose from the cliffs basking in the sunshine.

Robin, still intrigued by Mkize's challenge, said, "Jabu, you are an expert. How can we catch the hawk?"

Laughing Jabu shook his head. "No, no you can't do that. They too clever. Best we catch a fowl at home and take off the feathers. He think it a hawk."

"No, Mkize – too clever. We should get a rope, dangle over the edge of the cliff to the nest and give Mkize one of the young hawks. Miles, any ideas?"

"We tried that once, but the longest rope was too short and it was scary. Go with Jabu's suggestion."

Jabu, laughing, said, "Yes, yes! That best. I be right."

Clearly not satisfied, Robin continued to worry at the problem as if he were trying to solve a mathematical equation.

* * *

Only the interjection of oversight by well-meaning adults, the academic demands of schooling and my teenage self-consciousness detracted from the idyllic experiences that nature and the open spaces provided. One of the duties that I somewhat reluctantly performed was washing my father's vehicle. Once I got started, under the canopy of jacaranda trees, it was quite pleasurable. On one such occasion, I was busy with the final stages of polishing the car when the radio turned to unfamiliar orchestral music. The sounds captured my attention. I stopped to listen, enraptured by the harmonies tugging at inarticulate inner emotions. Despite my opposition to what I perceived to be adult music, my curiosity was aroused and I found myself wanting more.

Little by little, the music began to make sense and I became more discerning in my choices. To my mother's surprise, I asked whether I could take piano lessons. Progress in my lessons led to the purchase of a cheap piano to indulge my interest and her charming attempts at improvisation. Unfortunately, the work entailed to make progress was quickly brushed aside by more physical activities and my excursion into classical music went dormant.

Those first strains of music haunted me; I could not shake loose the inner stirrings they invoked. Juxtaposed with the experience of nature around me, the stars above and the threesome of Jabu, Robin

19

and me, the music anchored and sustained my growth and development as a person.

4

THE DIE IS CAST

It is a year late in the twenty-first century. The backdrop to the events that unfolded and each new discovery or development of our era captivated my attention.

With maturity came the humbling realization that my presence here was due to preceding events without which I would not exist. The asteroid that put an end to the era of dinosaurs left in its wake the emergence of mammals, including me. Deviations from the expected arc litter the course of history, each potentially thrusting a different reality on the players. The events range from minor to major happenings, some all-encompassing and some specific to individuals.

I struggled to assert my self-reliance and to shake loose the burden of ignorance of my youth. This struggle for comprehension of myself was very much a part of my need to understand our place in the universe.

I need to speak about the creatures I encountered and the role they played. They formed an integral part of my imagination and the character that I am. Without them, my life would have unfolded differently.

While the biosphere as a whole is magical, I singled out two specific inhabitants of it that weave a thread through the story. First, though, a caution: The temptation is to declare creatures that do not conform to a recognizable form or differ from our preconceived ideas as alien, but they are not. Take the grasshopper, scrutinize it in detail, and you will see two bulbous compound eyes, three lesser eyes, legs that fold backward and an abdomen that extends to the rear while feathery wings protrude from shoulders. If a creature of such outlandish design were to make its appearance in magnified form from another world, we would instantly declare it alien.

Earth produces a staggering array of forms, fit for this planet. Another planet will produce creatures with forms and functions to match that world's environment, beyond what we can imagine yet firmly within the realm of the natural order. The grasshopper is not alien, but its existence differs from ours so much that we cannot remotely comprehend its day-to-day reality; it may just as well be alien. This alternative universe intrigued me.

My daydreams led me to ponder:

We inherit this Earth, unilaterally, unequivocally, indisputably by imposition; all else is of lesser value in our estimation. Where do we get this idea? The source, precariously balanced on our shoulders, lolls back and forth on a slender extension of the spinal cord, a swollen intelligence quotient in a bloated cranium. This is the origin of all our claims. Then, where is the corresponding wisdom? What measure is there for that?

We look at the deer, the rabbit and the snake and conclude that these are for subjugation. They cannot be intelligent: look to their accomplishments and to ours: there lies the proof. Where is their pencil and paper? They have none, no language to jot or sign to articulate, no power to raise by degrees or understanding of the value of π to help them compute in infinite decimals. They have only instinct.

Our bias is our loss: to measure inches, why use a scale; to measure temperature why use a ruler? Then why use intelligence quotient to measure wisdom; there is no universal measure for sagacity and no common tongue with which to transmit the comparison.

Oh, if I could but for a moment be the hawk, the sparrow or the finch, to know, to understand, to live through their fears and joys and return with the memory intact, then wiser I would be.

Hawk

I, Kite the hawk, gaze down from my ledge high on the sandstone cliff above the riverine. The stream forms rock pools and cascades down waterfalls, crosses sandy beaches with stands of reeds. Alongside are trees that reach up to me but without interrupting my vantage point. On the far bank, the slope rises to the foot of the opposite cliff, adorned with thorn-tree thickets and fallen boulders. Caves line the base. Warm in the afternoon sun, juvenile rock rabbits play their games, darting in and out, circling the boulders, taunting me. The adults stand watch, knowing that one lapse in concentration may prove fatal, for I, too, need sustenance.

These same caves were once home to brown creatures who stood erect on two legs and lived in harmony in our kingdom. As time passed, misfortune had them evicted from their home by a larger species who competed for the same venison, berries and roots. The little ones departed for inaccessible highland regions. The caves stood empty, for the larger ones built their dwellings on the plateau near pastures, where they cultivated crops and tended oxen of a variety not seen before in this region.

Ancestral lineage ties me to this ledge as domicile. It falls to us, Kite and Aerie, to be mates at this time. We rear our offspring here until we must fly to heights from which we will not return, leaving our offspring to inherit this lineage and our names, which pass unaltered from generation to generation.

I turn my head upwards, and there Aerie, a mere speck in the distance, gracefully circles, leisurely in the rising current of warm air. With a forward tilt in posture, I lean off the ledge, open my wings and embrace the ceaseless wonder of effortless flight, gliding to catch the nearest warm convection and lift higher and higher until I reach Aerie and gently touch wings in greeting.

From our high perspective, the horizon stretches into the far distance: snow-clad mountaintops to the west, and in the east the ocean demonstrates the curvature of the planet. As we circle, our view turns to the south. There rise unnatural structures that soar upwards, sunlight glinting from them through a hazy smog rising from adjoining stacks that belch smoke.

The land surrounding these structures is broken, trampled and torn, haphazard in form where these creatures build homes from many strange materials. Squalor and waste surround them. The rural sprawl improves with distance from its epicenter, but tentacles radiate out from the nucleus.

In days past, narrow footpaths sufficed, later broadening to permit beasts of burden to draw strange carriages with round legs. These carriages disgorged a white version of the creature. In due course, a foul smelling black sheen blanketed these paths and an even stranger carriage appeared, one with no beast to draw it along. It sped along these paths, at great speed, to new sprawling settlements.

The intruders leveled vast tracts of land with monstrous devices that coughed and roared, drawing furrows in the soil. They grew trees in straight lines and then tore them down when they grew too tall, carrying them away to a great structure that spewed a toxic smell from its pinnacle.

Even with these changes our Eden persisted, relatively untouched. Juvenile creatures of the type that came with these strange carriages would frequent our valley, frolicking in the sparkling waters as I watched from my ledge. Adventurously they climbed the low reaches of the cliff, chasing rock rabbits who took the intrusion as a threat.

One particular juvenile often strayed into the valley with a companion, a furry dusty-brown four-legged creature of the canine family. Enthralled by the birds as they orchestrated their songs, augmented by the acoustic echoes from cliff to cliff, the youngster makes its way through the acacia stands. In flight over the riverine, I watch their approach. As is its habit, it waves a farewell to an aged being with a staff and then follows the narrow, winding path that leads from its habitat through the long grass on a spur of land overlooking the valley. Unseen by the youth but visible from above, bushbuck and hares disperse ahead of their passage or stand in silent camouflage, following the pair's progress from a safe distance.

As they enter the riverbed, a leguaan, a large member of the iguana family, reluctantly ceases basking in the sun and soundlessly, unnoticed and slips into the water like a crocodile hoping for prey. Then, sensing the size of the intruder, the lizard abandons its strategy to slither into its den, a deep alcove in the smooth rock just above the water line.

Intrigued, I follow the unfolding events as I circle above. The youngster, alerted by the movement of the leguaan but not sure what it is, approaches at an angle to investigate. The stream flows over the smooth rock surface to the left. The dog, taking a low stance with head forward, hair on its back bristling, stalks the darkness under the overhanging rock protrusion. Its master stands frozen, gaping at the disturbing behavior. The child tensely draws nearer. Finally, fear wins over the natural aggression of the animal and it begins retreating. Its master follows suit. Backing away, they frantically scramble up the bank, out of reach of the unknown menace, running to distance themselves from it.

As the drama dissipates, the striking similarity of the antics of these juveniles and our fledglings comes to mind. They too paint pictures in their imaginings, fantasies so vividly lifelike in their youthful minds.

On other occasions a threesome, one brown and two of a whiter hue, wander down the same grassy path. Even at my distance, I can see the effect of immersion into this tranquil kingdom. All pent-up anger releases. A joyful liveliness replaces apathy, a sparkle glints in their eyes in anticipation of the adventures the day will bring.

Many are the activities that engross them as they follow the stream downward, each bend in the course bringing fresh excitement of discovery. Geese, taken by surprise as they round the corner, their foraging in the stream interrupted, emit an angry squawk and take flight low over the water to another location further downstream.

By end of day, weariness takes its toll and the creatures begin the long trek back to their home, regretting that they were enticed to go so far.

Aerie joins me in my rotations up high as the sun sinks to the distant horizon. Storm clouds gather on the far escarpment and spikes of forking lightning flash, piercing the darkness beneath the ominous underbelly of the clouds. The air fills with expectation; a hush falls, anticipating the summer downpour. Not long after a fresh breeze blows to bring the first large drops. Swallows and swifts gyrate with plea-sure, feasting on the abundance of insects in flight. We turn and spiral downward, in a flash dropping to the level of the sandstone cliffs, gently alighting on our ledge to watch, safe and dry, as the storm passes over.

A crack of lightning splits the air and the downpour drowns out all other sounds. The release of energy mirrors the great sigh of relief as the land drinks the pure elixir from the sky.

The storm passes and, as darkness settles over the valley, the loerie closes the chapter, delighting all that hear it with the rising pitch and fall of its call. A moment of silence, then a new chorus starts: frogs of every size from chirp to baritone to bass join in a nocturnal mass of calls that echo from cliff to cliff. The throng reverberates in a cre-scendo across the valley until, finally, silence reigns and bats hold sway, noiselessly locating ripened fruit, darting in their zigzag flight from the caves.

The morning sun greets a refreshed landscape. Intense perfumes radiate from a profusion of floral displays. Bees under the weight of their loads industrially shuttle pollen to hidden hives. The river gurgles its pleasure with renewed vigor. The downpour has refreshed rock pools and the marsh-reeds sway, heavy with moisture. Weavers parade their exquisite colors to their nonchalant partners, flitting from one woven reed nest to another. Strings of shiny beads mark the excesses of the frogs' orgy; their spawn litters stagnant water like confetti after a wedding, dormant until magically transformed into a wriggling mass that marks the start of a new iteration of the circle of life.

The purple-crested bird, shy to give away its secret of crimson wings, climbs the tangle of vines that twist their way up the darker reaches of the brush. Like a parakeet, it leaps from branch to branch to break its fast with the fruit hanging in heavy bunches.

Delicately clad in feathers of softest powder blue, a family of waxbill finches inspect the bark and leaves of the thorn trees for insects. They intently work their way from one bush to another, or nibble seeds of grasses in the intervening spaces, hanging on the slender stems that sway in the light wind. They maintain a constant dialog of subdued "Seee, seee, seee!" as if calling their fellows' attention to what they have found.

From my vantage, on the cliff at the bend in the river, I see upstream in one direction and down in the other, my sharp eyes witness to all that transpires in this valley. Nearby on the ledge lie the first rudimentary twigs, a start to the nest we will prepare for our next clutch. Tomorrow we will line the nest with soft mosses and lichen and, a week later, will start taking turns incubating our next generation.

Unfortunately, our paradise is not immune to encroaching distur-bances. Grassy paths that stretched their tentacles towards us soon broadened and a sprawl of habitats now lines the roads. All manner of people in every color of covering wander down the paths to our quiet corner. They carry off branches and logs, fell trees and, later, carry these off, too, to feed fires in their abodes in the winter, the plateau a haze of smoke curling up from each home.

The adventurous threesome, juveniles no longer, of a sudden disap-pear to places unknown. My watch for them is now forlorn, dejected at the loss and at the degradation wrought by the intruders.

I, juvenile no more, return from my imaginings, the liberation of flight but a fantasy, the reality of the imbalance of nature as concrete as the ground I am rooted to.

5

AGGREGATION

As I have said, "The die is cast": the world beckons, the rudiments are in place, with two more companions to come before the stage is fully set. But for now, we must go our separate ways!

Adulthood brings responsibilities, leads to paths not predictable during adolescence. Robin, Jabu and I find ourselves separated by circumstance, but maintain a tenuous contact for the next five years.

My parents, through example, instilled a work ethic and sense of responsibility that obligated me to follow their lead once removed from their protective umbrella. There is little doubt that Old Mkize's persistent belief in my worth reinforced my self-confidence too. Overnight, I underwent a fundamental transformation from self-indulgent dissenter to a serious commitment to conformity, progress and career. Immersed in the corporate world I quickly learnt that I had a bent for computer systems, with a particular emphasis on the installation of business systems with interfaces to robotic subsystems, coupled with the economics of cost and benefit.

I honed my skills at computing sciences and project management. The addition of Astronomy as an optional university subject satisfied my early and deepening interest in the universe. Combined with the intrigue of anthropology to understand our place in this world, it broadened my perspective. A fantasy futuristic world of computers, robotics, life forms and space travel formed part of daydreams, now with something of a basis in fact.

Utilizing the ingenuity and versatility learnt as an adolescent on the farm, with my newly acquired project management and computer science skills, I built a reputation of successful installation of information systems.

Retirement age and a land consolidation project required my father to sell his property and with that, my bond to the pristine valleys of Mount Elias was broken. Torn between career and responsibility to aging parents, I chose the former when my brother agreed to attend to their needs. I immigrated to the west coast of Canada – the attraction: a project to manage the interfacing of robots to the accounting systems in a manufacturing plant for a local company.

* * *

Robin in the meantime furthered his interest in mathematics, extending this to eventually receive his doctorate and take up a position as professor at a prominent university. His analytical nature found a home in this chosen profession, resulting in a mature self-assured personality. Due to his early dysfunctional background, to the casual observer he often appeared to lack empathy as he critically weighed answers to questions, coming across as clinical and austere with a certain rigidity obscuring his underlying nature. In music, he found the perfect mirror to reflect his clinical approach, where as a pianist he found solace. He excelled at Bach's Preludes and Fugues, the rationality typical of Webern, Berg and especially Schoenberg's discordant compositions, skirting around romantic and emotional music. It lent Robin a detached, ascetic character while conveying an iconic calmness. At a deeper level, he was dependable for advice and friendship, with a considered confidence. Age softened his attitude when, as he confessed, it was a Chopin Nocturne that penetrated the barrier he had constructed, revealing more of the likable personality that resided within.

* * *

Jabu left his ancestral preserve to provide for his extended family, who remained in their rural home. Like many of his generation, swept up by the insatiable demand for labor for the mines, he found himself in a dormitory suburb of a big city. Dividing his time between the exertions of hard labor underground and stripped of privacy in a residential men's hostel, very different from the rustic existence in the countryside, he built a strong mental and physical frame and sense of right from wrong. It did not take long for him to take up a leadership role in the labor movement, leading marches in support of better working and residential conditions. His interest in geology, rooted in his early days observing the stratification of cliff faces and learning about the geological upheaval that these represented, became apparent from his observations of the rock formations underground identifying metal rich seams to exploit. Management awarded him a university scholarship, which he pursued with characteristic fervor. Activism within the student body was a ready extension of his union work: keenly recognizing political flaws, he participated in exposing governance failings at a local and national level.

After completing university, Jabu specialized in feasibility studies for mining investments. The geological survey company that had sponsored his university education employed him as a consultant. He traveled internationally to complete these assessments for client organizations. His sturdy physical presence and jovial attitude made for an easy-going combination that rapidly endeared him to acquaintances wherever he went.

* * *

With Jabu, Robin and I established in our respective pursuits we went about our separate routines with periodic conference calls arranged by Jabu. Preoccupation with the technical details of our separate professions insidiously wedged its way between us, causing divergent lifestyles and values. Increasingly these distractions masked the underlying bond established in our youth and threatened to dissolve the relationship by operating, as we did, exclusively at a distance.

On the last of these calls, Jabu began, "Hi! How are you two? It has been a while. Miles, what have you been up to? Wait, let me guess: head down and looking at computer screens? Am I right?"

"You bet. That and preparing briefings for management. I am rather bored with Gantt charts and system testing not to mention go-live activities. Then there are the infernal post mortems, what went wrong or could be done better. It can be a pain at times. I wish I had your way with people."

"Don't sweat, throw in a joke now and then and they will forgive you for any errors in your projections. Believe me. And you Robin? Have you found that elusive equation for catching a hawk? Old Mkize is still waiting, you know." Laughing, he added, "A bird in the hand is worth two in the bush. Now there's a formula for you."

Robin, still using his clipped, abbreviated sentences to economize with words, responded, "Let me see. One equals two – not likely. You wait, there is a solution. It is exasperating dealing with inconsistent variables. We should equate human behavior and nature in an algorithm to predict outcomes. With enough data, we can predict anything and steer behavior along a course. The hawk won't stand a chance."

"Okay, Einstein. Give it to your students for their next assignment. Miles, what say you?"

"Yes, delegate, delegate and delegate again. That is the way to get things done and the hallmark of all good project managers.

"I am still working in Vancouver on that robotic project. Now that is interesting. I love the control we can exercise over inanimate objects. Make them do all sorts of things. We have just completed the interfaces to the accounting systems and as you say Robin – with enough data it is incredible how you can deduce all sorts of facts that are otherwise not apparent."

Jabu responded, "Interesting. I'm phoning from Jack Hills in Western Australia, north of Perth. We are finishing an assessment for a new mine in the area. Some of the rock formations are the oldest on the planet. They date back 4.4 billion years. Exciting stuff, and with 4.1 billion-year-old biotic life discovered nearby, it seems obvious that they should avoid these ancient formations. It goes back to the Hadean eon. It would be a crime to disturb them. They are after the zircon deposits.

"Maybe I am in the wrong profession. I would love to explore the formations instead of looking at computer screens."

"True, that part reminds me of the time we spent at Mount Elias. I can't get enough of it. The trouble is that I then have to spend hours writing up reports and the worst of it is the travelling - endless flights in cramped airlines. But hey! I will survive.

"Robin, what are you doing?"

"Lectures aside, I am introducing a new curriculum. You know, challenge the new upstarts. I must confess exasperation with the 'human' side to the work. Far prefer solving mathematical problems and working with data."

As the exchange rambled on, my attention was drawn to the project plan on my screen, worrying about delays caused by scope creep or some other anomaly.

Robin continued, "Privately, I have been working on a new piano piece. Chopin of all things, but enjoying his music. Miles, is your music getting along?"

A spark of interest, my attention returns to the conversation, "I never thought I would hear you taking on Chopin. For my part, I have bought a piano and am thinking of taking lessons. It is a struggle. I wish I had your natural talent."

With my attention fully restored, Jabu remarks, "I hope to be in Vancouver next year. Would love to hear you both playing."

"Okay, okay, I will start practicing."

Robin says, "Actually, Miles, I am due for a sabbatical. What do you say to me spending a couple of weeks with you next year?"

"There is nothing I would like better. Jabu, let's coordinate around your dates. How many years has it been since we last saw each other? We had just completed schooling."

"Yes, and how time flies. We must coordinate. I so look forward to seeing you two."

Robin, uncharacteristically, used superlatives to urge that he needed us to meet. As the call ended, I closed my eyes to conjure up an image of life and our friendship as it was in our youth and the calmness that it instilled in me. With an inexplicable certainty I knew that Robin and Jabu, like me, on this occasion sought to re-establish the anchor that sustained us to meet the demands of career and life in the 21st century. I imagined Robin's struggles with the demands of academia, Jabu having to convince greedy mining executives to do the right thing and the stresses imposed on me in having to contain project cost, control timelines and manage resources. The prospect of shoring up our relationship, even at the expense of a year's wait, energized me as I turned to my computer screen with renewed vigor.

* * *

Two remaining participants, for which destiny had a role, make their appearance before the drama unfolds. Chance throws the dice and Dimitri and Julia make their entrance.

The quiet city of Penza, in the heartland of the Russ-kaya Zemlya steppes, nestles on the Sura River midway between the Russian capital and the Caspian Sea. It has had its fair share of historical upheavals, situated as it is between the competing forces of east and west in this great landmass. Starting as a fortress under the tsar, it later featured in Lenin's twentieth century revolution where he notoriously dealt with the insurrection of five kulak districts by urging the public hanging of many property owners under an anti-Bolshevik uprising.

Russia's exploits in space inspired generations of pride in their accomplishments. Nikolai Chernykh, a resident, shone bright amongst this constellation, in 1978 discovering minor planet 3189 and naming it after the city to give Penza a distinct cosmological mien.

Dmitri grew up under this influence, keenly following the breathtaking advances in astronomy in the twenty-first century. His interest originated from the inception of Sputnik, the assembly and ultimate demise of Mir, the first modular space station, to the collaborative work on the International Space Station.

His parents successfully negotiated the Soviet era, staying below the radar of attention of the authorities and emerging with housing and other benefits of the ideology that persisted beyond the collapse of the Union. One of these was the country's educational legacy, producing high quality academics. This provided admittance for their son to a mechanical engineering degree at one of the many local universities. Dmitri graduated with excellent results but economic circumstances in the new political dispensation made for few opportunities for the glut of graduates. They found the attractions of the West a distinct career option. Canada proved to be the country of choice for Dmitri where, as an immigrant, he coincidently secured a position as a test engineer on the project that I was managing. His engineering background and its basis in logic was invaluable in solving the complex handshaking between robots and computers.

A shared interest in tennis led to weekly sessions on the courts where, during intervals, we discovered our mutual interest in astronomy and music. His devotion to the classical genre of his homeland manifested itself when, on special occasions such as birthdays, he frequently gave me recordings of compositions by Rachmaninoff, Stravinsky, Prokofiev and other notable composers.

Dmitri, the antithesis of my preconceived view of people from the historic land of Slavic principalities, was a kind and generous friend willing to sacrifice time and energy to help whenever a need arose, whether privately or at work. With time, his unassuming attitude and equanimity emerged as the hallmarks of his personality, endearing qualities that sustained our friendship for many years.

* * *

The enigma of Julia Woodruff: as I later discovered, on the one hand profoundly artistic of temperament and on the other grounded in the rigor of the natural science of biology. An appealing ambiguity, a mystery that invites scrutiny with no guarantee of clarification.

Julia related how generations of her family made the town of Lillington home, situated as it is in the English midlands, a place where John Constable would have been at ease in depicting the old-village ambience on canvas. Of late, urban sprawl had disturbed the vista with rows of terraced houses and encroaching factories, rendering the town unrecognizable from its former identity. It pained her to witness the insidious change through adolescence to adulthood. The earlier era inspired her artistic representation of the flora and fauna of the countryside with matching impressionistic piano music, drawing on her artistic insights to develop her sketching and music compositions. As the environment changed under the encroaching commercialism, her discontent grew. Her art and music expressed a restlessness. The art migrated from a specialty of painting local flora in biological detail to an abstract rendering. The music became more discordant with a staccato form.

To provide a steady income she established an art studio in the village, catering to passers-by, and offered music lessons to the locals between lecturing in biology on a part-time basis at the nearby university, in preparation for a fulltime position taking effect.

Fate must have had its say, disturbing the established order like an indolent child looking for novelty. The encroaching commercialism on the rural environs and mundanity of daily routine masked a growing restlessness. An old oak tree stood in the town square, which the villagers proudly claimed to be the very center of England. As a child, Julia spent many hours playing under its spreading branches. One morning, en route to her studio, she was saddened to find the old tree toppled by a windstorm. As if to emphasize her downcast mood, a Canadian tourist passing through her studio struck up a conversation, leading to a comparison of the open spaces of the islands on the west coast of Canada to the claustrophobic limitations of the local environment. Intrigued by the allure of what nature had to offer, Julia explored Canadian vacation options and in time found herself walking through leafy trails on Salt Spring Island and visiting the art and craft on display in the main village. Impulsive as usual, she immediately started emigration procedures. In a matter of a year, having relocated to the metropolis on the west coast and with a commitment to a lease on a studio overlooking a vibrant tourist promenade with a view of snow-clad mountains in the distance, she settled into a routine and launched frequent excursions to the islands, documenting the native flora. Contentment returned, restoring her original art and music styles.

While Julia was in the throes of relocating, my parallel life also unfolded. Having settled into my newly adopted country, I busied myself with career responsibilities and resumed my music interests with lessons. My teacher, a concert pianist despite a deformity in his left hand, was an inspiration to me, enabling me to make some progress notwithstanding my basic lack of natural talent. We developed a rapport that extended beyond the lessons. Inviting me to a musical evening he hosted, I braved my shyness to attend what turned out to be an informal gathering of his friends who each performed a selection of piano music. The range of skills on display was intimidating compared to my meager capabilities. Later in the evening, a captivating blue-eyed brunette took her turn performing Mozart, Rachmaninoff and a toccata for piano she had composed – a lively exciting piece with a refreshing naiveté. My teacher introduced her as Julia.

We departed the evening to go our separate ways. A couple of months passed and chance again intruded. Seeing her at a bus stop, I offered her a lift. It transpired that her studio and my place of work were in the same vicinity. The result was that we shared our daily commute on a routine basis, enabling us to become close friends with, from my perspective, the hope for more.

With that, the final piece in the puzzle is in place.

* * *

Summer months on the west coast are magical. By invitation as related earlier, Robin decided to spend part of his university sabbatical with me. Julia joined us and led us to her haunts on excursions to the many islands, snowy mountains, dark foreboding forests and bright emerald trails set against a backdrop of seascapes.

Ever busy is Dmitri, embroiled in the depth of a project-testing phase. Tied to his desk to confirm linkages between robots and our new business applications, he envied me luxuriating in the open spaces.

The missing fifth wheel, Jabu, as anticipated was on a geological assessment assignment, holed-up in a local hotel putting the final changes to his feasibility report. The completed product, sent to his superiors for review, came back with a positive response. Accompanying the reply was an invitation to a workshop open to professional acquaintances. Without being specific on details, it was couched as a no-obligation recruitment drive; it promised to be entertaining and challenging.

He extended the invitation to me.

"Jabu, I have a dilemma. I have arranged to have dinner with Robin and someone named Julia. She is a very interesting person. I would like to introduce her to you some time. I don't think I can make it."

Jabu cajoled, "You can always postpone the dinner for another day. The restaurant will not mind. Come on! It will be interesting. And you know me, I prefer not to attend on my own. Guaranteed – it will be interesting." Then he added, "Do I detect more than what you call 'an interesting person'? Tell me more."

Blushing despite being on the phone, I replied, "No, no. I err… You will see. Wait and see."

Somewhat reluctantly, I agreed, having looked forward to spending time with the other two. "Okay. I will postpone dinner, but I suggest that Dmitri be included. I know that he is at a loose end and it was my intention to invite him to the dinner."

As an afterthought I added, "Oh but that won't work. He is not an acquaintance of yours. They only want acquaintances of yours at the workshop, right?"

Jabu was quick to compensate, "How about this as a compromise. To lend some authenticity to the 'acquaintances' requirement, we could meet over lunch tomorrow. That way you have something of a dinner and it satisfies the workshop requirement." Laughing he added, "You see, I can then extend the invitation to the workshop to the other three as well. We will then all be acquaintances."

With that, I changed the dinner arrangements and on the following day, the five of us settled down at a lunch table.

Robin was quick to remark on Jabu's appearance. "Jabu, you have filled out. And can I say you have become a remarkable specimen," he teasingly added.

Jabu, jovial as usual, replied, "It must be all the lugging of equipment and the hard labor underground at the mine. Can't say I miss it."

After introducing Julia and Dmitri, we questioned Jabu for more details about the workshop.

He said, "I don't want to appear evasive, but I am really at a loss to provide more information except to say they have a record of being innovative and progressive. From all accounts, their workshops really are interesting. I wish I could tell you more. I find it intriguing that they would not give us even a hint of what the subject matter might be."

After exhausting a round of speculations as to what it might be about, we gave up and the discussion turned to other topics; discovering common interests, the lunch turned into a lively discussion on a wide range of topics. We thoroughly enjoyed the occasion and agreed to meet again after the workshop.

* * *

The workshop does not disappoint.

Supported by slides projected on a screen the speaker introduced himself as Stanley, Director of Operations, and explained the proposal while the audience hung on every word in rapt attention.

"I am proud to announce a joint venture between ECO Search Consulting and Bedrock Mining INC. We will be collaborating to establish a foothold on Mars."

The audience stirred, excitement palpable as he continued.

"Yes! You heard correctly. Mars!"

"As you know, there are over one thousand people already on Mars and more en route. This is the new frontier! A new world is opening up. Our intent is to be at the forefront of this, humankind's bold step to reach out beyond our home planet."

"The initiative is to service the escalating demand for raw materials to meet local needs and with the potential of one day exporting rare minerals to the Earth. The momentum for growth is definite. There is no doubt about that."

"The initial focus will be on basic needs such as mining ice for drinking water and for use by industry. We also intend to quarry for construction materials and later expand to other substances. The venture, characterized as a viability prototype, has a strong probability of permanence as Mars becomes fully sustainable.

"Well, you may wonder what this has to do with you. We need you!"

He allowed the full impact for his words to take hold, and then continued.

"The two sponsoring companies, operating under the name *Overture*, will invest in a group of voyagers with the proviso that they commit to a one-way journey. Yes, a one-way journey. That is unless *Overture*, abandons the endeavor. In this case, we will carry the cost of the return journey. Given the scarcity of supplies on the surface, provisions and accommodation will be included at no cost along with an attractive remuneration – essentially a fully paid-for expedition for twenty-five years. In addition to the core team, analysts and other support personnel are to be included. I am sure you will agree that it is a very generous proposal, if you have a pioneering spirit."

A prolonged description of conditions on Mars followed; a review of the surveys already done from orbit, new assessments, how resource extraction would proceed and the degree of automation used.

As the address continued, with the audience spellbound, I glanced over at Jabu and Dmitri. Mesmerized, I could see parallels drawn with their work experience. Most of the automation would use robotic technology and the surveys would need geological input, both directly related to their professions.

My interest was piqued both as a project manager and as a computer specialist, and I could see Robin likewise wondering what the analyst role would entail. Only people unmarried at the time of departure qualified for inclusion. Interested parties were to submit a résumé within two months, and the departure date was set as six months hence. Emphasizing the dangers of space travel, in particular the launch and landing operations, participants had to absolve *Overture* of all liabilities except for negligence. He cautioned that conditions on the surface of Mars, without a protective atmosphere like Earth's, may have negative health consequences that must be accepted, but medication will be provided that will virtually eliminate these effects.

In conclusion, he said, "In addition to being Director of Operations, I will be spokesperson for *Overture*. As such if you have any questions please direct them to me and I will try to give you answers. Thank you for attending."

* * *

As soon as the following day we were back at the lunch table, clearly aroused by the possibilities. I, for one, could not see any reasons for not taking up the challenge. The prospect of being among the first to explore a new world thrilled, as did the sheer audacity of the venture. Likewise, Jabu and Dmitri's credentials provided an absolute match for the requirements, but Robin and I would need to make a pitch for inclusion. Julia, while interested, lacked the qualifications given the paucity of life on Mars, if any, rendering her biology education, music and artistic background non-starters.

She accepted this and, excited by our enthusiasm, jokingly offered, "I can be the Earth-bound liaison, keeping you informed of developments here, back at home."

Jabu, every ready with his wit, put in, "War of the Worlds, the Martians came; now the Earthlings take revenge."

We resolved to submit our applications, stipulating that we be accepted as a group and that they deploy us as such.

The unreality of the prospect overshadowed the anxiety of acceptance, albeit a low probability for Robin and me. We waited with mounting anticipation. Finally, the response came; we had to present ourselves for separate interviews. Again, the interminable wait before the news that Jabu and Dmitri were accepted based on their respective professions. For Robin, his acceptance was in a data analyst role overseeing survey results and monitoring production parameters, the offer founded on his mathematical expertise. For my part, acceptance also came through; my role being project oversight stemming from the versatility I had demonstrated on projects to date, for which I quietly thank my early childhood days at Mount Elias. Final approval was subject to a psychological review for each of us separately and as a group since that was our stipulation. We passed these without problems.

It remained for us to confirm our decisions.

The other three did not take long to decide in favor of going. I must confess that in my case a factor that I did not anticipate was increasingly on my mind. I had developed an unspoken fondness for Julia. The prospect of a life without her overwhelmed my thoughts. I may have acted on my feelings towards her by then were it not for my general shyness, but a marriage proposal then would disqualify me from the venture. What to do? Torn between staying and going I vacillated without decision. The agony of indecision depressed, and I withdrew into a shell of solitude that soon became apparent to my friends.

Stating the obvious, Jabu was first to remark, "Now Miles. Why the downcast look." Glancing across at Julia to see her reaction he continued, "May I guess? Is there an 'interesting' person you are worried about?"

Turning red and stammering, I replied, "It is just that, I… there is a lot to worry about. Well…"

Dmitri came to the rescue. "Miles. I have aging parents back home and it tears me apart to think that I may never see them again. You like me have family that can take care of their needs. They will be okay. You seldom see them anyway, living here as we do on the other side of the world. You can still maintain contact with them."

Robin elaborated, "You guys are the closest thing I have to family. If you stay, I will decline as well. All four of us or I am out."

That took the wind out of my sails. "I know you mean well Robin, but that adds to the pressure of a decision."

Jabu persists, "I think there is more to it than that. Come on, to me it looks like the forlorn look of an abandoned devotee. Am I right? Julia, you are a biologist, what do you think ails this dear, dear specimen of ours?"

"Okay, since you ask. Miles and I have become very close, I confess. Miles is so, so dear to me that it hurts just thinking about not seeing him. Miles, am I right? Is this what is worrying you, because if it is, I think you need to be more fatalistic. What will be - will be. Providence will incline to the best outcome. Just give it a chance."

It surprised me to hear this from Julia and certainly raised my spirits. However, a committee decision did not do much for my self-esteem, but I was then not in a position to do otherwise and committed myself to the venture. On the positive side, Julia and I were inseparable for the remaining period.

6

EN ROUTE

Of minor importance at the time but with far-reaching ramifications for all of us came news of the sighting of an interstellar object approaching our solar system. This was Earth's fourth recorded interstellar visitor, astronomical designation 4I/2047 U1, later named Nuntius, meaning "the messenger." It entered our solar system at a diagonal relative to the ecliptic plane. Traveling at an incredible speed, the asteroid (later assessed to be a comet) picked up speed in its approach, narrowly skirting the sun. It slowed in its retreat but maintained an escape velocity compounded by the slingshot effect of the sun to re-enter interstellar space, lost to the solar system forever. The odd shape, a mere 230 X 35 meters, on closer examination appeared to be the resultant splinter from an impact in the relatively recent past – not a comet after all. It bore no sign of micro-cratering characteristic of life during the prolonged chaotic formative years of planets around stars, the burnt dark-reddish hue due to millions of years of cosmic ray radiation. Two years earlier the third recorded interstellar visitor had appeared, 3I/2045 BZ1. This one did not escape the solar system, but lies captive in a stable but retrograde orbit around Jupiter, believed by scientists to be unrelated to the 2047 visit.

* * *

Imagine: in six months, the very meaning of home, possessions and work transformed for all time. Friends, family and loved ones suspended in a virtual reality; physical contact a fiction. These thoughts surface periodically in the rush of preparations but quickly extinguish under a mixture of excitement and organization for the future. Those dearest to us, prepared as if for an imminent funeral, fluctuating between sadness and concerns for the dangers, but also sharing in the excitement.

My attachment to Julia deepened, creating a schizophrenic struggle between the predictable and the unpredictable, between a stable future potentially shared with Julia and the uncertain desolation of space. Julia, unswayed, stood firm in the trust that resolutions would come.

Life in this unreality persisted unperturbed outside the narrow confines of our existence. As the window of preparation quickly narrowed, a steady increase of news of catastrophic hurricanes, widespread drought and flooding of coastal regions abounded, global warming accelerating under the influence of humankind's onslaught on the atmosphere. Unbelievably, climate-change deniers continued in their discord despite the obvious and mounting evidence to the contrary. For us, the rapidity of developments cast a shadow over our venture, raising concerns for those left behind. How would they withstand nature unrestrained by a conventional biome? It was a question that exacerbated the internal conflict that raged in my mind over abandoning Julia to these events.

Turmoil surrounded us as the final day approached. Logistical matters took center stage – closure brought to so many loose ends, resolving conflicting legal priorities, accommodating family needs and attending to unavoidable operational needs. At last, the training sessions for the intrepid – some would say foolish – travelers was behind us and adrenaline ran high as we anticipated departure.

The plan was to ferry 200 passengers in groups of 10 to rendezvous with the orbiting transit vehicle, *Forerunner*. A private company contracted to carry the human cargo to a geo-stationary orbit stood at the ready at Kourou, French Guiana. We said emotional farewells at the airport in Canada, and once aboard the charter plane to the equator reality set in: we were on our way to a new beginning.

The turbulence en route, a legacy of the hurricanes that had passed across the Caribbean in prior days, jarred us out of our self-centered bubble; a reminder of the uncertain weather conditions our loved ones would have to endure in our absence. Finally, the plane put down to a bumpy landing in a clearing with launch infrastructure near at hand within a sea of tropical jungle. Our ascent vehicle stood ready at the pad, a stark incongruous presence, ready to whisk us away to another dimension.

Disembarking from the plane, we boarded a bus to the local village. Once there, in sweltering humidity, we spent a few nights at the hotel at Kourou waiting for the flight window to open. Forced laughter relieved the building tension of an impatient wait. When the hour arrived, dressed in safety gear and looking like astronauts, we walked up the gangway to the rocket. I found myself looking about at the surrounding lawns leading to the endless trees, the sky a deep azure blue and the ocean in the distance. Was this the last sight of Mother Earth at close quarters? The impulse was to freeze the image in the mind's eye, secured in place for instant recall in the event that I needed to reverse time.

We boarded the rocket and the hatches closed with finality. No turning back now!

The training did not fully prepare us for the rigors of crosschecks in the crammed space mandated for takeoff, but finally the countdown began. T-MINUS 10...9...8...7...6...5...4...3...2...1... We have LIFT OFF! Thrust of 12,500 kN in the first stage of the 35,000 KM elevation is nothing less than terrifying. By contrast, the weightlessness of space, once reached, offered a profound relief, a novelty to become blasé about by the end of the 200-day passage to Mars. As we coasted to the rendezvous point, we marveled at the receding sight of the Earth, locking in the memory of our birthplace. As Earth waned, our staging post crystalized from a point of light to a bright ring sparkling against a backdrop of a myriad of stars. It reminded us of our place in the universe, the limitations of one lonely planet in the entire expanse before us. Our decision seemed justified; we, the vanguard of human endeavor.

The *Forerunner* transit vehicle was constructed as a wheel: a central hub from which radiated spokes with pods tethered at the end, each linked to its neighbor to form a vast carousel measuring a kilometer in diameter. Rotating slowly to artificially provide 0.38 Earth-equivalent gravity, it simulates that of Mars. When underway the electromagnetic thrust centered on the hub propels the entire structure forward or provides braking capabilities. The pods each accommodate four people, and employ computer synchronized thrust of their own to maintain pace with the central hub, whether accelerating or decelerating, to ensure the integrity of the whole system. Each spoke, a flexible woven Nano-constructed cable of exceptional strength fitted with a module, ferries travelers back and forth between the pods and the hub.

Our destination was the central hub, then to our home pods at the extremities for the duration of the journey. The hub, pods and ferries are hardened to withstand solar radiation with a magnetized surface to deflect even the most energetic particles, simulating the protective magnetosphere around the Earth. The pods, individually detachable from the carousel, with a partial aerodynamic design, provide limited gliding capabilities in the latter stages of entry into the Martian atmosphere. They are reusable to the extent that they can be mounted atop a launching rocket should the need arise to leave Mars.

Like moths around a flame, supply craft frenetically completed the provisioning of the pods and hub as departure loomed. Robin, Jabu, Dmitri and I calmly settled into our temporary domicile while organized chaos surrounded us. We took stock of our new surroundings, each staking a claim to our preferred personal space. The pod comprised sleeping quarters, an ablution closet and a living room with open space to a kitchenette. The furnishing was sparse but functional, catering for the long journey with limited freedom of movement. It included a television with a range of canned viewing material, a library of electronic books and a digital piano, specifically included in all the pods at my request, to alleviate the challenge of boredom and to further creative inclinations. The sleeping quarters were near the nose cone, with each bunk aligned to provide maximum privacy. The ablution closet was sealed against dispersion of humidity with water purification and recycling where appropriate. Rationing of water to conserve the supply was mandated, although it could, to a limited extent, be replenish from the hub if necessary. An array of compact foldaway contraptions for exercise were at hand in the living room. A 10-inch telescope stood poised in front of a viewing window that looked away from the hub. On the opposite side was a smaller window that provided a view of the central hub. A touch panel provided rudimentary navigation capabilities, radio communication and status information on a display screen optionally doubling as a television.

Comfortable in our quarters, we settled down to a routine and watched the activity around the hub. Eager to be underway we waited for the optimum departure time to arrive, which was calculated based on the alignment of the orbits of Mars and Earth to minimize fuel and flight duration, timed down to a precise day and hour.

The countdown started. The dramatics of the rocket launch from Kourou were absent, as the centrifugal gravity provided by the motion around the hub continued before another movement augmented the sensation. Imperceptible at first, forward motion of the whole structure slowly took effect, avoiding stresses on any of the components.

We were underway!

After an hour, movement was more discernable as the pods adjusted alignment to a new center of gravity. An hour later changes in the scenery of stars and the sun, relative to the moon circling the Earth, were noticeable.

Mars at opposition was 55 million kilometers away, with 200 days and many hours to ponder our decision, to think of those left behind and wonder at what lay ahead. My first thoughts were of Julia. I dispatched a message, assuring her that we were safe and expressing the hollowness of not having her present. I missed her. Thus started a frequent dialog across the ocean of space as time, stretched by distance, caused each message to take longer and longer for the reply.

The first half of the journey was under constant acceleration but even at the incredible speed reached, we could barely make out progress as seen against the distant stars. Earth, however, slowly receded to the vaunted blue dot, its significance diminishing in importance to us as the center of our universe, subverted by Mars as it occupied the new epicenter. We began the mental transition from Earth-bound to the new focal point.

* * *

Did I mention one small contribution that I made to the coming events? Probably not, but my interest in foreign star systems and the planets they support, with the potential for life on them, led to my enrollment in the SETI@HOME program. As one of thousands who made their home-based computing power available to the initiative, I processed some of the voluminous data they have on file, looking for the telltale signature of extraterrestrial intelligence in the random noise of the universe. Inquisitive at my interest, it thrilled me to introduce Julia to the world of an imaginary alien civilization, and I found a ready convert. The possibility of biology, her field of expertise, beyond Earth intrigued her. True to form, as news broke of oxygen being detected on multiple exoplanets, Julia quickly expanded her interest into other online programs related to the subject, using spare time to indulge in this fancy.

Now as we hurtled through space to our destination, sitting at her desk, absorbed in looking at the data flashing on the screen, Julia examined patterns in the changing images before her. Her subscription to the publicly available Google Artificial Intelligence (GAI) system enabled the computer to learn from archival data obtained by NASA's planet-hunting Kepler telescope dating back decades through to as recent as a few months ago. Piqued by the inability to locate the origin of the two recently arrived interstellar objects, she directed GAI to do the unusual task of reviewing the background to the two objects, rather than using Kepler's normal function of examining the slight dimming of stars as potential planets transit a star to derive exoplanet candidates. Kepler gathered a dataset of 35,000 possible signals indicating planets. In order to help re-examine signals for potential planets that researchers had missed, the neural network, trained to look for weak signals in star systems known to support multiple planets, now looked at the outline of the interstellar objects. She directed a time-lapse review for the period when the objects arrived.

Interesting, they appear to be coming from the same direction, Alpha Centauri. Something must have happened there for them to be traveling along the same flight path, albeit nearly two years apart. I need verification before I can make a definitive statement of fact.

Frustrated at the proximity of the sun and the solar glare as the reverse time-lapse recedes further into the past, she could see why astronomers were unable to infer a source from the available data. She reran the data, running forward this time.

If there were two objects, why would there not be more? Perhaps they are still on the way.

Idly watching the progress, as the time-lapse progresses through the more recent data, annoyed at the degradation in image quality caused by a blind spot that appears at the fringe of the images, she reset the system and started again. Same problem. Irritated, she turned the computer off and attended to chores before heading for bed with thoughts of the travelers en route to Mars, wondering how they were keeping. The next evening, she returned to the analysis and instructed the computer to use inverse colors, giving black on white instead of white on black. The sun and stars receded to the background and the interstellar bodies showed up as bright objects, providing a better view of their progress across the sky.

The same conclusion emerged.

They are definitely coming from the general direction of Alpha Centauri. As they enter the solar system, their paths bend under the gravitational influence of the sun. Other observers have noted that.

Running the time-lapse further into the past, she tracked the objects into earlier time, getting smaller and smaller until they disappear behind the sun. Linear extrapolation behind the sun computed their passage as converging on our nearest stellar neighbor.

I wonder, is this sufficient information for a conclusive determination of the origin? The technique of using GAI must be unique. For confirmation, the results need corroboration by an alternative technique.

Double-checking her work, she reran the analysis forward. Again, at the final stages the blind spot appeared on the images at the fringe of the sun, this time even with the color inverted.

The transposed image should not do that; what if it is real? That would be unusual.

Skeptical, she recorded the location and size of the spot anyway, deciding to look again at another time.

The next day Julia repeated the forward time-lapse, including the new periodic overnight dump of data now available on the GAI, still a few months old. Surprisingly, the blind spot had moved slightly and become larger. Zooming in for a closer view, she could see details. They appeared to indicate rotation.

Could this be a third object? It is moving along the same trajectory as the other two but the size appears to be much larger.

A forward extrapolation beyond the available data put the object behind the sun in another day or two, where it would be lost to further examination for a while depending on the angle of attack.

Unless! What if a professional astronomer, with access from a different angle, such as from Hubble or James Webb, could view the actual progress and compare it with this information?

Stay calm, what do I have? Two sets of facts: One is the source of the two interstellar objects; and the second is a third object coming from the same location, implying it is also an interstellar object and – by the way – it is much larger.

She recorded the locational details and looked up the contact information of the observatory in Hawaii, the site of the first discovery. Before contacting them, she called the local daily newspaper, West News Inc.

"Hi, I would like to speak with a science reporter. I have some news that may be of interest."

"Hold on and I will put you through to Lilian."

"Hello! This is Lilian Ansley. How may I help you?"

"I believe that you are a science reporter. What area of science do you specialize in?"

"Well, generally we don't have a lot of science related news compared to politics and reports on other happenings, so I have to cover the whole gamut of science. My background is in the social sciences – you know, psychology and sociology – but I think I can hold my own in the basics of the other sciences. Is there anything in particular that you need?"

"This is to do with astronomy. I am curious about an object I have seen and need someone, a professional astronomer, to either confirm or reject the sighting."

"Where do I fit in?"

"Look, I have to acknowledge that I am an amateur. The trouble is that the information may be important, but could equally be the spurious imaginings of a layperson. I would like to discuss the findings with a professional astronomer, but I need a witness present in case the person usurps my claims. Are you willing to be that person?"

"It sounds interesting. Yes, I will be more than happy to assist. When and where would you like to go ahead?"

"The astronomer most suited to speak to is not local. He is probably in Hawaii. The person I had in mind is one who made a related discovery about two years ago. He identified an interstellar object passing through our solar system. Not something that happens often."

Lilian interjected, "You must be referring to Oscar Ayana. He is the senior astronomer of the Haleakala observatory at Hawaii. I was one of many journalists who interviewed him after his discovery. We ran a story on it in our newspaper. I still have his contact details. Would you like me to set something up?"

"Well that's a head-start."

"Would you like to meet over lunch and we can discuss the details?"

"No, no, I prefer to just get on with it as quickly as possible. I realize that you will probably want rights to the story if it comes to anything, but at this stage, I am not authorizing you to that effect. Are you prepared to proceed on that basis? We can discuss rights and other matters after we talk to Oscar."

"Okay. I have recording facilities in my office. I will phone Oscar on my other line right now and see whether he is available. Hmm, it is about 11:00 AM there now, so this should be a good time. Hold on!"

"Hi, Oscar. This is Lilian Ainsley. Do you remember me?"

"Oh, of course I do. How could I forget? You were very helpful."

"I have someone with me who wants to ask you an important astronomy question. Are you available, say in about an hour from now? We will phone you."

Putting down the phone Lilian said, "There, we can talk to him at 3 PM. See you at that time. Is that okay, luv?"

"Okay," she replied, wishing she would not call her 'Luv' but otherwise reasonably satisfied with the arrangement.

An hour later Julia found herself opposite Lilian, a tall professional looking person with sleek black hair and manicured fingernails. A video link displayed on a wall screen showed a handsome young man with a thick mop of curly black hair surrounding a Polynesian face. He sported a neat beard, which framed piercingly intelligent eyes. The recording was set to go.

Oscar said, "Pleased to meet you Julia. How can I help you?"

"I believe you have met Lilian, a local reporter. Are you the person who recently discovered the interstellar object transiting our solar system? I just want to be sure I have the right person."

"Yes, I am that person."

"Congratulations on your discovery... As I mentioned to Lilian, I am a complete amateur at astronomy, but as a biologist I trained to be systematic about the work that I do. In applying the same sort of rigor to my dabbling in astronomy, I observed something curious that may be important but equally, a professional such as you, may have an explanation. Lilian is here to vouch for me as the discoverer if it is something substantial. I hope you don't mind us recording this session?"

"Not at all, and I think you are wise to secure the rights to the discovery. I would have done the same. Just by the way, we welcome amateur astronomers. They provide a valuable addition to the eyes on the heavens."

Julia explained her methodology, findings and expectations, and provided a link to the analysis.

The astronomer listened attentively and when Julia finished, he thoughtfully pondered the information for a moment, then said, "I have to acknowledge that your technique is probably valid but just to be sure, I will check with a colleague for a second opinion. I do have access to James Webb, but I will have to reserve time on the telescope and have it pointed at the location that you provided. This could take a couple of weeks. I will get back to you."

Julia said, "That may be a problem, because time is of the essence given the movement of the object and that others may see it and claim the discovery for themselves. Anyhow, I will leave it to you to get back to us ASAP. Thanks."

After terminating the call Lilian repeated her invitation to lunch. Without a reason to decline, Julia agreed.

As they waited for the serving, Lilian asked, "What led to your interest in astronomy, luv?"

"Oh, a friend of mine introduced me to the online SETI and GAI systems and things progressed from there. I am a biologist by profession so it is a little out of my sphere but the recent detection of oxygen surrounding exoplanets really sparked my interest. You know, is there alien life out there?"

Julia added, "Actually, I have to confess, I am a little lonely at the moment and have spare time. You see, the friend I spoke of is at this very moment on the way to Mars. Can you believe it?"

"What! You have to be joking. First this interstellar visitor, and now you tell me this. You do surprise, dear. I would go to Mars at the drop of a hat. I believe there are about a thousand people already there. You could party all night and not have to worry about too many neighbors. Why didn't you go with him?"

Julia, laughing, replied, "Lack the qualifications. No work for biologists on Mars. The place is dead. Actually, three other people went along with him. Miles is his name. The foursome get along like a house on fire."

"Do I detect something more about this Miles person? Mind you, prospects cannot be too good if he is on Mars. Right?"

Laughing, she responded, "No, as I said to them, 'what will be - will be.' I wouldn't want to stand in the way of such an opportunity."

"That's a good girl; there are many more fish in the ocean. I have to admit to one failed marriage, and I do not want to fall into that trap again. The next one will have to be something special. Lucky for me, no kids from the first one."

Julia and Lilian found likable traits in each other despite their differences, with Lilian being the socialite and Julia the focused questioning personality.

* * *

The widening gulf between Julia and our craft en route to Mars was now such that we could no longer hold meaningful real-time discussions; all communications were now by text messages, email or video recordings. Julia found the agonizing wait for the astronomer to respond with findings too much to bear on her own so she shared her findings with us, on the condition that we kept the information confidential. Having read her account, we too were infected with excitement at the prospect of her discovery and impatient over the wait-time. The news provoked lengthy discussions between the four of us, exploring alternative scenarios to explain Alpha Centauri as the source and in speculating what the third entity might be.

The confirmation came from Oscar sooner than anticipated. This time, rather than commit to messaging as the means of communication, Julia called us on a video link.

We listened and watched, enduring the half-minute delay in transmission, as she explained, "Alpha Centauri as the source is correct for both the previous objects."

Then, astonishingly, she breathlessly explained, "The third object, the larger object, the one I thought may be a blind spot in the images. It turns out to be a planet! Yes, a planet nearly the same size as Earth! Can you believe it?"

There was silence beyond the thirty-second delay as we absorbed the news.

Jabu was first to break the pause, "All I can say is – Wow! Incredible work Julia. Well done!"

Julia explained that Oscar was working on the details of the discovery and that they would be seeing him for an update.

Between each communication delay, we wondered at the extraordinary ramifications the news brought and what led to the discovery at that time.

Robin summed up with some questions in his crisp manner. "Do you know how it evaded earlier detection? What caused it to be on a course from our stellar neighbor? Does it have an escape velocity to exit the solar system? If not, where is it destined to go?"

So many questions, and Julia did not have the answers, but she confirmed that credit for the discovery would be hers.

Lilian, also on the video cast, used the opportunity to have a say. "I am the journalist whom Julia has agreed will publish the findings. At the outset, I must state that the implications for Julia will be far-reaching. This sort of news will bring all sorts of people out of the woodwork. Our news organization is preparing a publication strategy for Julia to review, one that will not alarm people; the news may spark panic if framed incorrectly."

Turning to Julia, she said, "I should mention that the impact of the media on you needs management. We will have to discuss how best to handle this."

Returning to us on the video feed, she added, "We should be ready to go public tomorrow, so watch the news feeds. I am sure there will be blanket coverage."

The session ended and Julia, feeling drained, leaned back in her chair to recover from the excitement.

Lilian, bubbling with effervescent enthusiasm at having met the group, could barely contain herself. "What an incredible group! I wish I were there. Who is that, the one who asked the questions? He is so cute in a boyish sort of way. He seems sooo intelligent."

Adopting Lilian's idiosyncratic idiom, Julia rather curtly said, "Yes dear! That is Robin. He is a mathematics professor."

"Hmm, okay. That explains that."

* * *

With the newsbreak, as expected a flood of public interest unfolded, divided equally between positive and negative, acceptance and disbelief. Thankfully, Lilian shielded Julia from the adverse reactions and took on a role of coordinating the many requests for public appearances. At first, the commentary was subdued, simply another visitor, until its dimensions became apparent. Excitement mounted: it was not meteoric debris, like the other fragments. This was a fully-fledged planet.

The Rogue had arrived!

* * *

All eyes were trained on the object, its source clear but its destination wildly debated from every angle. Scientists and astronomers launched a more systematic scrutiny and measured look at the facts, as they were unearthed. Divergent opinions emerged.

One group claimed it would plunge into the fiery inferno on its second orbit around the sun. Another faction opined that Jupiter would swallow it. A third group predicted that the velocity was within parameters for capture by the gravitational grip of the sun. They forecast that it would find a home within the entourage of planets, but wondered how it would negotiate the crowded space without mishap. The latter possibility raised frantic demands for quick answers.

As the planet emerged from behind the sun, an analysis likened the trajectory to the other two objects that preceded it, their course bent through a ninety-degree angle placing them perpendicular to the ecliptic plane. Its speed rivaled that of Nuntius for an exit from the solar system, but the reconstruction revealed that its trajectory took it to a close encounter with Jupiter, which had moved to an intersecting path. The mighty planet reeled in the velocity of the planet as it passed in its wake, rather than a frontal approach that would have added to its pace through a slingshot effect. Slowed, it emerged from Jupiter's hold, firmly within the grasp of the sun.

Hermes the emissary and messenger of the gods, the divine trickster who outwits others for his own satisfaction or for the sake of humankind, the god of frontiers and the transgression of boundaries.

He moves freely between the worlds of the mortal and divine.

Who exactly gave it its name remains uncertain but presumably, like Mercury named after the Roman god for its speed, Hermes equated with the Greek god, in a more sincere belief in this divinity as the true traveler. It emerged from the cloud of public clamor, a de facto name appropriately given. A subconscious prediction of the righting of mankind's wrongs, or a cruel hoax that plunges our world deeper into despair – who can tell?

Julia and Lilian maintained a constant dialog with Oscar who increasingly took the lead on technical aspects of the emerging facts.

A video link from Lilian's office showed a disheveled astronomer at the other end.

Lilian was first to speak. "Hi Oscar, you look like you haven't slept for a week. Is Hermes keeping you awake?"

Oscar paced the room and stretched to relieve the effects of prolonged sitting. "Yes. This is absorbing stuff. Very interesting, intense! Not enough hours in the day. Look, I will get straight down to it. You have probably seen the latest reconstruction of its path, but there is more to come. I have run new measurements to adjust for the unforeseen braking exerted by Jupiter. From Jupiter it looped around the sun in a wide elliptical arc, but in time, the sun will drag it into a near-circular orbit. Julia, you discovered the planet as it approached Jupiter, but the sun obscured your view of Jupiter and the succeeding effects on the planet. Your opinion that it stemmed from the general direction of Alpha Centaury still holds water."

Pausing before committing further, he said, "From what I can see, an unusual set of circumstances happens to prevail at this time. Maybe I should use the term 'normal but very low probability.' Mars and the Earth are nearing conjunction in the next few months and the new planet is heading in the same direction. Circumstantially, conjunction does not happen that often, and for it to coincide with the arrival of Hermes is a chance occurrence."

Julia interrupted, "You are right about the conjunction. I have a friend, actually four friends, who are en route to Mars right now. They left Earth just a few days ago. The launch date for the mission was planned to optimize travel time around the conjunction."

"This is incredible! You first drop the discovery bombshell and now you tell me this. It adds a completely new dimension to your life."

"Well, it was one of my friends, Miles, who introduced me to GAI and I was lonely in his absence. I was dabbling with GAI when – you know what followed. The two events are therefore somewhat linked."

All vestiges of sleep deprivation now dispelled, Oscar continued, "I don't want to alarm you but the arrival of Hermes may have its effect on your friend. You see, from my calculations, Hermes in its current slightly elliptical orbit will skirt around the outer edge of Mars and gravitationally draw Mars away from the sun. How much, I cannot say just yet. I need to do a few more calculations to give you a more precise estimate."

"You mean that Mars will retreat as their space craft approaches?"

"Yes, something like that, but it is not like they will never get there. It may add a few more days or weeks to the journey."

Lilian interjected, "This is incredible! Should we be contacting them or their sponsors to forewarn them? What about the people on Mars? They need to know as well. There is now a whole human-interest dimension to the story."

Oscar settled into his chair and shifted to a comfortable position, "I have shared this with you on the basis that these are estimates at this stage. It would be premature for you to publish anything now."

Rubbing his eyes as if to emphasize his tiredness, he continued, "I need more time to finalize my estimates. Think about it – nobody's life is in danger just yet, so another day will make little difference. I am sure that many people around the world will be coming to the same conclusion that I am, but we all need time, more time."

"Sorry. I don't mean to put pressure on you, but you know from past experience how the news networks rely on being first with breaking news."

"I have a whole team of astronomers dedicated to this, working around the clock. Because of the significance of the event, and, well, my previous discovery, we have continuous and exclusive access to James Webb. It places us at a considerable advantage over other ground or space based observatories and I have two other implications to follow-up on. Wait, let's see, let's meet again tomorrow, at this time 11 AM, and I will let you know about them."

Julia and Lilian exited the building. Lilian could barely contain her excitement at the prospect of a major news event while Julia pensively reflected on the dangers of the mission on its way to Mars. It seemed beyond extraordinary that events could conspire to coincide as they have done.

Rattling on with overlapping thoughts Lilian said, "My god, this will take the news world by storm. Oh, I just hope your friends will be okay. We will have to track their responses to the unfolding drama and publish as the story unfolds. The people on Mars – I wonder what they will think. They will…"

Julia interrupted, "Lilian – please just shut-up. Get a grip; this is more than just about you and your confounded newspaper!"

"Sorry luv. Yes, you are right. I must be more considerate, and patient."

They walked on in silence, with Lilian glancing over at Julia peri-odically to check on her mood.

As they approached the lunch venue, Julia stopped and says, "Lilian, I think I will skip lunch. I need time to think. Sorry, I don't mean to be rude."

"No problem, dear. We can meet again in my office tomorrow. We have that appointment with Oscar. You take care. I will start work on a report, just preliminary. You and Oscar will have to vet it before it goes anywhere. Okay?"

Julia turned and made her way aimlessly to the promenade. Blankly she looked over the water to the distant mountains, a strange depression overwhelmed her. Thrust into the middle of a firestorm of public attention, uncertainty around the voyagers and the loneli-ness without Miles, she struggled to stem the contending thoughts and emotions, longing for an overdue visit to the quiet forests of Salt Spring Island and the comfort that solitude with nature brings.

As if to expel the mood, she shrugged. "Yes, Miles you are special."

Time stretched, and she shook loose her inner turmoil, speak-ing into the gentle breeze. "Lilian, you are so exasperating with your mindless chatter, but I guess your intent is well-meaning. In some ways you are a godsend."

A semblance of normality eventually returned and she turned to go home. Practical chores around her apartment brought a sense of control and later sleep came as a welcome relief to the day.

Rising early, looking into the mirror, she consciously braced herself for the new day. "What will today bring? You can handle it. Yes. Just say 'Yes.'" With renewed bounce in her step, she made her way to the lobby and into the street.

Back in Lilian's office, with Oscar looking more relaxed and refreshed on the video link, he began, "Okay, I can say with some certainty that Mars will shift outwards by quite a distance. It is much smaller than Hermes, and as such, it is at its mercy. In your terms, I think you are looking at a transit-time of up to two hundred and sixty days instead of two hundred, for your friends. That is quite a lot but I imagine that is surmountable."

Julia said, "Can we communicate this to them? Forewarned is forearmed. They can adjust plans accordingly."

"Yes, I will send you more details; distances, orbital changes and the like. If you like, I can liaise directly with the mission controllers. They will need a ton of detail and I can give them as much as we have available. We now know the mass, velocity and trajectory of Hermes, which enables us to compute its future path with a high degree of accuracy."

"Thanks Oscar, the Mars controllers will also need what you have."

"Lilian, you can prepare a report and Julia and I can review it for accuracy. I will provide you with a link to the details right after this meeting."

Oscar continued, "Yesterday I said I would update you on two projections. The effect on Mars was one; the other is the effect on the Earth."

Pausing to gather his thoughts, he continued, "After your sighting of Hermes, which actually dates back a few months because of the lag in the GAI data uploads, Jupiter arrested the flight of the planet both in terms of speed and direction. Firstly, it dialed-back the speed to within the sun's escape velocity. Secondly, it bent its course so that the orbit now lies at a sixty-degree angle to the ecliptic plane. This latter effect is why it escaped detection by astronomers. You see, most of the activity they look for is within the ecliptic plane. There is very little action elsewhere, so they don't tend to look there."

Julia asked, "Going back to the first question, can you explain why Mars will be pushed further out?"

"Yes of course. On leaving the vicinity of Jupiter, Hermes skirted around the sun in a wide elliptical arc and we project it will reach aphelion, the most distant point of its orbit around the sun, on the other side of Mars. It is there that it will exert the maximum gravitational effect on Mars, pulling it away from the sun and elongating its ellipsis. The two planets happen to be at conjunction at that point in time, which is a coincidence."

Julia said, "Yes, I see, that makes sense."

Pouring a glass of water from a pitcher he continued, "That brings me to the second projection. The sixty-degree angle of its orbit to the plane is significant. Within two months from now, the angle places Hermes and Earth at their closest before its onward journey to Mars. Hermes will pass Earth on the sunward side of Earth and ahead of Earth's path. These are two large planets by comparison to Mars. They will attract each other, speeding up Earth's passage and drawing it closer to the sun. After they pass each other, the effect on Hermes will dissipate quite quickly because of its outward momentum whereas Earth, impelled by centrifugal forces around the sun, will not be drawn along by Hermes and settle at its new orbital location. In the long run, Hermes' orbit will lie between that of Earth and Mars but nearly perpendicular to the ecliptic plane."

Lilian could not contain herself, "That is incredible. It will virtually be our new neighbor."

"Yes, but you will have to be patient, and one more thing: the moon will not be left unscathed. It is very likely that its orbit around the Earth will also change. Tidal changes will have all manner of effects on Earth. One last point is that Earth's magnetic field may be disturbed. It is common knowledge that the southern magnetic pole has been in the throes of a so-called excursion for a few decades. Historically an excursion sometimes results in the flipping of the North and South poles. This usually takes a few hundred years and sometimes comes to nothing, but the effect of Hermes on Earth may be enough to speed up this process. It will have severe effects on electronic communications and solar radiation reaching the Earth's surface. I will research this further and get back to you with more detail."

* * *

Hermes, under forces over which it has no control, powerless to advocate for one fate over another, helpless under the duress of chance, tumbled through the unknown awaiting its calling. Earth loomed larger by the day as it bore down on yet another obstacle in its way, oblivious of the consternation, the elation, the oscillating siren of noise reaching fever pitch, as Earthlings anticipate the interstellar visitor's passage through its domain.

A probe, hastily dispatched to reconnoiter the strange intruder as it passes at ten times the distance to the moon, returned the first details. In their relentless pursuit of information Oscar's team uncovered exciting fact after fact to amass a picture of the visitor. Lilian, saturated with newsworthy material, diligently relayed the news to a spellbound audience around the world. She masterfully managed access to Julia, who swung between excitement and emotional exhaustion, putting on a composed front for news interviews and seeking elusive privacy and solitude when out of the glare of attention. Under Lilian's coaching, Julia cultivated a specific persona at interviews, hair tied back in a severe formal fashion, then alternating to a more casual appearance as a disguise for her private life. It brought a measure of success, as photographs in the newsfeeds generally showed the formal Julia and provided less recognition when in public.

* * *

As Oscar's projections manifested themselves, crowds gathered for vigils to spot the approaching visitor in the nightly skies. First, as a new evening star, to the naked eye it grew perceptibly each night until visible even in the glare of sunshine during the day. Assurances from scientists quelled rumors of catastrophic effects during its passage. They cautioned to expect climate changes in the aftermath because of the effects on Earth's orbit and that of the moon. This somewhat stilled the alarm and a festive atmosphere took hold as people watched and waited.

Julia and Lilian took to spending evenings in the seclusion of a clearing in the forest, with less light pollution, at the lower reaches of the escarpment leading up to the local mountains. As calmness settled on the two after another hectic day, Julia said, "Lilian, I need to thank you for supporting me the way you have. It would not be possible to manage without you. Thank you, so much!"

"Not to worry, luv. As you can see, I am in my element with all this interaction with people. I love it and it is a bonus to be supporting you. Oh look, there it is! Just rising above the horizon."

"Wow! It is such an alien sight, the moon waxing gibbous overhead and a similar sized object emerging over the horizon at the same time. Miles used to show me artists' depictions of alien worlds. I must send him a photograph of this. It is such a unique moment in time. The contrast of the cratered moon alongside the featureless brilliance of Hermes – so stark. I wonder; Hermes must be blanketed in ice."

"They say it will be larger than the moon tomorrow night and then begin receding."

"Yes. According to Oscar, they will appear to converge on each other as full moon approaches but by then Hermes will have receded and diminished in size. At that time, the sun's reflection will show the full circle of Hermes, a kind of full Hermes. Two bright lights in our sky. Amazing!"

"It is strange to think that it is speeding to a rendezvous with your friends."

As Hermes made its way across the heavens, the stillness of the evening took hold and for long moments, the spectacle held their attention, each deep in thought; the object that brought them together, the distance that separated them from the four friends and the imponderables of what the future held. Some claimed that they could feel the tug of gravity as Earth shifted from its designated lane in the celestial dance, but as humanity grappled with the imposition of a universe that dictated outcomes, humankind had to stand aside, helpless to intervene.

Lilian's comment stood in stark reality in the following nights as Hermes rapidly distanced itself from the Earth, speeding to its destiny. Within a week, it shone as just another star, albeit the brightest in the firmament. In its wake, the Earth strained to a new proximity to the sun and the moon's orbit took on an elongated ellipse around its host. Events had passed a point of no return: a new chapter lay ready to bend the routines of daily life.

The control center for the probe disseminated its cache of data to a global audience hungry for detail. Combined with projections from Oscar's team, Lilian's publications featured entire sections devoted to the unfolding facts.

The planet was similar to the Earth in size, with a diameter of 12,000 compared to 12,742 kilometers, surface gravity estimated at 90% and atmospheric pressure 75% of that of Earth's.

Estimates predicted that Earth's year would decrease to 328 days, while Mars' would increase from 687 to 756 days and Hermes would settle at 567 Earth-days per orbit around the sun. Where the 55-million-kilometer trip from Earth to Mars at opposition was 200 days, this would now increase to 260 days and a similar trip to Hermes would take about 150 days. Hermes' daily rotation around its axis was 26 hours and its tilt relative to the sun was only 15 degrees compared to approximately 24 degrees for Mars and the Earth.

Excitement rose to a frenetic level when spectral analysis revealed an atmosphere of 20% oxygen and an Earth-approximating proportion of nitrogen; could Hermes be supporting life? Coincidentally, Hermes would lie at 1.7 Astronomical Units, the distance between the sun and Earth, the extreme edge of the life-friendly Goldilocks Zone. The analysis also detected a thin veneer of ozone (tri-molecular oxygen) in the stratosphere, probably formed by the action of ultraviolet light and electrical discharges of lightning on regular bi-molecular oxygen. The paucity of ozone would offer a fraction of the protection from the damaging effects of ultraviolet light that the Earth does. Scientists speculated that Hermes had been stripped of some of its atmosphere during its journey through the cold void of interstellar space and wondered at what its original state was. Telescopes trained on the surface revealed a blanket of water ice, its depth uncertain without closer examination.

The diversion of probes currently circling Mars to meet Hermes received consideration. Having largely exhausted their supply of fuel to reach Mars, limiting acceleration to a slow burn for a transit-time of months instead of weeks proved to be feasible. Fortuitously, the window of opportunity as Hermes at opposition to Mars made this possible rather than launching new probes directly from Earth.

7

MEANWHILE

As the influence of Hermes took effect on Earth and the attendant climate changes manifested themselves as predicted, the prognosis for Mars was certain: warmth would leach from Mars in its more remote location once Hermes has wrought its effects.

Earth, already in the throes of global warming, found itself under additional duress nearer the sun. Temperatures rose by degrees as climatologists scrambled to understand the full impact. Without historical reference standards on which to base predictions, models underwent continual revision as data became available. Oscar's research into the polar reversal confirmed that the excursion of the magnetic South Pole was worsening. He was not alone in this assessment, as scientists around the world now tracked the phenomena in detail and measures to safeguard electronic communications received urgent attention. The focal point in the south had split from two to three. The rapidity with which the southern excursion deteriorated correlated directly with Hermes' passage near the Earth. The magnetic North Pole remained intact, and consequentially telecommunications in the northern hemisphere were unaffected but labile, precariously balanced in this state. Solar radiation levels penetrating the south were on the rise under the diminished protective magnetosphere in that area.

Mars did not have an ocean and a comparable dynamic hydrological cycle of evaporation, condensation, advection, precipitation and runoff to ameliorate the climate like on Earth. Its orbital change would therefore deepen the cold and only marginally decrease radiation penetrating the thin atmosphere. The cold would bite, adding discomfort to the inhabitants and further limiting their mobility. Extra-habitat excursions would require additional resources for warmth, cutting their range by as much as fifty percent. The prospect reached a tipping point, with inhabitants evenly divided between those who wished to remain and those for a return to Earth. They could either endure the coming frigidity or face the chaotic climate conditions on Earth. The question was, how to balance two negatives?

Julia provided periodic updates to our group on events back at home. She could not disguise her alarm at the speed at which the climate was changing under global warming. Further changes to the climate seemed likely as phases of the moon brought tidal extremes, with high and low tides already markedly different, affecting the fishing industry and crop production.

News channels that now devoted entire segments to events as they happened and scientific analysis supported her accounts. Projections of expected temperature changes on Earth by the end of the century required revision on almost a monthly basis as a runaway greenhouse effect set in. In the months since we had left, soaring temperatures had stripped Greenland of a tenth of its ice covering, raising sea levels and flooding enormous areas thought to be safe for many more years. Temperatures in areas where in the past cycles of drought created humanitarian crises had reached levels that made these areas unlivable. Massive migrations of climate refugees fleeing drought or flooding threatened the stability of entire countries. Relief efforts had little effect.

Under the relentless heat, tropical conditions reached high latitudes, bringing diseases that knew no boundaries. They struck where the masses gathered, instilling fear of these invisible enemies and decimating the population.

Hurricanes were prevalent in what normally would be calm periods, and the reach of the tempests was not limited to the traditional zones. In a diabolical twist, arctic conditions swept across parts of Europe and North America, exasperating climatologists' weather prediction models.

While Earth struggled to understand a changed world, the other two planets approached the point of closest proximity to each other, now within a matter of weeks. As Hermes looped around the far side of Mars, a gravitational tether would draw Mars along with it. In a cruel twist, at its maximum extent the bond would sever, leaving Mars to its own devices in the cold while Hermes returned to the warmth of the beckoning sun. Thereafter, Hermes would find its home in the entourage of planets between Mars and Earth, forever at right angles to the ecliptic plane as a statement of its foreignness. The two would greet at opposition every fifteen months and wave at each other at a distance in their semi-annual passage every seven and half months.

* * *

Developments on Earth increasingly confused the course of action to follow as we transited space. The first news came on day fifteen of our trip, and as the facts unfolded in the subsequent weeks our options swayed between a return to Earth or pressing on to Mars, each fraught with complications.

Working from the communication control center on the hub under the jurisdiction of *Forerunner*'s pilot, we reached out to *Overture*. After a number of attempts to link up with the Operation Director, Stanley finally got back to us over the time delayed link.

Hedging his words, he began by stating the obvious. "We don't know what to make of this. It is entirely unexpected. We will have to see."

Struggling to contain my frustrations, "You cannot leave us in limbo. The least you can do is to maintain contact. We need a decision soon! It is simply a question of whether to proceed on to Mars or return to Earth."

Showing signs of stress, "I need to confer with my superiors. Can I get back to you?"

"Stanley, you should have already done that. As Director of Operations, aside from also being the spokesperson for the venture, is it not your decision?"

"Well yes, but we have shareholders to consider. Look, I will set up a meeting with the board and get back to you."

At the next conference days later, initiated by us in the absence of news, he again vacillated between the options.

I made my point. "We, the passengers, feel that we have a say in the matter. The original mandate stands in jeopardy. Mars at its new location will be colder and more inhospitable than it was, whereas the change in Earth's location will exacerbate its climate. We are now over half way to Mars. Time is running out for a decision."

Allowing for the distance-imposed time-delay between exchanges which served only to exasperate matters, Stanley annoyingly offered, "Okay, I will convene a board meeting and get back to you."

"I thought you had already done that?"

"I tried, but we could not establish a quorum."

Frustrated, I elaborated, "I don't need to tell you because you should already know. The original window of opportunity still lies ahead of us, getting closer every day. Mars at opposition provides an opening that, if not taken, will translate into more than a year of procrastination. We will be in the doldrums here in space. Do you know how that feels? The consequences on our health and your costs will be far-reaching. Remind them of the costs. Yes, the costs!"

"I do realize the predicament. I will press for a decision. It is just that no one knows what the full impact will be on Mars. Every day brings improved data and information."

The frustration of indecision reached a head when after a week we remained without direction.

The tension, even in our small group, periodically spilled over into short-tempered jabs at each other. The effect of prolonged lack of privacy tested our tolerance for each other's quirks.

Surprisingly, it was Jabu who was first to lose control, directing his anger at me. "Miles, you are too soft with Stanley. You are the project manager. Act like one. Don't just take his nonsense." Standing over me, he says, "I have managed many projects in the past. Let me have a go at them. You will see; I will get results."

"Look Jabu, back off. No amount of threatening is going to help, whether against them or me. You should know better than that. You are a geo-whatever, stick to that."

Robin intervened, "Miles, Jabu is right. A rational approach will do the trick. Spell out the consequences. Use a logical format. They will listen. Present alternatives. Do it forthrightly, as Jabu suggests. Articulate the logic of each option. Be more persuasive."

Feeling cornered, unfortunately my pent-up irritation spilled over. "Robin, stay out of this. It is between Jabu and me. I have seen you – all eyes for Jabu. Do think it is not obvious? Are you his toy-boy?"

With embarrassment showing on Jabu's face, Dmitri tried to come to the rescue, but with English as his second language after Russian, he missed the nuances of the interchange. "The problem is not with any of us. Think about it, what has happened in the last few weeks is not anything that we could imagine. I am sure that Stanley is doing his best. Da, yes, he should get back to us more regularly and I think you have made that clear to him."

Jabu took up my challenge, "Where did that come from? Yes, I will stick to geology and do it well, but you need to do likewise as project manager. We need leadership and now you resort to demeaning both Robin and I."

Dmitri, still focused on solving the Stanley problem, continued at cross-purposes, "How about asking Julia and Lilian to take it up with Stanley. They can knock at his door every day and..."

Robin entered the fray again, "Sorry to interrupt, Dmitri. I need to come clean. My sexuality has been confused for some time. I did not have the best role models as parents. Maybe it was just me."

Continuing after taking a moment to steady himself, he continued, "When we met in Vancouver, in my sabbatical, I saw Jabu for the first time since our school days. His strength of character and robust looks surprised me. It stirred something – something dormant for a long time. During our teens, it was unfathomable. As an adult I realized that I am different."

Jabu broke the tension, laughing, "Robin, I will take it as a compliment, so don't let it worry you. But just to be clear, unfortunately – for you, that is – I am not that way inclined."

Robin responded, "Okay, I realized I was barking up the wrong tree. You would have had to respond for me to engage further than my admiration for you."

Dmitri finally realized what had transpired. "In my country you would have been nailed to a tree by your thumbs. Just joking. I think you are brave to admit to this, but in a strange way our differences are our strength."

"Thank you, Dmitri, you are right. And Jabu and Robin, please accept my apologies."

Jabu, waving aside my concerns, returned to the issue at hand. "Dmitri's idea of enlisting Julia and Lilian is a good one. We should do that, but I also think we need to call a meeting of all the passengers of the *Forerunner* to gain their input. No pod on its own can impose a decision, but a unified response to *Overture* may be enough to force the issue. I suggest that we draft and dispatch an agenda for a meeting to the attendees for as soon as possible. You Miles, as project manager, are and should remain the interface to *Overture*."

Robin concurred. "Tomorrow is day 120 of our trip. We are at a crossroad. As Dmitri suggests, we need all the alternatives that are at play. Prepare sound arguments in favor the most logical course of action and consider what will meet with the expectations of *Overture*."

After further discussion, we agreed to a notice that I dispatched to the voyagers.

At the designated time, we boarded our shuttle and set off across the intervening distance to the hub. Other shuttles were doing likewise in recognition of the importance of the meeting. An hour later, with nearly two hundred people crammed into the conference room, the meeting got underway.

Jabu opened the meeting. "You probably all know the dilemma we face. Hermes' passage has exacerbated Earth's already dire climate conditions under global warming. Astronomers and climatologists predicted the difficulties and the results are the proof of what they foretold. These same experts are even more certain in their forecast for Mars. The outward shift will cause extremes of cold when compared to what we expected."

I could see the audience shift under the uncomfortable message they all knew was coming.

Jabu continued, pausing between each sentence. "We have repeatedly contacted our sponsors, who have failed to reach a decision on a way forward. It seems simple." He waved his fingers in the air for emphasis. "There are only two options: return to Earth, or press on to Mars. We are at a juncture in our voyage where each day of inaction diminishes the choices we have. Our health and wellbeing are at stake. We need a unified voice to take to *Overture*; otherwise, they will impose a decision on us. I put it to you, what do you want: press on or return?"

Until this point, the meeting had been relatively calm, but obvious anxiety at the situation we found ourselves in began to spill over as camps formed around each of the two options. The split seemed to be an even 50:50, with tempers rising as each group became more insistent. There were even scuffles between the more vociferous antagonists on both sides. Chaos threatened to disrupt the entire purpose of the meeting, which was to reach an agreed-on approach, without which *Overture* would have a legitimate reason to impose their will on the situation.

The strongest protagonist for the Return group took a stand, shouting, "I am Jude. We only have one opportunity for a return at no costs to us. Only one opportunity! If we continue to Mars with the emerging dangers that are becoming apparent, we will not be able to argue for a return when conditions become unbearable. In signing up, we accepted the dangers as they stood at that time. But now, under these new conditions, the risks are more pronounced. We need to stop and turn this boat around."

He held out on this opinion and began to sway the audience in this direction, but the ringleader for the Press-On group became more adamant for his cause.

He was a slightly overweight, scraggy red-haired miner with a ruddy complexion and green eyes, which at this moment were flaring with anger. Jumping up, in an equally loud voice he argued, "I am Michael. No way! You cannot make a decision based on the flimsy information that we have. No one expected a joyride. We fully anticipated difficult conditions – maybe not as bad as those now forecast, but difficult nevertheless. I say get on with it, we are almost there. We can adjust for inconveniences as they arise." Hesitating he continued, "I am with *Overture* on this. They obviously have not responded because fundamentally nothing has changed. We are on our way to Mars as agreed to, and that is it."

Jabu, on the defensive, said, "With all due respect, one thing has changed – Hermes has changed everything and will have a decisive effect."

Michael, increasingly agitated and egged on by colleagues around him, retorted, "So what! Earth is in a mess and Mars will be a little colder. Just press on. We can deal with the cold, no problem. Nothing in our contract gives you or anyone the option of returning to Earth, especially not on a whim."

The equally distraught Return spokesperson in the seat behind Michael confronted him. "I have to disagree with him; conditions on Mars may be a lot more difficult than what we signed up for. I think we have a strong case for arguing for a return to Earth at the sponsor's expense. We need to exercise our rights, right now, or foot the bill ourselves later. Here is what…"

Michael interrupted before he could say more. "Jude, or Judas did you say, yes, you traitor. Sit down. Oh I can see, you are regretting your decision and want to get out of it without consequences."

Jude's reply was as quick, dripping with sarcasm. "Look, mister archangel, you are sooo virtuous? What are your ulterior motives? Come on, do tell. A girlfriend waiting for you on Mars?"

The Press-On group then shouted him down, at which the fracas turned into an all-out brawl between the two ringleaders. Security personnel eventually had to manhandle them from the auditorium.

As if removing the oxygen from the room, silence briefly descended on the meeting.

Jabu took the cue, honed under taxing conditions of union leadership on the mines; his innate skills came to the fore. He quickly brought the meeting to order with his calm affable voice and assurance that a solution would be found. He spelled out the consequences of discord and appealed for better senses to prevail. His rapport with the audience was noticeable as they increasingly deferred to him for leadership.

"Here is what I suggest we do. We need a list of the pros and cons of the Return and Press-On options. If we do that systematically, it will show what makes the most sense. We can then vote on the two options."

After exhaustively cataloging the good and the bad of each course of action, it was obvious that a deadlock would result. A second review of possibilities produced minor additional considerations. Jabu then proposed that the group reconvene after a break for an hour to cast a vote. He required that all participants accept the outcome and commit to the chosen course of action. With no dissention to this, the meeting disbanded, but gravitated into like-minded clusters. The hubbub rose to a din as they each reinforced their respective stands.

On reconvening, the vote resulted in the feared impasse, a deadlock from which there appeared to be no solution. Even if the two individuals removed by security were to vote, the outcome would be unchanged, given that they were of opposing opinions. Disappointment showed on everyone's face; *Overture* would decide the future, an unpalatable prospect. A muted despondency spread, infecting all, helpless under the spell of indecision.

Jabu asked Security to allow the two expelled individuals to rejoin the group then. Reluctantly, he offered a compromise resulting from the vote. "I suggest that we ask our project manager to contact *Overture* and explain the situation. An even fifty percent of those present here prefer to return to Earth and the other half believe that the mission should continue. We can ask them to accommodate both groups. In other words, an all-expenses paid return journey for one group and a continuation of the contract for the other. We will have to leave it to them to figure out the logistics of how to accomplish this because it will no doubt be complex; expect delays both in their response and in the execution. By show of hands, do you agree with this as the way forward?"

After cheerless agreement, people slumped back in their chairs and dejectedly considered the misfortune that had befallen the endeavor. It seemed unlikely that *Overture* would be able to afford to proceed in half measures; casting both options in doubt.

Eventually some stirred to leave but Robin, who had been unusually silent even for someone as austere as he could be at times, took to the floor, saying, "Wait, wait I have another solution!"

It was strange to witness his demeanor. The preceding emotionally charged atmosphere stood in stark contrast to the mathematical precision devoid of passion that characterized him, as he spelled out a solution not considered thus far. The audience, immediately arrested by his manner, stopped to listen as he spoke.

"We are twenty days past what was the midpoint of the journey to Mars. We are at day 120 of the journey. Based on the projected changes in the orbits, which have bought us an extra sixty days, initiation of the deceleration protocol is due for activation in a few weeks. We have a choice."

He paused to ensure that he has everyone's attention, then continued, "Hermes, in its orbit around the sun, is heading for a rendezvous with Mars. Its closest point to Mars is on day 260 on the far side of the planet. If we divert course in the direction of Hermes we will meet Hermes on day 200, the original date for arriving at Mars, sixty days short of the new rendezvous date of Hermes with Mars. Expenditure of additional fuel for the braking maneuver and course correction will be required to achieve the destination change. If the velocity is carefully controlled, our craft can enter a stable orbit around Hermes at that time. This will allow us to coast to the nearest point to Mars under the momentum of Hermes with us in orbit."

The audience listened in rapt attention, then gasps of surprise greeted Robin's next suggestion. "Our destination, our new home, it should be Hermes!"

It took a while to quieten the din.

He continued: "The logistics of achieving this requires the diversion of the supply spacecraft currently en route to Mars, to Hermes instead, for the establishment of a base on Hermes. The cargo includes launch capabilities, construction robots, food supplies and general supplies. The passage of probes, those that are en route from Mars to Hermes to investigate, will arrive ahead of our craft. Once we are in orbit around Hermes, time will no longer be of the essence. The orbiting probes can reconnoiter for an optimum-landing site on Hermes for us to execute when we are ready. This can be after Mars and Hermes are at their closest. It does not matter, but the option of landing on Mars diminishes as we leave the vicinity of Mars. There is therefore a decision point when we reach proximity with Mars."

Continuing with the audience fully in attention, he said, "There are many uncertainties that need clarification before confirming feasibility, but many issues inherent in this proposed strategy appear to be less onerous than the other options."

Pausing for everyone to grasp the logic, he continued, "*Overture* can be convinced to go along with the Hermes strategy by pointing out that surveys will likely reveal mining opportunities on Hermes. Besides, construction of housing is a prime and lucrative responsibility of *Overture*; something they would have had to do on Mars anyway. Being first to arrive on Hermes, they would have a distinct advantage over other missions.

"The cargo of launching rockets on the supply craft, reconfigured to support entry into Hermes' atmosphere with a chain-link of up to five pods per entry, can be used. The icefields observed on the surface of Hermes may need leveling. This means that robotic graders will have to precede the landing by humans. The pods can decouple from the entry train inflight and glide down to the landing sites. Indications are that temperatures on the surface of Hermes, despite being frozen, are considerably warmer than that of Mars. Hermes also offers surface water ice, a significant advantage over Mars, where mining of ice for conversion to water is expected to be necessary. Limited breathing without the need for portable air is likely on Hermes, given the 20% oxygen content in the atmosphere, another important benefit."

With that, Robin concluded his monologue by offering a way out, "At any time, if conditions on Hermes prove to be untenable, for any number of reasons, we can leave to return to Earth or continue on to Mars. Acceptance of a period of up to fifteen months on Hermes, one orbit around the sun until the next conjunction, is required for you to commit to this option. I realize that the unknowns are a concern, and there are many, but all the options are fraught with this."

There was stunned silence as the passengers considered his words. Then, first one, then another, then half the audience raised their hands, clamoring with questions, which Robin answered to the best of his ability. There seemed to be general acceptance that this was the best way forward, as many of the questions were about detail. In many instances, there were no answers, and such topics therefore required further investigation. Jabu recorded the outstanding difficulties with the promise to convey these to the appropriate experts and communicate their response back to the group. One item would make or break the proposal, and therefore needed urgent attention. The presence of oxygen in the atmosphere implied photosynthetic activities on the planet, and therefore that there may be a lifeform on the planet if it mimicked the Earth. The consequences could be bi-directional, contamination of humans or infection of the indigenous lifeform with potential for being lethal to either species.

The meeting broke up after voting in favor of the Hermes route by an overwhelming majority. Responsibility for clarifying outstanding questions was assigned to our pod. They chose me to manage the process and report to a steering committee made up of eight volunteer pod leaders in accordance with an agreed-to communication protocol.

8

DESTINATION

Our pod reached out to *Overture* to discuss the decisions. With the frustration of long delays between sending and receiving responses, after initial displeasure at our unsanctioned group meeting, they saw the logic in the proposal, agreed to its merits and allocated budget to facilitate clarification of the outstanding questions. We insisted that Julia act as liaison with the passengers and that she receive regular briefings on the progress, because the effort would be Earth-based. In the interest of transparency, at her discretion, Julia was given authority to pass information to Lilian for publication once certain of any facts and to keep the passengers and sponsors in the loop.

Two days later, an invitation to attend a follow-up briefing came through.

With our appointed steering committee seated around the communication console in the Hub, Stanley, the Director of Operations, brought the meeting to order.

He said, "We have not committed to a change in destination, namely Mars versus Hermes or a return to Earth. Until we have answers to the outstanding questions, Mars remains the focal point of this endeavor. The controller will explain the immediate steps required to get answers to the outstanding questions."

Handing the floor over to the Earth-based Mars Mission Controller Mr. Estrange, who was also in attendance, the controller clarified: "The probes that are en route to Hermes from Mars are already equipped with a range of capabilities to test for the presence of biology. Their intended use on Mars was for exposure to the atmosphere to measure atmospheric composition and scan for traces of life. Various gels, growth media, bacteria and viruses onboard serve this purpose. The normal intent is that once they reach the end of their life and their orbits decay into the atmosphere they have a specific role. The miniature onboard science laboratory takes measurements of the atmosphere at the higher elevations before the heat of entry and again after the atmospheric friction subsides. A parachute then deploys, partially arresting the speed for a controlled crash landing, which penetrates the ground to the extent of a few inches where it completes a final set of subterranean tests. After relaying the results to the control center, the probe self-destructs in an implosion, the destruction designed to seal it from exposing its contents to the atmosphere to contain contamination of the planet.

"Reassignment of one of the Mars probes diverted to Hermes can assess the atmosphere immediately on arrival and analyze the results while the other probes complete the surface survey, all before the *Forerunner* arrives.

"A choice of potential landing sites on Hermes, based on topographical and human habitat considerations rather than mining concerns, will drive the decision of where to land – if landing is in fact the decision. This survey, done in parallel to the atmospheric test, will use the one remaining probe. As part of the clarification process, we agreed to sacrifice one of the probes for the assessment."

"The rationale for this decision is that, by hitching a ride on Hermes, so to speak, we are prepared to divert the flight path of the *Forerunner* to Hermes where, as you pointed out, we can remain in orbit until conjunction with Mars. The cost of this diversion is minimal. On reaching the vicinity of Mars, the probes will have completed their assessments. Then, with the assessment information to hand, our choices will be whether to land on Hermes, proceed to Mars as originally planned, or return to Earth."

Returning control back to the chairperson, Stanley, on behalf of *Overture*, approved the diversion as an alteration to the mission and timeline. The meeting disbanded.

* * *

Proceed! The plan was set in motion, the course correction initiated, the deceleration burn started for the *Forerunner* and we anxiously waited for our rendezvous with Hermes.

As expected, the probes arrived at Hermes ahead of us. The results of the atmospheric test, transmitted to the control center, would take a couple of weeks to analyze while in the meantime the survey of the surface got underway.

After many orbits around the planet, the survey reported the initial findings. Using ice-penetrating radar, they established what appear to be four major continents, two clustered close to each other, one in a central area and the other in the east spanning the north–south equatorial divide. The central continent stretches northwards from the equator to the polar region, while the eastern continent forms a sickle-shaped pair, one scythe in the northern hemisphere and the other south of the equator. The fourth continent lies at a distance in the far west. A number of smaller landmasses were apparent. A lengthy rift valley on the central continents suggests the possibility of active tectonic plates. Mountain ranges run along the backbones of three of the continents and frozen sea ice dominates much of the planet. A semi-circular archipelago off the southern edge of the central continent shelters the continental shoreline from ocean waves, making for a good landing site, and being on the equator it is likely to be the warmest place on the planet. Conversely, from a wind perspective, the island archipelago sheltered by the surrounding mountains offers the possibility of a reasonably flat surface between the islands and the continent due to calm seas when freezing started. Therefore, only minimal grading would be required for it to be suitable as a landing strip.

As day 245 approached, our objective loomed larger. Hermes grew from a speck to the size of the moon as seen from Earth; it shone brightly, reflecting the dominant complexion of a planet gripped in a cold vise. Land features gradually emerged, dark ridges of mountain ranges and the reported rift valley running along the spine of the central continent. The excitement was palpable as we keenly tried to identify the suggested landing site, but it was still too far to make out the features in sufficient detail. In the distance, we saw Mars, no longer the shiny reflection of the sun, now an opaque red with distinct polar caps: the world that would never be home to us.

9

LURKING

All eyes focus without seeing, near-sighted; blind to consequences, for beyond the orb of Mars lies a restless horde, silently circling. A vast wheel of misfortune balanced for eons to a truce observed through the millennia. Now stirred from slumber, perturbed, awakened by the intruder, stealth its motto, it shakes loose first one then another and another of its restive minions as Mars transits in its new proximity to the belt of asteroids. They jostle for equilibrium but find none. Cast aside, some wander beyond the confines of the wheel. The vagaries of chance control their course as they now aimlessly roam, vindictively seeking a prey on whom to unleash their awesome power. Jupiter's attraction embraces some while discarding others, randomly flinging them in lethal trajectories. They bide their time, patience their only virtue. Too numerous to name, anonymously numbered, but each with a defined destiny writ large in the mathematics of angle, timing, velocity and mass for any who care to focus, forewarned but unable to forearm in the insufficient time available to them for deflection.

In wide elongated paths, they circle their prey tethered to the sun, those bound to the orbital plane most precarious. Mars, Earth, Venus and Mercury: beware; prepare, prepare, prepare. Brace for impact – or else!

* * *

While the hordes gather, Earth writhes. Cowed by the dangers from afar, it braces, but another threat builds within its own confines. The once docile moon exerts its will on the unsuspecting. Like a vulture circling its prey, it alternatively reaches down from its distended ellipse to claw at the quarry then retreats to a distance for a renewed lunge at its erstwhile master. The tidal exertions force the dynamo within to squirm, pitting North against South till the compass points to a duality of magnetism in the South as the polar excursion already in effect moves to a new dangerous temporary truce with the North. Will North and South trade places?

10

CORRECTION

While we marveled at the scene of Hermes at increasingly close quarters, the juxtaposition of humanity's calamities with the climate, profoundly disconcerted, dampened our excitement.

On a private connection, I urged, "Julia, you must explore the possibility of joining us on Hermes. If only I could have a way to make it possible, but I see none. I feel trapped out here. Is there anything you can do at your end?"

A long minute later, her assurance reached back to me. "Please don't worry. I am quite safe. Where I am there are no day-to-day effects on our activities."

Exasperated, I responded, "There are two or even three carousels like the *Forerunner* in various stages of readiness for a journey to Mars. We should convince *Overture* to divert them to Hermes as a matter of urgency."

"The trouble is that the authorities are struggling with climate impacts. Space exploration's not going to be high on their agenda."

With rising concern, I implored, "A small window of opportunity is open right now with the planets aligned as they are. They have a choice to act now before political conditions worsen. The alternative is that their project will remain stranded on Earth. The whole thing will be mired in an uncertain future."

My mind was in a turmoil. A case had to be made to direct the next launch at the partial conjunction of Earth and Hermes on the far side of the sun in seven or eight months. The distance between the two planets, although not as close as the present conjunction, would increase for a number of years before again converging. Julia had to use her newfound celebrity to make a case for inclusion on a trip.

To my relief, she agreed.

I needed to convince *Overture* that associates of our pod had been exemplary: Julia's discovery of Hermes, Robin's proposal for diverting to Hermes, and our coordinating role. The initiative on Hermes needed an embedded reporter to document the first impressions of the planet, and I could think of no one better than Lilian. The gearing of the sponsor's first wave of Mars colonists was for mining and construction built on an expectation of utilizing existing infrastructure on Mars. Hermes would need infrastructure-support personnel for a variety of purposes, such as maintenance, logistical coordination with Earth, communications and medical support. *Overture* needed to charter a carousel devoted exclusively to provisioning the expedition with these types of people.

The inclusion of Julia would be paramount: evidence of oxygen in the atmosphere could be the greatest news event of all time. The ramifications of discovering life on the planet, no matter how rudimentary, would be far-reaching for humanity and the reputation of the sponsors and their joint venture under Overture. Julia's celebrity and her biology background, with the potential to uncover the source of oxygen, made her an ideal candidate for inclusion on the journey. I put these thoughts to her.

Of course, I had my ulterior motives. I was missing Julia and wished she were already with us. Was it too much to hope that she would be of like mind?

She quickly came to the same conclusion and we agreed that I would take the matter up with *Overture* after she got Lilian to agree to the reporter role. My task was to explain to Jabu, Robin and Dmitri.

Wasting no time, I updated them. As expected, they were thrilled at the possibility of having the two along with us. Robin reminded us that the plan was contingent on the biological assessment of the atmosphere and surface conditions on Hermes. If we could not safely live on the surface, the strategy was moot.

Lilian too had no hesitation in agreeing. In fact, she was quite excited at the prospect, noticeably infecting Julia with enthusiasm as the three of us met one final time before approaching *Overture*. The fact that they would be traveling as a pair was an added bonus. I resolved to make sure that our masters were convinced.

Rather than schedule a special meeting to persuade *Overture* to launch a support team, to Robin's point, I decided to wait for the session at which they would release their findings. The assessment of the livability of the planet from a contamination perspective was pivotal to the question of a support team, and even of Hermes as a destination.

A nail-biting week passed before we heard that the patrons were ready to talk. The meeting included our pod, Julia, Lilian, the local steering committee and a number of representatives of *Overture* including Stanley. Mr. Estrange, the Mars Mission Controller, and a member of the United Nations also attended.

Stanley got straight down to business. "I would like to introduce you to Dr. Vespucci, who leads the secretariat of the United Nations Office for Outer Space Affairs UNOOSA, and Dean of the Faculty of Biology at the University of British Columbia. Their mandate is to promote international cooperation in the peaceful uses of outer space. I must however stress, this is a private venture and as such, mission related decisions are the purview of the mission sponsors. *Overture* is however committed to abide by ethical ground-rules set by the secretariat. Thank you for attending Dr. Vespucci. I would like to hand over the meeting to Mr. Estrange, the Mars Mission Controller to relay to you his team's findings."

With bated breath, we listened as he presented their findings.

"The probe took atmospheric samples during the descent. Oddly, at the higher altitudes there was evidence of what appeared to be bacterial residue in the form of dead microbes, the husks of bacteria with damaged cell membranes. As expected, these did not show signs of propagation during the limited time in culture trays. As the probe descended the incidence of these husks diminished to near zero at the surface. The explanation that provided the soundest logic was that prolonged exposure to ultraviolet light during the interstellar journey probably sterilized the free-floating bacteria and that precipitation at lower reaches washed the atmosphere of the residue. Once on the surface an accumulation of snow turned to ice likely buried the deposit. The probe was not able to penetrate the surface ice by more than a few inches to confirm the logic or establish what lay below that level. From a human perspective, the risk of lethal infection appeared to be virtually zero, although, if encountered in a concentrated form, the husks could result in chemical poisoning, something that was not tested."

"As with the presence of oxygen in the atmosphere, indirectly the inference of the dead bacteria was that life existed on the planet at some point in the past but a direct claim without encountering actual living material was not possible, albeit an intriguing possibility. The converse, contamination by humans of indigenous life, was equally not likely unless a lifeform remains hidden from observation. The normal protocol for protecting the environment would need to be in force."

Stanley asked, "I take it that there is therefore no technical impediment to proceeding with the landing. Is that correct?"

Mr. Estrange confirmed this assumption.

Other factors remained to consider, namely cost, profitability, political considerations and competition for resources used to carry out the endeavor versus directing these resources elsewhere. They evaluated these and although the risk was assessed to be high, the potential gains were substantial. *Overture* acknowledged that there was pressure to stop space exploration for now and that this window was rapidly closing. They were anxious to proceed before overwhelming local environmental factors and pressure from shareholders to focus elsewhere took center stage. On balance, they favored pressing on with the landing. One caveat was that, in order to ensure the viability of the mission, they required a minimum number of construction, mining and support personnel to agree to settle on Hermes. A breakdown of 75 construction, 60 mining and 10 support staff would be the minimum to continue.

To limit their risks they required the landing volunteers to indemnify them, holding *Overture* safe from litigation and absolving them from arranging specific return charters. Returnees would have to wait for seats on return trips in the normal course of charter flights. Passengers not interested in participating in the landing could return to Earth on the next shuttle. Destination Mars was effectively no more. They could not support a three-choice scenario.

Dmitri, who had been listening to the exchange until Stanley made this pronouncement, questioned Stanley. "It should be easy to accommodate the group who want to continue to Mars. They can disconnect their pod from the carousel as we near Mars, and all that will be required is for a support craft to assist in the landing after they make their way to the Mars orbit. An autopilot can control the pro…"

Stanley interrupted. "No, no, definitely not. We cannot entertain that. We have no work for them on the surface. Surely, it will only be twenty or thirty people. No, the group would be too small for us to manage as a separate venture. No!"

Stanley's insistence left Dmitri no choice but to accept his decision.

With the green light effectively given to a Hermes rendezvous, I drew their attention to the need for a support flight to provision the settlers with supplies, as well as the rationale behind an Earth-Hermes rendezvous on the far side of the sun for the shipment.

Pressing on, I added, "As far as we know, transit vehicles similar to the *Forerunner*, with supply craft in the ready, are still in orbit around the Earth. They should be available for use, something that will also probably not persist for much longer."

Stanley replied hesitantly, "We understand that the decision to land on Hermes has limited opportunity for success without a supply mission to support it. We have been thinking along these lines anyway."

With relief noticeable on his face he added, "It is a good point you make. We should have thought of the option of a rendezvous on the far side. The shortening of the trip down to eight months will be a boon in many respects. The associated cost benefit of an early departure and shorter trip will go down well with the board."

With some uncertainty, he questioned the mission controller, "Let me get this right. Do you concur that it will be possible to meet at the next conjunction? In about eight months?"

Mr. Estrange clarified, "Yes! Yes, of course that is possible. The conjunction will not be as close as the current one but it definitely presents an opportunity. The two planets will be partially mis-aligned in time because their orbital speeds differ but, yes, that will be possible."

Stanley continued. "Short-circuiting the trip will help relieve the mounting pressure to divert attention to earthly matters. I must say that it tilts the venture into positive territory."

Turning to one of his colleagues and hedging his bet, he continued, "You can probably take it as a foregone conclusion that the board will approve the trip. Once the board agrees I will signal to you to proceed. In the meantime, please go ahead and plan accordingly. It is just as well that we had this meeting. We are on the same page. Is there anything else we need to address?"

This was just the opening I needed to make my case for the inclusion of Julia and Lilian on the voyage. It took a little convincing, especially Julia's role. No question, a reporter they could understand, but biology and exploration for traces of life was another matter, since the focus of their business model was on mining and construction, not life sciences.

Improvising, since Julia and I had not discussed this, I launched into a long explanation, making the most of my time-slice in the back-and-forth of the communication delays. "Governance of the protocol to protect indigenous life forms will require a monitoring capability. The person you appoint will also need to set guidelines and enforce them for emerging circumstances. This will require someone with the expertise to conduct this aspect of the endeavor."

I stressed, "Failure to do so will, without doubt, raise the ire of environmentalists, which will not reflect well on the company. Conversely, if done correctly the company can expect congratulatory praise for progressive actions." I added, "The cost does not need to be prohibitive, merely the addition of one more person together with a properly equipped laboratory."

I put forward Julia's name and biology credentials. She did not require introduction given her acclaim for discovering the planet in the first instance.

There was an immediate appreciation of the value of her inclusion based on the rapport she had with the scientific community and, to some extent, with the general public. The bonus was her biologist designation. Through the time-delay video, I could see Julia's relief at the acceptance and Lilian's delight at the outcome.

The tension dissipated as matters turned to the details of logistical arrangements. In for a penny, in for a pound, Dmitri pressed for mechanization of the construction effort in the form of additional robots suited to the change in topography compared to Mars. Jabu concurred and asked for the wherewithal for additional core-sample drilling to support penetration of the ice layers for mining and in the search for life, only having one to use in the meantime. He also asked for a fleet of drones to conduct a wider search for opportunities and to enable unmanned sampling of minerals.

We came away pleased with our efforts and the agreed outcomes. Our immediate anxiety was to build the stipulated quorum of construction, mining and support personnel.

* * *

News of the bacterial husks rippled through the news channels on Earth, raising as many skeptics as believers in life beyond our home planet. The *Forerunner* voyagers were not immune to the same conclusions.

With the hub again crowded to capacity, Jabu started with the feedback, declaring, "Three decisions arose out of the meeting with *Overture*. Firstly, they agreed to a diversion to Hermes, but the decision on where to actually land on the planet will only be made when we arrive in the vicinity!"

A cheer went up as the audience excitedly considered the news, shaking hands with likeminded fellow travelers seated alongside them. It took a while for the noise to subside.

As calm returned, Jabu continued, "Secondly…, secondly they will entertain a return trip for those who prefer to do so, but that group will have to wait for a routinely scheduled shuttle to be able to return to Earth."

The smaller subset of the audience who favored this option were clearly delighted.

Taking a breath, Jabu went on, "Unfortunately, I have to inform you that they have declined a continuation to Mars. They cannot afford to undertake all three options. But, I have to say…"

Before he could elaborate, Michael, one of the two people who had to be constrained by the security person during our first meeting, backed by a vociferous group seated around him, wasted no time to challenge the decision. "No way – this is a travesty!" they shouted. Barging forward to the lectern, he ranted, "We signed up to go to Mars, not some new rock that happened to cross our path. That is where we must go. Once we reach Mars, you can ask for a return voyage or go to the confounded rock."

Others chimed in from the floor: "This whole process is a sham. The outcome was inevitable given the slanted composition of the coordinating committee."

Jabu tried to rein in the disarray: "I fully understand that you have rights that need to be considered, but a vote at the earlier session led us down this path and there was overwhelming support for the plan and on the composition of the steering committee. I suggest that you form your own committee and approach *Overture* with your perspective. After all, it is for *Overture* to decide where they want to spend their money and weigh up their initial commitments in relation to events that intervened. You definitely have a case."

Pointing to Dmitri he said, "I might add that at the meeting Dmitri here specifically advocated on your behalf to allow for you to continue on to Mars. They said they could not manage a separate and smaller work group."

That seemed to take the wind out of their sails and Michael reluctantly sat down, signaling to his followers that they can talk later.

With that apparently out of the way, we updated the group with the details of the sponsor's decisions and the required risk commitments to participate in the landing as well as the minimum composition of the landing party. This generated a few more dissenters before we settled on about 152 pro-landers, just seven over the minimum. The breakdown was heart-stopping close, construction 76, mining 64 and 12 in support roles.

A majority of the balance of 48 favor a return to Earth leaving the Mars group without a sufficient voice to make a case to *Overture* for continuing to Mars, knocking the wind out of their sails for their cause. With disappointment written on the faces of this minority, the meeting disbanded.

As we made our way out of the venue, Michael, his shock of red hair looking more disheveled than ever, was approached by Dmitri. In the din as the throng funneled through the exit, I overheard Dmitri voicing his regret at the outcome but lost the rest of the exchange.

Back in our pod, we wondered at what their next move would be. They were clearly disgruntled, but what obstructionist tactic could they employ to get their way? Their strongest argument was that Hermes was so newly arrived from the void that the unknowns far outweighed the known; it would make more sense to allow at least two years for conditions to stabilize before venturing to the planet. This would seem to be a valid argument, although counterbalanced by equally uncertain conditions on Mars and Earth. In addition, there was the rising public sentiment for preferably attending to conditions on Earth first. As always, the window of opportunity was usually short-lived, and in this case, in particular, needed acting on right away. Procrastination would close the window for many years. We thought *Overture* would have considered these opposing viewpoints and would come to the same conclusion that was already on the table. From the perspective of those holding out for a continuation to Mars, having exhausted a rational route, it left them with only some form of sabotage to get their way. What could that be? Our suspicions were piqued when we heard that they had given up on approaching *Overture*: it seemed unlikely that they would give up so easily.

11

NOAH

As Michael and Noah, his colleague, left the auditorium, Noah could see that he was in a quandary, wondering what to do next, when a person with a Russian accent interrupted them, addressing him. "Hello, I am Dmitri, the Dmitri that Jabu referred to. I just wanted to tell you that I think you should not just let matters lie as they are. At minimum, they should hear you out. At the meeting with *Overture*, I tried to explain to Stanley the Director of Operations that the cost to *Overture* need not be much, but he would not let me even finish my explanation."

Michael said, "Well thank you Dmitri. It is very considerate of you. This is Noah, a friend of mine."

Dmitri continued, "Anyhow, if you come along with us to Hermes, I am sure things will turn out okay."

Michael pulled Dmitri aside, glancing around to ensure that they were out of earshot of anyone who could overhear the conversation. He said, "You are right and I think you have made the correct decision for yourself, but you see" – he paused and looked around before continuing – "I am married to a person who went to Mars with the earlier group. She is a nursing sister. That was after we had an argument. We kind of separated. When the opening came up for me to go to Mars, I secretly communicated with her and she agreed that we could get together again if I joined her there."

"I see your problem. Only single people were supposed to volunteer for the venture."

"Yes, I should have been honest about that, but what could I do? They would have declined me."

"Da, yes I see."

"Please don't tell anyone about this, otherwise I will be in trouble and she may also have problems. Noah here has a similar reason, except he was not as dishonest as I was."

Noah felt a need to clarify and said, "Yes, I have a younger brother on Mars and I was worried about him, especially now that we know that the conditions will worsen. He was always so impulsive; set off for Mars only to regret the decision now that he is there. I joined the voyage mainly to be near him. Fortunately, I was already working for one of the sponsors. With my mining expertise and some navigation experience while in the Air Force, I was readily accepted. Our father died many years ago and I have been playing a father role to my brother."

"Of course, eez not easy for you. I will not tell others. At the meeting with *Overture*, I suggested to the director that you could detach your pod from the carousel as we approach Hermes and you could go on to Mars if they help you with landing. He would not listen. If you contact them and explain this, I am sure you can convince them."

As Michael and Noah left the Hub and Dmitri returned to his friends, Michael said, "Noah, you know I think Dmitri has something there. It is all a matter of timing. Could you have a look at the console in our pod and see whether you can make sense of the navigation options."

"Sure Mike, what did you have in mind?"

"Just see how easy it is to take control of the pod. You remember, during our training, they said the pods could operate autonomously, if necessary. Well, could we fly unassisted to Mars?"

"Look Mike, just because I have limited navigation experience, does not translate into controlling an object in space. I …"

"Noah, do you or don't you want to see your brother? Just have a look. We can decide after that. I am not for a minute suggesting that you should put us in danger, okay."

* * *

Hermes grew, ballooning; it dominated our view as gravity drew us in like a fish on a line, the grip of a magnet so powerful, its allure mesmerizing, funneling our imaginings to a life on its foreign surface.

The autopilot applied subtle velocity and directional changes to position us into our orbit around the planet. With only days left to rendezvous, the course adjustments clearly set us up for a close encounter. Each change focused us on the reality of the hazards of entry into the atmosphere and an unknown world that awaited. The final tunings took us into a low orbit around the equator, from where we could see our landing site. The experience of seeing a new world at such close quarters with a myriad of stars as a backdrop was overwhelming. Struck by our place in the vast expanse of the universe, cocooned as we were in our pod, it reminded us of our insignificant status in the order of the natural world. How we came to exist and the odds of surviving the forces aligned for and against us challenged our resolve. The impact on our group was both elevating and sobering; expanding our minds to encompass the possible and impossible, each instance in time a celebration of life infusing us with a determination to succeed.

* * *

Michael was like a dog with a bone. Once he made up his mind, there was no changing it. They made their way to their pod and Noah spent some time on the console. The screen was quite rudimentary and, with a little difficulty, he could see where the guidance system accepted parameters for steering purposes. It was designed as a point-and-shoot tool. One would point at an object, such as a star or, in their case, a planet, and the AI handled the trajectory to the object, taking into account velocity and gravitational effects of nearby objects. A feature allowed for a graphical simulation on the screen. They ran it through based on the current location and indicated Mars as the destination. The display executed the maneuver flawlessly. It curved around Hermes and followed a trajectory that compensated for the moving target, to converge on Mars further along in an optimum flight path. Noah repeated the simulation an hour later to test whether it recognized the movements in space since the last simulation, and it again performed perfectly.

Noah called Michael over and demonstrated the simulation to him. "I have to say that this is amazing. If it works in practice as it does in the simulation, it should be safe to proceed."

Michael was ecstatic, the disheveled red hair accentuating his wild elation as he danced around the limited space.

In moments he had all twenty of the Press-On group on a private video channel. "I have excellent news. Noah has simulated taking control of our pod's navigation system and steering it to Mars. It works perfectly. Even I could do it; it is so simple, watch…"

He ran through the steps and the simulation a couple of times.

"I would like you to try it for yourselves on your consoles."

They did so and soon reported that it was like child's play.

Michael challenged them. "As you can see, you can put yourself on a path to Mars. Here is the issue. We do not have the permission of *Overture* and we do not have a means to land on Mars. It is one thing to get there, and another to land. This needs expert support. Based on the simulation, the pods will arrive at Mars and go into orbit."

After pausing for them to understand fully, he continued, "Now! I am relying on them, the Mars Support Operation, to assist us once we get there, but I cannot guarantee that they will. I am presuming that they will not be so callous as to abandon us in space. *Overture* will not be happy with this that is for sure; it is essentially an act of mutiny. The decision is therefore yours. You have the means to get there and it is now up to you to decide what you want to do. Each pod can come to their own conclusions. You have to accept that there will be risks."

After an exchange of a few questions, Michael said, "Our pod will decide for itself and at precisely 13:00 GMT we will begin our maneuver if that is in fact our decision. That is about two hours from now. Five minutes prior to that time we will signal to you whether we are going or not. We must all act in concert for this to have any chance of success. Is that okay? Good luck and … see you on Mars!"

* * *

Absorbed as we were by the spectacle of Hermes before us, a surprise shattered our dreamlike state; an object crossed our path, veering off in a straight line as we proceeded in the curve of the orbit.

Dmitri was the first to notice: "Look there! And there are three more!"

Recognition dawned on us as we discerned that the shapes were pods from the carousel. What could the explanation possibly be?

Dmitri was quick to realize. "It must be them, Michael and his group. Surely, it can only be them. They exited the trajectory of the *Forerunner* with their velocity still sufficient for Hermes' gravity not to capture them and become a satellite. They are using the speed as a slingshot for an onward journey. It eez just as I imagined it could be done." Dmitri was agitated by the unfolding event. "Mars eez their objective judging by the angle they exited the orbit. Their timing was perfect, but do they have enough momentum to reach Mars, before the end of conjunction with Hermes?"

With rising concern, he added, "They have taken a gamble that they will reach Mars. I hope they know what they are doing. From what I remember from our training on the navigation systems, they must have used the onboard AI."

As we watched the receding pods, he went on, "Surely they could not have secured the permission of *Overture* so quickly. My guess is they decided to go alone. Without the sponsor's agreement and without commandeering the whole *Forerunner* system. No mutiny, no endangering all voyagers, just act alone in the individual pods."

With some relief, he added, "They have chosen the safest solution. Yes, that eez it, they have some control and no one else eez affected."

We realized that if they were able to reach an orbit around Mars, their next challenge would be the heat and turbulence of entry into Mars' atmosphere. Without support, the dangers would be extreme. The pods had limited aerodynamic capabilities for gliding purposes but a leveled landing site would need to align with their trajectory. The autopilot capabilities would need human intervention at key intervals and they did not have this expertise.

Soon they receded and disappeared into the distance, lost to visual contact; it would be up to the crew of the *Forerunner* to monitor their progress.

It would take a few days for them to traverse the distance to Mars. During that time, they would need minor course and velocity corrections to enter a suitable orbit around Mars, which no doubt the autopilot could do. For the time being, they were safe. As the hours passed, alarmingly, we learned that *Overture* was leaving them to their own devices because they did not have control over the support facilities on Mars and therefore could not direct activities.

* * *

Julia informed us that the news channels, alerted to the events, were giving it widespread coverage. Somehow, the mayday calls had been intercepted by the news media. Interviews with *Overture* and the Mars coordinators generally ended up with them pointing fingers at each other, refusing to take responsibility. If this persisted, a catastrophe was in the making. It became apparent that the dissenters had assumed that once they had successfully detached from the *Forerunner*, sympathies would turn their way to sway authorities to lend support. Recordings of their pleas for support went unanswered and time pressures mounted.

Dmitri, in concern for them, hesitantly admitted, "I had a conversation with Michael the leader of the dissidents. He and a number of others in his group were heading for Mars not so much for the mining and construction work; they wanted to meet up with relatives and friends. They asked me to keep this confidential because *Overture* had explicitly selected for the venture based on each person having no encumbrances."

Going on, he speculated, "Michael's group might be silent on this even now. I am sure they fear blacklisting of family members. It can only be the connection to family and friends that is motivating them to do this."

Jabu exclaimed, "Shit Dmitri, you should have said something sooner! How could you just remain quiet all this time? What if something happens to them, what then? This is space, you don't play with it!"

"Jabu, it is no use pointing a finger at me. At least I was approachable enough for them to tell me their dilemma."

Unimpressed, Jabu responded, "You should have said, 'No', when he asked you to keep it confidential."

On the defensive Dimitri replied, "By then it was too late. He had already confided in me."

Robin came to Dmitri's rescue. "Jabu, it is unfair to have Dmitri shoulder the responsibility for this." Turning to Dmitri he said, "You expected Michael to discuss this with *Overture*, didn't you? As far as I can see, you had no idea that he would take matters into his own hands. Am I right?"

"Da, yes. I told Michael that *Overture* would consider the matter more favorably if he spoke to them directly. Stanley would not even allow me to explain what I had in mind." Turning to Jabu he said, "You know that Jabu, you were at the meeting."

Concerned that Jabu's accusation would threaten our usual cohesiveness, I suggested, "Look, when Dmitri advocated on behalf of the Press-On group that was prior to the discussion he had with Michael. It did not have anything to do with the confidentiality question. That came later. Here is what I suggest; Michael should use his family connections as an added argument to convince *Overture* to take a more active role in facilitating the landing process."

Robin concurred. "We have localized audio connectivity via the central communication system to all the pods in the carousel, which includes the departing pods. We could patch them in. With an open line of communication, Dmitri could talk them into doing this. The time-delay would be minimal given our proximity to them."

Dmitri vacillated. "On the one hand I promised not to repeat my conversation with them, even to you, and on the other hand they are in danger. I don't know what to do."

Jabu, regretting his earlier accusation, said, "Dmitri, I am sorry for accusing you as I did. It was unwarranted. I am truly sorry!"

"Thanks Jabu. We are probably all stressed by what is happening, but what do we do now?"

"Matters have now reached a point of life and death. Michael will not hold it against you if you tell him that you spoke to us. I think Miles' suggestion is worth considering, but I would go further; since he has already gone over the head of *Overture*, he could appeal to the public on Earth directly. Many would take a more compassionate stance and advocate for assistance with the landing."

Dmitri agreed.

Fortuitously the link was still operational; they were still within hailing distance. Dmitri apologized for breaching his confidentiality, which Michael accepted provided we did not discuss it with anyone else. Dmitri then went on to explain our suggestion, but Michael was still against the idea, plainly nervous of the consequences. With this impasse, the parties went quiet.

I signaled to Dmitri to mute the call.

He did so, and turned to me.

I said, "I suggest that we make contact with Julia and Lilian. They could appeal to the public over the head of the authorities in charge of the Mars landings. A carefully phrased article by them may win support. Oh, but I must caution, we must avoid negatively influencing our sponsor's decision to allow Julia and Lilian on the next shuttle."

Jabu interjected, "It would need some delicacy. Fortunately, the Mars landing authority is separate from our sponsoring organization. Dmitri, try that. It is the only way out."

Over the unmuted connection, Dmitri explained our plan to Michael, but he remained undeterred.

"Michael, this is Robin. This has gone far enough! What do you think the answer would be if your wife or other family members of your group had a say? They would have no hesitation in agreeing."

Michael responded, "I think it is a matter of time and the authorities will agree to support us. We just have to be patient."

Robin angrily replied, "Time is fast running out. Leave it any longer and the choices you still have will be gone. Gone, do you hear?"

Noah interjected, "Michael, the tension is too much to bear. Let's just get on with it. We can deal with the consequences later."

There was silence. Then, reluctantly, Michael agreed.

Lilian drew up a communiqué and shared it with Michael, who made minor adjustments. The article, released on the Internet, read as follows:

Mars colonists left stranded in space

A dissident group of settlers elected to continue their voyage to Mars. Four pods broke away from the main journey, which is destined for Hermes, the new planet. They now face the dangers of descent to the surface of Mars unassisted by mission support from Earth and Mars. Their predicament is serious. They stand very little likelihood of surviving entry into Mars' atmosphere unless the authorities lend support. An appeal for help has so far gone unanswered. Only a few days separate them from certain disaster.

A number of newspapers picked up the story and published it widely. As expected, there was an uproar over the callous treatment of the dissenters. After all, they and their families represented the vanguard of humanity's first steps beyond Earth. To their credit, the authorities reached a decision quickly and dispatched an ascent and landing vehicle from the surface of Mars to meet the incoming pods. News commentaries welcomed the change, mirroring public sympathy, as they followed the unfolding events.

* * *

"Hello? Hello? Is that you Michael? Hello? Can you hear me? It's Ella."

"Ella, oh Ella, how I have missed you. How are you mo chridhe?"

"I am well. I cannot wait to see you. When the news broke, one of the news organizations contacted me. I have no idea how they knew that we are married. I miss you, love!"

"It will be only a few more days. I am so terribly sorry I lost my temper with you. I promise, I promise that will never happen again, never."

"Dearest Mike. That is long forgotten." Laughing, she continued, "Please don't do anything rash – I mean, that you have not already done. I wish you were not so impulsive, but I guess that is why I love you."

"Just a few more days, love. You take care."

* * *

Safely in our pod, we waited the remaining days as Michael's fleet of pods covered the distance to Mars and met up with the support vehicle as they moved into orbit. Docking the first pod required some adjustments before it connected to the support vehicle. That done, the other three pods then maneuvered to couple behind it into a train, with the landing vehicle upfront. They were ready for entry.

We watched the three-way split screen live-feed of events. One screen showed Noah and Michael strapped in, and facing each other. Two colleagues sat alongside them. The second screen was a forward view from the window of the support vehicle. The third screen was a view from an observatory on the ground overlooking the proposed landing area, showing the red sand stretching into the distance with a rudimentarily leveled landing strip in the foreground.

We watched with interest, because our entry process to land on Hermes would be similar, except that we were to glide to a strip of leveled ice, whereas the pods approaching Mars had to use parachutes in the latter stage of the entry. Each pod would separate from the train and deploy parachutes separately. Our descent would have two well-trained pilots to conduct the first two landings manually and then use the data recordings to program the autopilot for the subsequent landings. For us the train of four pods would remain intact, including the touchdown on the ice where a single parachute would deploy to halt the slide over the ice before the end of the runway.

* * *

"Michael, please stop fidgeting and strap down. Have a look at the view through the portal. Mars is more beautiful than I imagined."

"Okay, okay, I am struggling with this helmet; my hair keeps getting in the way… Wow Noah, what a sight! Oh, look there! Look at that, Olympus Mons poking through the atmosphere and there, there is Valles Marineris!"

"Incredible! Just breathtaking…"

"If you look to the left behind you, you can see Phobos and Deimos, both in the sky at the same time. That has to be special. Ha, ha, Fear and Panic – get behind us. Only a few more minutes and I will be holding Ella in my arms."

Tensions rose by degrees with the jolt of the support vehicle as it made the first of a few attempts to couple to the front of their pod. Then, with a sharp snap, it was in place. It took a few more minutes to link the other pods into a train behind them. At last, they were all set as they rounded the curve of the planet with one final lap of the magnificent world, the well-known topographical features easy to identify.

The first wisps of turbulent air streaked across Noah's window under deceleration, G-forces thrusting him forward in his seat, the atmospheric braking dragging on the craft. Shuddering increased to a calamitous noise; the only sensation he could process. Gripping the arms of the seat, concerns for their safety elevated with each passing second. Jerking lurched them uncontrollably, endurance seemed impossible; either the pod or they in the pod would succumb. The heat, from the friction outside, added to the pool of perspiration in his suit, drenching him and clouding his visor. The unnatural forces, the violence of the passage, when would it end? Endure, endure, that is all they had to do. Just endure. It must end, surely! Blackness began to intrude on Noah's vision as he slipped from consciousness, but just as his life seemed in balance the ferocity subsided as they declined, and with it their speed. A sense of elation took over. The sensation of having negotiated the very edge of what is humanly possible, so profound, contrasted as it was with a planet spread below. It served to magnify the experience to that of the miraculous. Incredible!

Gliding in the slipstream of the descent vehicle gave them a few moments to marvel at the rusted gullies and dunes below. Moments later a backward jerk against the headrest marked the release of the rear pod from the train, then the second pod. As they anticipated the discharge of the third pod, Noah turned to Michael whose green eyes mirrored his expectation of the next jerk. His face register a change before, puzzled by the unexpected, a thunderbolt echoed through the fabric of the pod, followed by a bump, a lurch and a whoosh. The angle of descent began to veer to the left and the view circled from the horizontal across the landscape to the distant horizon then up, up into the pitch-blackness of the heavens as stars swept across the view. The spin sped up, alternating between sky and land, sky and land, faster, faster, faster. Noah's head and whole body jerked from side to side. He could see the alarm reflected in Michael's visor.

* * *

From our vantage in the pod safely circling Hermes, we watched transfixed as the dissenters began skimming the atmosphere of Mars. The red glow of intensifying friction, viewed from the leading descent vehicle, transitioned to yellow as they plunged into the meager atmosphere until white with heat; the blistering exterior finally obscured the view. Switching views to each pod showed only an outer glow as they safely flew in the wake of the vehicle in front of them. As the atmosphere arrested the momentum the radiance lessened, revealing a spectacular view of the rusted surface of Mars. Still traveling at a significant speed, the landscape flashed below until, in the distance at the edge of the shallow horizon, a manmade construction became apparent, their destination; the observatory.

The pods began their separation sequence, starting with the rear pod. A parachute ripped open, the force plucked the pod from its predecessor, the pod slowed until all momentum was lost, and the pod dangled in a vertical aspect to drift down to a soft landing some distance from the structure. While the first pod settled to the ground, the second pod ripped loose and followed the same pattern to the ground. So far, so good, but as the third pod readied for separation the video link showed that the pod in front of it prematurely released its parachute. From our perspective, it was unclear whether the release of the parachutes required manual or automatic discharge. The third pod immediately deployed its parachute, successfully separating from the front pod, pod four, to drift to a landing. With a gasp we realized that the parachute of pod four was tangled and could not fully open.

The commentator with the view from the observatory could be heard to inhale sharply and from the background a female's voice repeated in sheer alarm, "Oh my god, oh my god, oh my god!" She trailed off with, "Michael, Michael…"

Pod four spiraled away as the leader in the descent vehicle realized the situation and forcibly ejected its docking mechanism from its trailing pod to execute an independent landing. Pod four careened off at an angle, its speed too high. A deathly silence followed as the scene unfolded in what seemed like slow motion; a cloud of red dust billowed as the craft plowed into the ground until the veil was fully drawn by the enveloping obscurity. The onboard camera went dark.

* * *

Strapped in as they were, there was nothing they could do, their fate lay in the balance. Each revolution of the spiral showed the ground nearing, the angle too steep to expect anything but the worst outcome.

Above the screaming din Noah heard Michael's voice, faintly, "Noah, this is it!"

Taking a deep breath, Noah watched as the wing on his side struck the ground, sheering it from the body as if made of paper. This somewhat righted the craft to plow into the dust of Mars. The screech of metal on rock obliterated conscious thought until, in a finale, the nose found purchase. The force ripped through the vehicle, tilting it up and over to crash on its roof. Then nothing, nothing but blackness.

* * *

Ella in the observatory was first to react. She scrambled down the stairs to the waiting ground support vehicle. "Drive, drive," she shouted at the man behind the wheel, who was still processing what he had witnessed. Within minutes, they entered the cloud of dust, slowing down to better navigate the murk until the silhouette of the pod lying on its hood lay before them. Entry was easy: the severed wing had ripped away the hatch to the interior. Inside, four men hung from the inverted craft, still strapped to their seats. Ella gently released the unconscious Michael from his harness and lowered him to the mound of sand in the cockpit. She applied first aid to her unresponsive husband and proceeded to do the same to the other three. The biting cold was her next concern; they moved them to the warmth of the support vehicle and sped to the clinic where a doctor attended to them.

* * *

Dmitri immediately reached out to the Mars Controller and within hours established a communication link. He maintained a daily dialog with Ella, in attendance at the clinic. All four individuals were severely injured and initially unconscious, and one person's condition was critical. Sadly, after a week, the critically injured person succumbed to his injuries, thankfully attended by the one he loved so dearly. Michael was the first person buried on Mars. As Ella said in a message to Dmitri, "He was irrepressible, spontaneous and impulsive, a unique person; ultimately the red sands of Mars merged with his red hair and ruddy complexion as though preordained. I will always love the memory of him."

Noah emerged from unconsciousness after two weeks and slipped back into an insentient state on hearing the news that Michael had died. He later gradually recovered, under Ella's care. Daily physiotherapy for a year returned him to full health, but for periodic episodes of headaches. The other two, although seriously injured, recovered over the next six months.

Overture ultimately honored their commitment to support the dissenting group under the original twenty-five-year contract despite their mutiny. They established a scaled-down construction facility on Mars which they executed in exemplary fashion.

12

WORLD

Our initial shock of seeing the four departing pods gave way to mounting tension as the dangers they faced confronted them. The events so mesmerized all onboard the *Forerunner* that all thought of Hermes lying at our feet was secondary. With landing plans shelved, we circled the planet as an automaton, all control vested in the autopilot. Days passed as we watched, riveted to the unfolding drama.

The initial emotions of shock gave way to determination to find a solution for their predicament. Relief followed as the authorities took up the challenge of landing. Hope and anticipation of the reunion with the loved ones was paramount for a few days, until replaced by the angst of the looming entry. Then came the nail-biting dive into the atmosphere and the shocking failure of the chute. Concern for their wellbeing stretched into hours before the news of their condition reached us, and days lapsed with hope of a recovery being our main concern. Finally, the distress of hearing of the loss of Michael brought grief and sorrow.

Dull resignation hung over us, and all the voyagers on the *Forerunner*, as we endlessly circled the planet that beckoned. The confluence seemed to exact the full measure of cruelty that the universe could mete out on us. The smallest degree of change in the trajectory of Hermes through the void would have separated us from the destiny that lay before us. The chance that Hermes should reach apogee in its elliptical orbit on the far side of Mars confounded logic and what is plausible.

The fate that befell Michael imposed a heavy burden on us, as did the prognosis for his colleagues. Even as we looped around the circumference of our orbit, Mars would come into view, larger than the moon seen from Earth, questioning our adoption of the intruding planet as home. Hermes, the planet that usurped eons of tradition in the hierarchy of planetary resonance to occupy a prime location, pushing aside Earth and Mars to lesser status, compounded the climate distress of heat and cold these two already shouldered. Earth glinted in the distance, reminding us each day of the dire future that loomed for our loved ones.

Of all of us, Dmitri took the loss of Michael worst. He blamed himself for intervening, despite the fact that their predicament had been dire to begin with. He could not reconcile his actions with the consequences. He withdrew for a long time as he processed the loss, even with our assurance that his intervention may have averted the loss of all twenty people. Ultimately, at a superficial level, he accepted Michael's fate. However, his usual thoughtful engaging demeanor, though it returned, masked an underlying tinge of introverted seriousness. Jabu's countenance conveyed signs of certain guilt for questioning Dmitri's initial silence, but Dmitri bore no ill will and both drew nearer as companions.

Noah, Ella and Dmitri maintained contact despite the gulf between the two worlds. I, to this day, shudder at the memory of the events.

The experience emphasized the dangers that confronted us as we approached our destination, sobered our enthusiasm, reminding us of the risks we so blithely accepted. As vassals of the broader drive of destiny, we felt helpless to direct its course. Our singular focus became the immediate next steps, leaving fate to have its way, whatever that may have been. A single step at a time.

* * *

Events so absorbed our attention that as Mars receded into the distance, the knock of opportunity was lost. By omission, Mars faded as an option, defaulting to Hermes as the destiny we were to pursue.

No longer bound by time constraints, we circled Hermes as captives of its gravity. Bound to the sun, we left Mars in our wake as the desolation outside the ecliptic plane lay before us. The survey probes continued their work from orbit, mapping the surface of Hermes, providing fine detail to us and our sponsors. We saw images suggesting continents, seas and islands under a blanket of ice. The data included the probable distribution of mineral deposits, fault lines and seismic activity. Mountain ridges and trenches stood in stark relief, while predictions of ocean currents and likely wind patterns provided a sense of climate. The diverse topography, not unlike Earth, offered an environment with potential for a permanent home. Continuous monitoring revealed a gradual rise in temperature from which to extrapolate projections. Its proximity to the sun was having an effect. Forecasts expected navigable seas within a decade, but estimates needed considerable refinement, drawn from more data, for the predictions to be considered reliable.

All the while, frequent communications with Julia told of an audience captivated by the unfolding information providing a distraction from the worsening climate conditions on Earth.

* * *

For us, preparations were underway. Dmitri was ferried to one of the supply craft where he reconfigured a mobile robot to provide excavation and grading capabilities to use for leveling a landing strip for our pods. With that done, he returned to our pod where we waited for the next step in the choreographed countdown to entry. The flotilla of unmanned supply craft detached themselves from the vicinity of the *Forerunner* mothership, taking up new orbital positions for entry to take their cargo to the surface. With a number of survey probes circling Hermes, they provided a continuous video of the supply craft as they prepared for entrance into the new world. The angle and velocity adjustments showed on our video feed as each of the four craft dropped to the first wisps of atmosphere. Arrested by the increasing air pressure, their velocity slowed, a fiery tail built and trailed each craft in a spectacular meteor-like display as they entered the depths of the stratosphere. The view then switched to the lead craft just as the furnace subsided and visibility cleared, opening a panorama before it, a picture of land, sea and mountains covered with a white blanket. A schematic of the landing zone superimposed on the terrain showed an oval representation of the target area on the televised image. The craft appeared to overshoot the objective, but the deployment of its parachute precipitated the required deceleration as its attitude changed to the vertical. Dangling from a tether it floated over the oval, sinking down to end the maneuver, positioning itself for an accurate landing. Balloons, released at the last minute, absorbed the shock of touchdown. The other three vehicles followed in quick succession as they completed the foothold on the planet. On the ground, the cameras panned through 360 degrees, showing the vehicles on a narrow, level area, presumably a shallow sea, with outcrops of ice-covered rock about a kilometer due south. To the northeast, the landscape gradually rose to a rocky peak, also about a kilometer away. The northwesterly view was flat for some distance. Despite the probes findings, one question was foremost on everyone's mind, is there life here? Fully expecting the contrary, intense scrutiny revealed no sign of movement, no lifeform, nothing but a palpable sense that the landscape harbored a hidden secret for surely an entire planet cannot exist purely to be shrouded in white.

Once the anticipation subsided we could see that, all in all, the site was well-chosen for a landing strip for the pods that will follow. The cargo doors swung down, forming a ramp from which a succession of tractor robots emerged. At his command, Dmitri's reconfigured robots mechanically got to work with leveling an east-west passage. The surface was relatively soft, so progress was quite rapid, but it would require compaction for it to suffice as a runway. Down the track a distance, a series of small rocky outcrops presented danger to the landing if left as they were. Using a radio link and the onboard cameras of another robot, Dmitri directed it for closer inspection of the obstacles, then issued some commands and the robot got to work on breaking up the rocks. As it worked, it dug trenches to one side and buried the debris at a depth that would not interfere with the landing traffic.

The work was slow but methodical. Gradually a clear and compacted runway of three kilometers formed on the ice. Electronic beacons deposited along both edges formed a communication channel to guide the autopilots in their approach to landing. The robots then dragged the supply craft to the incline to the north, out of the way of the landing strip.

Two weeks had passed since the first landings and Mars had receded into the distance following conjunction with Hermes. We were alone in the void of interplanetary space, each hour separating us further from the ecliptic plane of the other planets. There was an intangible loneliness knowing our course had diverged from the common path, our decision irreversible as we flew headlong into an indeterminate future.

* * *

Fresh determination turned our attention to the matter at hand: a successful landing on our adopted planet. With meticulous care, the entry protocol was reviewed repeatedly, eliminating errors and formulating strategies to counter unforeseen events.

Our sponsors had the forethought of comparing the colonization of Hermes with that of Mars. On Mars, infrastructure in support of the sponsor's mining and construction venture was in place, albeit rudimentary. This was not the case on Hermes. As an outcome of the comparison, they negotiated with the owners of the *Forerunner* and concluded the purchase of the central hub of the carousel. Built for use as a Mars entry vehicle if needed, the issue that arose had to do with the fact that the Martian atmosphere was significantly less dense compared to that of Hermes. To land on Hermes would require sustaining the heat of entry for longer and at higher temperatures.

The engineers believed that the design specifications were just sufficient to survive entry, but they could not rule out the possibility of destruction at the peak of atmospheric friction. If successful, the benefit would be the possibility to use the hub on the ground as a central habitat interconnected to the pods and serving as a common area for the inhabitants, one that would have had to be constructed onsite anyway.

There was also sufficient fuel onboard the hub for a return trip to Earth, which the colonists could instead use for heating and other purposes. The greatest benefit was that the hub was fully equipped with all the necessary communication devices for dialog with Earth and orbiting satellites. Without this, *Overture* would need to organize a separate mission to provision these capabilities. With the bargain struck, plans were underway to ready the hub for entry, but it would first service the pod landing communication needs from orbit before it too landed.

Personnel who elected to return to Earth and therefore were not included in the landing party would transition to one remaining supply craft, where they would unfortunately wait out the eight-month period in orbit before the next shuttle arrived, the one with Julia and Lilian onboard, then return to Earth on that vehicle.

A trained pilot by the name of Lester would remain on the ground after landing, as one of the construction team. He boarded our pod to oversee and record landing events as they occurred. His purpose was to build a repeatable procedure for the autopilots of each successive train of pods. Buckled in and dressed in space suits, we watched as our pod and three others detached from the carousel and maneuvered into a coupled train under guidance of the pilot, autopilot and the command center on the hub. To avoid the need to control multiple trains simultaneously, each train would enter the atmosphere and execute the landing operation alone before the next train moved into position for a repeat of the operation. There were forty pods, making up ten trains with ours being the first in line for entry.

We were at the head of our train with a full view of proceedings before us. As we circled the equator, we eagerly watched for our landing site relative to our orbit. The pod gradually shed altitude, enlarging the landscape until we could see the supply craft and robots in miniature as they continued to toil for us below. The view of the landing site was brief as we continued around the curve of the horizon. On the far side of the planet, the craft began to be buffeted as it dipped into the atmosphere. Our path would loop around half the planet to touch down at our terminus, the end of our long odyssey. Never for one minute did we imagine that our destination could be so exotic.

Images of the supply craft's entry into the atmosphere as relayed to us did nothing to prepare us for actually living through the scorching entrance. The recent mishap on Mars remained etched in our minds, a reminder of the precariousness of what we were about to experience, serving only to heighten our apprehension.

The chatter of preparations on the intercom went silent. Mentally we braced ourselves, immersed ourselves in an envelope of anticipation, our bodies taut, rigid with expectancy as if to shield us against disaster.

The deceleration G-forces tore at every fiber in our bodies, threatening to rip us from our seats, pushing us to near-unconsciousness, while encased in a ball of fire. The heat was so intense that the temperature inside our cocoon rose. Sweat poured from every pore, from a combination of heat and adrenaline. Clattering and jangling as every nut and bolt strained to remain in place, we felt like the craft was about to disintegrate. Unnerved in the extreme, we could but hope for deliverance. Finally, after what seemed like an eternity, the peak passed and the banging gradually subsided. The relief of emerging from the firestorm was profound, but the buffeting continued until we shed sufficient velocity to begin a steep glide. The tension dissipated, washed over us like a soothing balm.

By comparison, the exhilaration of the rest of the flight was profound. Burned into our consciousness was a picture of our future spreading before us. The passing scenery drew us in, mesmerized by its enchantment and wonder at what secrets it hid.

Wide-eyed, we watched. The landing strip materialized in the distance as the horizon loomed nearer. The sliver of smooth ice welcomed our approach.

Jabu was first to break the silence. "What topography! Wow, amazing! The rift valley, there to the right, look how it stretches into the distance; the way the glacier slices off a side of the mountain, it must expose the strata."

Robin joined in, "The air, so clean, pristine; uninterrupted view for miles. I could barely make out the dividing line between space and the stratosphere as we entered. No such thing as pollution here! Just pure air."

I rejoined, "Yes. Look at the string of islands to the left, and more, further on, all the way to the south. They look like soft downy bumps. Have you ever seen anything so white, crystalline?"

"Here we go; it looks like Lester is ready for the landing. Hold on!"

At a signal, the pilot released the small speed-arresting parachute of the rear pod, detaching it from the train. It slowed while we maintained our speed. The second pod from the rear did likewise, and the next until it was our turn. The four pods, now separated from each other, flew as wild geese in an abbreviated V-shape formation, and lined up for a clear run at the landing strip. Lower and lower we descended as the whiteness outside flashed past the window, down, down then finally, touchdown! We plowed through a layer of snow and ice, spraying a wide arc on either side of our craft until, with a jolt, we came to rest well short of the end of the elongated runway. Within seconds the other pods slid to a stop on either side of us. Our train had safely negotiated the descent! Outside the window, the graded marking of the leveling work showed on either side of the pod, and further on tracts of undisturbed snow and ice glistened in pearly reflection of a distant sun.

It took considerable will to redirect our focus to relieving ourselves of the seat harnesses and working our way through the vehicle and spacesuit integrity-check procedures while the pilot completed his final log entries. All was good. The robots drew near, attached themselves to each pod and dragged us to safety at the edge of the runway, allowing the next train of pods a free approach to the landing strip.

* * *

Expectantly, we opened the rear hatch, a ladder descended to the ice floor and I, as project leader, carefully stepped down the metal rungs until the crunch of ice confirmed the first human footprint on this foreign land.

As cameras recorded the event and transmitted it to Earth, the cradle of humanity, my three colleagues stood beside me to survey the bleak landscape before us.

Led here to this remote outpost on the leash of chance, no prepared speech, no "One small step for man, one giant leap for mankind," no orchestrated fanfare, only silence. Hermes spoke for itself. It invoked in every human a different message: our diminutive place in the universe, beckoning worlds, the sparsity of life or its abundance elsewhere, the secrets of the void, the emergence of instinct, the persistence of consciousness, the daily grapple with the mundanity of survival, of love, joy and sadness. To all these, it spoke.

For me, a picture came to mind of the robot lander that reached the surface of Titan some decades prior and surveyed its surroundings. The video of that event, imprinted on my mind, was breathtaking in its foreign bleakness: a methane sea and aerosols coloring the sky, reminiscent of what was before me now, an alien landscape. Here the stark whiteness was a brilliance so translucent it magnified every feature like a glistening dream.

We gaped in long silence at the magic of this world and the humbling privilege of being the first on it. The magnitude of an entire planet, uninhabited by any discernable lifeform, beckoning, inviting exploration. That it should fall to us of all of humanity was beyond comprehension. Images filled my mind; artists' impressions of fictitious alien landscapes that covered my bedroom walls as a youth. They did no justice to the actuality before us.

Slowly the mind turned to the present moment. Detail not apparent from the supply craft video resolved into a glacier leading down a ravine from a stark mountain peak to our right, down into the sea at our level, frozen like a still photograph of a cascading waterfall. The glacial ravine was buttressed on either side by ice-covered ramparts. One dropped away to a low-level platform and then swung around to ease into the frozen sea. The other ended in a cliff at the water's edge with broken ridges disappearing along the coastline. Looking south, the sea stretched beyond the leveled landing area to a row of brilliantly white islands strung along the horizon from left to right, dimpling the flatness of the sea. The sky was a pale blue with gray clouds skidding along the distant horizon as the diminutive sun winked at us from behind a cloud. The similarity to Earth brought a reassuring lump to the throat; conditions were not too alien. Turning off the whirr of air circulating in my suit, I listened; the silence was absolute. No rustle of leaves, no cry of seagulls or chirp of insects. We were alone!

I willed the solitude to continue, for time to stand still in this moment of wonderment. My mind reached out like tentacles to embrace the whole of it. Lightheaded, I soared, elevated in spirit to merge with the surroundings as though unified as one composite entity. It was as though the sole purpose of my entire being was configured for this moment alone. All my dreams and imaginings, distilled into this single moment in time, dispelling all shadows of doubt, worries and concerns, banished to insignificance by the majesty of the moment.

As the metronome of time insisted on its intrusion, my mind turned to my friends surrounding me and I saw that they too had begun to shake loose from the spell. Dmitri, with moist eyes, choked out the words, "Home from home, the frozen plains of Russia. How is it that our journey leads to the beginning; a full circle?"

My thoughts concurred entirely. "Yes, the solitude of the valley where I lived, now re-presented in this form, a reverse image like a negative. Wholly desolate where the other was so vibrant. It is a circle!"

I could see the echo in Jabu as he stammered, "The peacefulness... It seems to wipe out decades of time and with it all the struggles, gone... A world in waiting. Waiting patiently for this introduction; it seems to be asking us to do something, but what is to be done?"

Robin broke his austerity, moved by the experience. "It is a new beginning... For once, I feel a home, our claim to it, the possession of it; it is an anchor, as illogical as that sounds... It is as if the force of gravity has drawn us here, to another Earth, barren of life except as an inheritance for us as the only lifeform... Why do I feel that it is an offer made, thrust on us and we accepted so willingly, or were we tricked? We will have to rise to the occasion."

Silence returned as we each grappled with the stirred emotions. At length and finally, the spell was broken when practical matters intruded. In unison, my colleagues all pointed to a slightly elevated plateau and over the radio intercom enthusiastically proclaimed its suitability as a campsite. Minutes later, joined by members of the other pods, loping along at 90% Earth's gravity, all sixteen of us, and the pilot, congregated around our pod to take in the view. Like children, we animatedly gesticulated at each new observation. There seemed to be consensus that the level plateau is the best spot to pitch camp.

We began carrying our belongings to the area, soon dubbed "The Podium" as the robots started hauling our pods there. This would be our home until we built structures that were more permanent.

While the robots assisted in setting up the basecamp, successive pod trains followed our landing process in intervals of thirty minutes. By late afternoon, with all safely grounded and moved to the land at the edge of the sea, a confidence pervaded our bearing; without mishap, we had firmly established our presence on this new world.

Meanwhile the hub readied for descent. Preparations checked off; tethers used to connect to the pods retracted, parachute and balloon systems checked. Supply craft that would remain in orbit detached from the main body. Essential communication devices needed to communicate with Earth and the Hermes ground party were transferred to the supply craft, leaving a substantial communication capability on the hub to service our needs on the ground.

The hub ponderously positioned itself for plunging into the atmosphere following a path similar to ours. The minutes passed before we saw it approaching over the horizon, trailing the speed-arresting parachute before deploying the main chute. Lacking any aerodynamic form, it dropped to the vertical. Dangling from the huge umbrella, it drifted over the landing site then slowly descended before the balloons released and it bumped to an awkward stop in the middle of the runway. A cheer went up at yet another success, and the relief of knowing a crucial component of our safety and wellbeing was at hand.

With our home secured, our footing established, we settled down as the sun set in the west. With no moon to shed light on our movements or dispel doubts of our chosen path, we were alone on this vast uncompromising world. Weariness of an eventful day drew the blind on day one.

* * *

The morning light welcomed us to a new day. The long night had calmed the excitement of yesterday. It would certainly require adaptation to acclimatize to the 26-hour day.

We spent the day moving the pods up the slope to the Podium. Next, we focused on the major task of manhandling the hub to a central position surrounded by the pods in a north, south, east and west configuration. Interconnected prefabricated covered and sealed walkways taken from the supply crafts and assembled for this purpose linked to the central hub. The final steps were to start the generator to activate the air circulation system and, most importantly, set up the external air monitoring equipment to measure air pressure, oxygen level and assess for toxic content. By morning, we hoped to confirm the earlier findings of a benign environment, spelling the difference between livability and the discomfort of constant clothing changes.

Exhausted from the day's work, the higher gravity had not helped, having acclimatized to the low artificial Mars gravity on the long trip from our home planet. It would take a while to rebuild our strength. By late afternoon, we settled down and for the first time since landing, removed the space suits in the safe confines of the pods. Although the suit design used lightweight flexible material with a semi-flexible hood, it was a relief to rid ourselves of the claustrophobic costume.

A bright day dawned with a dissipating mist hanging over the landing strip. Eagerly we congregated in the hub to review the results of the atmospheric monitoring equipment. The readings were similar to those taken by the probes. Oxygen and air pressure were the same as recorded and there was no toxic content or living matter such as viruses or bacteria. Dispelling pent-up concerns, harbored in anticipation for bad news, everyone heaved a unanimous sigh of relief.

Then, like a switch, with one voice we all simultaneously volunteered to be the first to exit the hub without a suit. Sense prevailed: recognizing the need to reduce the risk to one individual, we drew lots to select the person; it fell to Jabu. To avoid bi-directional contamination, the agreed-to precaution was that we would shower before and after exiting the hermetically sealed living space. In so doing, Jabu emerged from the shower wearing a sterilized thermal jumpsuit and stepped out of the airlock onto the ice. Cameras mounted on the outside of each pod recorded the event for transmission to Earth, where an audience of billions would watch.

Jabu provided a commentary of the sensations he was experiencing. The first followed a shallow intake of air. We waited for a reaction. He resumed normal breathing and declared, "Pristine, as fresh as a meadow. No smell, just plain exhilarating air. I can only describe it as completely free of anything foreign. Very refreshing, especially when compared to the recycled air we have been breathing on the space craft."

He walked in a loping gate to the slope leading down to the sea while the cameras tracked his movements. Speaking into the radio he said, "Movement is naturally a bit of a struggle given the artificial gravity en route, but I can feel that it is less onerous compared to Earth. It is naturally quite chilly given all the snow and ice around me, but nothing that ordinary warm clothing cannot overcome. I am going to walk up this ridge and have a look around. Don't worry I will look out for any surprises. I don't see anything untoward though. The snow is completely undisturbed. The most striking sensation is the complete stillness when I listen through the acoustic receptors. No creatures, no sigh of the wind through grass or trees, and the frozen sea emphasizes the quietness; no lapping waves. It is, so to speak, deafening. Your voices, when you speak, are dampened by the soft snow."

After thirty minutes, he indicated, "I am experiencing a sensation of slightly labored breathing but I think I can endure for an hour or more before it becomes more noticeable; the low atmospheric pressure is having its effect. We may have to allow a period for acclimatization. I would like to stay longer but I guess I need to head back in."

He returned to the hub for a shower and an automated medical examination including a blood sample. The results were all negative for any adverse effects; they compared with what high altitude mountaineers typically experience. There was some, very minor, evidence of sunburn; damage by ultraviolet light detected by our sensitive equipment, pointing to the weak ozone layer. After thirty minutes in the partially pressurized environment in the living area, his condition returned to normal. The results once transmitted to Earth for analysis returned with guidelines that unsuited excursions must be limited to one hour followed by at least thirty minutes in the pressurized area. Exertions above normal walking activities required less time outside. The results were better than we expected, allowing greater freedom of movement than anticipated.

The probes conducted a detailed orbital survey within a ten-kilometer radius of the landing site. They documented topography, located mineral deposits and identified construction materials to guide our activities in the coming days and weeks. Eager to confirm the virtual beacons of the survey, with the maps on their handheld devices a group of four set out in a robot modified to provide transportation. The vehicle had an enclosed space, pressurized, sterilized and oxygenated to provide mobility without the need for space suits. Two hours lapsed and they returned having located each beacon in the immediate vicinity and checked off the survey results.

From our vantage point at the Podium at the basecamp, preparation were complete to embark on the next stage: exploration of the broader environs of our base.

12.1

JULIA

Lilian and I decided to share my apartment for the remaining days of the lease while we waited for our departure to join Miles and the others on Hermes. I had to vacate my studio last week to avoid a six-month extension of the rental, a decision I regret because all I can now do is fret over whether the voyage will go ahead with nothing to distract me. I should have extended the lease and incurred the loss, which would have been entirely affordable since the sponsors of the trip are carrying my costs on the same twenty-five-year term like Miles and the others. Lilian will remain in the employ of the news organizations. Even practicing the piano is a lost cause while my mind is elsewhere, and when Lilian comes home from the office she never stops talking. Bless her soul, she intends well.

The door closed with a bang, disturbing my thoughts. "Lilian, please, please. Gentle with the door. You startled me."

"Sorry Luv, the wind caught it... I am sooo excited. Only a few more weeks and we will be on our way. Do you think the spacecraft will be ready? We need to start packing, you know. I must tell you about our meeting at the office today. We..."

"Lilian, one thing at a time. It is still a few weeks before we leave and there are strict guidelines on what we may take with us. There is no point in packing until we receive the guidelines."

"Sure, okay, you are the boss. But it is still exciting."

"I don't want to dampen your spirits but you probably know better than I do that the public has become aware of the date set for the departure of the shuttle."

"Really? I didn't know that. I thought it was a well-kept secret."

"No, the secret is out, and protesters want the departure aborted. They are quite vociferous. They believe that directing expenditure at space related activities should stop in favor of alleviating climate related effects. In a way I see their point, with the mounting adverse effects of global warming."

"What! You can't be serious. Do you think we should cancel our trip?"

"No, no, it is just that they have blockaded the entrance to one of the launch facilities, at Kourou, French Guiana. I spoke with Stanley; he said that acting on guidance provided at a sponsor's shareholder meeting on the subject, they remain unmoved, they want to proceed. They have organized a diversion to distract the protesters at the time of the launch, which is scheduled for early hours of that particular morning."

"Well, thank god for that. I would be terribly disappointed if the whole thing was cancelled."

"I agree, but the uncertainty is nerve-wracking. I wish we were already on our way."

"I was saying, we had a meeting at the office and the newspaper wants to launch a website, to get the public to propose names for key features on Hermes. You know, features like continents, islands, mountain ranges, oceans and seas. Now that these orbiting probes have identified them. They want me to coordinate the information."

"Wow! That sounds interesting. You must be very pleased with the appointment."

"Yes, I am, but it is a little daunting. It will help pass the time until we depart."

"I wish I could say the same. I cannot stop worrying about the blockade; it is the only thing I can think of."

"The results of the survey will be passed on to the International Astronomy Society IAS for a final decision."

In the final stages of preparations for departure, two emotions dominate our last days, my anxiety and her ecstasy. Every evening she updates me with the latest developments at the office. To her it is a relief from the anxiety of whether the launch will proceed or not. She spends her remaining days organizing the website under the auspices of the news organization. Further orbital surveys confirm the main continents and smaller landmasses, assuming that sea levels will settle at a certain level after the anticipated thawing of the ice sheets. Based on maps she publishes on the website showing the projected geography, the naming competition proceeds.

The response is far more than Lilian had anticipated. Fortunately, the system collates the responses automatically and ranks the preferences for each feature according to popularity for each name. With a couple weeks to spare before the launch date for our trip, she submits the ranking to the IAS. Four days later the results of the scientific panel tasked with adjudicating the responses publishes the results, which Lilian transposes on to her website.

"Julia, I feel exhausted. The results that the IAS gave us to publish have generated more problems than the whole exercise. It seems like everyone expected his or her preferred name. One of the main objections is that many of the names are English."

"Why don't you just allow each country to provide a translation based on their language? That way you can stick with the same names."

"Not a bad idea. I should have thought of that. I will suggest that to them tomorrow. Anyhow, one of the rules to participate was that the decision of the IAS is final, so it seems like they will not consider changing the names. They did not always settle on the most popular names, often resorted to ancient Greek or Latin names. Maybe that was to avoid the need for translation."

* * *

Recovering a sphere[2] from her bag, Lilian explains and shows me the decisions. "Look at this. They made a globe, a little rudimentary but quite good at showing the features. You can see Farland lies in the far northwest, separated from the other continents by an extensive ocean; it is a major landmass and has a westerly adjoining island.

"Riven is a five-sided continent and lies to the east of Farland, extending from the equator to the North Pole and partly beyond. You can see this valley; it is a rift valley, which they named 'The Rent'. It runs down the center of the continent, spilling into the ocean not far from the Podium basecamp where your friends are. The glacier near the camp is the southern extremity of the rift valley. The land to the east of the Rent, which divides Riven into East and West Riven, has broken mountains and valleys stretching to its east coast, and you can see here where this long northerly strip of land protrudes into the sea; it links to North Falcate, which is another continent. West Riven is mainly undulating hills with extensive plains.

"South of Riven is this ribbon of islands called 'The Pearls', which extends along one side of the pentagon shape. We will be able to see them off our coast when we are there. South of the Pearl Islands, these scattered islands, all of varied size, they named them 'Dracon Islands', because of their dragon shapes. They extend far south. The seas in this area collectively go by the name 'Oceana'.

"On this side is Falcate, which as you can see forms a fairly major landmass. There is a North Falcate and a South Falcate. You can see they are two semi-circular sickle-shaped continents with hills or mountains along the rims of their perimeters with plains in the center. They each provide a roughly topographical mirror of each other. I love this, the Middle Sea. It is a shallow depression separating North and South Falcate with an island in the center called Iris

---

2   See Chapter 39.1 Sub Paragraphs 1, 2, 3 & 4 for diagrams.

Island. Can you see the eye? The two continents form an eye shape with the iris in the middle. Cool!

"The largest ocean was named 'Hadean Ocean.' Apparently, it's named after the primordial conditions when the seas first formed on the Earth, with likely parallels on Hermes. They thought the name seemed appropriate for the harrowing journey through space that the planet had to endure. It lies west of Riven, running from pole to pole, with the largest stretch in the southern hemisphere including a frozen South Pole, which they say may not thaw, even with the warming.

"On this side is the Salacia Ocean, the female mythological divinity of the sea. I got that from the notes that they provided. It lies between the west coast of Farland and the east coast of Riven. The Priscoan Ocean, which is an alter name for Hadean, joins the Hadean north of Farland, as you can see, and is apparently the smallest water mass on Hermes."

While the naming process absorbs Lilian's attention, I, having completed my departure arrangements, have nothing to do but fret about the protesters, wondering whether the launch will proceed. The demonstrators have a point: expenditure on alleviating the severe effects on the climate should take precedence, but on the other hand, humanity has failed to address many priorities in the past despite the means being there to do so. I think both should proceed.

The countdown to the day continues until eventually Lilian and I board the flight from North America with other voyagers, headed for the launch facility. En route to French Guiana, we see at first hand the incredible devastation wrought by the warming climate. Large swaths of island nations in the Caribbean devoid of settlements, agriculture nonexistent and in the distance another wave of destruction in the form of an ominous looking hurricane cloudbank seems headed for coastal USA. Earlier we passed the smoldering ruins of fire damage to forests, buildings and infrastructure. Tent cities straddled the hills as refugees from the meteorological conditions streamed in for shelter, echoing similar news accounts from the rest of the world.

"Lilian, it is worse than I thought. No wonder the agitators want to stop us."

"Yes, I can see that. Julia, we have to look to ourselves. We have to press on, surely?"

"I don't know what to do. I feel bad, being the person who discovered Hermes. One word from me could put the trip in doubt."

"No, no, no, please, all our plans, and then there is Miles and your friends to consider. You have an important role to play on Hermes. What if there is life on the planet? Only you can answer that. I am not big on these things but humanity, as a whole, needs an answer to that question. Think about that Julia! It is important."

"Yes, but if the protesters find out that I am going to Hermes, they will think I am a traitor. Who knows what they may do? I don't like being in the center of attention."

"Julia, you are normally philosophical about these things. What happens will happen; we can deal with it when it comes about."

"Funny you should say that. I remember saying to Miles that providence will incline to the best outcome. I guess I must take my own advice."

Lilian's insights surprised me; she is usually so superficial. Swayed, I procrastinate until events simply overtake the possibility of changing my mind. I wish Miles were here to help with the decision.

To evade the protesters, the pilot avoids the recognized airport to land some distance away at a lesser-known aerodrome. From there, frisked away in buses over a bumpy side-road, we enter the launch facility through a rear entrance. Instead of the comfort of a hotel, lodged in a backroom, we wait out the remaining time before launch. Unlike the initiation process that Miles told me about, due to circumstances, we receive only abbreviated training while armed guards are deployed around the perimeter of the launch platform to keep the protesters at bay if they attempt to sabotage the launch.

Fortunately, there are no delays for technical or logistical reasons and at the scheduled time, we lift off to the thunderous acceleration we dread.

As we rise above the spread of jungle surrounding the site, I catch a glimpse of the protesters in the distance. The diversion that Stanley spoke of seems to have worked. Survive we do, but the harrowing at the hands of forces so extreme leaves us drained, depleted of the adrenaline that sustained us during the experience. I slump back in exhaustion and relief when gravity finally gives way. They allow us to move about in zero-G for a while. What a liberating experience, floating about and changing direction at the slightest touch against the walls. Lilian is enthralled, giggling like a child; she cannot get enough of it. I have to smile when, at the end, she turns to sulking as preparation for transfer to the carousel began.

Before long, we find ourselves safely in our pod shared with two other travelers. Before unpacking we stand a while looking at the central hub, the activity around it, and the pods slowly rotating in a carousel. From our geo-stationary orbit, we can see the Earth, a sparkling blue orb, taking up the whole of the viewing window. Even Lilian is quiet, seemingly captivated by the grandeur of the view. I later realize that her reaction to the zero gravity and her quietness are the effects of the traumatic ascent. She remains numbed with shock for a few days, frequently having nightmares about it. For my part, Miles' description of the launch somewhat steeled me against the worst of it.

Ours is a lonely trip outside the ecliptic plane: over 200 days in transit for the *Forerunner II* to converge on the rendezvous point with Hermes circling somewhere on the far side of the sun. For eight months I have to contain my impatience to see Miles and his friends.

Lilian overcomes her terror of the ascent only to transition to boredom at the confinement in the pod. At a loose end she complains, "Not another day. I will never survive this. It is just too much.

I should never have volunteered... I could do with a drink but no, no alcohol allowed on the trip. Can you believe it?"

"Lilian, we are only fifty days into the flight, you need to do more than watch videos. There is the exercise machine; keep at it, for your health's sake."

"I need more variety; why don't we go over to the hub? We can talk to someone there instead of just the four of us. I know; we could organize a party, anything. This is mindless, sitting around here looking at the stars. I just hope things are better on Hermes."

"You go. I am brushing up on my old biology notes. After that, I have to do my usual two hours at the digital piano. Not to worry, I will use headphones. I may join you next time."

"Okay, I'll get changed into something more appropriate." Turning to the two fellow travelers, she asks, "Beth, Ingrid, would you like to join me?"

They decline and in a few minutes, Lilian boards the shuttle. Much later, she returns with a new sparkle in her eyes, having met some people and obtained a promise for more interaction in the future. These jaunts become more frequent and soon evolve into daily excursions, sometimes visiting other pods. Lilian is back in her element.

I occasionally go along with her, meeting her acquaintances, exchanging motivations for taking on the journey and their expectations once on Hermes. It proves to be a welcome relief from the confines of our pod and makes the trip more bearable.

12.2

CONSOLIDATION

The new inhabitants of Hermes are not idle as Julia and Lilian travel the expanse of interplanetary space. Our task is to map out an aggressive exploration pattern of ever broadening concentric circles around the Podium. The first objective is simply to traverse the mapped circles to get a lay of the land, document observations and allow for diversions for anything of interest. Using the detailed orbital surveys of a ten-kilometer radius around the Podium, four robots are prepared as four-man rovers, one per selected pod. To overcome the prevailing powdery snow conditions, Dmitri fitted the rovers with continuous rubber tank-like belt treads originally designed for sandy conditions on Mars. With the consensus to proceed with caution, looking out for surprises that an alien world may harbor, we set out.

Our pod's exploration assignment is the easterly quartile of the circles, including the two buttresses on each side of the glaciered Rent rift valley, the valley itself and east of the valley. The elevated peak in the northeast, somewhat resembling a volcanic cone, is also our jurisdiction for later in the plan.

We head due east from the platform, mounting a gentle rise to the first buttress to reach a vantage point, from where we see the glacier as it slides into the sea, which spreads to the south with the string of Pearl Islands scattered along the horizon. The desolation of this world is profound. Nothing moves and no evidence of activity disturbs the landscape. Absolute stillness. A pale blue sky has greeted each day since arrival and today is no different. A soft breeze off the sea chills the air even as the miniaturized sun tries to warm the ubiquitous blanket of ice. Continuing with caution, we step out of the controlled environment within the mobile robot to descend to the glacier as it pushes unobstructed into the sea, disappearing below the ice covering. Jabu, with his eye for geology, observes that the glacier must be quite deep and slow-moving, given that the terrain is relatively flat and the glacier appears to originate from further inland, slicing through the edge of the mountain peak. We resolve to bring along the only ice core-drilling equipment that we have to test his theory after completing the plan to traverse the concentric circles of our quartile, a process that will take a few months. Jabu explains that an analysis of the ice cores should hint at the age of the ice and may reveal the historical content of oxygen and level of carbon dioxide. It may divulge the seasonality of melts and deposits. Inclusions in the ice such as rock, sand and debris could uncover other secrets, including the originating source of the material, the duration spent being carried and from that the speed of transit. These latter details would need a more extensive survey of the upper reaches of the valley.

Returning to the vehicle, we descend to sea level to negotiate a passage to the larger eastern buttress by traveling on the sea ice then heading back to the land further along the coast. To reach the summit of the buttress we circle back in a westerly direction, the direction of the camp, using a gradual incline leading up from the sea. Broken terrain makes for slow progress until we have to abandon the vehicle in favor of walking by foot. At the summit, the ubiquitous desolation greets us. We have a panoramic view towards the Podium, the leveled landing strip and the sea stretching beyond the islands. A dark bank of clouds lies on the far horizon, and judging by the wind direction it may be heading towards us.

Looking inland, we see the mountain peak looming large, its western escarpment severed by the Rent glacier, which forces a tributary around the amputated section to merge back with the main stream at the southern foot of the mountain.

With sunset approaching, we wrap up our sightseeing to return to the vehicle and head for camp. The wind has picked up and the cloudbank is a little closer. The temperature seems to have risen from an earlier minus fifteen degrees Celsius to minus three degrees – quite balmy compared to the previous days. Being virtually on the equator, planetary scientists claim that we are currently in the mid-winter period. Seasons on Hermes will however not fluctuate as much as on Earth due to the shallow incline of the planet on its axis.

Still unaccustomed to the longer days and nights, and despite being tired, the four excursion teams meet in the central hub to compare notes.

The westerly team report undulating ice-covered hills as far as the eye can see. Characteristically, low elevations mark the coastal stretch with numerous would-be streams entering the sea if it were not for their frozen state.

The southerly team made their way over the sea ice to one of the Pearl Islands. Each island is about five hundred meters in diameter and uniformly spaced in a row. Scrapings reveal a smooth rock foundation two feet below the surface where the ice is not very salty, indicating precipitation as the cause of the ice deposit as opposed to tidal influences in the past. They too could see the approaching bank of clouds. A meteorological check with the orbiting vessel confirms that a storm is advancing from the south. We decide to postpone further excursions until we have a better impression of the effects of the storm. Tomorrow will be a boring day if we are to stay camp-bound.

The northerly team covered low-lying terrain in the west of their quartile, leaving the more mountainous region that rises to the edge of the Rent for later. They traversed up a frozen river valley for about five kilometers before turning westwards and crossing a hill to the next river. They descended into the valley and then angled across to return to the Podium. Hard ice characterized the lower reaches and fresh snow was evident at the higher elevations. The conclusion drawn: fresh snow fell at the top of the hills whereas rain or wet compacting snow characterized the shallow areas, indicating a warming trend.

Our team covering the easterly quartile reported on the glacial slice through the western escarpment of the mountain, forcing a skirting tributary. The terrain looking eastward is a series of impassable mountain ridges as far as the eye can see with deep intervening valleys. Many mountains are bare of snow, the incline being too steep to hold the precipitant on the sheer slopes.

None of the teams found evidence of life in any form and the need for caution dissipates.

* * *

Twenty-fifth hour and the storm strikes. A steady wind drives the snowfall for a couple of hours. The snow mounts against our pod, emphasizing the stillness of our world. The window reveals an intense darkness beyond the shaft of light from the pod. Surprisingly, snow gives way to pattering rain on the roof of the pod. A temperature check reveals a reading of plus four degrees. Quite remarkable: a warm front must have brought the rain.

Dawn brings a landscape of fresh snow pockmarked by raindrops from the shower that followed the snow. The spent storm leaves only wisps of clouds in the far north. We marvel at the change in temperature and venture that it foretells the predicted warming of the climate generally. Will we be walking around in short sleeved shirts soon?

After breakfast, having decided that the weather has stabilized, the teams set out on their excursions. The southerly team again heads out across the ice-covered sea. After two hours they radio in that the rain has left pools of liquid water on the surface of the ice. We concur: there is a trickle of water over the surface of the glacier in the Rent but it solidifies quite quickly as the temperature drops from three degrees to one degree at higher reaches. Using drills that they took with them, the team finds that the sea ice is only two feet thick. At this rate of warming we will have a liquid sea on our doorstep quite soon.

Impatient to know more about the Rent glacier, we decide to use the core-drilling equipment now rather than on later journeys crisscrossing our concentric circles. We first select a site in the center of the glacier, parallel to the edge of the sea. This would be the oldest ice. As expected, the top layers are relatively soft, gradually becoming harder the deeper we penetrate.

At fifty-five feet Jabu shouts, "Okay, I think you need to slow down now. Judging by the slope of the land on either side of the valley, we must be nearing the bottom."

Having barely completed his warning, we hit bedrock.

With his prediction spot on and high-fives all round, Dmitri jokes, "Hey Jabu, were you born here? How could you know how deep the valley is?"

Jabu responds, "Must be from a previous life."

We haul out the ice core, cut it into marked segments and store them on the roof of the vehicle where they will remain frozen, like the rest of the landscape, until we get back to the Podium. We decide on a second drilling a little closer to the edge of the glacier. This time it is a few feet into a part of the river of ice that projects into the sea. We progress as with the last hole, but to a depth of sixty feet, before reaching the substratum, at which point the drill shudders to a stop, the depth being too great for the device to continue further.

As we lay out the segments of the ice core, Jabu points to a mix of calcium-like particles in the ice, wondering what the source could be. Without an immediately plausible answer we stack the samples on the roof and prepare for our return journey. The day is done.

Back at the Podium we arrange the core samples in the laboratory refrigerator for analysis over the coming days.

The evening discussion in the hub with the other teams concentrates on the presence of liquid water in the sea and on the glacier, as well as the layer of fresh snow. We enthusiastically speculate on the warming trend.

Our second resolution is to get the robots to work on releveling the landing strip for the next landing, which is now only a few weeks away. The strip needs to be maintained as a regular task. We need to correlate the depth of ice with the daily temperature and ensure that the ice will bear the load of any landing craft, be they supply vessels or pods. If the ice becomes too thin another landing site will have to be found, or the feasibility of landing on water needs to be explored. Lastly, temperature changes need to be communicated to Earth, where they have more sophisticated modeling capabilities to project what the future holds.

Results of the core samples are intriguing: the oxygen content increases with depth, while the carbon dioxide level decreases. The findings imply that the atmosphere is currently representative of the top layer of ice or near to it, and that historically there was more oxygen in the atmosphere. We also know that the planet spent a considerable time in interstellar space. If the standard model is to apply, the planet was accreted from a gas cloud circling a star. It seems unlikely that the oxygen content was developed while in transit across interstellar space. The oxygen must have originated while the planet was bound to a star system. The mystery is that the only biological evidence of the source of oxygen is the remnant of bacterial husks, dead bacteria, found in the stratosphere and very little to none lower down. Exoplanetary specialists, back on Earth, come to the conclusion that the most plausible explanation is that some form of rudimentary life existed on the planet or in the atmosphere while the planet was still in its original solar system and that it has been sterilized during its transit to us. They add that the thaw may reveal more detail at ground level. A fascinating aspect of the analysis of the core samples is that the bottom three-quarters is uniformly dated at half a billion years old in barely distinguishable layers, as if it was rapidly deposited over a short period of geological time. A few inches on top of the base is a strange mix of ice and dust particles. It appears as a micro-fine accumulation over a protracted period of time since the base deposit was laid down. The very top sliver is recent, namely since the planet has been orbiting our sun or been in this location. Our interpretation is that the planet navigated the void in a frozen state with the noted anomalous ice and fine particulate matter occurring during transit in the void. The dust bears the signature of interstellar particles.

The remaining days before Julia and Lilian arrive is spent completing the exploration in the concentric circles. While the specialist's theories seem valid, we bear the brunt of the icepack frustrating meaningful investigation to ground level. We too eagerly anticipate when the warming of the climate will uncover more of interest, but patience will be required; it may take weeks or even years.

* * *

The pod members not involved in the exploration effort remain at the basecamp formalizing a rudimentary layout for a village. They supervise the start of work by the robots or intervene manually where the robots lack the ability.

Commencement starts with a decision to remove the surface layer of ice down to ground level and map the proposed village on this as the foundation. The ice is found to be two feet deep, with the last six inches stubbornly hard, making progress slow but steady. The robotic equipment has to be used cautiously to avoid damage to the relatively lightweight fabrication material used. The village is intended to accommodate at least 600 people. There are already 160 onsite and Julia's contingent will bring another 200. The sponsor's construction and mining operation will be limited, pending successes achieved by the initial commitment. It is hoped that the base will attract other migrants and, if so, *Overture* will expand operations to meet demand. The plateau is a kilometer wide and four kilometers long, sufficing for expanding the village well beyond the initial design parameters.

The layout of the village includes a living space, a community center, greenhouses to supply food, work sheds, laboratories, robot repair facilities and an electronic monitoring and software development center. These amenities are all interconnected with walkways, warmed and sealed against the environment with a number of entrance and exit airlocks.

The construction material for the village was originally intended for use on Mars, a dry cold environment compared to the cold wet frozen state of Hermes, with a warming trend and where the ice may give way to water. The supply craft carried prefabricated thermally insulated wall, roof and window panels that require a concrete foundation on which to build the structure. A lightweight chemical that expands to a thermally insulating solid mortar when mixed with water was also onboard the supply craft but needs to me mixed with sand to add volume. The layout of the village needs to be vetted by *Overture* before work begins, so, while *Overture* reviews the design, the teams concentrate on leveling the plateau of any boulders and ridges. The confirmation to proceed comes within a few days but with minor changes. They require the buildings to be centered on the plateau rather than the planned westerly concentration. Their assessment also considered the elevation above sea level. Factoring in a rise of ten feet for global ice melts and adding in for a high tide surge and severe weather conditions, the village still has a ten-foot safety margin, so the go-ahead is given.

Dmitri wastes no time in configuring the robots to begin sifting the soil to a fine grain and mixing in the concrete. The recent snowfall provides a convenient source of fresh water, salt water being unsuitable to mix with the concrete to form the required slurry. The slurry is poured over the foundation area and allowed to set. The assembly of the buildings using the prefabricated panels proceeds at a pace only requiring minimal human intervention for the more complex fittings. The greenhouses are built first, to give us an alternative to our supply of dried and canned food. Dedicated hydroponic specialists proceed with sowing the seeds. They are fortunate in being able to use local soil as a source of trace elements to derive nutrition, there being no evidence of biological compost in the ground to support the growth. The compost will be cultivated over time from decaying plant matter from the farm. Frozen fish spawn has been included in the cargo shipped with the *Forerunner II*, to establish fish farming as a source of protein, but that will have to wait until the supply ship arrives. A portion of the greenhouse complex is readied for this so that the fish can be introduced as a priority when the supplies arrive.

Warmer days with temperatures above zero persist, providing ideal work conditions for the construction teams and enabling them to stay ahead of the planned timeline that I had set out for them as project manager. The warmer temperatures are also softening the ice layer, making for easier grading and leveling of the village site. Liquid water is now readily available; we simply top up the interior water reservoir with ice or snow, allowing it to thaw within hours.

Small waves now lap the shoreline, spilling over the underlying crust of ice and exposing protruding rocks. Every evening, progress review meetings are punctuated with palpable excitement at our good fortune at inheriting a world with so much promise. Time passes quickly despite the long days and the weariness induced by the change in biorhythms induced by the twenty-six-hour cycles. It will take a while to acclimatize.

12.3

JULIA

Lilian, our fellow travelers and I are in our final approach to Hermes, which looms large in our view. Despite the magnificence of a pristine planet before us, our anxiety mounts at the prospect of the blistering heat of entry. Lilian in particular is overwrought, having found the ascent taxing in the extreme. She abandoned the visits to the hub and other travelers as the descent drew closer, this being her singular concern.

Pacing the confines of the pod, she mutters, "I know we won't make it. I just know it! The way everything, the whole craft, shook when we took off; this pod is much smaller, how can it survive?"

"Lilian, these are the same types of pods that the others used and they all managed to land on Hermes quite safely."

"I have a premonition that something will happen. Look at what happened on Mars with Michael and them. All it needs is for the parachute to malfunction and that is it."

"Yes, but they did not operate by the book; they had to improvise because of the circumstances. You should know that. Your coverage of the whole lead-up to their arrival and then the descent was extensive. You, better than anyone else, should know that."

"Yes, but why do I feel that something will happen?"

"Lilian, you are panicking unnecessarily. They should have provided training and prepared us better. I will tell you what: I will talk to the onboard doctor and see whether he can prescribe a sedative of sorts for you. It will help you. Is that okay?"

"You are right; I need to block it out. Okay, please do that. I can barely breathe. Whew, calm down girl!"

A call to the doctor secures the required medication and Lilian becomes more settled. I must confess that I do not feel much better than she does, but seem better able to hold myself in check.

As if in response to an internal cry for help the radio crackles to life. "Julia, are you there? It is Miles here. Can you hear me?"

"Oh thank god, you could not have called at a better time. We are so worried about the descent."

"Yes, I know. It is dangerous. The consolation is that we managed it without mishap. The pilots are good at what they do. I am sure that Lester, our pilot, will have discussed the whole entry process with your pilot. I feel sure that you will be okay."

"Thanks, Lilian is here too, listening. The doctor has provided a mild sedative to ease her nerves."

"Oh, that is a good idea. You should take some as well, but I would not overdo it. It is an experience worth enduring to the full. If only for full appreciation of the experience that follows, when you begin a more conventional glide. You will come through it safely, of that I am sure… Lilian, you will be fine. We are waiting for you! We look forward to meeting you in person."

12.4

EXPECTANT

Only seconds now separate communication interactions between the *Forerunner II* and Hermes as they draw near, enabling verbal discussion instead of relayed text. I can barely contain the excitement at hearing Julia's voice directly but feel anxious at being powerless to ensure a safe landing. I hope my reassurances sufficiently disguise my forebodings.

The landing strip is now a watery slush, which necessitates a different strategy to that taken by us. Fortunately, the underbelly of the pods is reasonably flat, sloping upwards towards the front and protruding below the level of the wings such that they should absorb the initial contact with the slush without nosediving. The mush is also not deep, solid ice being a few inches below water level, thereby preventing the craft from sinking after coming to a standstill. We have prepared the robots with extended cables to winch the pods to shore after they are stationary. All is ready, we just have to wait out two more days as they decelerate towards the target and loop into orbit. The weather conditions are ideal as they start the descent.

We follow the synthetic voice of the *Forerunner II*'s autopilot providing a radio commentary of each step as the entry unfolds. The unemotional report provides an artificial sense of control that is both calming and nerve-racking.

12.5

JULIA

Lilian is now quite calm from two days of taking the sedatives. It certainly helped. She is able to share in the excitement of the view as we circle Hermes, looking quite inviting in its sparkling mantle of white.

The radio chatters away as the various control personnel make final adjustments to the trajectory. We feel the maneuvering as the pod, having detached from the carousel, aligns with three other pods for coupling. With meticulous care, the interacting voices execute a series of coordinating commands until a gentle click locks us to the rear of our train. The whine of hydraulic gears secures the link and the attitude changes as the hiss of the navigation system discharges gas to align the craft for descent. Our train is ready!

For some minutes, the sensation is of Hermes spinning below us while we are stationary – strange! A technician interrupts our attention with a bark of command and a perceptible downward trajectory begins. The horizon shimmers pearl-like against the backdrop of stars standing in relief in the blackness of space.

"Steady, steady, prepare for entry!" he shouts as the first wisps of air stream past our window. The craft shudders under the arresting atmosphere. My body tenses up, the grip on the armrest fastens like a vice. The turbulence rises, the shaking increases, the noise level escalates and the tension mounts; every part of the craft is tested to the extreme. Surely, the weakest link must succumb; first one part then another in a cascading failure. How can it endure? A crescendo of noise blots out everything. Just as we seem to reach the impossible, flashes streak past the window, first red then orange, rising to white. The air literally burns in the intensity. The finale is a test, human versus physics. The outcome seems indisputable, but as all hope appears lost, the terror subsides.

Miles' words spring to mind: a 'full appreciation of the experience that follows.' So true. The sense of safety marks the contrasting aerodynamic glide. The panorama below and the exhilaration of flight combine to make the experience unforgettable. Even Lilian, next to me, embraces our emergence from the trauma with elation at having survived against what seemed like all odds and to marvel at what follows.

She is first to exclaim, "Look down there! I can see the facing sickles of North and South Falcate... Julia, this is so exciting. Look there; you can even see Iris Island in the middle of the Middle Sea, between the two sickles, just as the surveys reported and we named them in our contest. I cannot believe that I am actually here. This is amazing."

"Incredible! Imagine what it will look like when all that ice melts and the ocean and land stand out against each other."

"It is as if the contest prepared me for this. I can see all the features that we named. We are crossing the Salacia Ocean next, then we should see East Riven coming up soon."

"It is as if the model you worked on is coming to life. I wonder what secrets lie under all that ice. Maybe there are sea monsters. I can't wait to start looking into the biology of the planet."

"Look. Riven, there in the distance. Can you see the mountains? They must rival the Himalayas."

As we sink lower, the release of the speed-arresting parachute jerks our attention to the imminent landing.

Lilian's excitement dispels the looming danger. "There, that must be the volcano near the camp; it has a conical shape. Do you think it is active?"

"Not sure. We should be able to see the camp soon. Look there on the left, the Pearl Islands; so realistic, just like a string of pearls. It is like a dream world."

We again brace ourselves while the frozen landscape flashes past the window. Nearer, nearer to the icy platform until, with a long-extended whoosh, the belly of the pod touches down and slides to a stop. Our journey is over; we are safe.

12.6

BASE

From our view on a knoll overlooking the Podium, the four of us with a crowd of onlookers expectantly search the skies for the arriving trains of pods: thirteen trains of four coupled pods, each train carrying a precious cargo of sixteen people, four per pod. Robin is first to see them using his binoculars. Their tiny shapes glint off the morning sun as they travel from east to west above us, evenly spaced in a string. A remarkable sight, it silences everyone, an occurrence so unique, standing here on this foreign land watching and waiting with bated breath. They disappear over the horizon to orbit the planet one last time.

Reappearing in the east, the first of the trains separates from the string formation to brave the fiery plunge into the atmosphere while the others continue in their orbits. The glint off the first turns to a glow as it passes overhead, deeper, deeper into the obstructing stratosphere where the glow turns to a bright red then orange and white under the searing heat. It streaks across the sky at an astonishing speed, trailing a long contrail, gradually shedding momentum as it disappears in the west to circle the planet before its approach to the landing strip. This time it emerges low over the eastern horizon, the four separated pods of the first train in characteristic V-formation. They hang suspended in the air at the slowest possible approach-run, each with a ballooning parachute at rear. Spectacular sprays of slush signal touchdown as they glide to a stop further down the strip and the watching crowd applaud with relief. Some rush down to the edge of the sea to help the robots winch the pods off the landing strip. Once there the passengers disembark and on unsteady legs embrace their friends, family members or acquaintances.

We know that Julia's pod will be in the second train, arriving thirty minutes after the first group. It is our turn to hold our breath as we see them appear low over the horizon and, like the first, elegantly complete their landing. A robot speeds over the leveled ice, nudges up close to the pod to attach a cable and proceeds to winch the pod to the shore. Disregarding the other pods, my focus is on the first one ashore. The exit door swings down, providing stairs to the ground. Four eager faces peer down at us. I only have eyes for Julia; she is safe!

Long embraces welcome them as they disembark; dispensing with the need for spacesuits now that contamination is no longer an issue. Thankfully, Julia looks in good health. Her alert eyes, misty at the reunion, reflect mine. It has been a long absence fraught with anxiety and thankfully without mishap. Internally I silently pledge that this will be the last separation and coyly proclaim, "Julia, I have missed you so much. An eternity seems to have passed since we were last together. This time I won't let you out of my sight."

"Yes Miles, I should never have agreed to you deserting me but my words proved to be prophetic, 'Providence will incline to the best outcome.' So all is well that ends well. Strange how those words, said so lightly at the time, proved to be correct. I definitely cannot claim to be clairvoyant."

Lilian steps forward, taking my hand, "Miles, I am so pleased to meet you in person. Julia told me so much about you. She makes out that she is so calm and collected, but believe me, she pined for you."

Blushing, I deflect the conversation. "I need to thank you for looking after Julia, warding off the reporters and agreeing to accompany her. I imagine it made a world of difference having a friend along for such a long trip."

"Actually, I owe Julia a debt of thanks for keeping me sane. Thanks Julia."

Julia turns to look about her, her gaze straying to the strange surroundings, and I watch as her mind absorbs the unfamiliar setting, the Podium, the mountains and the sea. It was interesting to observe as her mind at first struggled to grasp a land shrouded in the white acoustic blanket then gradually embraced it with acceptance, her delight and intrigue apparent as her hand strayed to cover her mouth in muted wonderment.

As a group, we make our way up the incline, with Lilian and Robin walking ahead, exchanging words. Lilian hangs on his words with exaggerated attention as he explains, "Jabu and I do the geological exploration. At least he does the technical part and I document the information in a database. We examine the information to plot out how best to exploit the minerals based on the extraction effort, likely yield and salability back to Earth or for local use."

"Julia told me you are, or were a mathematics professor." Giggling self-consciously, she says, "One plus one is two. You must be good at arithmetic, or is that too simple for you, luv?"

Robin turns to her quizzically. "We are all professionals in what we do here, hence our selection. You are a journalist, is that right? Which university did you attend?"

"Oh Robin, you are so modest. I wish I had half your brain... Yes, I am a journalist, but my qualifications would be nothing like yours. I did psychology and sociology at UBC, no doctorate or anything like you. Should I call you 'Professor,' dearest?"

Robin, clearly uncomfortable at all the attention says, "Please, please none of that," and he strides ahead, with Lilian lapsing into quiet as she struggles to keep up with his pace.

* * *

The new landing party comprises a diverse skillset unlike the construction and mining personnel that made up the bulk of our group. As settlers, we now have a full array of service expertise at our disposal, bringing a sense of comfort to our colony.

Julia and Lilian take up residence in their pod, positioned a short distance from ours, along with the rest of their cohort. It will be another few weeks before we all move into permanent structures. The first evening is nothing less than perfect as we exchange stories of our experiences since parting. There is a sense of settled wholeness in being together, the curtain of separation drawn, the missing half of our beings restored. Despite an angst-plagued day, we stay up late, relishing each other's company before finally retiring to peaceful sleep.

We quickly establish a new routine of starting each day over breakfast at the hub, planning the day's excursions, setting out for each new adventure and returning in the evening to discuss events over dinner. We become very familiar with the surroundings, ever widening our daily jaunts until, exhausting new areas to explore, we decide on a two-day excursion. Robin, Dmitri and I postpone other responsibilities, whereas this is a part of Jabu's geology assignment. Likewise for Julia, hers being the need to understand the source of the oxygen and for Lilian, to communicate findings to an insatiable audience back home. The trip requires modification of the robot to sleep six, allowing Lilian and Julia to join the party. After a couple of days of preparation, we set out, cramped in our vehicle. We elect to navigate a route up the Rent, starting at the sea.

The warm front that brought the rain continues to dominate the weather; temperatures up by as much as ten degrees Celsius lay bare large swathes of land previously covered with ice. Rivers and streams tumble down ravines swollen with meltwater, carrying muddy silt far into the sea, clouding the otherwise crystal-clear waters. As we progress up the valley, Jabu, in his element, explores rock formations. It is reminiscent of times spent with Robin and I in the ravines back at Mount Elias. In places, cliffs hang precariously along the edges of the gorge. No longer supported by a foundation of glacial ice, they raise the specter of landslides, but Jabu is quick to distinguish safe from unsafe routes. Progress is slow, the broken landscape difficult to negotiate with our overloaded and underpowered cruiser, which requires manhandling over stretches of difficult terrain. Rock striations provide Jabu with subject matter for a fascinating commentary on the passing formations, pausing to explore ore-bearing rock and giving a history of the probable origin. Occasionally he stops at the escarpment to chisel samples for analysis or curse at not having drilling equipment to hand, swearing to be back for evidence in support of our mining mission when the supply craft arrives.

As the sun sets, we prepare a rudimentary pressurized and transparent tent attached to the robot to provide an adequate supply of air. This is our first night in the wilderness of the planet. With lights turned off, we marvel at the immensity of the Milky Way spread out before us. Each deep in thought relives the journey that brought us here, pondering what lies ahead. I recollect lying on the lawn at Mount Elias as a teenager, the drone of the electricity generator turned off and, like here, no moon to compete with the stars, the spark that ignited my dreams of other worlds and, arguably, what led to this moment and place.

The following day takes us further upriver where the steep margins, scoured by glaciers to a typical U-shape, give way to sloping westerly banks and the easterly side rising steeply to the mountain peak in the distance. It is cooler here. The sheet of ice on the slopes has receded to a patchwork where the sun does not reach. The soil on the west side is less rocky, almost loamy; one could imagine agricultural pursuits carried out here.

Late afternoon, in this world of extended days, we retrace our steps back to the Podium. At the mouth of the river as it spills into the sea the rush of sediment-laden water continues unabated, the sea no clearer than the prior day. We look forward to when we can examine the floor-bed more closely. Does it hold secrets that the land stubbornly refuses to yield about the elusive source of oxygen? Back at camp, Lilian catalogs the photographs taken during the outing, overlays commentary and dispatches the communiqué to news outlets back on Earth for sharing with the public.

It has been an interesting two days, and since Julia and Lilian arrived, life has taken on a feeling of permanence not there before. There is a distinctly more settled homely character. Julia and I have resumed our relationship as though there has been no intervening time since separation now months ago. Content in each other's company, I am silently reminded of her confidence of a fitting outcome; providence could not have provided better than this.

* * *

The following weeks focus on completion of the settlement. The structures quickly take shape from the prefabrications once the leveling and foundations are in place. Relays move into their quarters as they are completed, our turn amongst the earliest. Each pod attaches to the new assemblages to provide an expanded area of habitation and privacy. With little coercion, Lilian and Julia join our group, completing the aggregation of disparate parts into a group in this unlikely place, not remotely conceivable only two years ago.

Few of the others of the newly arrived group have direct mining experience. Their areas of expertise range from medical (a young intern by the name of Doctor Levisohn), farming and catering to repair and maintenance personnel for a variety of specialties. Interestingly, people from each discipline congregate with their own kind in the new living space, creating an artificial divide between the original group and the newly arrived. True to human nature, even in this unlikely setting, factions form and distill into groups with their own peculiar preferences, dislikes and agendas. Overarching alignments organically emerge into those that work with their hands, the deskbound people and the independents who consider themselves free-floating intellectuals who blur the distinctions and allegiances. A complex mix of people but ultimately cohesive, with tolerance brought on by a common intent to make the most of the opportunity to create a new order that avoids the mistakes of Earth. Responsibilities to our sponsor takes precedence over these divides as we each focus on our obligations.

* * *

Jabu and Robin focus on their mandate. They use the orbital surveys as the basis for exploration. They document the geology in layers of detail revisiting promising sites as needed, taking samples and recording analyses of mining opportunities when back at the laboratory.

Lilian provides a steady stream of reports to Earth, showing progress with the construction, views of the surrounding landscape and the domestics of the settlers. Her Earth-bound audience, mesmerized by each episode, get relief from the dire conditions brought on by the worsening climate. Lilian and Robin maintain a strange interaction. Lilian's effusive attention to Robin, matched by his dismissive nonchalance, is puzzling to observe; they seem so mismatched, yet each satisfies some deeper need than is apparent. Completing an obscure triangular relationship, Robin is preoccupied with working with Jabu, enjoying time spent with him while holding off on anything other than the responsibilities of their joint assignment.

Dmitri is central to the construction effort as he programs and reprograms the robots for the tasks as they evolve. He takes pride in the quality of output with his usual attention to detail. Equipment limitations require novel adaptations to the robots to accomplish challenges presented, an exercise he relishes, testing the limits of his skills. He maintains a regular exchange with Noah and Ella on Mars, providing us with firsthand accounts of developments on the planet that was to be our home. Sadly he learned that Ella contracted a rare form of cancer usually carried forward as a hereditary trait affecting offspring. In her case the effect is direct, affecting her life-expectancy. They said, the damage is genetic, caused by solar radiation due to the poor protection offered by Mars' meager atmosphere. Even with the preventative medication, she and five other Martian pioneers contracted the disorder. In his concern for them, Dmitri redoubles his contact with them, frequently sending encouraging messages of forbearance in the hope that advances will bring relief.

Management of the construction project and tracking excursion teams falls to me as project manager. The enlarged team since the recent arrival has expanded my responsibilities to near-fulltime to include expanded oversight of the network of computers, integrated radio infrastructure and linkages to Dmitri's robots.

Julia is in her element. Daily outings along the coast and up river valleys remind her of jaunts to Salt Spring Island and other west coast forests and inlets, except of course here there is no vegetation, the verdant replaced by the austere. On occasions I accompany her. Setting out early, we climb steep inclines, wade in creeks and marine coves or stop to marvel at the beauty of the stark panorama. Returning at dusk, we collapse into bed, sleep beckoning our aching muscles to rest from the long days.

On an excursion such as this, distracted by many deviating interests in our path, and finding ourselves some distance from camp with dusk settling, we decide to head for home. In the light of the remaining day, we make for the shoreline, an easy route from there back to the Podium. Without a moon, only stars light our way as we stop at a river inlet for a breather, sitting on boulders with the sea at our feet and the stars circling above. All is still in this world without creatures. Except for the peaceful lap of the waves, the profound silence endures for an eternity. All concerns seep from our consciousness as we let the minutes stretch, at peace in the hush of our thoughts.

13

ELEMENT

Julia startles me, pointing to an ember of light, the size of a dusk particle. Pulsing as it rises from the placid waters, floating like a bubble in the still air, drifting upwards, upwards, the throb of light continues out of reach. We track its progress as it blends in with the stars, adding its glint to the firmament spiraling above us. What can this be? Mute, we watch as it climbs, now a tiny speck in the distance, then abruptly, as if caught by a breeze, it turns inland and disappears from view.

"Julia, it looks like a firefly."

She responds excitedly: "No surely, a chemical reaction of some sort. It can't be a firefly."

Before long a second ember rises. Dumbfounded, we watch as it follows the same pattern, again catching the breeze to disappear up the river valley. Mystified, we wait for a repeat, but nothing comes until eventually we must leave. Julia marks the spot on the shoreline opposite the point at which it emerged from the water. Further investigation is called for. As we trudge back to the camp I recall lying on the warm lawn of Mount Elias marvelling at the stars spread before me and the pair of fireflies adding to the wonder as they danced, flitting over the vegetation in the exuberance of their mating dance. How strange it is to witness a parallel but chemical event in this foreign place.

To Julia the desire to root out the cause is insatiable. Spending many evenings at the spot we marked, waiting for a recurrence, her patience is finally rewarded. The glow emerges, not from the sea itself but from a protruding rock formation a few meters from the mark and thirty meters from the shore, too deep for wading. The throbbing emission follows the same pattern, rising vertically, turning and moving inland; her attempt to follow the crystal of light is thwarted as she stumbles up the rocky incline only to see it disappear out of sight over the ridge. Undaunted she returns to base, seeking out Dmitri to customize a robot for use as a pontoon to navigate the waters to the rocky outcrop.

Fortunately, the robot lends itself for use in water. Designed for the cold, dusty Martian environment, it is air tight, sealed against the atmosphere. Dmitri fits the wheels with rudimentary paddles to provide forward motion in the water. Julia and Dmitri as pilot set out. Partially submerged under the weight of the boat, the windows provide a view under the water. Slowly, cautiously they approach the outcrop. Through the still murky waters a formation looms, ghost-like, larger than as seen from the shore but still only a few meters in diameter and of similar height. As they advance, their eyes widen as though mechanically controlled by the encroaching proximity. Spellbound, they stare, incredulous at the spectacle before them. It is an artifact, a formation of exquisite detail, like a coral structure with a web of branching fernlike leaves extending from a central column. Its rigid form is patterned in charcoal, calcium and clear silicon coloring, too elaborate to be of a crystal of chemistry or of inorganic origin. The object reaches up to a pinnacle protruding from the surface of the sea in what appears to be a spout, a funnel.

Keeping their distance, Julia and Dmitri circle the formation, photographing its geometric structure. They marvel at its intricate design, cautious lest they disturb its inhabitants, for surely this must be the work of intelligence. But there is no movement to reveal what lies within, if anything.

They resolve to wait for dusk to see whether the glowing particles emerge from the funnel, which appears likely to be the point from which they exit. As the light recedes they wait in the gloom, but in vain. After an hour, there is still nothing, and they return to the shore and make for camp.

Barely able to contain their excitement they show us the photographs. Even in the murky waters, its configuration is unmistakeably by design. Surely its formation would require an intellect? Or is it a crystalline formation unique to this planet, foreign to Earth sciences?

Dmitri tries to explain. "The pictures are a little murky. We didn't want to get too close, in case we disturbed it. It also could be poisonous, but I can tell you it is not natural."

Julia adds, "Yes. It looked like it was deliberately constructed. My first reaction was that it is a coral reef and I suppose it could be that, but somehow, there is something more uniform about it. It is not haphazard. Look here; you can see the uniformity in some places."

Jabu asks, "Do you think it is alive?"

"There was no movement so it is hard to tell."

Jabu laughs. "I know, I think it is the exoskeleton of a creature that is inside."

"You may be right. I have no idea but it is not like a petrified artifact. There is a certain glow to it that suggests that it is self-sustaining, even now."

Robin offers, "We need to figure out whether it dates back to some distant time. You may have to take a scraping and have it carbon dated."

Lilian adds her thoughts, "I agree with Robin. I can check with the lab whether they have carbon dating facilities. This is so exciting!"

Julia reluctantly interjects, "No, we should not disturb it if at all possible. At least until we know more. Besides, as Dmitri suggests, it could be poisonous. It is a pity that the water is murky; the runoff from the river since the rain and the warming is clouding the water."

Lilian asks, "I need to communicate this to Earth. What should I say?"

Julia replies, "It really is premature to say anything right now. I need more time to make sense of this. Give me a few more days and I will see what I can come up with."

"But if you send them the photographs the pictures can speak for themselves."

"True, but some will just say that they are pictures of corals, taken on Earth. The last thing you want to do is make us the laughing stock of the world. Just give me some time."

Robin concurs, "Yes, you are right. As the resident biologist it is your call. I would go so far as to say that even broadcasting this to the other settlers is also premature. You can't have people trampling all over this."

Jabu enjoins, "Yes, Julia, I imagine that you also have a responsibility to safeguard what you find. It probably includes securing the site. Making sure it is not damaged or overexposed."

"Thanks Jabu. I am not an expert on preserving rare or endangered species but common sense says that we should proceed cautiously."

My feeling is that the matter is in Julia's capable hands and that she will do the right thing. There are so many questions that we cannot and may never be able to answer. Is it an artifact of some distant origin in time? Did it survive the age of ice, locked in its cold embrace, or is this a recent construct?

We finally agree to contain the news to our group until Julia has more information, at which point a communiqué can be prepared.

* * *

Oxygen, that illusive molecule, what is its source? In Julia's mind, the connection is made. Can this be the explanation, hidden in that rocky outcrop? What secret does it hold? The election of Julia to investigate is but a formality. Neither heaven nor hell could have contained her. From morning until late evening, she explores the seaboard, the shoreline, the hills, slopes and the many riverine waterways leading to the beach.

Binoculars in hand, she starts by patiently waiting for the emergence of the glowing particles. From her observation point on the hillock over which the phenomena disappeared after their vertical assent and abrupt turn in this direction, as evening approaches the reward comes. Not one but two simultaneously appear and, yes, they rise from the funnel structure. Up, up as before, they then turn and track in her direction, as if preprogrammed. Encumbered by her protective clothing she follows. The objects proceed up and over the slope then turn in the direction of the Rent, floating over the escarpment and into the valley. To follow is impossible as the steep banks carved out by glacial action block the trail requiring a detour; the pair of lights disappear up the valley. Noting their path, she returns on another day, this time waiting in the valley, but a rise in wind seems to discourage further events for many days.

The return of calmness rewards her with a new sighting, tracking along the course of the Rent River. Unable to maintain pace due to the many rocky obstacles, she loses the object as it continues ahead and around a bend. Day after day, her trail extends, but then at a hunch, she decides to start at a point further along in the general direction they are taking, where the U-shaped valley gives way to sloping banks on the westerly side and rises to the mountain peak in the distance in the east. The soil is less rocky, almost loamy, she recalls. To get there requires the rover and an overnight stay.

As is our habit, we convene each evening to exchange experiences of the day. Our curiosity is on Julia's progress, excitedly anticipating an update now that calmer weather has returned.

"I continue to track them up the rift valley. Until we know what their destination is, there really is nothing new to report, so that has been my focus. Every day I track them a little further. I follow as quickly as possible but usually lose them because of boulders strewn in the valley. I can keep doing this, but I suspect that they are heading for the stretch where the western side flattens out a little. This is the first change in topography, so they will either stop there or move on to some other objective."

Robin asks, "You make it sound like they are rational beings. Surely there's a possibility it's just a haphazard flow with no destination in mind?"

"You are right; I should not jump to conclusions. By the way, as far as I can make out, they are tiny bubbles with some sort of particle of light inside them. The emission of light may be explained as a chemical reaction of some sort, but the predetermined flight path tends to rule out an inorganic process. It is simply too early to say. I can't get close enough to see in enough detail."

Intrigued, I ask, "Julia, what do you have in mind? If you need to go that far up the valley, you would need two days to cover the distance. I seem to recall that we camped near that spot when the six of us went on our excursion?"

"Yes, I suggest that I do another one of those excursions."

"I won't be able to go for a few days because of my duties here. Robin and Jabu are in the same predicament, which leaves only Dmitri to go. Can it wait?"

Robin interjects, "We have an obligation to communicate this to *Overture* as soon as possible. Dmitri is ideal; he would be able to attend to any malfunction of the robot. Without him, you would be stranded."

Jabu says, "I agree. You need to press on." Laughing, he adds, "We still don't know what monsters are lurking out there."

I stumbled through my agreement, struggling to hide my embarrassment at the jealousy I feel at the thought of Dmitri and Julia being alone together for two days.

Unfortunately, Jabu is quick to notice. "Do I detect some reticence there, Miles? Come now, Dmitri also needs a turn with Julia."

I feel like strangling Jabu, particularly when Julia walks over to me and says, "Don't worry Miles, we will behave ourselves. Right Dmitri?"

That only confuses me more, leaving no option but to retaliate. "Okay, I confess, I am jealous. Dmitri, it will make me feel better if you spend your time working on a modification to the robot, a jamming device that silences Jabu whenever he opens his mouth."

The next day, with Dmitri as pilot, they start out. By late afternoon, they pitch tent on a promontory overlooking the sloping bank on the opposite side of the riverine. Soon after sunset, as darkness descends, no less than six of the objects make their way up the valley and without hesitation navigate to the slope, settling on the ground and extinguishing their radiance. As they watch, another pair arrives, following the same passage to the destination. By late evening, at least twenty have landed on the slope. Illumination by starlight is not conducive to seeing detail, so switching the binoculars to infrared shows the terrain more clearly. Julia notes land and rock formations near each object, as a guide for exploration in the morning. More than satisfied with their observations, they turn in for the night. Julia's hunch has paid off.

Twilight sees Julia setting out for the opposite bank, eagerly anticipating what the day will reveal. The intervening river is broad and fast-flowing, requiring them to cross further downstream at a narrowing. After a few casts the robot anchors a cable in rocks on the far side to provide a taut bridge across the stream. They cross the rushing waters hanging from the cable, then climb to the slope and begin their search for the remains of the glowing embers. Much to their surprise, no dull embers greet them. Rather, there is a fine veneer of green in patches, evident across the loamy soil and only apparent after a careful search. On closer examination, they find areas of pronounced sheen development forming moss-like growth. Careful not to disturb the green fungus, Julia studies a particularly advanced patch of growth. The development is roughly circular in shape, spreading from an epicenter around the apparent castoff remains of the glowing ember, somewhat like a very small pebble in appearance. Once identified, it is obvious that all the patches are of the same construction when viewed through this lens. She photographs at close quarters for comparative measurement for any observed growth when next visiting.

They break camp and return to base, excitedly showing us the camera images. The connection between the pulsing embers and the green sheen remains a mystery, and discussion elicits no plausible explanation. Julia will have to delve deeper for answers.

Dmitri's robotic responsibilities at the camp demand attention for the next days, an obstacle in Julia's progress. Undeterred, a few lessons in operation and navigation of the robotic vehicle overcome this hurdle to enable her to travel the distance alone. However, for her part, she also has to attend to her base responsibilities of checking that all protocols to prevent contamination of the environment are in place and operational, a safeguard seen as paramount now that we have observed what appears to be a lifeform in a world previously thought to be sterile.

At my insistence, the vehicle has two working radios included to contact us in the event of a mishap. At her first opportunity, she sets out. Starting at the shoreline, she works her way up the Rent to the field of moss. Once there she notes that in the intervening days the moss has grown quite considerably. Areas previously just a sheen stand ten millimeters tall, now clearly mossy in appearance rather than the algae-like veneer. Former moss growths now stand twenty millimeters in height; the growth has been vigorous. Earlier bare patches show a verdant coating, giving the entire slope a definite green hue. Comparison of the current growth with the photographs from the previous visit show small fernlike leaves typical of moss emerging from the initial growth.

Zooming in to the structure of each circular growth shows some without the pebble-like center previously observed, especially in areas of more advanced growth. Brushing aside the fernlike petals to look closer, she is startled to see movement: an insect the size and appearance of a small beetle stands its ground in plain sight, the two species, human and alien, apparently sizing each other up.

Is the universe giving up its secret? Imagined but never before encountered. Forms of life separated by the gulf of space suddenly thrust into each other's reality.

Long moments pass, an age, as the silent confrontation stretches, the magnitude of the occasion indiscernible in the view of each stranger, so foreign are their respective perspectives to comprehend whether intelligence is present.

Finally, Julia moves. The gesture is mimicked by the other and the spell is broken. She quickly records the insect on her camera before it disappears under the foliage, noting its appearance: six legs, the front pair not used for mobility; a shallow hemispherical carapace covering the top, strangely multicolored; a dull opal-like appearance; no obvious eyes and an elementary mouth; the whole being just three millimeters in length.

Alone in this strange land, Julia is compelled to communicate her findings. She calls me on the radio and excitedly describes what she has seen. "Little beetles. Yes, beetles. I can only describe them as beetles!" she exclaims in a rush of words.

"Julia, what are you saying? Are you safe?"

She tries to compose herself. "The glowing lights. They seem to hatch beetles. I just cannot believe it. It saw me. Seemed to register my presence."

In my amazement, for lack of words, I can only gasp at her account.

Concerned for her I finally say, "Please take care. They may be poisonous. Keep your distance."

She agrees, "Okay, you are right. I will take care. They are so beautiful."

Despite having provisions for a single overnight stay, she says she will sojourn for an extra night to better study the site.

That evening holds further surprises. Darkness brings a steady stream, many hundreds of pulsing lights, making their way up the valley to settle on the slope. Observing from a distance, the hours pass; a scene wonderful in its execution, thought provoking in its ramifications. What are the implications for the settlers inhabiting a world already reserved by this species?

Despite little sleep Julia is up early having decided that her time is better spent finding the source of this stream of insects. Surely they could not all come from the sole coral outcrop discovered earlier? By evening, she is at the shore waiting for their appearance. It is not long before the pageant starts, first from the funnel already identified, then from further out and along the shoreline.

She rationalizes that these insects are emerging from eons of hibernation in interstellar space. Now in a secure orbit around our sun, they are resuming their pattern of life under this foreign star. To understand their lifecycle will require many hours of observation. What mysteries will be revealed only time and perseverance will allow, a task she is eager to undertake. She returns to the Podium with determination to pursue this endeavor with vigor.

By the time Julia returns, I have already relayed her encounter to our group, who reacted in amazement just as I did.

The immediate question is whether we are ready to communicate the news to *Overture* and Earth. The answer seems obvious - we cannot hold this secret any longer – but Julia is of a different opinion, believing that we need to know more about their lifecycle before we say anything.

Jabu is first to react, "Julia, you open yourself to criticism if you withhold this any longer."

"Yes I know, but I am certain that there is more to this than meets the eye. We still cannot account for all the oxygen in the atmosphere. This may contribute to it, but that depends on how widespread it is."

With Lilian nodding in agreement, Jabu says, "You can always provide an update later, surely?"

Robin adds, "We also don't know what effect they will have on us. If, as you earlier suggested, they are increasing in numbers, the full effect may only be felt further down the line. Our silence will be difficult to explain."

Torn between communicating and waiting for additional information, I vacillate. My trust in Julia's judgment versus what logic seems to dictate; blind loyalty or standing on principle – it is a juncture in the road ahead that I do not enjoy. I once trusted Julia's challenge to providence and here we now stand in each other's company. What better proof could there be of where my loyalty should lie? Is there a middle ground, a compromise? Either provide a snippet of information with a promise of more to follow or allow Julia an extension of time before we issue a more complete salvo.

I put these choices to the group but they only serve to entrench the divide. Further arguments solidify the impasse. Faced with the stark choice of black versus white, ultimately, the compromise is the only way forward and the group agrees to an extension of time for Julia to complete her work.

Once we are alone, Julia says to me, "Miles, thank you for being sympathetic to my stand. Actually, they are right; strictly speaking we should communicate this to the public now."

"Why then were you in favor of waiting? Is there something that is worrying you? I felt that there was more to your hesitation than meets the eye. What is it?"

"You are very observant. Yes, I must confess, it is all the public attention. The endless questions! Some engage as professionals, which I enjoy, but others get quite antagonistic. The discovery of Hermes was enough for me. I realize that this is not about me, it has to do with humanity as a whole, but I am the messenger. I guess I am trying to postpone the inevitable. Maybe I shouldn't have volunteered for this."

"There is one difference; in this case I am here to support you through it all and I am sure the others in our group will do likewise.

I think you should be open with them. You may find that they will be supportive. Lilian helped you through the initial stage and will most likely do the same now."

"Maybe you are right."

"Look, I know that you, of all people, are best suited to explore and report on these creatures. I am also quite sure that you will find an explanation for the oxygen. Just take it one step at a time."

"Okay, thanks. We can see what happens. I think it is best that we talk to them now; see what reaction we get."

On opening up to the group, Dmitri and Jabu immediately appreciate Julia's position; a delay will build confidence and has the benefit of allowing more time for her to solidify the facts. Robin, however, remains unmoved, arguing that a delay will bring criticism. But this only exacerbates Julia's position. Lilian predictably agrees with Robin, but despite a lack of consensus, everyone agrees to support Julia through the process and we default to the earlier decision, which is to delay communication for a while longer.

* * *

After a few days, Julia, still reticent, asks for more time. Days turn to weeks and Robin's agitation rises. Weeks turn to months while the insects proliferate. The nightly displays are at first modest, only apparent to the keen observer, but later become more obvious until unmistakable. Julia matches the rising tide of insects with time spent trying to understand, to find the underlying explanation of the behavior. She blots out all other concerns by immersion in her passion for uncovering the secrets. Deep into the long nights, she connects patterns, speculates and makes inferences, retracing her steps and circling through her logic until at last a plausible explanation begins to take shape.

A miniature iceberg breaks from the glacier as it melts. It crushes one of the coral habitats of the scarabs as it floats past, fortuitously revealing the contents. This provides Julia with the opportunity to inspect the habitat at close quarters. It exposes an intricate labyrinth of tunnels within the coral structures and a larger central assembly point in the lower center. The material is a combination of carbon, calcium and silicon crystals. The creatures, absent from sight, do not immediately rebuild the broken formations. Instead, unobserved, they simply seal the gaps using the crushed debris and return in later days to reconnect the tunnels. The carcasses of the dead are cleared to lower reaches of the structure, out of sight, very quickly, before Julia's intrusion began. On close examination of the broken fragments, parts of some beetles appear as if deliberately embedded in the clay compound.

All this while the settlers in the community continue with their allotted responsibilities, oblivious to the growing excitement in the group of six. We are all too aware that the secret will out if left untold for much longer. Matters reach a head when Dmitri relates a conversation he overheard in the cafeteria: one person, to the disbelief of his colleague, claimed to have seen glowing lights in the sky the previous night. He planned to explore further.

Julia has to this point provided only snippets of information to us, working as a recluse for much of the time. At Dmitri's report and our relief, she emerges from her cocoon: "I think I have figured them out!"

The mild equatorial winter turns to summer, the sun spills its light onto the inhabitants for an hour longer each day and the warmth dispels the last vestiges of ice at the lower reaches, leaving only the mountain peak to the east, the shadowy parts of the Rent and the grind of the glacier still covered. We gather in our residence to listen to Julia.

At the outset, the biologist in her comes to the fore. She emphasizes, "Think of this as a speculative precursor to my findings. Call it a preface if you like. Further work will be necessary to solidify the assumptions into facts. A lot of the information is difficult to prove with the limited resources at our disposal. Speculation is necessary to build the framework and for the logic to hold water. I have to acknowledge that if this preface is disproved much of my theory will evaporate."

Robin's attention, stirred at the prospect of the flow of logic to come, sits upright to listen.

Julia explains, "The moss on the riverside and algae in the sea are one, differentiating only in the stage of their circle of life. Viewed from the perspective of the algae, their lifecycle is as follows. The algae survives only in weak saline water, where fresh stream water mixes with the salinity of the sea. Here, at the mouth of the streams and rivers, extending into the ocean to a depth where sunlight penetrates, the algae photosynthetically derives energy from sunlight, absorbing carbon dioxide and expelling oxygen. It soaks up nutrients in the water through pores. Seasonally it releases microscopic purple spores, which in stark contrast to the parent plant are averse to prolonged exposure to salt water. For survival, the spores require transportation out of the saline habitat within a matter of days. The beetles step in to assist; acting with urgency, they encapsulate the free-floating seeds in a bubble, constructed using algae pulp as a fine membrane. Safe from the harmful effects of the seawater, the bubbles, when ready with other ingredients, take to the air, released into the atmosphere and guided by some unknown means to settle on suitable land near river streams. What guides them there is still a mystery to me. Once there, the algae membrane with nutrients from the soil provide sustenance for transformation of the spores into moss. Typical of moss, the plants remain small. They have only poorly developed tissue to build rigid internal structures to grow tall or for transporting water and nutrients to the extremities, but growth is vigorous."

"Juvenile beetles gorge themselves on the moss, depleting the growth in a single season. Remnants of the moss dissolve as nutrients and leech back into the soil, enriching it for the next iteration, leaving no visible evidence of their existence. Fat on moss, the beetles return to the sea via the rivers and streams, where they disgorge their contents into the water, which aggregates into algae in the saline water to complete the lifecycle."

"On the other hand, the lifecycle, seen from the perspective of the aquatic beetle, is as follows. Their parallel life starts in the sea. As mature creatures, with sunlight for energy, they seem to photosynthetically separate carbon dioxide from the air for internal metabolism in a process similar to plants on Earth.

"Near life's end, coinciding with one of the seeding cycles of algae, the aquatic beetles shed particles of their skin, wrap the skin around the algae spores as protection against the saline water, and place the combination in a bubble with salt water, for reasons not yet known. A second bubble attached to the first has air for buoyance. The pair, less than three millimeters in diameter, released into the air settle on slopes leading to rivers and streams, guided there, as I said, by some means not yet identified. Emerging after a few days, juvenile beetles develop from the skin particles of the adults as amphibians, in the process changing color from dull opal to a bright iridescence. They consume the moss grown from the algae seeds until sated. Bloated, they make their way to the streams to swim downstream to the sea. Here, they disgorge the contents of their stomachs as algae paste. They lose their amphibian status to mature and live out their lives as sea-bound creatures. The orifice used to eat moss seems to close; all further intake is now via their skin in the form of energy from the sun and moisture and nutrients from the sea. The beetles are wingless and the dome-shaped carapace curves over on all sides, partially obscuring the underdeveloped mouth and a part of the head. I estimate that they live for about three years, after which they shed particulates of their skin for the next generation, completing the lifecycle, and the interdependence of beetles, algae and moss. The two species maintain this symbiotic relationship, entirely dependent on each other."

We listen in rapt attention, impressed by what Julia has uncovered in such a short time, understanding the need for the extended time.

Even Robin, enthralled by the scope of findings, says, "The conclusions you reached certainly make sense. It is very compelling. I am amazed at how these creatures coexist."

After a period of silence, as the implications sink in, Lilian asks, "How do we communicate this to Earth, how will the public react?"

Dmitri agrees and adds, "Da, yes, the consequences on their psyche, is that the word? The first evidence of life beyond Earth; we have known for a few months and yet I still find it unsettling."

Julia says, "Now that we know more about them I feel better able to answer questions from the public. I feel mentally prepared. Thank you, all of you, for your patience."

Jabu points out, "Because of the delay, and I am not being critical of it, I think we need to first let the residents here know. If one of them has seen the lights, it is possible that others have also. We need to tell them first, or at the same time, update *Overture*."

I concur with Jabu. "Yes. Here is what I think we need to do. Firstly, convene the residents and update them. Secondly, have a briefing prepared for transmission to *Overture* directly after we inform the residents. This should take the form of a news release indicating that detailed information will follow. The third item should be the detailed description of the findings. This can follow after a few days."

Lilian says, "I can assist with the news release, but there is a need to authenticate Julia's findings. Supporting evidence, photographic and the like, needs to be provided."

Robin, who published many papers and reviewed numerous dissertations for his students at university, points out, "You need to write up the findings in a paper and find a sponsor to review it before publication. I suggest that this be after providing the detailed information. So, the residents first, the news release second, the detailed information third with a paper leading to a dissertation."

He suggests, "The compilation should be written as a precursor to a dissertation for a doctorate that can follow later. The magnitude and depth of your findings warrant the rigor of scientific method for communicating serious subject matter. I must caution, though: there is some urgency. You need to get the initial word out before someone else does. The prospect of someone beating you to the detailed report seems limited because there is no one else onsite to do the required research. It is the first step that is critical. Any number of people stand to see the creatures and break the news, albeit in an amateurish format, diminishing the impact of your report."

Lilian volunteers, "For the paper, I can use my science reporting contacts to approach any number of prestigious science journals to arrange for the publication. Maybe one of the university professors associated with the journals could review the article."

We agree to the overall strategy. My task is to convene the residents on the morrow. Dmitri suggests, "Julia, you should give these creatures a name. The legacy will record this for posterity. As the person who made the discovery, now is the time to solidify the discovery with a name."

"Thank you Dmitri, you are kind. I would prefer us to arrive at a name as a group. Any suggestions?"

After considering various combinations of "Hermes," "Insects," "Beetles," "Scarabs," "Aquatic," and "Flotilla," we settle on "Betilla" and hope that it will stick. That will be their name.

14

NEWSBREAK

The crowd, now swollen to nearly 400 people with the arrival of Julia's cohort, having congregated in the meeting room at the heart of the burgeoning village, eagerly wait for the news that warranted the assembly. Julia stands at the podium, nervously fidgeting with some papers as the audience quietens to start the meeting.

Julia collects herself, introduces herself, and with a smile gets down to the main message. I see the persona of the practiced university lecturer that she was, take over to hold the audience's attention as she explains. "I was recruited for this mission to identify the source of the oxygen in the atmosphere that enticed some of us to this planet and which we so freely breathe. Well, we have identified a pair of sources. The lifeforms that we have discovered, having been here first, now have us as neighbors to share this planet."

She waits while murmurs of surprise circulate then with their attention fully back on her she continues, "There is no need for alarm. As I said, there are two lifeforms. The first are creatures the size of small beetles that are, for the most part, aquatic. The second is algae and moss off which they feed. The habitat of the aquatic beetles is very similar to coral reefs. They line the coast. They are photosynthetic, much like plants, absorbing carbon dioxide and discharging oxygen. A symbiotic relationship exists between the creatures and the algae, which grows in the sea. The creatures transport algae spore from the sea in small glowing bubbles, along with juvenile beetles to the land where the spore germinates, resulting in moss. Juvenile beetles feed on the moss and disgorge the paste back into the sea, where it grows as algae to complete the life cycle of the moss and algae. As you would expect, the moss and algae also contribute to the oxygen in the atmosphere. We decided to call the creatures 'Betilla.'"

Julia answers the many questions that follow to the best of her ability. Some people report sightings of the glowing bubbles and wondered what they are.

She ends the session with directions to the locations of creatures and appeals to the audience to avoid disturbing their habitat while further investigations proceed. In conclusion she says, "The news is being dispatched to Earth as we speak and more detail will follow. We will keep you informed. Thank you for your attention."

With *Overture* forewarned, Lilian dispatches a news brief to Earth that captures headlines across the globe. News organizations clamor for more, choking the communication lines to *Overture* and Lilian's news organization, West News Incorporated WNI. Without an appointed media spokesperson to handle the unexpected volume of enquiries, the two organizations decide to collaborate, resulting in Stanley the spokesperson for *Overture* being appointed to act as intermediary between the public and Julia. To our dismay, Julia once again finds herself at the center of attention. Fortunately, it being an arms-length arrangement shields her from the worst of it; the detailed paper will answer many questions, so to that end we assist Julia to expedite its completion. Three weeks later, with the paper ready and science journal having agreed to publish it, we release the details.

* * *

A jolt stuns humanity, deposed from its anthropomorphic throne. The first concrete news of life beyond Earth is another blow to the long-held belief that we are the center of the universe, that all must bend its knee to us. The consequence is polarization. Fundamentalists shout heresy, scientists glow in vindication, liberals bleat agreement with scientists, ecologists warn of contamination and conspiracy theorists seek sinister motives while the masses, silent in their personal shelters, struggle with the catastrophe of climate, oblivious to the noise. Coalescing under their banners, groups form, placards for the vociferous. Police barely contain the anger. Riots sweep across the country led by newly minted leaders long waiting for a cause. Hastily printed pamphlets proclaim their message while science journals feed pyres to their belief, sweep like wildfire across the globe.

Triggered by the news and under the umbrella of chaos, a group calling themselves Earth First forms. Made up of disparate religious fundamentalists and climate change deniers finding common cause, they mobilize behind this new contentious front and launch their assault on law and order. Their charismatic leader eloquently stirs emotions, calling for the dismantling of all space facilities and a return to the natural order.

14.1

FAUST

Born on the twenty-ninth day of February, William Faust II always considered himself to be special, an idea instilled in him when his drunken father, William Faust I, on many occasions stumbled into the house to loudly declare with a flourish to his namesake, "Ah! William my son! You are destined for greatness. Mark these words." His father's eloquent ramblings, at whoever would listen, had a profound impact on the young William. He relished the attention, but his mother would unknowingly dash his pride by lovingly calling him "my little Willy." To his dismay, the name stuck and throughout his juvenile years, this designation followed him. His father died in a car crash while inebriated, causing extensive damage to property, with the costs falling to his mother to settle. Destitute, she too died just two years later, leaving the teenager to the vagaries of officialdom. Ultimately, a benefactor, impressed by his eloquence in a school play, provided for him, enabling him to attend university where he enrolled in a course in effective communication. To advance his debating skills he joined the Flat Earth Debating Society, surprising himself at how convincingly he could argue for or against the topic. A turning point came with the award of the lead role in a stage rendition of Goethe's *Faust*. Mesmerized by the theme he immersed himself in the persona of Faust, enthralling the audience who clamored for more. Demand for his talent grew. On completing university, he decided to break with his Little Willy nickname for good. He moved to another city and when introducing himself dispensed with the name William in favor of a single word, Faust, officially changing his name to this.

As the climate worsened, he found a ready audience in the aggrieved populace to attach religious overtones to their plight with militaristic nuances, the means to right wrongs. A growing reputation for drawing large crowds to hear him speak led to a lucrative following. The arrival of Hermes and its effects on Earth provided the final spark that launched him to the stratosphere. He stoked the fires of discontent with messages of hell, damnation and vengeance.

* * *

A rented sport stadium, filled to capacity, impatiently waits for the speaker to take to the podium. As the minutes tick by, they begin their mantra, which rises to a deafening roar when a meticulously groomed bearded man with long black hair takes the stand; Faust surveys the crowd. No words pass from his mouth; he raises his arms in salute and the raucous chants of "Turn or burn" reach a frenzy. On and on, he stirs the emotions of his captivated followers. Then, bowing deeply, he signals his intent to talk. The crowd instantly falls silent, mesmerized. He speaks slowly, pausing between each sentence, "I say to you, take heed: The heavens will not be trifled with. Ruination is at hand lest you change your ways. The devastation wrought by the climate is but a token of what is to come."

The crowd bear the cathartic flagellation, hanging on each word.

He continues, "The serpent is rising from the cesspool of deceit and unless you right your wrongs and throw off the yoke of science, it will devour all in its path. This is a warning: Abandon Mother Earth for the stars and you will surely perish under your delusion. All hell will rain down on you and there will be no salvation for you!"

He then riles them with a call to action, "I say to you, rise up and defend what is yours. Spare none."

14.2

CONSEQUENCES

Inundated with a flood of callers of every denomination, Stanley frantically dispatches a message to us: "We are under fire, barricaded in our offices! These barbarians, religious and climate nuts – they are threatening our launch facilities. Even attempting to take members of our staff hostage. Any form of intimidation is possible. Chaos everywhere!"

He stammers through the rest of his recording, "Speculation is rife on what they will do next. We expect the menace only to rise."

Later, a second communication comes through. He is slightly calmer: "We convened an emergency board meeting and for now they have decided to ride the wave. We hope sense will prevail with time. Will keep you informed!"

They maintain contact, providing update bulletins periodically preparing us for eventualities that may arise.

A disconcerting bulletin comes through. "Stanley here." His voice strains to complete the sentences. "Things have not improved. I ... we suggest that you strive for self-sufficiency in all needs including possible disruption of communications with Earth. We cannot predict what the antagonists will resort to next. Ss.. sorry to be the bearer of bad news."

As if to underscore the message, barely hours later the radio link breaks. Silence prevails.

Our pilot Lester, who navigated us to a safe landing, fiddles with alternative channels. Try as he might, only white noise results. Frustrated, he makes contact with the orbiting supply ship.

Lester explains: "Activists have sabotaged the communication link at French Guiana. Can you try for a link to the European Space Agency? They may be listening or our sponsors may have alerted them to our need for assistance."

The supply ship answers: "Thanks for the explanation. We have been struggling to contact headquarters ourselves to no avail. Let me try the ESA – hold on!"

Minutes later the backchannel crackles to life. "ESA here, we hear you. We know your difficulties. Hold on and we will patch you into Guiana. Hold on!"

Again the delay, then: "Operations here! Good to hear from you. HQ wants to speak with you. Hold on! "

"Hello, hello. This is Stanley – Operations." White noise interrupts him before he continues. "Look, I hope you can hear me. Hello, hello. This transmission through Europe and Guiana is the best we can do for now. Matters have not improved. As I was saying, you need to assume that it will be a while before normality returns."

There is crackling noise again as the transmission fails then recovers, "They have breached our facility and sabotaged the premises housing antennas at the launch facility. The backchannel will have to suffice for the time being. We suffered damage to the launch pad itself as well. This means a delay of the imminent launch of the supply ship. Importantly, you have to assume that it will be a long time before supplies reach you."

The video link shows Stanley taking a deep breath, as if to collect his thoughts before continuing. Intermittent pauses interrupt the transmission as it struggles to maintain the connection. "You probably know that the magnetic North and South poles are unstable, especially in the south. The north is now also unsettled and worldwide radio communications are affected, in particular those that rely on geo-positioning. The effect on interplanetary transmissions is severe, as you can judge by the quality of this link. Probes to Mars, Jupiter and Saturn are in trouble. It is impossible to say how long this will last and what the full extent of the effects will be. The satellite systems that relays transmissions are disrupted by changes in the Van Allen belt as the magnetic field around the Earth fluctuates."

A full minute of noise intrudes before he resumes, "I better speak quickly. As I said before, you must assume the worst; plan for self-sufficiency, rationing etc. We will keep you updated to the best of our ability."

"One final thing: I have dispatched an audio recording taken a few days ago. You can listen to it in your own time. It is from Dr. Vespucci. That is all I have to say for now."

He closes the connection.

As silence returns, for lack of words to express our reaction, we listen to Dr. Vespucci's recording.

It starts with Stanley speaking, "I have Dr. Vespucci with me; you may recall meeting him on a previous call. He is the head of the UN Office for Outer Space Affairs. Dr. Vespucci, you can speak now."

"Hello. Our mandate is the peaceful use of space. While not related to your discovery of life on Hermes, environmentalists at the UN requested that I congratulate you on your discovery. As you know, I am the head of the Faculty of Biology at my university so I have an interest in your work. The UN environmentalists urge you to take care of the environment there, especially since you are primarily a mining operation. My colleagues asked that I pass this request on to you directly."

Stanley responds, "We, as an organization, are committed to follow the UN guidelines on the environment. Thank you Dr. Vespucci."

* * *

The delay effectively shuts the window on the next close approach of Hermes to Earth at opposition. The result is that, at minimum, it will be two orbits or sixteen months before shipments arrive, assuming conditions improve. Fortunately, another supply vessel, the *Accouter*, left prior to the publication and is en route to Hermes. However, on arrival in eight months it will not have support from Earth for landing procedures if the communication problems persist. The autopilot and local facilities will need to carry out these maneuvers or place the craft in orbit around Hermes and await conditions that allow Earth to take control; a review of options is underway.

While in transit from Earth, Lester our flight engineer and pilot was the commander in chief, a role he was to relinquish to ground personnel on arrival at Mars. With our diversion to Hermes, our pod group tacitly took charge, having taken the lead on a number of occasions. By his own admission, Lester lacked the expertise to manage a ground-based operation. In the absence of an official leader, we decide to call a meeting in the hub of all the settlers to coordinate a plan for the next year.

I open the meeting with an outline of the news from Earth and audio extracts from the meeting with the sponsor. We inform the audience of, first, the sabotaging of the launch site and with it the harm done to communications; and secondly the influence on transmissions caused by the polar excursions. The reaction is as expected: alarm at the perverse coincidence of two events of grave consequence for the bond we have with Earth. Many are shocked and concerned for friends and relatives who have to withstand the worst of these events, mounted as they are on the already devastating climate changes. We urge against despondency and encourage the maintenance of contact with loved ones for as long as possible. Anticipating the need for continued individualized access to Earth, we set up the communication link to queue files for transmission with automatic receipt acknowledgement and resend on failure. We urge the audience to use pre-recorded audio or video in preference to real-time dialog, which somewhat dispels the prospect of being entirely cut off from Earth and noticeably reduces anxiety in the room.

Turning to the need to build self-sufficiency, the audience express a broad range of concerns, from mild inconveniences to questioning our very chances of survival. By prior arrangement, Jabu takes over and expertly solicits the enumeration of essentials, identified as food, water and electricity to power air scrubbers and the need to keep hydroponic equipment working. Some requirements are in abundance; some, like the food, are adequate, if monotonous. It transpires that the shortcomings are mainly luxuries such as failing electronic gadgets but also parts for some essential equipment, many of which are en route in the supply ship due in eight months.

The discussion turns to the need for a governing committee, one that will ensure fairness in disputes and ration commodities in short supply. An election by show of hands votes Jabu as chair of the committee, Lilian secretary (to take charge of communications), and Robin mediator of disputes. Logistics of supply rest with me, being a project manager. The four of us constitute the initial core group, the Management Committee (MC). Four other people – Graham, Luke, Susan and Vivienne – are members of the committee who rotate in as the core group after six months. Graham's nomination to the committee seems to be prearranged judging by the number of people vouching for him. Word is that he is fixated on autonomy from Earth and has a following who are of like mind.

Graham, a portly balding man, wastes no time in playing this card, using the congregation of all residents to sow the seed. "We must establish Hermes' political separation from Earth. They have no idea of what is important to us. Our needs are opaque to them. With time, this will only get worse, I am sure you can see that. I say we need to take control of our destiny for ourselves."

Cries of "Yea! Yea!" echo from a substantial number of settlers. His view gains support from the audience as they listen to his arguments.

Bolstered by the response, Graham wipes the few strands of hair from his face, and flushed with excitement expands on his view. "They have virtually absolved themselves of any responsibility here. We should formalize this without delay."

Jabu counters. "In the long run you may be right. I suggest that we let the year pass before considering this further and let it then be on the basis of the success or otherwise of the first year. We will essentially be autonomous during the period anyway. This way we will avoid antagonizing them, particularly when they are so vulnerable."

Jabu's view receives traction from many present, leaving Graham to bide his time. He agrees to wait out the year, and the meeting ends with a resolve to take Jabu's advice.

Hermes now has an elementary structure in place to coordinate the future.

* * *

Julia remains puzzled by aspects of the fieldwork; parts of the publication beg further explanation, or is that all that there is to know? Restless for comprehension she reviews her findings, cycling back through the logic. She wonders whether there are gaps.

How do the insects find their way from the sea to their preferred slopes for tending the moss? Is this happening elsewhere on the planet, and if so, what cumulative effect does it have? How do the Betilla survive without a means to feed themselves once back in the ocean? What material do they use and how do they build their castles in the sea? The biggest riddle is the purpose of the iridescent carapace.

Now that the only communication open to her is restricted to using the backchannel radio link to dialog with peers back on Earth for input by means of recorded sessions, a laborious process, progress to finding answers is a challenge, but will have to suffice. Undaunted, Julia prepares a list of anomalies to solve and sets out to attack them one at a time.

The easiest to discover is how widespread the Betilla habitats are. To do this she prepares for a multi-day excursion along the east coast, probably adequate for a general picture of their distribution. The rest of the team is busy with routine tasks so she intends to travel solo, a risky endeavor given the unknowns beyond the reach of past trips. I urge her to wait for one of us to join her, fully knowing Dmitri will likely accompany her. Reluctantly she agrees, so the date is set for the following week for a ten-day trip, with Dmitri being the fortunate companion.

Jabu cannot pass the opportunity by. "Dmitri, you lucky devil you... Oh, and Miles, what are you going to do for ten days without Julia? Julia, remember to focus on your responsibilities, nothing else; your focus is on the Betilla. Right?"

With my cover blown, I deflect, "Robin, what did you say you and Jabu are doing this week? An excursion of your own? Just a question."

Jabu laughs. "Okay Miles, you win. Will you chaperone us?"

Lilian blushes bright red. "Robin luv, can I come along and Jabu be our chaperone?"

Robin merely shakes his head, exasperated, at a loss as to how to respond.

Dmitri simply changes the subject. "I suggest that we use the robots as pontoons again. They are slow, but faster than traveling over land. Walking is not an option because the protective suits can't provide a breathable environment for that sort of duration."

A pontoon it will be, so Dmitri prepares one and loads tools to solve any mechanical issues that may arise. The day dawns and they launch their boat. Motorized, it paddles along at a steady pace, just faster than walking. Fortunately, the sea is calm and has been since our arrival, even during storms. The protective barrier of islands provides shelter from wave surges.

Hermes, without a moon, has only limited tidal changes, the gravitational effects of the distant sun being the only source. They steer the craft near a stream inlet where protruding rocks, character-istic of the formations created by the Betilla, extend from the water.

Julia examines the shapes for telltale funnel structures and easily finds them. The evening watch confirms the appearance of the glowing embers, and noting the direction of their flight, they proceed to the inlet. In this manner, they traverse a fair distance and on each identification of formations with cone shaped outlets, the glowing bubbles emerge in the evening.

Julia is able to surmise that the funnel outlets are directly associ-ated with the Betilla and that the little bubbles travel up the river valley to locales similar to the moss fields found earlier. The need to wait for confirmation in the evenings falls away as each bubble siting directly relates to Betilla habitats and the funnels. This enables them to navigate along the coast during daylight, marking off the funnel sites and making rapid progress along the shore. With minor exceptions, all streams entering the ocean have Betilla habitats, and the glowing bubbles usually travel up the nearest valley. Some travel vertically to disappear into the clouds, or too high to track even with binoculars. On one evening, they beach the craft to follow the bubbles and not surprisingly, each valley has its own landing site. The Betilla systematically head for these locations and preferentially settle on loose soil, although in some cases if there is no loose soil they colonize rocks.

Working on the assumption that all valleys leading into the ocean have a similar population of Betilla, the contribution of observed oxygen to the atmosphere must stem from the photosynthesis by the moss. Thinking ahead, Julia plans to confirm the hypothesis using long-range drones, which are en route from Earth with the inbound supply vessel. The drones will be able to fly at low altitude, hover over selected areas and range across most of the planet. Checking with the data emanating from the orbital survey probes, there is more oxygen in the atmosphere now than when they first arrived and there is a direct correlation between the spread of moss and the increase in oxygen. This appears to support the theory that this is the source of the oxygen and that it is probably widespread.

Julia turns her attention to the question of what directs the bubbles to the same spot, like salmon to their spawning grounds. Unlike on Earth, they cannot be relying on the sun or stars for navigation because this is a new sun to them, as is the star-scape. That leaves magnetic fields. To prove this is not simple, and besides, the bubbles seem to follow an erratic path to the location, as if an imprint of the geographic coordinates at birth directs their travels, but there is no evidence of a birth or eggs.

On the return journey, she captures a few intact bubbles and examines them under a microscope when back at the Podium. Each bubble has two compartments, essentially two bubbles fused together, and each compartment has different constituents. Curiously, the first has tri-molecular oxygen or ozone; the second contains a saline solution with a particle floating in it. It turns out that the particle is algae spore wrapped in a sample of Betilla skin. DNA analysis shows that the Betilla shed skin particles as micro DNA, probable equivalents of the complete Betilla. The skin wrapping around the algae spores protects it against the saline water while the combination is in the bubble. Julia confirms this with tests, showing that they otherwise would dissolve in the seawater; the algae spores need this protective layer.

Brushing up on the chemistry of salt water and with reference to experts on this subject, Julia concludes that the salt water in the second bubble is a conductive medium that transmits electrical charges. The sodium and chlorine ions in the salt gain or lose an electron so that the electrons are free-floating and able to carry an electrical charge through the water. The Betilla use the repelling effect that diamagnetic materials have on a magnetic field. An applied magnetic field creates an induced field in the opposite direction, causing a repulsive force. In this case they use the properties of the ozone molecules in the bubbles to change direction. They effectively manipulate these properties in the bubbles to navigate where they need to go.

Released into the air, the two bubbles in combination, less than three millimeters in diameter, settle on slopes leading to rivers and streams, guided there by alternating the electrical current in the seawater. It is effectively a switch between the natural magnetic field of the planet and a polarity change to navigate or steer to the desired location. Julia sees that, like plants that capture photons of light in the process of photosynthesis for use in splitting water molecules into oxygen and hydrogen, the Betilla use electrons normally used to metabolize sugars to enable plants to grow, to produce electricity when directed to do so. From literature on the subject, she notes that the production of electricity and transmission of electrons in the fluid medium at this quantum level is over five times more efficient than using solar cells and as such, offers an effective means to control navigation.

The DNA skin sample seems to inherit a conduit to the memory repository of the parents and from that, the location of the fields. The magnetic coordinates of deviation and inclination, passed from one generation to the next, enable them to locate the destination to which to navigate. The inheritance of the memory is an assumption that she notes will need confirmation. The shedding of the skin explains the lack of a reproductive process, multiplication occurring by cell subdivision as opposed to the need for eggs or live-bearing offspring.

Once in the sea, having negotiated the streams from the slopes where they gorged themselves on the moss, the Betilla lose the ability to eat, as their mouths practically close over. From then on, driven by photosynthetic processes similar to plants, they sustain themselves as essentially solar powered beings, having no need to ingest food other than nutrients absorbed from the water through their skin, much like a plant. Like phototrophs on Earth, organisms that carry out photon capture from light to acquire energy, they use the energy from light to carry out various cellular metabolic processes common in photosynthesis. More than that, the Betilla are oxygenic photosynthetic organisms using chlorophyll for light-energy capture to oxidize water, "splitting" it into molecular oxygen for release into the atmosphere.

Applying her understanding of photosynthetic processes common to plant life on Earth, Julia is able to stitch together the underlying logic of the Betilla's life support processes and their effects on the environment. The photovoltaic skin enables them to absorb and emit light or generate an electrical current, the same electrical charge that the skin particles also possess enabling navigation to the slopes while in the bubbles. The Betilla use the energy derived from the light for internal metabolic processes and to break down air and water into constituent parts of molecular oxygen, ozone, hydrogen and carbon dioxide. Oxygen released into the atmosphere persists as such while ultraviolet light and electrical discharges from lightning forms tri-molecular ozone from some of the oxygen. Like on Earth, some ozone finds its way to the stratosphere, where it provides a protective shield against the excesses of ultraviolet damage to living plants and organisms. One compartment of the bubbles contains ozone for buoyancy while in flight, which is then released into the atmosphere after reaching the slopes. It also potentially finds its way to the stratosphere, adding to the protective shield. Like plants, the Betilla use carbon dioxide to support internal metabolism, in the process sequestering the greenhouse gas from the atmosphere, preventing runaway global warming. After shedding their skin to the bubbles, the body succumbs and dies. The carcass, combined with silicon and calcium from the environment and the inherent carbon in carbon dioxide, forms the mix to build the coral-like reefs.

Julia manages to develop these scenarios through observation, with validation being provided in the laboratory and dialog with Earth-based scientists. One part continues to elude her, however.

She wonders: *What is the purpose of the iridescent carapace? Unlike insects on our home planet where mating has a role to play, here the propagation is not through sexual interaction. Cell division is the means of replication. Does the coloring and light-emitting property provide a means for communication? If so, how can we interpret it and what are they signaling, or does this have some other purpose?*

Drawing a blank on the remaining questions, she updates us on her latest findings. By now, we are not surprised by the extent of the revelations and the level of detail; Julia does not cease to amaze. The breadth and depth of information is staggering given the limited resources she has to conduct her investigations.

As with the newsworthiness of the earlier communication on the presence of a new lifeform on this planet, this detail also needs announcement, but the content in this case is more technical in nature and therefore will have a different audience. Robin suggests that she add this information to her original dissertation towards the doctoral thesis.

* * *

On publication, arranged by Lilian as in the initial case, the scientific community on Earth, astounded by the news, clamor for more, but the poor communication channel frustrates their efforts. Tensions rise between the scientific community and the Earth First climate deniers with their fundamentalist partners, who feel emboldened by the magnetic polar excursions. Our sponsors, more and more skeptical of the merits of continuing the venture, find themselves in the middle between the contending forces. The authorities, stretched beyond their limits in dealing with the consequences of global warming, are barely capable of maintaining law and order.

Meanwhile other nations, woken to the potential on Hermes, consider missions of their own to the planet but challenged by populations on the move, disintegrating infrastructure and political pressure to stay clear of this as a venture, have difficulty in mobilizing for a mission. It leaves only the richer authoritarian regimes that can override public pressure to launch a project to the planet. The future of Hermes as an oasis in the sky, a refuge from the extremes of humanity's excesses, hangs balanced against the threat of unscrupulous development.

In the meantime, the Betilla, having emerged from hibernation, are re-establishing their preserves, enriching the atmosphere with oxygen and rebuilding the ozone. All while the ice continues to melt, raising sea levels, adding moisture to the atmosphere and thickening its density. Life for the human occupiers becomes more comfortable, diminishing the need for prolonged use of protective clothing against ultraviolet radiation and extending the durations for which they can engage in open-air breathing. Their existence is increasingly like that on the Earth, except for the complete absence of organic life other than the Betilla with their moss and algae.

Construction work to support the community at the Podium is now complete and our sponsors telegraph the requirement to start mining operations. Their plan is to focus on the harvesting of rare Earth minerals that are in short supply on Earth, those that will fetch the highest price for the least weight to minimize transportation expenses between the planets. They reiterate the mandate of zero pollution and interference with local flora or fauna, minimal excavation and full restoration of intrusive work at completion of the mining operation in affected areas. Their intent is for the stockpiling of output in readiness for future flights back to Earth. Mining work is soon underway, giving *Overture* a year to build up stocks before the next outbound flight.

15

COMPETITION

An oligarch, rich beyond imagining; illegal proceeds of the state handed out to cronies on a whim, mining rights in the land once part of the great union fall to his kind in return for favors. Anuar surveys his vast empire. Recently allocated on a promise of loyalty, his trump card, compromising information like cards held to his chest. The mountains rise to the south where construction work on his favorite pastime stands complete: a telescope pointed at the heavens to indulge his fantasy, a look at other worlds. With a bitter shrug of his shoulders on his large frame, his only regret is that it was not ready earlier. His smaller telescope's inadequacy to resolve the coming planet in its approach led to this construction to improve his vision.

Simmering anger, suppressed for so long, tortures his mind: *"Long before that girl – what is her name? – Julia Somethingorother announced its presence, I saw it in vague outline. But before I could commission this new telescope, to confirm the finding, she claimed the prize. Why, why, why did I not think of using the Internet facilities as she did? I would be famous by now. Maybe all is not lost. That Tunguska event, maybe it too was a precursor to Nuntius, the intruder from beyond the solar system? Next week I will hike the region with my mobile laboratory; see if I can find the asteroid in the flattened forests using my adapted mining equipment; penetrate the bog to locate the body. Then fame will come. Of that I am sure."*

Turning his gaze to the south-west, not far from the telescope, there stands his other pride and joy, years in the making, the rocket loaded and ready pointed at its original destination, Mars, but equally ready to go to Hermes if need be.

Shrugging off the bitter recollections, he laughs into the wind. *"Laundering the ill-gotten funds was easy, investing in mines on Hermes! Hah, who could have dreamed of such an opportunity to obfuscate the public behind a national symbol of advancement? Sure, the vessel may be rudimentary and pose real dangers to the crew, but why worry? Good fortune favors the brave. Explanations for failure are many if it comes to that. Space travel remains a dangerous game, and disasters happen."*

* * *

History repeats itself. The lessons learned ignored, plunder is the motto, expedience the byword. The sponsor's promise to preserve the planet in the state as inherited could not, will not, last. With the news of improved habitability on the planet, hostile players like Anuar, with their interplanetary launches in the works and nearing completion, are destined to rape the new world of its riches. Profit is the sole motive. Scientists lobby various United Nations forums for the establishment of ethical ground-rules for preserving the planet but penalties are few. They are either not punitive enough, or difficult to enforce except through sanctions, but these never reach their target. The cries of those suffering under a climate gone berserk drown out all conversations, leaving only a whisper.

Anuar is the first of the hostile players. Like others that may follow, he is unscrupulous even in the quality standards built into his spacecraft. His craft stands ready for launch. With the word "Destiny" ironically emblazoned on its side, he secretly launches from an obscure site. It will travel under extended burn to make up for lost time; its course, his latest obsession Hermes. Arrival at its destination with Hermes in opposition will coincide with that of the *Accouter* supply vessel, which he knows to be en route. His ship, with landing and relaunch capabilities, will carry the bare minimum of equipment necessary to support mining and of necessity bear supplies for the crew for a year on the surface. He has no intention of building a permanent base initially, deferring this to a future date. The main objective is to establish a foothold on the planet and secure mining rights in specific areas. The *Destiny* will return to Earth with the mining output as soon as the Earth and Hermes are again in opposition.

16

MEANWHILE

Communication difficulties with our home planet continue to plague contacts with our sponsors and loved ones, the absence of information raising stress levels, especially in relation to family and friends. The trickle of reports that reach us are increasingly alarming, casting a shadow over the safety we fortuitously inherit on this planet, a reversal of all expectations at the outset of our journey. At a personal level, my brothers, who fortunately reside in areas less prone to the effects of the weather, contend with an influx of refugees. Their messages tell of a world in chaos, fraught with the dangers of desperate people at the limits of their means. Reliant on crumbling social services, they invade islands of calm, spreading the calamity. Behind fortresses of walled enclaves guarding against intrusion, they lead anxious lives, only venturing out in convoys to work sites or to replenish supplies. When out in the open, with an ineffectual magnetic shield, solar radiation strafes them from above, forcing them under protective umbrellas to avoid the cancerous consequences. Helpless but to observe at a distance, we hope for a plateau, arresting the downward spiral, for restoration of order. We understand that life will never be the same again.

* * *

Faust gleefully follows the unfolding drama. With each new calamity the numbers at his rallies swell. His coffers overflow, people giving freely as they desperately cling to every threadbare hope he offers, disguised as they are in false pronouncements of victory.

"Salute our brothers in arms," he rants, "they obstructed the path to space. Brought delay on delay and now the spinning magnet is coming to our defense as even the poles object to those who willfully seek to bring nature to its knees."

He paints pictures of gloom artfully juxtaposed on promises of paradise for those that hold forth; a future circumscribed by the natural order in balance.

"They staunched the wound, severed the link to space. Persist and persevere; this is our motto, and victory will surely come. Earth will be returned to the faithful, but first turn from your evil ways and a new Eden will be yours."

He alternatively chides and praises until, like Pavlov, they become like clay in his hands. He molds them to his design; conditioned responses result. His signature salute provokes a rising tide of hysteria that sweeps through the masses as they chant, "Turn or burn, turn or burn, turn or burn!"

By the end of the session, a peak of ecstasy is reached. The faithful, invigorated, make their way home, where the mundanity of a deflated existence confronts them.

* * *

Julia, Lilian, Dmitri and I tussle with common distresses while Robin can only sympathize with us, not having family to worry him, having long lost contact with his mother. Jabu, who supports aging parents with a monthly stipend, is distraught at what they may be enduring. Periodically we spend entire evenings fruitlessly looking for possibilities, options and opportunities to bring relief to their situation, some means by which we can have them join us on Hermes, but nothing comes to mind given the discontinuance of flights. Discouraged, we inevitably turn in for the night empty handed.

* * *

In Mount Elias, the old man Mkize is not immune to the unfolding catastrophe.

As the sun rises in the east, he stands under the blackened branches of the tree on Dry Tree Hill, surveying the sea of fog flooding the valley below, obscuring the blight humanity has wrought on this once beautiful valley. Like a prophet he stands erect, his ever-present staff in hand as if a permanent extension of his arm. Oh, that he could with one stroke, as Moses divided the sea, part the clouds below to reveal the old world beneath, restored to its former beauty. Since those bygone days all manner of people have occupied the land, destitute under the force of nature. They have built their temporary dwellings, stripped the land of every branch and tree to feed the fires of their discontent. Smog and fog now intermingle to build an illusion of morning mist as smoke rises from the clustered dwellings. Gone are the days of feeding the fowl as dawn breaks; gone the shared joys as each attended to their respective allotment in the machinery that sustained the settlement from day to day. Yet, up there, the enemy of past times still circles, the hawk; now a fond reminder of the innocence of that era. All forgiven now that the fowl, duck and geese are no more.

He stirs from his melancholy.

As he turns in reluctance to trudge the path to his home, an inner voice cautions, "Turn left not right. Remain a while longer! Remain! Listen to the portent of danger that lurks. Listen; listen; listen, do as I say. Remain a while!"

Shrugging off the restlessness within, he makes to resume the path.

"Stop a while! Look at the hawk; he sees from a distance, a vision of the future, of what is to happen! Look how gracefully he turns. Stay a while. Stay!"

202

To dispel the disconsolation Mkize strikes the skeletal tree with his staff, from where the voice seems to emanate. Moving forward with a determined stride, he proceeds down the path to the spur and the remnants of the old farm. En route, he waves at his neighbor who responds, "You were not home so I left a little something for you."

"Thank you – God bless you!" he answers with a flourish of his knob-stick in a salute as the oppressive mood lifts. Continuing down the path, he closes the rusty gate to the yard behind him, and proceeds to his home.

Entering the gloomy interior of his domicile of many years, he hangs his coat on a hook and stretches out his gnarled hands to the glowing embers of the fire that warmed him through the night. Alongside, a pot of stew simmers in the radiant heat and half a loaf of bread adds to the aroma. "God bless you!" he repeats.

Meanwhile humanity stirs from its fitful sleep in the valley now usurped by shanty dwellings. Voices penetrate the murkiness as they reluctantly face a new day. One, a new arrival to these parts, with malice in his heart at yet another day without prospects while hunger gnaws at the disgruntlement of what fate has handed down to him. Listlessly he dons a faded denim jacket and exits his dwelling in search of relief. Hoping for scraps, he skirts the knoll and wanders along the spur to the old store. A steel door bars his way from entering and the windows barricade against just such an intrusion. The shed too is impenetrable. As the murkiness begins to lift under the warmth of the morning light, he sees a standalone concrete blockhouse. Dull light seeps from the two small soot-darkened windows; there must be activity within. He approaches in caution and peers through a corner of the windowpane. An old man stands there with his back to the window, warming his hands over the remnants of a fire. Next to the fire a three-legged cast-iron pot steams, wafting a blend of flavors. His stomach rumbles at the prospect of food. The door stands open a fraction, inviting entrance. He tests it gently so as not to disturb the old man, but the door creaks under the weight of his hand. Startled, the old man turns in shock. His staff knocks over the pot, which spills its contents into the fire and produces a cloud of hissing steam. The intruder dashes in to right the pot and in doing so both men slip on the spreading broth. A tussle ensues until the younger of the two relieves the old man of his staff, but not before their clothing catches fire. In a rage of pain, the intruder strikes the old man a single blow. Mkize falls to the ground as the spreading fire snakes up his garment to his neck and hair. Frantic to stem the scorching pain he diverts his efforts at extinguishing the flames. The young man stands back to take Mkize's jacket from the hook and smothers the cinders on his denim jacket.

The malevolent fire finds the nearby straw bedding to renew its vigor, engulfing the room with its acrid breath, lapping up the tatty drapes to the ceiling. Mkize writhes in agony as he fends off the consuming conflagration.

The young man takes the opportunity to grab the bread and the half-empty pot and makes for the door. A final glance back at the unfolding tragedy stops him in his tracks. He turns to drag the old man from the room, smothers the fire on the man and disappears into the adjacent shrubbery. The pot, later found abandoned, lies empty in a trench.

The inferno reduces the building to a shell as the smoke rises to mingle with the fog in malicious irony of its earlier beauty.

Fortuitously, the neighbors, alerted by the flames, rush to the scene. Mkize is barely conscious at the doorstep, with serious burns across his neck and forehead. Once removed to the safety of their home, they tend to the wounds and revive Mkize from his stupor.

His recovery takes many months and his once bright eyes dim from the scalding. A scar marks the blow that struck his face. Periodically, as they nurse Mkize to health, a young man in faded denim jacket appears at the gate, anxiously enquiring as to his recuperation.

Mkize's mind often strays to the premonition that he ignored while on Dry Tree Hill, but he buoys his spirit with recollections of the pristine valley and the sea of fog that magically transformed the valley below. His irrepressible spirit holds no desire for vengeance against the man whom misfortune brought to his door.

Through it all, a gnawing uncertainty challenges his reserve. He struggles to comprehend its source. "There are many like him, the intruder, in desperate straits; the flux grows with each day. What is this world coming to, what form is this demon, this climate of extremes? I must hold my head high, stand firm; never bend to its will. Fate may challenge but we, the noble in spirit, we will emerge insurmountable and turn the tables on its foul design."

* * *

Mars struggles with its own circumstances; the biting cold a constant challenge in this frigid world. The dependence on energy is under renewed stress as demands for heating increase; the micro nuclear generators operate at maximum capacity, forecasting a need for the provision of one or more supplemental reactors. Water locked in rock-hard ice at the new lower temperatures and extracted at significant cost results in frequent equipment failure, brought on by operating beyond the stated specifications. This in turn increases the dependence on resupply missions for replacement parts, but the launch facilities on Earth are under siege, surrounded by fortresses of protection to keep out the invading force of demonstrators and activists. The rising sea levels gradually encroach on the facilities positioned as they are near the coast, a new threat requiring investment in dykes or raising the launch platforms. Tidal extremes resulting from the moon's elongated ellipse threaten the dykes on each swing in the pendulum of its phases. The unreliability of communications brought on by the magnetic polar excursions add a further wrench in the works, aborting launches on a frequent basis and requiring elaborate countermeasures to circumvent disruptions.

Dmitri continues his correspondence with Michael's colleagues on Mars, Ella and Noah. Their view echoes the newsfeeds that we have trickling in through our communication channel. Fortunately, they have a reliable supply of food from their hydroponic farm, provided they are able to mine enough ice for conversion to water.

Noah indicates that there will be an exodus of about a hundred people on the next return voyage; not a trend yet, but it will erode confidence in their ability to maintain a presence on Mars. Some felt alarmed at the continued deterioration of Ella and five others, caused by radiation and for whom recovery was all but ruled out.

* * *

For now, we seem to have made the correct choice in deciding on Hermes. The climate is better than expected, living conditions are comfortable, water is in ample supply and the planet appears to be stabilizing at its location in our solar system. Tectonic consequences of the change in geological stresses may still manifest themselves in the future, but volcanic activity remains dormant, as reported by the orbiting probes. Equipment as a means to measure quake activity in the planet's crust has been included in the supply mission that is en route to us at this time. A definitive answer to the internal workings of the planet will have to wait.

17

DESTINY

Anuar proudly watches as the *Destiny* takes to the sky. His ego, like the craft, soars on the hope of impressing his political cronies.

Leaving the details of managing the space flight to his stooge Grigori, who sullenly attends to his whims, Anuar's attention turns elsewhere. He sets off in his private jet for Tunguska, in a remote area of Siberia near Lake Baikal, to indulge his other frivolous pursuit. The advance party with the equipment already there are waiting for his bidding. As they fly over the site, they see the fallen trees. Resembling a gigantic spread-eagled butterfly with a wingspan of seventy kilometers and a body of fifty-five kilometers, they have been knocked down in a direction away from the center, with those at the epicenter still upright despite the passage of time since the occurrence. Anuar compares the sight with the Kulik survey conducted in 1927 and finds a direct correlation. The possible impact zone is his destination.

While the *Destiny* accelerates to Hermes, days turn to weeks as Anuar explores the epicenter of the Tunguska event of 1908 but finds nothing. Like a murder without a body. The implication is that he can only confirm the known. The object exploded in the atmosphere, as determined by other investigations to explain the leveling of the forest for thousands of square kilometers, leaving no evidence of its presence. Even using his ground penetrating radar to find the object comes to nothing, rubbing salt in the wound of his ego, evaporating his dream of fame once again.

Vexed by yet another failure and as a last straw, he attempts to reconstruct the trajectory of the object by the angle of the fallen trees and implied direction of the entity based on their fall-pattern. Together with the rotation and orbital position of the Earth on that eventful day, on return to his telescope in the mountains, he points in that direction hoping against hope to find some new insight into the source of the object. Alone in his observatory he scans the skies, soon realizing that some random vector other than the source would apply given the passage of lightyears' pertinence if this was an interstellar object. He is about to abandon the idea when Mars happens to travel across his line of sight. In its wake as it journeys inside the orbit of the asteroid belt, he notes a slight change in the path of some asteroids. His curiosity piqued, he follows Mars as it travels its more distant orbit, displaced nearer the belt of rocks by the arrival of Hermes. The disrupting effect on the asteroids continues. Even Ceres is drawn in by degrees. The consequences are obvious; each loosed object, too many to track individually, pose a threat to the equilibrium enjoyed by the planets in this system.

Comfortable in his seclusion, he murmurs to himself in his native language: "*Hmmm, here is the glory I sought for so long. Oh for shame, that fame should come couched in infamy. What an irony that I be the bearer of ill news. Me, when all I want is recognition. Okay, who cares? I will be the compounder of misfortune and twist the screw of the spell held over the Earth as it grapples with a hostile climate. Why should I not profit from this tribulation? While all sleep, I can prepare. I will hold my tongue, alerting none. The disaster will come about, there can be no doubt, and I will be ready. I will build a fortress to survive even the worst, and when the cataclysm is past, I will emerge the victor to inherit the Earth.*

"*For insurance, I will build another rocket, a rocket to take me to Hermes if the fortress cannot withstand the devastation.*"

"I must remain alert, watch for the coming doom. Gage its impact from the size of the threat and if too large, launch 'Satyros.' He will fly me to the fledgling planet Hermes to rule over it and be the master of the new world. There I will build my empire, leaving my legacy for all time."

Elation overwhelms him. Sardonically he chuckles, guffaws from deep within his imposing girth: "Fortune has again favored the brave, my motto holds true. Here is confirmation of my destined greatness. By now, the *Destiny* must be approaching its destination. I will soon have a foothold on Hermes. They will prepare the way for me. My plans are working to perfection!"

* * *

ESA is the first to report sighting a craft entering space from what appears to be a rudimentary launch site in central Asia, north of the Himalayas. All attempts at communicating with the vessel or its ground support organization are fruitless. Monitoring reveals its direction as Hermes. All they can do is track its progress and provide the Overture organization with its progress towards Hermes. Disquieted by the news, we wonder at what their intent is. We realize that the arrival challenges our seclusion and growing sense of right of ownership as first occupiers of the planet. Unease at having others staking a claim threatens our independence.

An uneventful few months pass before the unnamed spaceship and our supply craft *Accouter* arrive separated by a week, entering trailing orbits to prepare for landing. The *Accouter* crew report that they have distant sight of the other craft and for the first time we learn of its name, *Destiny*. It displays suspiciously militaristic elements such as what look like torpedoes attached to the side panels and cannon-like contraptions tightly coupled under the wings designed with rotating engines for hovering capabilities. The aerodynamic outline with oversized exhaust and rear engine gives it an aggressive look. The craft shows no provision for artificially induced gravity for the occupants, and we therefore presume that they have lived through near-zero gravity during the entire transit period. By implication, acclimatization to the planet's gravity after landing will be a protracted exercise.

A friendly hail by the *Accouter* pilot goes unanswered for over an hour before a curt reply comes back, acknowledging the communication and bidding the *Accouter* a safe landing, but in a tone to discourage further dialog. The *Accouter* team decide to let the *Destiny* descend to the surface first, but start their maneuver to position for their own entry, drifting to a different orbit, losing line of sight to the *Destiny*. The orbiting surveyor probes take up monitoring the movements of the *Destiny* and its whereabouts, updating the ground station on a continuous basis through a secure line.

Three days and many circumnavigations of the planet pass before the *Destiny* begins its descent. On a signal from the orbiting probes, we see the craft's fiery entry streaking across the sky from east to west, their landing trajectory guiding them to the Farland continent across the expanse of the Hadean Ocean. We wonder how they decided on a landing site, how they assessed the surface conditions and what method they will use to achieve touchdown. Their alternatives are to use balloons, parachutes, aerodynamic gliding or to hover for a vertical descent. They also have a choice of whether to alight at sea or on land. As we watch, they disappear over the horizon, lost to sight, but the orbiting probes track their progress, reporting an apparent successful vertical touchdown on land near the sea, using their hovering engines. On each pass overhead the probe reports, disgorging activity and some assembly of structures, then all goes quite for two days before activity resumes.

The decision on landing options for the *Accouter* undergoes a final review. The ice landing strip originally used is no longer a choice, having melted under the rising temperatures. This leaves a combination of parachutes and balloons for landing the entire craft or the cargo on its own. The latter with five drops is the preference, one on each circumnavigation of the planet. A small descent pod will penetrate the atmosphere for each cargo drop and a balloon will provide a soft landing on the surface. This has the advantage of leaving the mother ship in orbit to await the next supply craft as a backup for the return trip to Earth. The craft will be placed in a stable orbit and remain there, unmanned. The crew will descend in the final orbit around Hermes, using a manned descent module expressly available for this scenario. This will use parachutes and balloons for the final stage to touch down.

As preparations reach finality, the twenty-two people still languishing in orbit in their *Forerunner* pods awaiting a return flight to Earth reach a decision. Eight of them have a change of heart, electing to descend to Hermes using the pods for landing as we did, except they will hydroplane on the last stretch where we had ice to land on. The remaining fourteen still prefer a return to Earth. After approval comes through from *Overture* on Earth, they couple their pods to the *Accouter* thruster and set off for the return flight, leaving the inhabited descent stage and supply modules behind.

Despite the understanding that there will be no radio support from the Earth, the decision is to proceed with the landing. The *Accouter* descent stage enters an elliptical orbit, releases the first cargo module at the closest approach to the atmosphere and signals to the ground control group to take over guidance through the entry, parachute and balloon stages. We watch as the module appears, hangs in the air held by the parachutes, and splashes down buoyed by the balloons for a perfect landing a few hundred meters from our observation point. Recovery from the sea lands the module on our beach and within thirty-minute intervals the other supply modules splash down followed by the crew module. The two pods with the eight who decided on Hermes rather than a return to Earth are soon winched to shore to augment our settlement.

All are safely down, crew and supplies. After welcoming the new arrivals, we start unpacking the supplies. Aside from general supplies there are packages containing personalized items, permitted within weight constraints. These include gifts from friends and relatives as well as items we asked them to source for us.

Amongst other items, Dmitri and I requested tennis rackets and a supply of balls designed to compensate for our lower gravity. The recreational center has floor space for basketball, badminton, tennis and other team sports, which we intend to utilize fully. Ignoring other items, I rummage through my package, intent on finding a small parcel secreted there at my request. With some relief, I find it tucked away under miscellaneous items and pocket it for opening as soon as I am alone. Later, impatiently, I open it to find two beautifully designed rings: a ruby engagement ring and an accompanying gold wedding band; my brother selected well. Unfortunately, they are rather useless until I pluck up the courage to broach the question with Julia.

18

EXPLORATION

With the supply ship came the drones. At Jabu and Julia's insistence, their assembly for operations takes priority. We decide to allot ten of the twelve drones to specific areas on the planet, retaining two on standby at the basecamp. Being solar powered as a rule they need a day of charging for two days of continuous ranging. As a start, we dispatch them to their allotted areas. Once there, they remain in standby mode, for use as needed.

With Dmitri's assistance, they are soon navigating over land and oceans, over mountains, seas and rivers, flying high or at low altitudes, hovering over areas of interest and landing for close inspections where necessary. They range widely within their designated areas under guidance from the control center, exploring the planet in detail, indexing video recordings with notable places for review.

Jabu directs his time-slice to the exploration of areas of geological interest based on the orbital surveys. He examines rock formations, looks for signs of minerals, considers the feasibility of extraction and accessibility and maps out a plan that will be the most profitable while having the least impact on the environment.

In Julia's time allocation, by day and with night-vision at night, they traverse the routes of the Betilla. They follow their habits, watching from a distance, parking at close quarters in the moss fields or floating alongside their coral constructs in the seas, silently and unobtrusively observing their every move.

It falls to Robin to produce a quantitative analysis of the geology and biology, combining disparate facts, adding logic and factoring in qualitative information. Jabu uses the analysis to prepare a plan and schedule for mineral extraction built on the availability of resources, machinery and personnel derived from my master plan. Julia uses the information to examine the distribution of Betilla across the planet. She confirms that they are indeed widespread in all areas where the ice has thawed. There is one exception, the land adjacent to the Middle Sea. Here, Betilla activity is strangely absent, probably, we assume, due to unsuitable soil conditions for propagating moss. It is also apparent that the Betilla lie dormant under the ice in areas not yet melted at the north and south polar latitudes.

The remaining matters of intrigue are the carapace coloring and the light-emitting capabilities of the Betilla. Julia continues her observations of the creatures. One notable error in her previous investigations is that those bubbles that rise from the conical aper-tures and proceed inland have the characteristic pulsing glow, while those that rise vertically do not glow. She has difficulty trapping one of the rising bubbles, but succeeds after many tries. Not surpris-ingly, they do not contain the algae seed wrapped in the Betilla skin. Instead, they contain traces of bacteria, and there is only one bubble, not the typical joined pair. She presumes it must be a flaw in their spawning. However, it confirms conscious navigation of those with seeds to their destination. Those without the seeds and only a single bubble contain ozone, giving them the required lift to float and only directly upwards. Using the drones to track the vertical progress is not helpful; they rise to a height beyond the range of the drones, disappearing from sight at altitude. Other than these revelations, the purpose of the main quest for an explanation of the coloring and glow stubbornly refuses to release its secret.

214

On an excursion to the Farland continent, based on coordinates provided from orbit, the drone ventures near the base camp where the *Destiny* made landfall. In stealth, the craft approaches, maintaining an elevation with the sun at its rear. Details of the camp layout are more apparent than when viewed from space. A haphazard group of modules lies across a plane not far from the sea; the landing craft is in the middle, dwarfing the habitats. Robots rove in close proximity carrying out further leveling and assembly tasks. Periodically a person emerges from a hut only to disappear back into the prefabricated building after a few minutes.

We notice tracks leading from the camp up an incline and over the hill. Following the path for about two kilometers, on a hillside opposite a river, we see three robots are busy with excavation activities. Dmitri compares the coordinates of the location with the aerial surveys; it corresponds with a concentration of rare Earth mineral deposits. They have evidently started mining operations there, based on the publicly available survey data. This explains the choice of landing site, but the terrain has striations of granite making it less than ideal to quarry. Julia points to a patch of moss not far from the pit that they have dug. She expresses concern at their disregard for the indigenous biology.

After a few minutes, a person emerges from one of the robots, notices the drone and signals to a colleague in another robot, who joins him or her. They wave aggressively, seemingly gesturing us away. We retreat out of sight, their message clear: "You are not welcome."

To maintain a presence in the vicinity to better monitor their activities we decide to park the drone in a secluded area some kilometers distant.

* * *

215

Julia's quest to understand the coloring and pulsing nature of the Betilla fades for lack of a strategy to unravel the mystery. She focuses on updating her thesis, and life settles down to a routine of daily chores, talk of the latest mining and construction operations, excursions into the stark environment and visits to the string of islands. Julia and I have resumed our close relationship, spending all our free time together, and my jealousy towards Dmitri fades; our relationship deepens. She returns to her hobby, sketching the landscape and close-up views of the moss and their partners, the Betilla.

The electronic piano has been a godsend. My favorite pastime is to listen to Robin and Julia play their intricate music with such depth of feeling. Being immersed in the sounds, so exquisite they tug at the heartstrings, is a privilege beyond imagining.

The new settled feeling, a strangely welcome relief from the hectic days of exploration and the excitement of discovery of the new lifeforms, brings contentment. The endless space journey, the unexpected appearance of Hermes out of the void and the decision to take the risk of diverting from Mars to Hermes are all now a distant memory. Why then the persistent twinge of doubt that this cannot last? What surprises lurk in the future? What are we to make of this new world in the time to come?

The answers do not take long in coming. At first, events seem unrelated. The habit of fate is not constrained by convention; it exercises its will at random, the only certainty being its uncertainty.

Of an evening, Julia and I walk along the coastline to our favorite viewing site to watch the throbbing lights as the Betilla make their way from the ocean over the hill to sow seeds in the fields alongside the rivers. I feel the tension in my hand as I cling to the ring in my pocket; will I have the courage to propose to Julia this evening? The time seems right.

The Betilla seem more active than usual tonight. Many thousands rise from multiple sites along the line of sight. From our vantage point on a small rise with a backdrop of dark clouds, the glow shines with awe-inspiring brightness. Speechless, we watch the radiant dance of light. Gradually a pattern emerges, made more apparent by the sheer number in flight. Interspersed in the pulsing glow, a lesser pulse of irregular and fluctuating brightness and color shines at variable intervals, offsetting the regularity of a dominant pulse. As the swarm forms a cloud, the density shows the dominant pulse as a synchronized throb while the lesser one changes apparently randomly. Julia is fascinated, as am I. What can this mean? We watch, captivated as the cloud begins to swirl, forming a knot in the center surrounded by an empty space then nine concentric rings of concentration radiating outwards from the central bulge. The concentric rings each begin clumping together into knots of their own, one group per ring, until we see a slowly rotating mass with each clump a different size. Aside from the overwhelming size of the central bulge, the fifth ring develops into a nub about a tenth the size of the central clump; it begins to separate out into a set of minor knots of light rotating around it and displays a throbbing red brightness offset to one side in its swirling interior. The second largest in the ring, the sixth, does likewise, displaying a circular band of Betilla around it with rotating clumps apparent beyond the band.

The stately pageant revolves around us in grandeur as we breathlessly take in the spectacle. The outer rings circle the central bulge slower than the inner groups. On and on the majestic pattern persists then slowly dissolves into a mist of lights. Turning to Julia I see that she has had the forethought and time to capture the images on camera before they dissipate into the nebulous cloud, subsiding as the Betilla returned to their fortresses. What can this signify?

Julia gasps, having held her breath for much of the time, sets the camera aside. Her hands cradle her face in wonder: "There was something unmistakably deliberate about what we just witnessed. There has to be an explanation."

I am too dumbfounded to reply and can only nod in agreement.

We wait for a recurrence, but none comes. The exhilaration of the moment fades and darkness descends on us as the show ends.

We wait a little longer, then move to head home in silence, meditating on what we have seen. As we walk, my hand strays to my pocket. There the object of this stroll, the ring, feels alien; will these momentous events overtake my personal yearnings? Has the opportunity been lost forever? Plagued by feelings of a certain decisive finality seemingly to have overtaken my endeavors, my wishes, we walk on under the guise of thoughtfulness, despondency my companion. The juxtaposition of my emotional response to the event and my longings tear at the very fabric of my sensibilities. I struggle to separate the two, to fend off the spiral into dejection.

At the camp, Robin, Jabu, Dmitri and Lilian watch the recording, amazed at the spectacle.

Robin is first to reach a conclusion. "From my perspective, the pattern of rings and the central object is the solar system. The knot in the middle is the sun. Jupiter stands out, correctly proportioned relative to the sun, complete with its moons. And look there – there is the anticyclonic storm producing the red spot. Saturn is next, correctly positioned in the sixth place out from the sun."

Jabu laughs. "How do you come to the conclusion so quickly? Now that you point it out, it is obvious. I wish I had your mathematical brain, or is it pattern matching, Venn diagrams? What is your trick?"

Lilian's admiration shows on her face. "Wow! Robin, you are so clever."

Robin shrugs in irritation, bringing a despairing reaction from Lilian. "Well, I think you are clever."

Where the spectacle was beautiful to observe, the meaning behind it is even more astounding.

Julia points out, "The angle of the presentation is not accidental. It was created specifically for us, the viewers, from our vantage point."

Dmitri elaborates, "Yes! The only conclusion is that it is a message, an attempt to communicate with us. It's got to imply intelligence!"

Continuing, he says, "Robin must be right, except, one planet is missing, Hermes… Could it be because we orbit the sun at an angle to the ecliptic plane?"

A rush of questions come to mind, the foremost being how they can possibly know the location of all the planets. How do we answer them? How do we tell them we have heard them? Surely, after the first salvo a repeat or elaboration will follow. They cannot be certain that we heard or understood them.

The group working as one, in rapid fire theories flow. Conjecture solidifies known facts, which leads to inferences, suppositions and ultimately to ideas worth exploring. Intelligence is indisputable, dialog their goal, visible light the conduit and pictures the language. What do we not know? Being aquatic for much of their life, are they able to communicate underwater? To know the structure of the solar system, visual or magnetic detection capabilities must exist. Then again, how? Are the iridescent carapaces light sensitive for dual purposes, photosynthesis and for sight? Can this be part of the explanation?

Julia clarifies: "On Earth, bioluminescence is a form of chemically produced emission of light by living organisms. It occurs widely in marine vertebrates and invertebrates, as well as in some fungi, micro-organisms and terrestrial invertebrates such as fireflies. In some animals, symbiotic organisms such as bacteria produce the light and in others, production is by the animals themselves. Here the opposite may also apply; does it double for light detection purposes?"

I interject, "Yes, but to resolve distant objects, such as Jupiter and Saturn, a wide aperture lens of several meters is essential to image the planets, let alone the red swirling storm clouds on Jupiter. Where or what telescopic features do they have? The carapace just does not fit that description."

We are back to the drawing board just as we thought all surprises had been exhausted. This not only confirms other lifeforms, but sentient ones at that. There are degrees of intelligence, in a range from inherited instinct to rational thought, self-consciousness and beyond, if that is possible. Where in this range do the Betilla lie? Steeling ourselves against further surprises, we acknowledge that they could tilt the scale of intellect in any direction.

Round and round the discussion circles until we build a rational pyramid, one block of logic on the next. A plan emerges: we need to take one step at a time, from the simple to the complex, and knit a coherent whole.

Starting with the easiest of puzzles, Dmitri rigs up a watertight microphone attached to a computer to simulate a hydrophone, and with Julia onboard the floating robot they venture into the sea where Betilla reefs are in abundance. The device immediately records sounds, birdlike twitter that carries long distances underwater. The pattern of sounds is similar to the light emissions of the bubbles with the glowing lights, a regular pulse with variable sounds between the metronomic beats. The volume rises and falls in beautiful waves of patterns, with multiple Betilla participating, best described as music. It is as if directed under the baton of an orchestral conductor, strangely harmonic with unaccustomed overtones. Eerily atmospheric sounds intersperse the pointillist birdcalls while retaining a broadly melodic continuance. To the untrained ear, it does not correlate with the back and forth of a language between two in dialog, but rather an expression of a mass choral work, synchronized beauty that may still convey a message. The sounds persist for many minutes, undulating, progressing imperceptibly from one form to another dissimilar one. Julia and Dmitri record the sounds for over an hour for later analysis.

Conclusions later drawn from the examination of the sounds in comparison to the visual displays shows a direct correlation: the two are some form of communication, one for when submerged and the other for dialog while airborne. The production of sound implies an auditory capability, in short, a means to listen as we do with our ears. The visual component can only be via the iridescent carapace, a light detector, since they do not have eyes. This leads us to speculate that the tracing of planets in the solar system must be possible by means of this capacity, for light detection. The riddle of how they are able to resolve the distant planets continues to elude us.

To find out more about their habits with minimal intrusion, we need to penetrate the coral structures to see what they do inside their habitats. Dmitri, with his technological bent, comes up with a solution. He requisitions a colonoscope from the medical unit and extends its reach by the addition of a length of rigid fiber-optic cabling. The cable, inserted into a fine aperture drilled into the coral, reveals the interior. A labyrinth of tunnels radiate out from a central cavity that accommodates hundreds of Betilla. They tend to crawl along the floor, walls and roof in preference to swimming, although their tiny feet are partially webbed. The iridescent shells illuminate the cavern and tunnels with multiple colors and the characteristic pulsing continues, but at a lower intensity. The sounds they produce seem to come from the remnants of the mouths used to feed on moss in their amphibious stage alongside rivers on the surface. A part of the roof of the cavern is transparent silicon allowing light to enter, providing a sun-facing window to the outside world to energize their metabolism using solar power through photosynthesis. The Betilla tolerate the intrusive fiber-optic cable, as if understanding our curiosity.

We leave the cable in place to record the activities over time, attaching the colonoscope to a floating buoy anchored to a rock, and thereby free the robot pontoon for other purposes.

The intrigue of figuring out what lies behind the Betilla's activities is enough to absorb our attention fully. For other matters to distract us from unraveling the mystery seems like an imposition. Yet this is precisely what happens.

On arriving back at the camp, we hear of news that the orbiting probe detected an explosion on Farland, detonated by the *Destiny*'s crew. Jabu immediately surmises that they are using dynamite to expose the minerals embedded in the granite strata, as noted by the orbiting surveyor. The cameras confirm this as they pass overhead.

Annoyed by the news, Julia recommends reporting this to Earth as a violation of the broadly accepted principle to preserve the planet from harmful effects of activities such as this. They need sanctioning and steps taken to discourage recurrence. Especially now, with life, and potentially intelligent life, on the planet, everyone needs to act in a responsible manner. After all, we are occupying land that belongs to other beings. Lilian dispatches a notification via the circuitous backchannel and troublesome communication link to an overarching scientific control forum as well as Dr. Vespucci the secretary of UNOOSA, informing them of events. At this stage, we remain silent on the question of intelligence still under investigation.

Aside from an automated confirmation of receipt of the notification, no response is forthcoming despite repeated attempts. The wheels of authority no doubt turn slowly while we impatiently wait. The inaction is confirmed when we register another explosion a week later; they, the *Destiny* crew, must have decided to ignore directives from Earth, if they received any.

We launch the drone from hiding to take a closer look. Sure enough, the hillside shows the scars of a blast. Strangely, at a safe distance from the blast area, people clothed in spacesuits appear to be evacuating three or four individuals without the protective suits, who seem to be dead, unconscious or immobile. How can the blast affect them when they are well outside the range of any ejected debris? We radio an offer of assistance but all attempts at communication go unanswered. After discussion, Lilian dispatches to Earth a more urgent request for intervention. Again, there is little reaction of any significance. They are having trouble tracking down someone in the *Destiny*'s command structure to solicit a response, let alone an agreement to desist from their destructive actions.

A day or two after these events we return to our adapted colonoscope-monitoring device to download an extract of the data record. An examination shows normal Betilla behavior up to a point in time when, with a flurry of activity, they begin sealing their end of the aperture, leaving the recording blacked out. A discussion on the significance of this explores a few possibilities, none of which explain why they would be closing us out.

Robin questions the timestamp: "Look, the date and time is two days ago. Can you think of an event that happened at that time? There has to be an explanation."

Jabu ponders aloud: "There have been no weather-related effects. A storm surge may explain this but the weather has been the usual relative calm. The calm has persisted for weeks now. That can't be the reason."

Dmitri concurs: "Yes. Even the forecast, the weather predictions – I am not aware of an approaching storm. If bad weather were on the way, it may explain this; sort of like shuttering of the hatches, so to speak. Actually, the only thing I can think of is the incident on Farland with the *Destiny* crew dynamiting the hillside. That was about two days ago. Could it be that?"

Robin wastes no time in comparing the time of the two events, and leaves us astounded; the blast coincides to the minute with the Betilla's blocking of the aperture.

Jabu exclaims, "Incredible! The detonation must have disturbed the Betilla; the shock waves have some effect on them. Surely, they have experienced seismic activities in the past. Maybe they were sensitized in the past and this has triggered a panic response, a previous trauma."

Julia ventures: "How can we find out? We have no means of asking them unless we open some form of communication channel. It would be worth doing this just to get an answer on their solar system presentation. I think we need to focus our attention on a means to communicate."

We explore alternatives and come up with two options, audio or visual. They seem to use both, but their opening communication used light, so this may be the preferred medium. A picture seems too simplistic as a response. Their use of a picture in the form of the solar system may have been to draw our attention, while at the same time, knowing that we are space travelers, they knew we would know about the planets. Their opening dialog served two purposes: to draw attention and to provide hidden meaning. The latter to solicit a response of equal intellect. A reply in picture format would need to do likewise, but what can we tell them in this form and how?

Robin points out, "Think like an alien; the Betilla's response to the blast was to seal off the optic cable into their coral nest. This means that they knew this was a visual observation tool. What if we used this as the conduit for further contact?"

Julia says, "We need to start an education process, a language that both can understand. But how do we do that?"

With no clear path forward, we settle on reconvening in the morning, providing time to think up other possibilities.

Events overtake yet again. In the morning, broadcasting on multiple bands, an SOS message from the *Destiny* comes through on our radio. "An accident has occurred; four individuals are unconscious, resulting from inhaling an unknown toxic gas. Please can you supply a broad-spectrum agent to resuscitate them?"

Before we can dispatch a reply, a second communication comes through. "The individuals are showing signs of recovery. Not to worry about providing a remedy; we will monitor their progress and get back to you if needed. Thank you – out!"

Jabu exclaims, "What on Earth? They seemed seriously injured yet here they are recovering in next to no time? One extreme to the other... Anyhow, thankfully, they seem okay, but my guess is that we probably will not hear details of what actually happened. They seem so secretive."

With the interruption behind us, leaving us wondering about the event, the days pass. The questions subside and we revert to the task of how to establish a communication with the Betilla. We have not been able to figure out a way to start a dialog.

Robin speculates, "As an example that may apply here, historically, when two civilizations met for the first time, as in the case of the Incas and the Spanish, they benefited from being in each other's presence to point to objects and naming them. This must have enabled them to build up a vocabulary. In our case, light and sound are the two channels available. They can only operate remotely; we are not in their presence. So, question: how do we simulate this?"

This gives me an idea. "Wait! That may be the secret. If we send them a picture, static or in video, using sound or a split screen picture, we can point to the objects and name them. The inverse can also apply; send a sound recording and use a picture to display the object."

Julia makes the point, "Sure, but unfortunately, in this world, lacking in living creatures to picture, aside from the two species we have identified, few objects produce sound."

Robin expands, "Better still, if we send a picture of a letter from the alphabet we can articulate it with its corresponding sound, for example the graphic of the letter 'a' corresponds to the sound 'AAEE,' then string letters from the alphabet together to form a word such as 'p-e-r-s-o-n' and audibly say the word 'person.'"

Jabu adds, "Usage would have to be limited to real world objects familiar to both of us, like mountain, river, sea, planet and cloud. You know, this could work."

We debate the merits of each alternative and settle on simply displaying a picture and sending the corresponding audible equivalent, one at a time, acknowledging that nouns will be easy, verbs would require a video of the action.

Trials start. We insert a fresh fiber-optic cable into their inner chamber, and transmit separate pictures of moss and a juvenile Betilla feeding on the moss on a hillside. Then, using a submerged speaker system, we echo the image with its auditory equivalent. Repeating the pairs a few times, we finally get a consistent response on our microphone. Every time we show the picture of the moss and say the word "moss," we hear, "TMMTZZ." It should not have come as a surprise: they cannot articulate words as we do since all the recordings we have of their musical sounds resemble twitter-like bird sounds.

I give pause. "Wait, I think I have a solution. If we use a translation application, one of those that are common on all our communication devices, especially since they are now enhanced with the latest artificial intelligence algorithms, we could learn their pronunciations and translate them into English and back to the Betilla language."

Building on the rapport Julia has established with the Betilla, she serves as spokesperson. Very quickly, we compile a vocabulary and are able to speak increasingly complex sentences and receive intelligible responses. Within a week, we are able to speak fluently. We speak English, the translator sends the words in the Betilla language, they speak in Betilla and our interpreter translates into English. After initial pride at our accomplishment, deflation soon follows. To our utter surprise, we receive a communication in English and the sound is as if Julia is speaking, perfect diction and emphasis in the right places. It is not in the Betilla language and we have no need for translation. They have taken a step further than we have: not only are they able to translate our language, they have formulated a means to translate before sending. Amazing! What technology do they possess to do this, and while submerged at that?

With the communication barrier removed, we are able to speak freely through the submerged audio listening and transmitting devise, with nothing to hinder discussions other than the slight distortions of the sounds traveling through water.

Naturally, all the questions we compiled, fraught with articulation difficulties, are suddenly in reach. We can ask and responses will be forthcoming. The prospect is at once exciting, and their obvious intelligence intimidating.

As the days extend to weeks, Robin increasingly shows signs of discomfort until finally he says, "We have been so engrossed in these creatures that we have lost track of time. It is the same as when we first discovered the Betilla. We held off informing Earth for too long, in my opinion. Here again, same thing, we should have informed them of our discovery of their intelligence a long time ago, let alone the extent of it."

Julia defends, "Yes, it is the same as last time. On that occasion, we had to understand their full lifecycle; in this case, there is no point in just saying they are intelligent. We need to present the evidence in as much detail as possible."

Robin remains concerned. "You open us to severe criticism. The delay on its own, how do you explain that? Worse than that, what if the Betilla have some form of harmful effect on us. You know what? The people here on Hermes have a right to know. They will lynch us if they come to any harm, something preventable. We cannot with-hold this any longer. If you don't say something, I will!"

I feel obligated to intervene, find some means to compromise. "Robin, yes, we have delayed and we are collectively responsible for that. The discovery has been intriguing on so many levels. To this point no harm has been done."

Looking ahead, I question, "Assuming we do inform Earth. What happens next? Will they recommend a cautious approach, allow us the freedom to speak with the Betilla at will, or will they demand that we shut down all communications? At some level the initiative is ours."

Continuing, I say, "For starters you can expect the usual spec-trum of responses from intrigued scientists, quarrelsome activists, hawkish militarists, dovish pacifists and the range of religious affiliations; any and all are likely."

Looking for the compromise, I suggest, "It is one thing to share this solar system, galaxy or universe with low-level life forms, yet another with an equal or superior intellect. Who are we to steer the response to the Betilla in any particular direction? Even amongst ourselves, we have differences of opinion on the way forward. Robin, I take your point, there is urgency. Equally, there is a right way to announce this and a wrong way, and a right time and a wrong time. I suggest that we give ourselves a little extra time to come up with the correct solution."

We call a hiatus while we resolve what to do. The message is clear: we need to act quickly in informing the world and the residents, but while preparing a communiqué, we must maintain the dialog with the Betilla, so as not to raise suspicions by abruptly discontinuing interactions with them.

On reconvening, we conclude that given the unprecedented nature of the discovery, there is no model on which to draw for equivalence, nor any organization equipped to advise us on the best course of action. Essentially, we are the temporary guardians of the information; we decide on the manner, format and timing of the release. Our overriding objective is that the information must be accurate, timely and state only the facts, without inferences. As such, readers must reach their own conclusions on the display of the concentric circles, whether this represents the solar system.

To this end, we give ourselves three days to provide a summary of events, written as a cover story by Lilian, for dissemination to the news outlets and for our residents. Secondly, Julia must expand on her thesis for transmission to a scientific journal. In the initial communiqué, we will not elaborate on the fluidity of our communications with the Betilla, limiting it to the solar system display and the strange 'TMMTZZ' response to our rudimentary dialog via the auditory channel. Our reasoning is that piecemeal information will still the alarm, and allow gradual absorption with acceptance built in stages. We will provide a more complete update for the news media when the thesis is ready.

After initial reticence on the part of Robin, we finally reach unanimity on strategy and three days later Lilian completes the communiqué. With a copy to our sponsors, the news outlets and the residents of Hermes, the dispatch provokes a storm in response. Reaction from my brothers, who are incredulous at the news, reaches us first through a privileged channel we had set up. They say that the prevailing sentiment is that our evidence implies intelligence. This they question, skeptical of the local so-called experts on Earth who provide insights and interpretations based on the slender facts we provided. Some question our methodology, others vehemently oppose inflaming society with dubious claims when they are already in crisis with worsening conditions on the ground. The Earth First group uses the news as fodder to incite its followers, calling for an extraction of all settlers and the permanent quarantining of Hermes. The residents however are excited to know that this stark planet supports at least one or two lifeforms.

Taken aback by the response from Earth, we are unsure what to do next. The initial report only hints at the magnitude of our discovery, and yet the reaction is so extreme. A consolation is that we limited the information to the bare minimum and drew no conclusions. We conclude that a measured approach is necessary; our next bulletin must stay firmly within the bounds of verifiable facts. To my brothers we indicate that further developments have confirmed our findings and that supporting information will be forthcoming as soon as we have concluded our research. We hope to hold the audience at bay for the time being while we solidify the evidence, because the next episode will challenge even the most open-minded.

During the intervening two weeks, Julia frantically updates and strengthens her dissertation. As designated spokesperson with the Betilla, she also maintains a steady dialog with them, cautious not to ask penetrating questions. With the range of responses from Earth now known, we delve deeper with the Betilla to provide unambiguous clarity and factual certainty in our next update. This allows us to consolidate our thoughts into a coherent response to their obvious intellect. We surmise that the Betilla too must be considering the implications of sharing a planet with intelligent beings and wonder what the long-term implications will be.

Before the follow-on dispatch is ready, circumstance intervenes yet again. A third explosion at the *Destiny* site, reported by the orbital surveyor, comes as a surprise and needs examination. We are flabbergasted at the disregard for the rules, which they must have received by this time. To investigate, we scramble the drone from seclusion for a closer look. As before, we see a section of the hill laid bare. Two manned rovers are shifting rubble resulting from the explosion from the base of the hill, sifting out promising debris for mineral extraction. The workers remain inside the sealed vehicles, obviously avoiding toxic gasses released by the detonation. A third robot stands immobile at the foot of the hill. After a few minutes, the two active vehicles cease their operations and approach the standing vehicle as if to clarify why it is immobile. They remain at a safe distance for a while then one starts out in the direction of the base camp while the other stays in place a few feet from the motionless robot.

Our drone settles on a rocky platform and we turn off the rotor blades, silently observing proceedings. Minutes stretch into an hour before an unmanned robot makes its appearance from the direction of the camp. It draws up to the immobile vehicle, couples it to its rear and begins towing it to the camp with the occupants still inside. The other vehicle follows suit. The drone starts up and follows the convoy at a safe distance, watching as the immobile vehicle stops at a prefabricated building. Personnel dressed in protective clothing enter the vehicle and carry four unconscious miners into the building. Further activity continues in and around the building, apparently attending to the patients inside. We return the drone to its secluded hiding.

We have obviously witnessed a repeat of the previous episode, except that the effect has penetrated the sealed vehicle.

"I just don't understand this. How is it possible?" Robin asks. "Is there a relationship to the Betilla?"

Julia responds, "Puzzling for sure! The only way to know whether the Betilla are responsible is to ask them a direct question."

Robin says, "If the Betilla directed the immobilization, the message is clear: they object to the use of dynamite. There are at least two possible reasons that I can think of: the explosion distresses or disorientates them physically; or they dislike the effect of the explosion on the environment. Which can it be, or are there other possibilities?"

"I can ask the Betilla, and they probably will answer, but I doubt that they will explain how they manage to immobilize them inside the sealed compartment. If the affected people revive, then we have yet another mystery."

We quickly set off for the Betilla site and before Julia can broach the subject, without prompting, the Betilla immediately address the subject with a question: "Why are you damaging the environment?"

Taken aback, expecting to be the first to ask, it takes a few minutes for us to recover. Julia is at a loss for words, and I can see the dilemma: a lengthy explanation is required. I urge her to say that we will get back to them, which she does, and they hesitantly agree. We try to organize our thoughts. Naturally, their perception is that, as one species, the *Destiny* group are indistinguishable from us. How could it be otherwise from their perspective? This is informative and implies that, unlike humans, Betilla are seemingly multiple discreet creatures that behave uniformly, apparently like a single monolithic entity. Our task is clear: we will need to explain the autonomous nature of groups within the Homo sapiens genera to clarify the divergent behavior.

A good thirty minutes later and Julia responds at length, describing the individuality of each member, the pairing for reproduction, the grouping of likeminded, the divergence of logic and rational conclusions and potential for conflicting viewpoints even resulting in physical clashes where one group attempts to impose on another through force. As we formulate this response, it strikes us how these traits account for so much of both the best and worst in us. She goes on to explain that the *Destiny* group do not conform to norms recognized by the majority of groups from our species. Contrary to recognized standards, they are here to exploit the planet for gain. Their objective is the extraction of rare minerals by the most expeditious means possible, keeping costs down without regard for the damage they do to the environment. They do not have the long-term interests of the planet at heart.

The Betilla's reply is unambiguous: "We only condone activities that are benign to the environment. The reversal of the nonconscious state of the affected individuals will occur after they confirm their acceptance of this requirement."

The stunning dictate raises more questions than we can fully process. The Betilla are able to exert their influence over us in a manner that we are unable to counter or even understand, yet the promising interpretation of the mandate is clear: avoid hostility through reasonable behavior, and they are not overtly dangerous.

To build trust we signal back our concurrence with the conclusion they have reached but inform them that the *Destiny* group are not yet aware that the Betilla are an intelligent species. They have probably not linked the effects on their personnel to anything other than gasses released from the rocks dislodged by the explosions, although they will be wondering how it penetrated the sealed vehicles after the most recent incident. We request time to inform them and our principals of the discoveries, and that this is the first evidence of extraterrestrial life that we have encountered.

Then comes the big question: dare we ask how they were able to render the people unconscious, and how they reverse the effect? After some consideration, we conclude that we have nothing to lose by doing so, so we submit our question.

The answer is frank. "Our members in the vicinity direct an electromagnetic pulse at a specific wavelength, locking their cognitive abilities while allowing fluid circulatory systems to continue unimpeded. A second pulse unlocks the biological signals within the being, permitting a resumption of mental abilities. The pulses are able to penetrate the material used in the sealed compartments."

We look at each other; a follow-up question seems superfluous. We are not knowledgeable enough to understand even the rudiments of their abilities and assume that we are merely touching on the tip of the iceberg. The knowledge gap between them and us is probably significant. What surprises us as much as the technical details is the derivation of the words "electromagnetic pulse" by their translation? Technical words usually require specific interpretation on the initial use of the words. This did not happen, so how did they derive these words? Seemingly, they had prior access to the translation, a question we should direct to them at some future time.

Now what? Our strategy to provide the information to Earth in a piecemeal fashion is in tatters. We should have said more.

Robin takes the high ground. "I don't want to say 'I told you so,' but that seems absolutely the point. Now, not only do we have to explain their intelligence, we also have an actual crisis on our hands. How do we explain that we withheld information?"

Lilian adds, "Yes, Robin is right. We should have said more."

Since the implications are somewhat directed at Julia, I feel the need to come to her defense. "Wait a minute. It was a joint decision and, think about it, nothing has really changed; the *Destiny* group are actually none the wiser as to the cause of the problem. To them, it is still some form of poisoning. We need to proceed as before, one step at a time."

Jabu agrees. "Yes, you cannot now admit to earlier shortcomings. Move forward, remain factual and explain how we learnt to communicate with them; provide auditory examples. Julia, did you record the latest dialog with the Betilla?"

"Yes, I did."

"Well, there you go, but I think your dissertation needs to take second place to the news update. People are unconscious over at the *Destiny* site. Until we get their assurance that they will cease using dynamite, they will remain like that; we need to act urgently."

Julia admits, "I agree. It will need a relatively long explanation, but we need to come clean with all the solid facts."

The outcome is that we draft a fresh news release with the latest developments, the discourses with the Betilla, their ability to learn, the fluency gained so quickly and – most importantly - their dictates and ability to enforce them. Another week passes before the dispatch to Earth is ready. This time the news serves only to deepen entrenched views, with a large contingent believing we fabricated the whole story, using the distance to preclude independent validation of our claims.

In the apparent absence of a directive to the *Destiny* group on the need to stop using dynamite, we agree to take matters into our own hands and send them an electronic copy of the article, drawing their attention to the section covering the immobilization of their personnel by the Betilla. We ask them to acknowledge the contents so that we can inform the Betilla to trigger the reversal of the condition in which they remain. The confirmation comes quickly and we transmit the agreement to the Betilla. Predictably, the *Destiny* group advise that their people have returned to normalcy. At our request they also inform the publication organizations on Earth, which somewhat diminishes the disbelief in the Betilla's abilities, in certain quarters. On enquiry as to the lack of response to our earlier notification to Dr. Vespucci and others on our concerns at the use of dynamite, they claim that they never received our message, likely due to the communication difficulties.

* * *

Turmoil festers in the *Destiny* group. Their mining mandate undercut by developments, they are at a loss as to how to proceed without the right equipment for excavation without dynamite. Their options are either to abandon the venture and return to Earth or revolt against their master, mutiny and join our group. To voice this option, a localized communiqué reaches us exploring unification.

In consideration, we convene a long overdue meeting of our Management Committee to decide on the advisability of consolidation. Graham, Luke, Susan and Vivienne join Jabu, Robin and I to deliberate on questions around the Betilla and to address the *Destiny* group's request. Both are far-reaching, influencing so many aspects of life on Hermes that careful consideration is called for.

Predictably, Graham translates events into further reason for autonomy from Earth. "Conditions on Hermes are diverging from Earth's through no fault of ours. They somewhat brought on the calamities there themselves. I venture that any decisions they impose on us will lack local perspective. Besides, the Betilla probably view themselves as equals or even the dominant partner here, and decisions may fail without their support. Then what? They have the means to enforce their preferences if necessary; we would be back to square-one."

Jabu draws us back to the matter at hand. "You are right about the Betilla; they have aboriginal rights that need to take precedence, but autonomy from Earth – that is another matter. The decision we are trying to reach is merely on whether to absorb the *Destiny* group."

"For my part," I say, "I have to agree with Jabu; these are two separate issues. The absorption of the *Destiny* group extends our capabilities, and adds to the workforce and equipment resources.

Speaking for Julia, I can also say that it would bring greater uniformity to our presence and behavior in our interactions with the Betilla. On the subject of autonomy, that discussion should be deferred to another day."

Graham asks, "Miles, your group seems to have a monopoly with the Betilla; are we able to speak with them directly ourselves?"

"I would not call it a monopoly; it turns out that the only person they respond to is Julia. In fact, when they talk to us, they use Julia's voice; it is quite strange. They seem to trust her and her alone."

To avoid antagonizing the *Destiny* group's backer we propose that the decision be reversible in the future, if necessary. They must operate to our rules, norms and standards while this arrangement is in force, the expectation being one of seamless integration. On communicating this to them, they accept and are relieved; it avoids the mutiny label and it transpires that their backer is willing to forgo control for the time being. Two weeks later, they relocate to the Podium using the hovercraft with which they arrived.

At our next session with the Betilla, we elaborate on our position. We propose cooperation, reciprocity in all dealings and dialog to resolve issues. We look forward to joint custodianship of the environment and are open to suggestions for corrective behavior at any time. We have merged our resources with the *Destiny* group to better function as a unit.

With obstacles apparently removed, we eagerly wait for their response, looking forward to delving into detailed questions, but their reply to our proposal has surprises embedded in it. They accept our terms and are pleased to hear that the *Destiny* group's backer on Earth will relinquish control.

Robin is first to respond, voicing our incredulity through Julia. "How did you know that the *Destiny's* backer is relinquishing control? This was not stated."

Obscure sounds emanate from the translator as it struggles to interpret the response. Recovering, it then gives what sounds like

236

chuckling followed by the statement, "We intercepted your electronic communications."

Jabu bursts out laughing, and the chuckling response echoes back from the Betilla as the two sides enjoy the moment.

Apparently, they have a sense of humor and technology we cannot expect from an aquatic setting. We obviously have a lot to learn, but how much are they prepared to share with us? In all instances they have answered our questions but without providing background, leaving us in the dark as to the means to the end. Noticeably, they have not asked us for explanation of our technology, leaving the impression that they are able to find answers without asking us. Is it possible that our technology is rudimentary by their standards, so basic that it is self-explanatory?

Confused as to where to start, we decide to defer questions to a later stage, caution being the watchword. But Robin, impatient for answers, prompts Julia to ask, "Can future communications be via analog radio or digital electronic means?"

The Betilla's reply is again direct. "You can use digital electronics using radio signals."

Directing us as to the form of address identifying them, they provide an unintelligible word, the name they give themselves, which we translate to the word 'Betilla.' With that, we break off the session and return to base where we send a wireless message to them using a computer to test the channel. They acknowledge receipt and thereby formalize the method for future communications – we send in English and they reply in English.

Our strategy is to allow events to unfold naturally without pressing for answers – the motto: time is not of the essence, patience will reward. With this as the basis we proceed. Never in our wildest dreams could we have predicted that we would share a world with these diminutive neighbors of an aquatic realm and sparkling intelligence, but here we are. Let fate take us where it will.

* * *

The *Destiny* group prove to be problematic. We soon learn that there are two factions in the group and they are constantly at loggerheads with each other. One group is led by the overseer Kostya, a middle-aged man with facial scars that suggest a previous life of violence. They believe they should have stayed on Farland to build their own community and should move back. The other is eager to integrate with our settlers. Matters come to a head when the two groups nearly come to blows, requiring our intervention to settle their dispute. We are not able to ascertain the precise details of their disagreement but it seems that they settle their differences after Kostya consults with their backer and they abandon the plan to move back to Farland. A fragile truce holds and a level of normality reigns. Under the semblance of order, they gradually begin contributing to the work effort that supports the community.

By contrast, life on Hermes for the rest of us settles down to a calm routine, but always shadowed by the distress on Earth and Mars, which continue to deepen. For them the chaos in their midst eclipses even the discovery of alien life to focus on critical needs. We operate as automatons carrying out their prescribed directives, bearing no ill will against them, but guilt lurks undisguised as we feel their despair. Stranded in this foreign land with no means to return, we diverge in our ways, independence foisted on us by circumstance. We long for the tall trees, the swaying grasses, the rustle of leaves, the flight of birds across the sky, the ubiquitous cries of the wild from birdsong to the chirp of insects and roar of beasts. Ours is a world of sand and rocks, cliffs, stark gorges, plunging waterfalls, sheer mountains topped with snow. And then there is the pervasive stillness at once calming and yet oppressive.

Julia disappears for days on end, seeking answers to questions not yet posed. Penetrating the mist of understanding, tugging at the veil of mystery and returning with a glistening sparkle in the eyes, as of an explorer unfolding the tapestry of comprehensions, we suspect. Bit by bit, drawing the curtain on the concealed, silent as she struggles with opaque insights, but driven by a patient certainty of prevailing.

Communication being the vehicle for building rapport, she progresses from radio text to digital voice over radio, now speaking freely as she nudges the correspondence towards trust and sharing. Gently, so gently pushing aside the cloak of the enigmatic, she grasps a means to an end. As curiosity is her chauffeur, so too with the Betilla. She paints pictures to them of valleys rich in a kaleidoscope of color, scattered displays of every blush on a carpet of ochre and green on open plains, dappled shade in verdant forests and a world where every niche is occupied by the vibrancy of life. Oceans, mountains, plains and skies teaming with the vitality of creatures of every shape and form.

A spark is kindled. Can it be nostalgia? They ask for more and Julia closes her eyes to paint portraits from childhood to adulthood, the quest for nature, art so dear to her heart, the oneness of self and creation. Moved by her own longings, tears come, emotion pulls at her as she grapples for control. Then, in a moment of silence, a rush of sound rises from the Betilla: unrestrained empathy, unrestricted by convention, in a profound beauty of song, birdsong speaking to the heart unencumbered by the need for translation, every Betilla in unison reverberates, echoes in the lonely space for what seems an eternity, then dies to a whisper and is extinguished. Exhausted by the compassion shown, a bond is forged that transcends species, an understanding of the inner self of each is struck and endures. An insatiable desire for more flows unimpeded from the little water creatures in their quest to visualize every nook and cranny of Mother Earth, inquisitive for the minutest detail.

In exchange, Julia learns of their distant birth, of life in transit gripped in the torpor of hibernation by the cold vise of the void with limited mobility, the anguish of its duration and the relief of the solar system, a new home and the coincidence of an optimum orbit far greater than any expectation.

A call from base interrupts their exchange; messages from Earth describe catastrophic events along the western and eastern shores of the Atlantic. All low elevation regions are under water, a hurricane and storm surge inundating vast areas. Cities are abandoned, damaged irretrievably. The unexpected speed of the onslaught traps millions, with uncountable numbers lost to the raging sea. Julia rushes back to camp to listen to the unfolding news; coastal North America, South America and Europe do not escape the destruction. Anxiously we watch as the satellite images show the extent of the hurricanes. Two separate vortices span the length and breadth of the ocean, one edging closer to Europe, the other heading south towards Brazil and Argentina. Kourou, French Guiana, our launch site, lies swamped by surging waves reaching far inland. It is the final nail in the coffin of Earth's support for Hermes and Mars.

Our Management Committee convenes to consider the implications for the settlers; with our lifeline severed, we are effectively alone. Future missions, whether for supplies or new immigrants, will not materialize for decades, if ever, under Earths worsening conditions. Our strategy must ensure continuity of our food as the primary objective. Secondly, we need to accept the permanence of the planet as our home. A long debate on the need to observe the protocols for safeguarding the environment from contamination ends in deadlock. The question is whether to abandon the hydroponic farm in favor of sowing seeds in land outside of the protected domes. The concern is that our foreign vegetation may find conditions ideal and spread uncontrollably or supplant the only local flora, the moss on which the Betilla depend. The landmass is our domain for sustenance, while the oceans are home to the Betilla, but they temporarily depend on the land for cultivating the moss, a key part of their life cycle. The Betilla now occupy all areas adjacent to terrain not under ice, and the moss lines proximate regions.

They have effectively annexed most of the planet. As our population expands, competition appears unavoidable. This presents a dilemma not easily solved and which we prefer not to broach with the Betilla until we have unanimity within our group.

* * *

Humankind is not alone in the struggle against the onslaught of the elements. Control earned over the millennia now reversed, Mother Nature holds sway. The primitive state once shared by all creatures for millennia, until the spark of fire wrought control and fended off the savage beast, brought warm to the hearth, food lost it poison under the kiln and the sapient being was elevated to the throne. Now humbled before the onslaught, equal under the great leveling, the mater is superior.

* * *

Hawks that we are, Aerie and I, Kite, look out from the ledge and wonder at the inexplicably enlarged sun, shortened days, curtailing of the annual, alternating hot and cold that confuses the incubation of eggs, the hatch again in disarray, infertility. Try, and retry, persevere but with the same results, we stare at a future without offspring.

Rising on the thermals, we look for cause from a great height. Our valley still a ribbon of pristine, we see the tentacles of discord reaching for this last Eden. A rising tide threatens a land once rich in flora and fauna. The clearing of the indigenous, supplanted by the monotony of the invasive, is plain to see. Its penetration is fortuitously suspended by the barrier of cliffs and steep valley banks that guard our preserve. The humankind who once escaped the great cities, now having raped the rural, begin the trek back to the cities, where they console themselves under the umbrella that shields them from the forces of nature unleashed on the land. It provides a measure of relief for our sanctuary.

Looking to the sea, a typical picture presents itself: a massive bank of swirling clouds foretells yet another torrent. The wind disrupting our thermals, flight labored, we steady ourselves and descend to calmer regions. As the sun sinks to its early setting, we return to our ledge and the new silence that pervades our valley. The raucous chorus of frogs diminished to a diminuendo, the few bees that buzz, once laden with pollen, now return to their hives empty-handed. Skeletally thin bats emerge from the caves carrying strange white fungi on their mouths, leaving many of their kind in heaps under their overhangs. Swifts and swallows fly their gyrations, but there are few insects to satisfy their hunger, and they return to their adobe abodes with little to feed their young.

With a heavy heart we turn to our empty nest, huddle for comfort in a fitful sleep as darkness envelopes us.

* * *

We decide to reconvene at a future time with new ideas for a solution to the question of farming the land. The status quo will remain in force, but we agree to discontinue all mining operations, recognizing that we are reverting to a form of subsistence farming, a practice long abandoned when technology and mass production took root. We will carry forward the use of hydroponic domes as a legacy of that technology.

To avoid degeneration into the abyss of ignorance, we need to build a society independent of Earth until there is a resumption of integration. We recognize the imperative of starting a program of collecting data, concepts, methods, scientific principles behind inventions and practice, knowledge, knowhow and the preservation of skills. Achievement of this goal requires the harnessing of talent, latent and actual, to participate, starting with the promotion of the cause and ensure adoption by all colonists. We need to catalog existing capabilities, and exploit these before branching into and addressing underrepresented areas. To solicit buy-in, we arrange a meeting of all the settlers. Two days later, with all the people in the auditorium, Jabu as spokesperson explains the background, referring to conditions on Earth and what the Management Committee has in mind, emphasizing that the prospects for success are bleak without full participation by everyone. He sketches how this may be accomplished. We need volunteers to establish a methodology to agree on the format and location of a repository for the information, and a process for recording new information as it is obtained. We need to use local resources for storage of the information, and ensure persistence, repair, maintenance and support of systems. We need to build redundancy while allowing for expansion, cross-train to build depth, and avoid reliance on a narrow set of people.

A minority who believe circumstances will change, allowing a resumption of supply from Earth, question his talk.

Kostya is the most vociferous of this group, shouting his demands. "This is all a waste of time. What is the point? Just a few weeks or months and you have to undo everything. No! I say, just ration the food for a while and we will be okay. Don't waste time and energy for nothing." Turning to the crowd he says, "Who is with me on this?"

Some hands go up but Graham defends the argument. "Jabu just explained the background from the sponsor. Disruption of communication, sabotage, climate, flooding, refugees, and add to that the distance to Earth and the alignment of orbits for flights, and you have a huge problem. It could be years before supplies arrive. Autonomy from Earth is not a choice; it is here now. Right now!" Challenging Kostya, he echoes his words. "Who is with ME on this?"

A large contingent enthusiastically clap and Graham bows in acknowledgment turning to Kostya. "I think you are outnumbered. Jabu, would you like to continue?"

Jabu asks for volunteers as working groups are set up, each with autonomy to decide on basics, a forum for thrashing out interdependencies between groups and a schedule for feedback to the

Management Committee. Over the next few weeks a sense of owner-ship in the venture is apparent, a new vigor and camaraderie. Even Kostya's followers participate productively. Challenges confronted in a spirit of cooperation translate into steady but certain progress; the dismal news from Earth is now balanced by the first signs of pride in our new home and way of life. Some obstacles prove to be insurmountable, but the search for solutions continues. Silicon chips for computer microprocessors and memory are in finite supply and production beyond our means. Radio components are likewise a challenge. Certain metals and minerals will need mining ventures and processing at some stage in the future. Undaunted, these items are temporarily shelved while other work progresses. Interestingly, novel solutions have to be found for everyday needs. Products usually taken for granted are now approached from first principles, whether for personal grooming, hygiene, decoration, maintenance and even clothing. Dormant skills and aptitudes are awakened, some surprisingly unexpected, others exercised to new levels.

Dmitri and Robin relish the challenges, with Dmitri delving into the depth of robot controls and integration to radio and computer systems, while Robin leads an experimental approach to solving problems, documenting outcomes and examining data output. Jabu and I coordinate teams, scheduling activities and tracking progress, while Lilian builds a repository of a wide range of subjects based on reported progress, indexing the information for fast retrieval. Julia continues her liaison with the Betilla, exchanging information on each other's worlds.

19

TELESCOPE

A standard review of the logs from the orbiting probes shows low intensity background electromagnetic radiation in the microwave hydrogen-line wavelength emanating from across Hermes. Technicians have noted an almost imperceptible by steady increase since our arrival on the planet. Its source, or an explanation, eludes all attempts at investigation, until gradually falling into acceptance as a normal feature of the planet and no longer questioned. Nevertheless, in characteristic fashion, Julia is unable to leave the unexplained phenomenon at rest, periodically returning to the anomaly, always inquisitive for a rational answer. On this occasion, she ponders the logs once more, looking for patterns or something that will give away its secrets. Progressing from day to day to day in the log since her last review, she stumbles on a spike in the pattern; the entire planet is alive with the signal, doubling, tripling in its intensity to a peak, and then dying away.

She wonders: *What can this be? The duration from start to end is approximately thirty minutes. Seismic records show no coincidental tectonics. Irregular weather is absent in the meteorological files and solar activity is normal. Human activity is concentrated around the Podium area, and highly localized. Besides, we have no need to transmit at this wavelength.*

Delving deeper, she looks into the literature and notes that the 21-centimeter hydrogen line represents electromagnetic radiation at the precise frequency of 1420405751 Hz. This is equivalent to the vacuum wavelength of about 21 cm in free space. It is within the microwave region of the electromagnetic spectrum and is frequently used in radio astronomy because these waves penetrate clouds of interstellar cosmic dust that are opaque to visible light.

I can see that it is a frequently asserted by the SETI organization to be a universal channel – one that extraterrestrials may use to announce their presence in the cosmos. They routinely monitor this spectral region for a signal.

What is the relationship to Hermes? Why here? Why does it emanate from Hermes rather than from elsewhere, and why is it increasing?

Hmm, extraterrestrials – of course. That is it! We have an alien species right here on our doorstep, and they are proliferating.

Why and how would the Betilla transmit a signal and, if they are responsible, why did it peak at this time?

She broods over this for some time, questioning. *What other aspects of the Betilla remain unanswered?*

An explanation for the iridescent carapaces remains inadequate. The pulsing lights as a means to communicate is valid, but seemingly incomplete. Light in the visible range is but one fragment of the full spectrum of electromagnetic radiation; is it possible that they are able to transmit in other frequencies, and why in this particular wavelength?

Looking back in time to the date of the spike, she recalls the event: the excitement, the elation, the Betilla's musical response to their emotional dialog. The day she wept in nostalgia for our distant Earth.

Yes, the time corresponds exactly. There can be no doubt that the source is the Betilla, but why would the frequency emanate from the entire planet. How can a localized event invoke a global response?

Before approaching the Betilla for an explanation, Julia decides to test out a theory. Using a directional microwave receiver, one that can point to and receive signals from a particular direction, eliminating extraneous noise from other sources, she returns to the sites where the Betilla are most numerous. Pointing the device at them and noting the intensity of the signals, she compares this to areas devoid of Betilla. She gets confirmation: the Betilla are continuously transmitting in the hydrogen line as background radiation. Her guess is that they use the iridescent carapace for transmitting in a wide range of frequencies, visible to microwave and perhaps more. No doubt, they are able to receive the signals using the carapace as well, so this must be a means of communication. Knowing that they routinely absorb light for photosynthesis, she wonders whether they manipulate the hydrogen elements in water or air to excite the atoms, releasing the photons and thereby producing the microwave radiation. It would be even more wondrous if they use quantum mechanics of photosynthesis to communicate instantaneously by means of Spooky Action at a Distance, a feature of this mechanism being the remote detection of communiqués around the curvature of the globe in an instant.

She speculates aloud: "If true, these creatures are truly sophisticated."

Contacting peers back on Earth, they confirm that an advanced civilization could well use this as a means for communication. Their experiments to achieve this have been frustratingly close to success. They explain that linking of pairs of particles by the quantum property of entanglement occurs naturally when two particles, created at the same point and instant in space, interact. The linkage can persist even if widely separated in space; a measurement on one immediately influences the other, regardless of the distance between them. The concept has been successfully tested many times. Can this be the explanation for the evidence at hand?

Going back through her earlier field studies where she recorded the absence of sex organs for reproduction, and noting that they use cell division to multiply, she realizes: *This means that each individual Betilla is a clone of another and a clone of yet another, making them all related in this manner, each uniquely discreet but singular as a group. Combined with the communication capabilities, this means that they operate as one virtual organism, local experiences transmitted across the planet and felt by all instantly, hence the global response that shows up in the log. Remarkable!*

If they operate as one, receptive to signals across the globe instantaneously, when looking at the sky at night in the visible light range, or a wider wavelength if necessary, they all effectively have the same view. Maybe they selectively eliminate parts of what they see on the other side of the planet to focus on certain areas of the night sky. They operate as a telescope with an aperture as wide as the planet's width, internally processing the view as a single image. The largest telescopes that humans have only measure about ten meters in diameter, making the Betilla telescopic capabilities far greater.

Excitedly, Julia realizes, *this is how they were able to perceive the nine planets in the first encounter with their intelligence that evening as they displayed an image of the nine concentric circles in the sky. I have got to tell the others.*

To test her theory, the following evening Julia asks the Betilla to describe details of what they see when looking at the Earth. Surprising and yet as expected, they describe the oceans, continents and the swirling clouds, two large vortices, one traveling in a south-westerly direction crossing from sea to land, the other moving in a north-easterly course crossing into the continent. The Betilla ask whether these features are normal, given the likely devastation they would cause. She realizes they are describing the two hurricanes the newscast brought and the destruction wrought by them.

After a pause to control her emotions she tells of the struggles humanity faces. First with their disregard for the planet's resources, industrialization, the rise of atmospheric carbon dioxide, and global warming, and then the exacerbation caused with the arrival of Hermes, displacing Earth nearer the sun. The Betilla listen in rapt attention. Julia can feel their misplaced guilt at the apparent welfare they reap from Hermes' position in the constellation of planets in the solar system while Earth writhes under these same coincident circumstances. At a loss for words, silence stretches as each party processes the magnitude of these discoveries, eventually parting and each returning to their separate realities.

Exhaustion weighs on each step as she returns to base. She knows that her theory is true, but she carries the pain that the Betilla hold to themselves.

Morning brings a new day and I note a pervading sadness as Julia asks me to convene our team to explain her latest findings. That evening, with our group of six convened, she describes her discoveries: the cloning features of the Betilla, and the consequential single yet discreet organism with interconnected minds that we have as neighbors; how they communicate using the carapace, the logs that support her theory; the concept of a globe-spanning telescopic aperture, their view of the night skies, the resolution of the hurricanes on Earth; and the sadness they feel for their part in the events.

Struck by the scope of her revelations, after a pause, we recover and quietly applaud the intellect it is our privilege to witness. Built as it is on the many discoveries that preceded this latest finding, adding to its scope and depth, it is a rarity by any comparison. As I listen in amazement, my hand strays to my pocket where the engagement ring remains, torn between sheer admiration for this person before us and a sense of loss as I realize that Julia may have slipped irretrievably beyond reach, her intellect, perseverance and capacity for empathy placing her on a pedestal out of reach. Her dogged determination, exacting more from an oversubscribed source of revelations, lends premonition that more is to come – or is depletion of the reservoir at hand?

* * *

Julia's next visit to the Betilla is markedly different to the previous meetings. Where previously they shared information hesitantly, usually providing direct answers to questions without elaboration, with a corner in their relationship now turned, they are forthcoming without prompting. This time they are first to offer explanations, providing background to the pain of sympathy they have for Earth's struggles. Elaborating on their history, the Betilla describe a distant past, eons ago in lapsed time, memories passed from generation to generation securely stored in their ancestral repository.

They tell of a time when, like Earth, they developed and evolved on a planet rich in diversity. Even under the glare of two suns paired in the sky, they thrived at a suitable distance from this dual source of energy. Chance would have it that an asteroid obliterated their home, flinging debris in all directions, coalescing into a sterile belt of rocks or falling to the ground on other planets. Embedded in a protective layer of rock and ice, providence conspired to seed an inner planet with a sample of their forebears and their main food source, the moss, survivors of the shock of the collision and the transit to the new planet in that distant solar system. Here the two species built and maintained a symbiotic relationship, entirely dependent on each other to persist, evolving for eons under the harsh radiation streaming from the binary pair in the sky. Life struggled for a footing under their dominance. Through the force of ingenuity, they found a way to guard against the onslaught, turning adversity to advantage, deficiencies became their merit, liabilities their assets, emerging with countermeasures. To secure life for their partner the moss, the Betilla mimicked its photosynthetic capabilities to combine in adding to the protective ozone layer. They hoped to encourage the growth of diversity on this barren planet but alas, to no avail. Attempts did not bear fruit in the harsh conditions, leaving them alone with their partners.

It happened that a giant inner planet merged with one of the suns, destabilizing the long-held resonance of the remaining planets, forcing theirs to the cold outer reaches of their solar system. It became a frozen wasteland. In time, the inevitable explosive merger of the two suns followed. As if to emphasize the end of a chapter, a cluster of asteroids caught up in the eruptive force wrought a reign of terror on what is now the Middle Sea. A shudder rocked the planet with finality as the last of these objects provided the impetus to cast their home world into the void. There they traveled endlessly before chance would again intervene, and they now find themselves under a welcoming sun with a chance to rebuild the lost diversity once enjoyed. It is the parallels with this history that generate empathy for the Earth.

Struck by diametrically opposite outcomes, destiny thrust Earth into an unfolding calamity with the arrival of Hermes while fate meted out benevolence for Hermes in its choice of orbit. A change in the flight of Hermes through the void by the smallest of margins could have offered an entirely different result. The intersection of two fates now in the balance, Julia wonders what course of events will unfold.

As if in answer, the Betilla muse on the irony of the situation: Earth at the doorstep of progressive degeneration while Hermes stands at the threshold of unlimited potential. Agonizing for a solution, she and the Betilla come up empty handed. In sadness, they again end their discourse, each returning to their own kind to consider what to do.

When Julia enters our residence, by intuition and experience, I see that she has further news for us. And so, shortly after her previous update, we again gather around to hear, expecting minor revisions or additions. Instead, we hear of the sad history of the Betilla, their excitement of newfound opportunities and the dampening realization of Earth's struggles, superimposed as it is on their good fortune. As has become our custom, we need time to digest this latest news before questions start, eager to learn more, to understand, fascinated at the smallest detail.

Robin probes for more, his mind always looking to solve conundrums. Sensing hidden opportunities he delves deeper: "If the Betilla helped in the production of a protective ozone layer, this implies that they did this by choice. At a biological level, they seem to be able to manipulate the environment to their liking, in this case using photosynthesis; quite a daunting task under the harsh conditions so close to two suns in their home system. Yet we witnessed how the ozone layer on Hermes has improved in the short time they have been in our solar system. Is this chance or by design? Are they preparing for the greening of Hermes? If so, theirs will be a long-term endeavor, many millions of years, especially to allow for the evolution of diversity."

Jabu interjects, reminding us of the discussion we had during the Management Committee meeting, "Remember, we considered converting the indoor hydroponic farm to a conventional outdoor farming operation. The concern was for contaminating the environment against the wishes of the Betilla, whereas it now seems that they would welcome this. It would, to some extent, fast track the spread of vegetation."

Dmitri adds, "Da, yes, and if you take it further; if we are able to import species of plant life and fauna from Earth, we could speed up the process and create a more diverse environment."

Jabu excitedly elaborates, "The greening of Hermes would occur in a matter of a few decades. We could create a biosphere; land, sea and atmosphere, all seeded with life."

Julia concurs, "Fortunately, unlike Mars, all the terraforming work to prepare the planet for life is already in place: atmosphere, temperature, water, atmospheric pressure, even the protective ozone and magnetosphere. The only missing ingredient is life."

I respond, "Yes, but the question is moot because flights from Earth are moribund under the challenges they are facing."

To explore the suggestions further, we task Julia with broaching the subject with the Betilla.

252

As she prepares for the discussion, she cannot shake Robin's pattern of thought. She recalls the orbital surveys that preceded our fiery entry into the atmosphere after the journey from Earth. Bacterial husks found in the upper atmosphere and a complete dearth of living bacteria at lower elevations, seemingly indicating a past where microbes may have been present but failed to survive the journey across space.

Her mind goes back to her fieldwork to review the material.

Has this anything to do with the Betilla habit of floating bubbles containing traces of bacteria in them into the heights? In an attempt to seed the atmosphere, the husks may represent failed attempts at float-ing microbes into the sky to distribute across the planet. They may have intended them to represent the initial stock from which life evolves. Why would they do this? Definitely another question for them now that they are more willing to offer explanations.

When she poses the question of farming in the open, they freely accept, even encourage, the planting of vegetation in the land outside of the enclosures currently used. Without her even needing to ask about the bacterial husks, they explain their experimentation with seeding genetically modified bacteria across the globe using their bubbles for increasing the likelihood of life taking root from the spore. The bubbles rise to the clouds and fall to the ground randomly dispersed geographically when it rains, as part of the hydrological cycle. In acknowledgment, Julia mentions the husks observed by the probes in the stratosphere. In response, they say that these were probably a legacy from their time in the void; they could not have survived the cosmic strafing and duration, and also at the higher elevations, the bubbles would burst and the bacteria would succumb, leaving only the husk, due to the absence of clouds in the area.

To Julia's surprise, they go on to explain that these bubbles serve two purposes; one, to initiate the evolution of life, as mentioned, and the other to seed the clouds with photosynthetic bacteria to seques-trate carbon dioxide and balance the oxygen and ozone levels in the atmosphere. Although they multiply, these bacteria are short-lived, needing the moisture of the clouds and a certain concentration of carbon dioxide to remain viable. They therefore need periodic replenishment based on weather patterns because the moss and Betilla alone are not sufficient to maintain the atmospheric balance.

Expressing surprise at their genetic manipulation of the bacteria, they explain their technique, which resembles gene editing. Unable to follow the logic she records the conversation for sharing with experts on Earth.

Back at the base, on revealing this information to us, our excitement is palpable. Jabu exclaims, "The Management Committee will be thrilled. Imagine that, real home-grown veggies."

Dmitri says, "First things first. We need grains; sorghum, corn, wheat and we will have vodka. The veggies can follow later. Imagine that, real vodka!"

Lilian too is excited, "I have been so bored. We should PARTY! Whoopy!"

Robin dampens her spirit, turning serious, "You know, historically, the theory was that the evolution of an advanced technology in the universe hinges on its civilization harnessing fire and utilizing metals; in other words; based on dry land. Yet, right before our eyes, contradicting all of that, we have an aquatic species that is not able to use fire, but is instead using biological resources to advance its technology. It is truly amazing."

I agree, "Yes, it just shows how life finds a way and how resilient it is under such severe conditions. I also find it startling that we know so little, even with all our advantages."

* * *

At a short meeting of the Management Committee where the Betilla agreement to allow farming in the fields is explained, there is no dissention to going ahead. Excited at the prospect of richer food

quality, the settlers start moving plants and begin seeding operations right away. Success proves to be elusive however, as the soil
lacks humus to support growth and chemicals such as fertilizer are
unavailable except in a form for hydroponic use. One of the settlers
suggests planting in the fields where the Betilla have moss growing,
which again needs approval from the Betilla who, it turns out, have
no problem with the suggestion. Success comes quickly, producing
bumper crops in the loamy soil while the moss spreads to adjacent
areas alongside the domesticated fields, allowing tilling of the soil
in the farmed land. The bubbles now navigate to the newly designated areas.

With the passage of time, the settlers note new improved varieties
of their crops growing in the adjacent fields. Julia establishes from
the Betilla that they have genetically engineered these variations
from samples taken from the original stock by the immature Betilla
as they fed on the moss. They regurgitate the samples along with the
moss, at sea. In the sea habitats they transform them into new varieties then cycle them back in the bubbles floated back to these locations. A partnership between human and Betilla is at its inception.

The Betilla take the next step, triangulating the DNA from multiple
strains of each crop to find the originating species that humans over
time selectively farmed to improve yields. Then, applying retroactive
techniques, they produce grasses from wheat and maize, nightshade
tubers from potatoes, grass from rice, biennial wild cabbage from
cabbage, woody-textured roots from carrots and many others. These
primitive species are distributed to moss fields adjacent to the fields
tendered by our farmers.

At the next meeting with the Betilla, Julia agrees to their request
for us to manually pollinate the emerging flowers. In the absence of
bees and other pollinators, this task must be performed by humans,
a function the Betilla cannot do. Without pollinators, wider distribution of flowering plants cannot proceed.

The greening of our adopted planet is underway, albeit limited, but the progress only emphasizes the widening gulf between Earth and Hermes. It draws attention to the guilt of one at the expense of the other, challenging the mind to find equity. Both Betilla and men dwell on the disparity, seeking ways out of the dilemma.

* * *

Julia has spent significant time on her thesis, progressively expanding it as new insights emerged, until it reaches voluminous proportions. After a review by Robin to check on the logic of her arguments and conformance to general standards, the document is ready for submission. Lilian suggests that we approach Dr. Vespucci to supervise and defend the thesis at the university's examining committee, since he is head of the faculty. They frequently use West News Inc.'s science forum, a division of the news organization for which Lilian works, for communicating with the public. He agrees and after a few failed attempts at transmitting the document, because of the intermittent nature of the communication link, he acknowledges receipt. Weeks anxiously pass during which corrective changes proposed by Dr. Vespucci are applied. Then, there is the wait for the defense in front of the committee.

Finally a message arrives: "The examining committee has approved the doctoral award but in an unusual step, they deny the right to publish under the university's name until certain precautions are met. The concern is the reception by the public at large. There will be consequences and they are unsure of how to proceed. The revelations will be of great interest to many in the scientific community. On the other hand, the implications of an advanced species challenging our dominance in the solar system will be met with disbelief, alarm, discord and potentially even violence. We are considering options and will get back to you ASAP."

Julia, troubled by the response, says, "Unbelievable, these gentle creatures at the center of a storm! You would think that a university would stand firm behind facts. What can they possibly want?"

I console, "They probably want to protect themselves against ignorant people. People who resort to violence when their beliefs are challenged. They probably need time to brace themselves against a reaction that could take any form."

"Why did I go to so much trouble to write up my findings? Would they prefer I remain silent? Let things become known simply by osmosis? The more I have to do with people the more disillusioned I become."

A few days later we receive a message from Dr. Vespucci: "The University reiterates that you have been awarded the doctorate. For this I congratulate you. The issue with publication remains a concern; the University is not equipped to handle protests at the level they anticipate. If you are in agreement, the UN can handle the publication. They have the resources to handle any eventuality. You may remain anonymous if you so choose. Please advise how to proceed."

As we discuss the message Julia says, "I think Dr. Vespucci is very insightful. My reticence at being in the glare of the public is hard to hide. I think we should take him up on the anonymity option."

I agree. "Actually, I can see the relief you feel. You have been very anxious these last few days. It also takes nothing away from your award."

Robin adds, "We are so proud of you, Julia. It is an honor to be associated with you. Well done!"

Lilian says, "It is fortunate that Dr. Vespucci happens to be associated with the UN. Congratulations Julia, you are the best!"

Dmitri and Jabu hug Julia in their admiration.

The UN announces the publishing of the document under the heading "Scientists uncover remarkable intelligent lifeform on Hermes."

The locals are quick to deduce who the author of the information is; Julia holds a special pride of place with the settlers. The discoveries on our doorstep bring a personal aspect to the unfolding news that they increasingly follow and feel a part of. A groundswell of recognition for her accomplishments leads to a call for a celebration, which is planned as a surprise for her.

As we congregate in the hub, round after round of applause greets Julia's entrance to the chant of "Doctor J, Doctor J, Doctor J," which she graciously acknowledges after her initial surprise subsides.

On being asked why the news makes no mention of her by name, she explains, "Please think of this as our discovery rather than mine. I am sure you understand that the news will be greeted with a wide range of responses. As such, I prefer that the reaction not be centered on me. I am ill prepared for that and am happy to share the recognition with all of you. Thank you."

The evening is a mix of pride, joviality and a relief from the concerns for the Earth. Music, played on surprisingly diverse instruments, either secreted onboard the transit from the Earth or legitimately declared as carry-on luggage, lends a certain nostalgia for bygone days and hope for the future. Alcohol is in rare supply, the first of hops and vineyards still a season or two away as we branch out into the fields. The hydroponically grown versions are not very popular.

* * *

The university was right: the news provokes the expected response. Faust leads the charge, taking to social media and unleashing a torrent of malevolent rantings, in a recording with him standing in a prophetic stance speaking against a backdrop of calamities, which expertly switch between pictures of serene pastures with glowing skies and firestorms alternating with catastrophic flooding.

"Oust the evil ones that spread untruths. Eden awaits the victors."

The UN building in New York takes the brunt of the attack. Placard waving throngs line the streets chanting, "Turn or burn!"

Days of confrontation eventually give way as the crowds turn to other priorities.

* * *

The images of discord increasingly intrude on Julia. Her moods shift from brooding to elevated excitement as she cycles between the calm of her solitary excursions along the coast and the agitation in response to the news events. The shock of the revelations of her dissertation eventually dissipates, receding to the background as other events overtake the headlines and stability returns to Julia. She returns to her quest for knowledge and understanding of the biology of the planet. These once again occupy a central focus that excludes other concerns.

Returning to the techniques used by the Betilla for gene editing, she and Lilian work on locating experts on Earth with whom to work to understand the methods used. With a reliable contact established, Lilian channels Julia's transcript of the techniques to them. The response is incredulous. The simple sophistication of the procedures is remarkable. They ask for clarification of advanced aspects of the methods, admiring the elegance of the solutions embedded in their practice. They have resolved problems that bedeviled progress on Earth for many years. Despite the erratic link between Earth and Hermes, Julia facilitates a staccato exchange between the two parties. News of the advanced nature of the Betilla's competence with DNA and how they engineered an ozone layer spreads, soliciting suggestions for a variety of applications.

One suggestion draws Robin's attention as he scans the news feeds. "Would the Betilla be able to sequestrate carbon from the atmosphere on a sufficient scale to bring the greenhouse effect under control on Earth?"

He poses the question over breakfast and the idea provokes a wide-ranging debate on this and other possibilities.

Jabu asks, "If we could transfer a population of Betilla, with a supply of moss, what do you think; would they be overwhelmed by other species?"

Julia suggests, "Clearly, ecological competition will be strong: some neutral, some cooperative, others antagonistic. The greatest threat will probably come from humans. People will probably feel that our position at the top of the food chain will be taken over by the Betilla."

I agree. "Yes, fears of dominance, whether justified or not, will likely surface, with unpredictable results. Mankind is irrational at best. Just look at the track record of mistreatment of the environment."

Robin cautions. "It is quite remarkable what Julia has uncovered about the Betilla, but I have a concern that I can't shake. Why is it that the Betilla only communicate with Julia? Julia, please understand, I have nothing against you, but I have to ask. They must have a reason for singling you out. Do they have ulterior motives?

"How do you mean? What motives?" I ask.

"Well, with the suggestion of sending Betilla to the Earth, is this something they anticipated? You just said that we are fairly predictable. Once they are located there, what then? Do they take over? I don't know, it just seems that they lack aggression, or is it just hidden? In a world where the fittest survive, one has to be suspicious of other species, or at least defensive. They are just too trusting for my liking."

Julia responds, "I don't know why they have singled me out as the intermediary. Could it be because I have spent the most time with them? It is my job after all. As to ulterior motives and defense mechanisms, they are quite well equipped considering what they did to the *Destiny* group. I think your concerns are unwarranted."

Jabu dispels the subject with a laugh. "Robin, I didn't know you were into conspiracy theories. You had better watch your back, there may be a beetle lurking there, ready to pounce."

But Lilian remains serious. "Where there is smoke there may be fire. Robin is right to ask. He is usually well ahead of the rest of us."

The discussion returns to the question of transporting a working sample to Earth. We recognize that it is somewhat hyper theoretical. With the exception of the *Destiny* group's space craft still parked near the Podium, we don't have a means to travel there, unless we can convince them to hand over the craft for this purpose. It is also dependent on the Betilla being willing to undertake the venture. To this end, we raise these possibilities at our next Management Committee meeting. Graham is quite enthralled by the idea. Unsurprisingly, he sees an opportunity to build further independence from the Earth.

He suggests, "We need to establish from the Betilla whether this is feasible, and if so, how quickly they estimate they will achieve a measure of success. We can then strike a bargain with Earth, bringing their climate under control in exchange for two requirements: DNA samples of a variety of species of flora and fauna for seeding planet Hermes, and secondly, political independence from Earth, with self-governance and the right to control immigration."

The committee is divided on his insistence on political independence, but since the Betilla are pivotal in the whole discussion my recommendation is that Julia approach them for their opinion, which we proceed to do.

Reporting back, Julia found that the Betilla are more than willing to play a part in averting the catastrophe unfolding on Earth, alleviating, as it does, some of the guilt they carry. She relays details of their proposed modus operandi for transferring a population of Betilla to the Earth and for facilitating the return trip of DNA samples from Earth. They provide information on the hibernation techniques used by them during the transit through the void. This would apply to both directions of the transit, from Hermes to Earth and back again.

It will reduce bulk and can be conducted as an unmanned operation. Julia is quick to point out that the transit part of the venture is achievable as described by the Betilla. The collection of DNA samples will however require extensive coordination as to the extent of the cargo. The diversity needed to achieve an ecological balance and the minimization of harm to the environment on Earth during the process is paramount. To ensure that the endeavor is carried out to our specifications it will need someone from Hermes to oversee the operation; she being most competent to do so as Hermes' only qualified biologist. There is general agreement. But a solo trip to Earth and back? That I could not stomach.

"We need to manage the venture as a project. As such I should accompany Julia as a project manager. Besides, Julia, you alone for all those months! It will drive you around the bend."

Hesitantly she responds, "It is long, but I should be alright, sort of. Lester will be there; I can't go without a pilot."

"But you have difficulty dealing with the attention, as recent events have shown. Anyone in a similar situation would have difficulty, the negative attention; how will you manage that? People won't just let you carry on undisturbed. Please reconsider."

"Lilian is quite good at managing me. What if she came along? We did quite well on the trip over."

Flustered I respond, "Yes but when you are there you will need a project manager."

Jabu, to my exasperation, enjoys the spectacle as always. "Now, now Miles. Be honest, what is really worrying you?"

I feel my face turning bright red. "No one should spend that amount of time alone. And, the hazards of space? What about them?"

Jabu says, "Hmm, do tell. Lester will be there."

"Okay, okay you want honesty? Okay, I would miss Julia. There it is."

Smiling Julia says, "Oh Miles, it was just a test. Of course, I need you to come along."

Lilian exclaims, adding to my consternation, "How cute! Miles so shy and Julia the tease. I would love to be a fly on the wall during the trip."

Jabu adds, tongue in cheek, to everyone's amusement, "There you go; we have a decision. Miles the project manager and Julia the biologist. Go, pack your bags. Go!"

Our first task is to secure consent with the authorities on Earth to allow the Betilla to establish a presence on the planet. The question is, who to ask? It needs agreement from a wide range of policy makers, ecology agents, governments and even the United Nations. We decide to start with the UN Environment Program and send their manager the request, including a reference to Julia's thesis on the capabilities of the Betilla. Their response is positive from the perspective of using the Betilla for carbon sequestration, but that they do not have authority to allow us to harvest DNA from member countries. This will have to be obtained from each country individually. Alternatively, an appeal would have to be made at a general meeting of members. We request this latter option asking permission to address the audience by means of a recorded video at which we would solicit cooperation and permission to travel to willing territories to collect the DNA. We emphasize the need for the appointment of assistants from each area to ensure safe travel and act as guides to provide the best chance of harvesting representative samples from each jurisdiction. We also detail locales where Betilla will take up residence along the shoreline near suitable river entry points, the selection based on areas where human interference will be at a minimum. Finally, three caveats are added to allay Robin's concerns: Betilla behavior is expected to be fully cooperative but we cannot predict whether they have other motives or agendas. Participating member states must accept this caution. Secondly, the intent is to restrict the Betilla to jurisdictional areas that agree to the proposal, but if the Betilla have other motives we cannot ensure that they will not spread to areas outside the designated places. Thirdly, the Betilla may seed clouds with bacteria to sequestrate the carbon dioxide. The bacteria proliferate in the clouds while the moisture content is adequate and carbon dioxide levels are above a certain threshold. The bacteria are short-lived, but winds may carry them to other areas. The latter two stipulations will require general agreement in principle by all the members at the meeting.

The manager agrees to the video address, which we prepare and send him forthwith. The meeting is coincidentally scheduled to occur in two days' time. The response comes back with most of the members agreeing to participate, but two countries are unwilling, expressing concern that the Betilla may have invasive tendencies. Some also express concerns at releasing bacteria into the atmosphere. An impasse. How do we solve this? Can we appeal to a higher authority, the UN General Assembly? The two countries are Australia and New Zealand, with Japan hesitant about the release of bacteria. In response we undertake to allow an exclusion zone of one thousand kilometers off their shorelines. Will they accept this? As we wait for the answer, assuming a positive response, we contact the *Destiny* group's backer through Kostya for permission to use their spacecraft. A day later, Australia and New Zealand reluctantly okay the seclusion-zone suggestion and the Japanese follow their lead. We also get the green light from the *Destiny* group to use their craft. With those two parts of the puzzle in place, planning for the journey starts.

On closer examination, it is clear that the collection of DNA samples will prove to be a daunting exercise, compounded by the need to harvest from as many species as is possible to ensure biodiversity. By necessity, we scale back our goals to levels that are more realistic, avoiding a looming sense of failure. Flora is less of a problem compared to fauna because we will not be contending with moving targets, the main challenge being the logistics of reaching remote places.

For fauna, we decide to work our way from small to large creatures and in doing so recognize the corresponding food chain. Sourcing from zoos and other animal conservatories will ease the need for extensive field trips. Clearly, Hermes will not be able to support large herbivores or carnivores until the hierarchy from small to large varieties is well established and on a progressive path.

Recognizing the superior knowledge of the Betilla on the subject of DNA, gene editing and metabolism while in hibernation, we turn to them for guidance. After some back and forth, we realize that extensive documentation on the evolutionary history of flora and fauna on the Earth already exists. We just need to tap into these archives, vast libraries built from evidence taken from field studies, supporting the tree of life. The Betilla require microscopic quantities of tissue, excreted fluids or particles taken from the species. They only need two or three specimens from the extremities of major branches of the evolutionary tree. Using gene-editing techniques, they can reverse engineer down and up branches of the tree to reconstruct new, missing or existing varieties by triangulation from the extremities to nodes in the earlier lineage, building inherited traits or new features. They are able to increase the sample material from very small amounts to any desired quantity using copying methods therefore needing only a small initial stock, making our task considerably lighter. We are now able to target specific species and the harvesting of material will be easier. The Betilla provide straightforward instructions for the freezing of the DNA, which also simplifies our tasks and reduces the volume of storage space needed.

A message from Dr. Vespucci furthers our objective. He has tentatively set up a visit to Norway's Svalbard Global Seed Vault where he promises to meet us. He has proven to be indispensable, advocating on our behalf to have the UN Environment Program cover the costs of our endeavor and his department will handle logistical arrangements. He crucially echoes our realization that the endeavor, even scaled back as set out by the Betilla, is of a magnitude that is probably beyond our reach; harvesting a meaningful sample of DNA of Earth's genome is not a two-person activity. He offers to recruit a team of specialists that can assist. We gratefully accept his offer and he indicates that he will have a team ready by the time we arrive on Earth.

As the day nears, I consider these latest developments and the trip to the Earth with Julia. I wonder about the geographic distribution of the Betilla that will ensure that they can do their atmospheric cleansing work effectively. I consider the fieldwork to gather the required DNA from as wide a population of flora and fauna as is possible as well as the return trip to Hermes. They each require a working partnership, but also an intimacy that is both exciting and daunting. If ever we are to marry, now is the time, or the opportunity will forever remain a remote dream?

Before doubts start creeping in, with the engagement ring in hand and we are alone on our favorite stretch of beach, I stumble through my proposal, expecting a kind, gentle decline or, at best, a deferment for time to think. Relief floods through my veins as I see her eyes lighten up and she accepts without hesitation. We hold each other in a lasting embrace. The rest of the time spent on the beach is a blur. I have no recollection of the details except that we decide to conclude the union as soon as possible and tie the knot before leaving for Earth. The trip will be our honeymoon. As evening sets, we walk slowly hand in hand along the shoreline towards home, each step a dreamlike trance, a lightness in our tread. Dispelled are the dark clouds of doubt that I previously grappled with.

The days that follow are probably the most hectic I have ever experienced. Aside from the preparations for leaving, the genuine delight of our friends at the news and their wholehearted determination to perfect the wedding arrangements bind us as a uniquely special group, committed to each other's wellbeing and thoroughly at home in each's company.

When we explain the concept of love and life partnering to the Betilla, they are baffled, needing a few rounds of explanation before the concept makes sense. Understandably it is an entirely foreign notion to them. It is interesting to witness the dawning of understanding, then the acceptance turning to delight at the pairing.

It takes a supreme effort to focus on anything other than Julia, but the demands at hand to prepare for the journey, now only days away, are daunting. Fortunately our comrades are understanding and insistent on relieving us of much of the responsibility. We make use of their consideration to frequent our favorite place whenever possible. There we deepen our relationship with intimate insights, exchanging ideas and plans for the future. But ultimately we have to tear ourselves away from our pleasures to prepare for the trip.

Refrigerated storage containers prepared to strict temperature specifications provided by the Betilla are readied to accommodate their DNA and a supply of algae spores. The transfer of the cargo to the containers requires us to travel over land to the northern coastal reaches of West Riven where ice still holds a grip on the land and sea. Here we carefully excavate blocks of ice with Betilla and algae still frozen in them, waiting to emerge from hibernation. We transfer them to the cold-storage containers while keeping the temperature constant with the ice at source. On returning to base we are instructed to add juvenile Betilla and moss from the local fields to the storage containers, embedding them in layers of ice. The refrigerator is then programmed to take the temperature down to minus twenty degrees Celsius and remain at that temperature until we reach the Earth. A redundant refrigerator is prepared as a standby in the event of a malfunction of the primary unit.

The wedding day is the evening before the departure, which is planned to make the best of the orbital alignment of Earth and Hermes. The pilot who landed our pod after leaving the *Forerunner* mothership is the closest we have to a captain to legitimize the marriage. With the villagers gathered to witness the occasion, he conducts the ceremony with the gravity the occasion calls for. Robin, as the mediator appointed by the Management Committee, produces a register for signing. We are the only names in the book, marking the first marriage on Hermes. As we emerge from the cubicle where the signing takes place, in crossing to the main building, to our delight, the sky lights up with a faint glow. The Betilla circle in their glowing bubbles above the small village, forming a pattern of concentric circles as they did when they first made their intelligence known to us, as a recognition of our nuptial ceremony. Alerted by our exclamations, the guests stream out of the hub to watch the display. Many are moved to tears in recognition of the status of the Betilla as partners and at an emotional level, a shared joy and sympathetic concern for each other's wellbeing. Waving and cheering in appreciation, the spectacle continues for a few minutes then fades as they disperse over the hill.

Nostalgia for Hermes will be a recurring sentiment Julia and I have for Hermes as we recall this evening in our long absence from the planet. Joy in the company of our friends we have grown to hold so dear and sadness at the prospect of not seeing them for such a protracted period will test our endurance.

Finally, the long day ends and the contrasting reality of the morrow takes center stage: a launch in a foreign craft of dubious refinement, with all the risks this poses.

20

HARVEST

A bright and clear day greets us in the morning and with some trepidation we board the *Destiny* group's antiquated spacecraft as the time for liftoff approaches. Rudimentarily appointed, the interior is no match for the accommodation on our flight from the Earth in the *Forerunner*, but with a pilot and only two passengers we will have considerable space to ourselves. Centrifugally generated gravity is minimal, but they have an extensive set of exercise equipment to keep us in trim and compensate for the lack of natural restraints. Takeoff and transit will be fully automated, with Lester there to attend to any anomalies.

Minor technical problems delay the launch, but we soon find ourselves accelerating away from the planet, Earth our destination.

The 210 days to transit to Earth are both restrictive in the confines of the craft and expansive in the intimacy of the experience. We indulge ourselves in long discussions on a variety of topics, wonder at the spread of stars in the realm, listen to a wide range of music and reread many of our favorite novels. On the serious side, we plan support requirements for our operations on land. We consider the flux of conditions under global warming, how effectively to disperse the Betilla with the moss to safe locations and the logistics of our return journey, four years in the future. As sporadic communications allow, Lester maintains contact with the *Destiny* ground control center to confirm our position and progress. He occasionally joins us for board games to pass the time.

Seven months in limbo seems long, but passes surprisingly quickly, as Earth and the moon loom ever larger in our sights.

As we approach rendezvous, the Earth-bound control center of the *Destiny*, for reasons not clear to us, fails to check-in at the required time to take over control of navigation. This leaves us in danger of overshooting the orbital coordinates, our velocity in excess of the gravitational capture parameters of Earth.

At the console, Lester tries to remain calm, "Control Center, this is *Destiny*. We are approaching the designated coordinates for you to take control. Please confirm! We are on standby."

A few minutes later, "Control Center this is *Destiny*. I repeat. We are in danger of overshooting the handover point. Please respond!"

Try after retry with mounting alarm, all efforts to make contact fail. After all that has gone before and lies ahead, is this our end?

With time running out, Lester resorts to the one alternative known to us. "European Space Agency, are you there? Can you hear us? This is *Destiny* en route from Hermes. We require assistance. ESA are you there?"

Fortunately, and to our great relief, they respond to our distress. "*Destiny*, we have been monitoring your communications. You only have minutes to adjust your velocity. Hold for further instructions."

"ESA this is *Destiny*. We hear you."

Nail-biting seconds pass as I watch the concern on Julia's face.

"*Destiny* – patch us into your control panel using the following override commands."

Then follows a set of codes that Lester enters into the system. We wait. An agonizing few moments pass before their message confirms they have control.

"*Destiny*, we have logged into your system. We have control!"

Barely seconds later, to our relief, the center of gravity shifts as the craft begins braking.

"ESA, our attitude is changing. Your maneuver seems to be taking effect. Thank you! Thank you!"

Not long after, we approach and pass the moon at close quarters. The desolation of the far side provides pause to gather our equilibrium from the receding danger. We emerge from the curvature of the satellite to see our trajectory adjusted and aimed at Earth.

At our speed, it takes a mere day and half to reach Earth. We circumnavigate the planet a few times before drawing near enough to pass an umbilical tether to the ESA space station. They prove to be very accommodating, having heard of our mission and its purpose. They propose that we use their facilities going forward because the owners of the *Destiny* are not dependable and have a dubious reputation. We are not surprised, given our experience with their Hermes expedition crew, and grateful for being safe in ESA hands. Thankfully, on inspection they confirm that the craft is sound, albeit rudimentary.

Our cargo is transferred to the docked entry vehicle parked alongside the space station. It takes two days to finalize descent preparations, and then we complete the harrowing dive through the atmosphere. We find ourselves bobbing in the ocean off the coast of Italy in the Mediterranean Sea. A tugboat with ESA emblazoned on the side draws near to take our craft in tow to a waiting frigate, where we are hoisted aboard for ferrying to the nearest port. We in the meantime strain under the unaccustomed weight of gravity, an adjustment that takes longer than anticipated even with the strict exercise routine we followed en route. At the harbor, Lester bids us farewell and good luck with our venture; he will rejoin us when we depart.

Paris in full spring bloom, oblivious to the raging climate conditions elsewhere, gives us the opportunity to recuperate slowly but surely while a privately chartered plane is readied for us and our precious cargo. Overflight permission for a direct flight to the islands of the Seychelles takes a while to reaffirm, as do the other legs of the trip, all professionally handled by Dr. Vespucci's department. He has secured accommodation at each stopover with strict instructions to maintain the anonymity of our identities and disguise the nature of our work.

Despite these measures, the UN being a public body cannot operate in complete obscurity; some details, such as our arrival date, are public. Faust is active; UN offices around the globe have to fend off their attacks. The effect on Julia is noticeable. Her mood swings return, requiring constant reassurances that her work is for the betterment of all.

Finally, we are ready and en route. News coverage recedes into the background and Julia focuses on the work at hand. After seeing the vastness of the Sahara below us, we reach the tropical islands of the Seychelles. The effects of climate change are immediately apparent from the air; shoreline erosion caused by rising seas, many islands submerged, coral reefs bleached gray from acidification but still holding forth in some areas as barriers against the sea, parched land from uncharacteristic droughts, the archipelago nation strains under effects brought on from distant lands. We have to dispense with our preferred location to another and here we deposit the first of the Betilla. The next leg is to the west coast of Madagascar. Then we make the long trip to northern Namibia on the west coast of southern Africa, and an even longer and turbulent flight across the Atlantic to the Falkland Islands. Chile is next, then all the way to the west and east coasts of Canada before returning to Paris.

Each stop entails the careful extraction of a segment of the ice containing moss and Betilla in hibernation from the cold-storage container. The thawing is carried out following the procedures supplied by the Betilla before leaving Hermes. Securing their new homes in carefully selected secluded areas is critical. In each case, we stay to observe their vital signs, and confirm unimpeded growth as the fledglings start to multiply in soil closely resembling the moss fields on Hermes. Interestingly, after a couple of days the juvenile Betilla are able to communicate with Julia, evincing an ability to take instructions from their parents, even while in a state of torpor on Hermes, clearly fully apprised of their tasks here on Earth.

Their primary task is to multiply. The magic of exponential reproduction rapidly expands their presence. They devour the moss as soon as it is sustainable, which thrives on the rich soils. They also feed on indigenous flora, taking care to maintain an ecological balance. Development is rapid and on reaching maturity, as is their custom, they migrate down rivers and streams to the sea. Here they build their castles in the waters after regurgitating moss-forming algae, which flourishes in the sea, spreading along the coastline.

Back in Paris, we swelter in unseasonably hot weather as summer approaches but we soon depart to traverse the loop initially completed to disperse the Betilla, revisiting the sites to ensure undisturbed activity and checking on progress. Already on the first cycle back to the sites, floating bubbles with the characteristic pulsing glow are seen taking to the air from the coast. They are limited in number at the first visit, but we project a firmly established routine within six months. After two cycles through the sites and five months into the venture it is obvious from local measurements of atmospheric carbon dioxide that changes are apparent. We attribute this, in part, to the seeding of clouds with engineered bacteria, the upward flow of bubbles into the clouds being the indicator of their strategy. Wrought by photosynthetic action on atmospheric carbon at ground level and in the clouds, hope rises for a wider effect. Ultimately, it must reach global proportions before improving conditions at the scale needed to bring calm to the world.

As summer turns to autumn, we note a remarkable change. The once murky waters surrounding the sites are now pristine. Clear waters invite a rich variety of fish to return to areas long abandoned. Moss fields show growth of indigenous plants previously absent. An influx of birds invade, with whistles of delight to reap the benefits of a renewed landscape.

Julia has an idea. We contact the Australian and New Zealand environmental authorities with before and after pictures and an invitation to witness the change for themselves. Maybe they will be enticed to join the experiment after all. With their curiosity piqued, after ironing out the logistics, we meet them at the Madagascar site and the change speaks for itself. The Australians complain of the Great Barrier Reef, now a dead zone, gray coral the skeleton of what was once a vibrant aquatic landscape, the pride of Australia's natural heritage. With nothing to lose, they agree to a transfer of some Betilla to the sheltered waters along the reef's coastline. New Zealand too offers parts of the sheltered east coast. Within a few short months, the word spreads of the successes achieved and Japan, once averse to the program, joins the venture with Korea and Russia following on their heels.

With our range now vastly extended, translating into long, tiring flights, we cycle through the sites at a steady pace, marveling at the transformations. News filters out from the hitherto tightly controlled environmental community to the public at large. Hints of optimism are apparent for the first time in years. A new willingness to engage in the recovery process becomes apparent. Demands to contain industry's egregious practices mount, along with an acknowledgment of the fragility of the natural order with a corresponding need to treat it well. Even Faust, with his strategy blunted, struggles to rally his followers; only his most zealous supporters maintain their admonitions. We sometimes see signs of vandalism at the Betilla sites, but never a repeat at the same site. On questioning the Betilla, they admit to discouraging the perpetrators with a disorientating electromagnetic pulse, unpleasant enough to eliminate a recurrence.

* * *

Anuar stares out at the sea from a rise. He murmurs to himself, "There must be a way. I underestimated how these creatures affected my men on Hermes."

He chuckles to himself. *Funny, the way the men staggered around like drunken idiots after breaking the corals.* Then thoughtfully, he ponders. *There must be a way... Hmm yes, maybe poison. Why not use poison? We can apply it where the current will take it to the sites. That way we can work from a distance, unobserved, and monitor the effect from this hill. Those bubbles, if they stop coming, we will know we have the right poison.*

I have two enemies; the people and the beetles, both must be dealt with. Guns for the one and poison for the other!

But there is Kostya, that useless individual. He needs to ferment more trouble. Preferring to return to Farland just will not work, laughable. I need them all in one place so I can control them when I get there.

* * *

Marine specialists get involved in studying the nature of the improvements. One such person observes a strange phenomenon: microplastics and microbeads in the ocean surrounding the Betilla sites appear to be in decline. Further studies confirm this, the scale and rate of improvement corresponding to the spread of Betilla habitats, appearing to link the two. Julia extrapolates the idea to consider whether they could address the vortex of debris, mainly plastics, in the Pacific, suggesting that we somehow have a presence of Betilla in the North Pacific Gyre as a trial. She broaches the subject with them and they explain that they have genetically manipulated the genes of certain bacteria to ingest plastics and excrete biodegradable material. The microbes decline to normal levels once they have exhausted the plastics in an area. Even a small population of these modified bacteria will proliferate in the presence of microplastics while this food source is available to them. There is therefore no need to translocate Betilla. A quantity of microbes, harvested from the sea where the Betilla are active, will suffice. With a marine biologist as a recruit, using a floatplane we head for the North Pacific Gyre from the western Canada site, the sample in hand. Amazed at the extent of the garbage field below us, we elect to land in open water to the south of the arena, where we transfer our invisible therapy to the waters. As we leave, we photograph the patch stretching to the horizon, hoping to use the image for before and after comparisons.

We emerge from winter with nearly a year of our mission behind us, and early signs are that carbon sequestration is working. An analysis shows that, although minimal, there is evidence that we are on the right track and gaining momentum by the month. If the trend continues on its current trajectory, in another year or two it will be conclusive. Equally though, balanced on a knife-edge, the trend may be an anomaly and the passage of a year may prove the opposite. Ozone measurements also show a marginal healing of depleted areas over the Antarctic, but still too early to be claiming success.

* * *

Our project turns to the collection of DNA samples. A call to Dr. Vespucci confirms that our invitation to visit Svalbard Global Seed Vault still stands and he indicates that he has arranged for the team that he recruited to meet us there. Excited at the prospect, with our itinerary altered and flights booked, we set out for the Arctic Circle. Our plane circles the austere landscape as we line up with the runway. A short distance away the deceptive structure greets us mounted at an angle against a bare rise, disguising the extensive underground facilities.

At the reception area, a distinguished looking man with graying hair steps forward to Julia. Offering an outstretched arm, he takes her hand and with a deep bow in an Italian accent says, "You must be our celebrated biologist and discoverer. It is truly an honor to meet you in person, Julia. I am Dr. Vespucci. This is Aksel, Vault Coordinator, who has kindly agreed to act as guide for us."

Julia and I in unison reply, "Pleased to meet you Aksel."

He shakes hands and indicates for us to follow to an adjoining room. Entering from the rear, the large well-lit auditorium has about ten people grouped near the front, quietly talking to each other. Aksel leads us onto the stage, where he welcomes the attendees and hands the meeting over to Dr. Vespucci.

Dr. Vespucci starts, "Julia Woodruff needs no introduction but to put a face to a name, this is Julia and this is Miles, partners in work and marriage. They have been very active these past months establishing the Betilla across the globe to help with bringing our climate under control."

Turning to the audience but speaking to us, he says, "This is the team I have been fortunate to recruit. Julia and Miles, you will be pleased to know that not only are they individually highly qualified but they also have significant experience in their respective fields. For the last year, Jeremy – please stand, Jeremy – has led the team, and will be handing the reins over to you now that you have reached the stage in your project that entails DNA collection. To date they have focused on desk-based research ahead of the fieldwork."

Dr. Vespucci then introduces each of the ten people by name, qualifications and experience. In combination, their expertise covers the world's biosphere, from plants to organisms that fly, crawl, slither, swim or fly, including their behavior, whether based on land, in water or the air.

With a wink, he says, "Indulge me for a minute; I have a surprise for you, one that you can turn down if you so choose. These people will assist in gathering the needs; we have agreement on that… In addition, everyone before you answered 'Yes' to the question regarding their interest in accompanying you to Hermes to help with the greening of the planet."

Seeing our surprise he continues, "Please, please do not answer that question now, and nor does the team need to commit to the journey to Hermes right now. I would like you to think about it. It seems that there is a mountain of work on the other side. My opinion is that you will need expert help. Over the next period of months, you will be working as a team and you can make your decision as the work nears completion. As to the cost, I will make a case for the UN to carry it. So, we all have something to think about and I will advise you on the outcome of funding in due course."

I can see Julia will have no difficulty in agreeing to Dr. Vespucci's offer. In meeting everyone over coffee and tea, the excitement is contagious as we discuss next steps and the future.

When we are about to resume the conducted tour of the facility I call for everyone's attention. "Firstly, allow me to thank Dr. Vespucci for all his work and putting this team together; it is appreciated. Secondly, the expedition needs a name; may I suggest 'Operation Noah's Ark,' and we have an 'A Team'?"

"Yea, yea," everyone agrees, with claps and high-fives. We have a team.

Aksel leads us deep into the bowels of the Earth, describing the purpose and function of the vault as we proceed. "Our objective is to safeguard Earths diversity. From what Dr. Vespucci has explained, I can see good reason for us to cooperate. If you are able to use our seeds on another planet it will independently safeguard our seed stock."

As we approach the secure areas with row upon row of shelves loaded with carefully labeled crates reaching to the ceiling, he goes on to explain, "We here have no real rights over the seeds. We merely act on behalf of the depositors. That is in fact the secret of our success. It makes them participants in the process."

We listen attentively as he goes on, "For you to take from the vault you will need their permission. It is simply a process; it should not be a problem."

Dr. Vespucci asks, "Would it expedite matters if there is an undertaking to resupply the taken seeds back to the depositors in the event of a circumstance that makes this necessary?"

Aksel replies, "That sounds like an extension of what we actually undertake to do for them. So, yes. It is very likely that they will agree."

I add, "I see no reason why the community on Hermes would not sign such an agreement. I can confirm this with them, and as a member of their Management Committee I can in fact sign on their behalf. You understand that the distance means a long response time to resupply the seeds."

"Yes, the distance is both a problem and an advantage... Yes, okay, I will consult with the members and get back to you. I think you should allow a week for the approvals and at least three months to extract samples; you understand we have over a million specimens. I take it that you would want a wide variety, yes?"

Julia then explains the Betilla's genetic engineering approach using triangulation to minimize the number of species to provide. In response to Aksel's interest in the genetic technique, Julia refers him to the appropriate organizations who are in receipt of the Betilla's technique. We spend the rest of the day learning more about the vast enterprise that makes up the vault. By the end of the day, fully satisfied with what we have achieved, we thank Aksel and Dr. Vespucci and set off for the next episode in our quest.

* * *

With renewed vigor, Julia now in her element, we visit far-flung natural reserves of marine, mountains, forests and plains, hiking along paths not often frequented. We adopt a policy of divide and conquer. The team fans out to places that minimize the effort and maximize the harvest, approaching zoos and formal repositories of DNA first before supplementing from nature. Periodically, we meet at certain locales to exchange notes and confirm harvesting plans before setting out to conduct the work. Our only burden is the refrigerated storage container. Our greatest challenge is the unpredictable weather and human interactions but with time, our treasure builds, augmented by samples from DNA banks. Julia compiles an extensive catalog of the plants and animals, their genus and relationships in the evolutionary tree. She also documents the habitat best suited to them, the microcosm from which they are drawn and their interdependencies from pollinators to creatures that recycle the waste of others.

Her best work is the sketches that accompany many of the specimens, artistically drawn, accurate representations with matching photographs. I quietly witness the sheer delight with which she conducts every aspect of the collection. Fully immersed in the world of nature, she seems oblivious of my presence. Singularly focused, unable to contain her excitement, words spill from her, a running commentary of an imaginary landscape for realization on Hermes. An artist designing a new reality on a distant planet, her pallet, each specimen carefully selected and blended for color, contour and balance, forming a tapestry of life; impatient to transform the barren to the fertile, silent desolation to pulsating vitality.

There were questions on the advisability of introducing alien life to the planet when the project was first proposed – whether the Betilla would have invasive tendencies, upset the ecological balance or have ulterior motives or negative effects – when climatologists reported seeing black deposits in the rainwater occurring as a fine sediment if left to stand. Alarm at the apparent contamination proved unwarranted when analysis by health advocates found the substance to be activated charcoal; a detoxifying agent with health benefits at the low concentration levels observed. The Betilla's bacterial sequestration process in the clouds proved to be the source of the deposits and it came as a relief to us that there were no harmful effects.

Time passes quickly and our departure date draws near. With just weeks to go, we stop over at Svalbard, where Aksel proudly hands over his samples, and from there we conduct a final lap of the Betilla sites. En route, as we fly over the land and sea, though we are biased, we note a certain calmness as Mother Nature begins to re-establish her foothold. The Pacific Gyre has measurably shrunk in size. Soaking rains bring relief to parched deserts, brown turns to green, lakes form in scorched depressions, calm winds replace raging storms in some places and ice flows begin to form in the open waters of the Polar Regions.

Meanwhile, humans like migrating herds hesitantly start their trek back to abandoned homes under a new optimistic prognosis for the Earth. The first signs of recovery are evident after four short years. After all, there are now only 327 days in the Earth's year at its new orbital location, but there is much yet to do – decades or even centuries of healing before restoration of order.

In our hotel, as we wait for the weather to clear to allow our chartered flight from Madagascar to Namibia to proceed, we occupy ourselves with incidental preparations. Julia, out of curiosity, sits scrolling through the SETI website that led to her discovery of Hermes.

Perking up she calls me over. "Miles, come, have a look; they have been tracking the electromagnetic radiation at the 21-centimeter hydrogen line coming from Hermes. Remember how we figured out how they use their carapaces; well there see, not bad hey? They have cross-referenced to my dissertation. They first noticed it at about the same time as when the probes circling Hermes picked it up. It seems that they exchanged the news at the time and agreed to monitor it jointly. Look there; there is the spike that alerted me to wider implications."

"Incredible, it just shows how thorough they are. It would have been quite an embarrassment to their donors to have missed that."

"Yes, and you know what that means? It probably means that the Betilla on Hermes are in constant contact with those here on Earth."

"I wonder what they are saying to each other."

Laughing, she replies, "As Robin said: plotting to take over the world. So much for ulterior motives."

As we fly from Madagascar to Namibia, I have a parting wish: to visit the land of my youth, to show Julia the valleys, mountains and streams that formed our playground at Mount Elias. We land at the nearest airport just two hour's drive to the Eden of my formative years. As we pass familiar landmarks, I have a mounting sense of excitement mixed with nostalgia, for those were carefree days. Much has changed, though. Humankind has an insatiable need to improve or modify his or her environment, often abandoning the old, littering the tracks with failures, advancing the new and latest. The rutted road leading to our homestead has deteriorated. A new and better road forks off the old route, a new lifeline to communities along its way, leaving those that benefited from the old abandoned. As we branch off the new way, a bus thunders past, emblazoned on its side in bold words: MAHARAJ'S BUS SERVICE, still in service after all these years.

Ten minutes later, we arrive at our destination. With profound sadness, I see an all but deserted cluster of buildings. The homestead a skeleton, its roof removed to feed a sprawling rural shantytown alongside the new road. The masses, seeking solace from over-crowded cities, flocked here to the countryside only to find jobless tedium. Out of necessity, they built temporary shelters that inevitably became permanent; their proud tradition of neat mud-walled thatch roofed dwellings giving way to the squalor of tin lean-tos.

* * *

We, Kite and Aerie, have adjusted, the shorter days and years our new normal. For the first time, a single healthy fledgling stirs from sleep on the thatch-work of twigs cradled on our ledge. Food will be on its mind soon. Our nest will not be barren, as feared, for there is a new breath of freshness that pervades our valley. Our fellow creatures sense it too. The swifts and swallows chase insects like before, their numbers swell and expectations for more are evident in their aerial acrobatics, carefree and untroubled. The loerie flashes its colors, celebrating the shyness it overcame under the spell of changes in the air. The bees, once more laden with pollen, are returning to their industry. Parents watch with a new pride as a pair of rock rabbits twins chase their short tails around the boulders a little distance from the caves where bats hang in new numbers from the ceilings. At night, even the frogs swell to a new refrain, their chorale works strangely calming despite the raucous overtones.

The fledging stirs again; food will be the cry shortly. Taking to wing, my search for victual is easier in these new days as I rise for a better view of prey. Up, up, there, at the optimum height, detail is visible. Circling in a broad arch, I see the all-but-abandoned farmstead on the spur. What is that? A pair approaches down the path to our valley. The one has a familiar gait. Who can that be? Can it be the youth, now grown, the one who frequented our world in days past? Food forgotten for the moment, I descend for a better view. Yes, it is the one, and the partner, a female, her long brown hair spilling over her shoulders, shifting in the breeze. Mesmerized at her movements, the confidence of bearing that speaks of peace and tranquility, at one with nature. The tinkle of laughter like water trickling over rocks, they touch and electricity sparkles in their eyes, their contentment obvious and a joy to behold. There is a certain deep attachment they have for each other, and he to their surroundings. For a brief minute, reminded of the freshness descended on us, the new optimism and resurgence of life in many forms, what can it be that radiates from these two; some subconscious linkage, a curious unfathomable bond, inexplicable but real? What is it?

Reminded of the needs of our offspring, returning to the ledge with Aerie we watch the approach of our unexpected guests as they wander along the ravine and settle in a corner to rest. Our fledging wakens with a cry for food. Aerie sets out to search while I hold watch.

* * *

The once manicured lawns of the farmstead, flower beds and orchard now stand tall with weeds. The elevated water tower that provided for the needs of the complex in days past stands at an awkward angle, rusted with gaping holes, its purpose long gone. We park the car and walk up the pathway to the entrance of the home that provided such comfort. Inside, the wooden floorboards are absent. In my bedroom the window is now a staring gap, and the boyish curtains and wooden frame gone, cruelly mocking the intemperance of my previous existence?

Turning to the trading store, in the bygone era a bustling hub of humanity, now a distant memory, it stands forlorn. The serving counters have been stripped and removed. The shelving that displayed a myriad of useful and not so useful trinkets has been torn from the walls. In a corner burns a fire over which a pot sardonically chuckles, brewing a scant meal for an aged man, his gnarled hands held out for warmth.

As we approach, his sight lacking, startled, he says, "Who is that? Who is there?"

That voice, that inflection, I immediately recognize. It is Mkize, our trusted resident caretaker of old, his loyalty beyond reproach?

"Mkize, Mkize, yes, it is Mkize. It is Miles, do you remember me? Miles... Can you not see?"

As our eyes adjust to the gloom I see tears come to his eyes as he recalls who I am, hoping that we herald a return of a prosperous past. A scar runs across his forehead and burn marks are evident on his hair and neck. In the corner a second straw bed with a pale blue denim jacket draped over the bedding shows signs of recent use.

A rush of questions: "Dear Mkize, are you well? You look injured. Are you okay?" Stooping down to inspect his condition more closely and pointing to the spare bed, I ask, "Do you have someone to look after you?"

With a deep sigh, Mkize draws in a breath and explains: "Yes! I met with an accident. My old home is no longer; burned to the ground."

Pointing to his face, we understand the consequence.

Shifting his position, he goes on in lighter mood: "I am blessed with the help of a young man who rescued me from the fire. He tends to my every need. He is out now, doing odd jobs for the neighbors to support us. He brings water, food and fire wood – you know we don't have electricity anymore, like in the old days."

Diverting the attention from himself, he asks, "I heard that you still see Jabulani. His parents told me. They said he sends them money, such a good boy. You know his parents nursed me to health after my accident. Such kind people! They are so proud of him. I believe that he does a lot of traveling – overseas to faraway lands."

With a distant glow on his face he says, "You know, his grandfather and I are brothers?"

I can barely contain my emotions, "Yes, Jabu and I share a house in a faraway land." I realize that it would be impossible to explain that we live on another planet. He would not understand.

Continuing, I say, "I did not know that you and he are related. I will have to tell him about your accident."

Before I can say more, he interjects, "Please, please don't tell him. I do not want him to worry. I am well attended to here and it gives me pleasure to still be on this old land."

Unable to adjust to the changing world around him, steadfastly refusing to move to the shantytown, he has held out here, supported by meager handouts from benevolent neighbors.

We reminisce a while, then alas, the best we can do is to comfort him with a share of our provisions and bid him well as we depart.

Saddened by Mkize's story and disappointed at the state of the settlement I decide to take Julia to my ravine haunts of old.

As we distance ourselves from the farmstead, I am encouraged by its increasingly untouched isolation. Nature still rules in its pristine self-sufficiency. Grasses wave in the breeze and the hawk circles above, elegant in its effortless flight. Wistful reflections on the past flow through my being.

We wander along rock pools and cascading waterfalls, ever deeper into the velvety green world, flanked by soaring cliffs of red sandstone that close in on us as we progress. Swallows reel as they swoop down from their mud nests, sheltered under overhanging formations, to capture insects in flight, their shrill calls echoing from cliff to cliff joining in the symphony of birdsong. Celebrating the absence of humankind, waves of crescendos and diminuendos, each vibrato and pizzicato randomly orchestrating an abandonment of form yet a blend for maximum effect. Then, as if on cue, the loerie flashes its scarlet wings as it launches from the secrecy of one thicket to another, striking across an open space, exposing its shy nature as though to flaunt the unveiling of its beauty. It vocalizes its presence with a protracted call that echoes above the chorus of sounds. Made more marvelous with Julia by my side, we listen in rapt attention. Resting beside a pool of quietly flowing water reflecting the shimmering blue sky, ochre and red cliffs and the emerald shades of green, we soak up the dappled warmth of the sun on the smooth contoured stone. As we doze in the spell of the moment time stands still, nature begins to ignore our presence, life resumes it cycle.

A group of exquisitely blue waxbill finches systematically preens every nook and cranny of a nearby brush for morsels of food, twittering as they progress. A field mouse, not ten feet from us, decides it is safe to emerge from hiding to drink from the running water. Cautiously it tests the open space, alert to any danger; tentatively at first, then more boldly, it creeps across the rocks to the pool, checks for safety looking left and right and then drinks of the refreshing elixir, a long draft. Too long, for overhead a hawk steps off a ledge far up on the cliff where it has been waiting for just such a moment. With one motion, it spreads its wings into the warm air and strikes across the ravine, unseen by the mouse. In approach, it folds its wings closely, dropping at a precipitous angle and gaining speed with each passing second. The little mammal stands no chance as it raises its head from the water. A terrifying glimpse of the approaching hawk, claws extended, is its last. It turns to defend itself, but to no avail. The hawk takes its struggling prey and the only injury is a single blood-soaked feather, dislodged from its underbelly, which gently floats to the ground in front of us. The blue finches, startled by the calamity, scatter in all directions, leaving feathers in their wake in their frantic escape. Soon, with calm restored, we watch as the hawk rises to the cliffs, its victim firm in its claws, food for its young on the ledge where it held vigil.

Silence stretches as our pulsing hearts return to normal. Julia solemnly takes out a plastic bag, pockets the blood-soaked feather and collects those of the blue finch, quiet reminders of the tragedy but an unstated hope that the specimens will live again on a distant planet.

As we start our return trip to the airport, I point out Jabu's proud home kraal alongside the old road, still holding out in the traditional style. Jabu has religiously sent a part of his earnings to support his parents and family, enabling them to maintain a stabilizing foundation, an important cornerstone to the burgeoning community. A short stop and with greetings we convey our joy at finding them in good health and happiness, then press on to the waiting pilot. As we approach the city, provoked by the feather samples and the DNA they carry, I suggest to Julia that we stop at the Natural History Museum in the town. I know from past visits that they have an extensive collection of wild bird eggs on display; just maybe we can secure loerie DNA from the curator. After explaining our intent, he reluctantly parts with a scarlet feather, on condition that we let him know what success we have.

Next is to our final stop before departing for the launch site. Dr. Vespucci meets us at the airport and conveys us downtown where the team of specialists are already ensconced in the hotel. All but one agreed to join us on the trip to Hermes and another recruit filled

287

the vacancy to maintain our complement of ten. All are both excited and nervous, as we recall being prior to our first flight.

We settle into our room on the fourth floor. On the following day, there is one last task to perform. By prior arrangement, we take a rented vehicle to a farm on the outskirts of the town, where, following instructions from the Betilla, we acquire a collection of frozen fertile domesticated fowl and pheasant eggs. They also provide incubators and miscellaneous supplies sourced for us and needed in the process to resuscitate our DNA treasures, all additions to our cargo, destined for Hermes.

On returning to the hotel, we find a large gathering at the entrance. Circling around to the back, we enter the premises through a rear entrance and park the vehicle.

Aghast, anxiety – even fear – writ large on her face, Julia says, "It is them. I am sure of it. Demonstrators! Somehow they have figured out that we are here."

"Julia, just stay calm. Are you sure it is demonstrators?"

"Yes, yes, I saw one with a placard. 'Turn or burn' or something like that. I remember seeing it on TV a while back."

"Look, we are safe here in the garage, at least for the moment. We need to get to our room; we will be safer in numbers with the rest of the team. I will call Vespucci from there; see what he can do. Is that okay?"

"Okay, let's take the stairs."

Leaving our supplies in the vehicle we silently, unobserved, make our way to the fourth floor. A knock at Jeremy's door opens to a crowd of all of our fellow travelers. "Thank god you are safe."

"What is going on?"

"It is the Earth First bunch. They arrived minutes before you. You have been lucky; they are busy surrounding the hotel to prevent our exit, or entrance for that matter."

From a window, we anxiously watch the proceedings on the street below. "Has anyone contacted Dr. Vespucci?"

"Yes. That was our first reaction and we contacted 911. They are sending the police over. We just have to sit tight. I am sure they will bring them under control quite quickly."

"But look, there are more arriving; controlling them will not be easy… Miles, look! Some have placards with my name on them. Somehow, they have figured out my involvement. That was the last thing I wanted. Look at what the placards read."

It is disturbing to see such vehemence: "Nuke the Invaders!" "Heretics are for Hermes!" and worst of all, "Burn the Witch of Woodruff!" How can they be so cruel?

The standoff takes days to bring under control with Julia's agitation showing no signs of abating until finally the chaos subsides, leaving her exhausted, moody and withdrawn. It takes all my resolve to comfort her and assure her that they represent a small fraction of people; the success we achieved will ultimately speak for itself, with the vast majority of people being appreciative of her contribution.

A week of delay and our attention turns back to the departure. Our treasure-trove of specimens is packed and ready for flight. In contrast to the demonstrators, an appreciative public and authorities show up, eager to compensate for the behavior of the protesters and to facilitate our launch to rendezvous with the *Destiny*, still parked in a waiting orbit.

21

DISTRIBUTION

Julia's mood turns for the better as we bid farewell to friends and relatives before setting out for the launch facility and taking to the air in the harrowing transit to orbit. In the weightless world we dock with the *Destiny*. Now not only fully serviced, it shows signs of new safety and communication features fitted by the ESA. Lester is there to meet us; he will be our pilot for the return trip. A day or two lapses for the transfer of the cargo from the assent vehicle and to correctly position the *Destiny* for a slingshot course around the moon to Hermes.

The twenty-first century version of Noah's Ark breaks with the shackles of Earth; we are under way. The voyage is uneventful, and we enjoy each other's company and the opportunity to relax after the hectic time on Earth. We cement our newfound camaraderie of specialists, founded on the adventure just completed and the new one at hand. Once fully settled and while our recollections are still fresh, our team itemizes the inventory, builds indexes and sketches a sequence for distributing the stock of life. A log of dependencies and prerequisites for each specimen, with annotations that others can follow, results in a voluminous repository for reference purposes. These activities absorb us for many weeks as we watch Earth recede in the distance. Excitement then builds as we count down the days to arrival and Julia and her team puts final changes to the catalog.

Hermes gradually grows larger, from a shimmering star to a blue and white orb. Then oceans and continents take form, articulating the coming adventure of seeding the planet while Earth shrinks to a shiny blue dot, a glistening reflection of memories of four years spent as husband and wife.

After the stress of entry abates, the welcoming party clamors for news, for details of our experience. News feeds provided hints at the successes achieved, but details were sparse. Introductions for the gravity-deprived travelers are somewhat cumbersome as the villagers assist us to our lodgings. Jabu is quick to suggest that we convene in the hub on the following day to allow us to somewhat adjust to gravity and there provide a more detailed update. Accordingly, we stand in front of them in the hub on the next day to complete the introductions, fully explain the purpose of the enlarged team and take questions. Some are personal, some are abstract; all proudly recognize the vital role and footing of Hermes as a contributor while also honoring the Betilla with a deepening respect.

The topics then turn to the future. Eager to reap the rewards of our trip there is no shortage of volunteers for the great greening. With care, we gently dampen their enthusiasm.

Julia explains: "As we harvested the specimens on Earth, we were amazed at the interdependencies of species. If you disturb one, there is a ripple effect through to other species; it is surprising just how delicate the relationships are. If we prematurely release one without its counterpart, it will very likely result in failure. It is important that we built and secured each ecosystem one at a time, incrementally."

After some questions, she goes on: "We will be releasing a plan of how the greening will unfold, but it must be understood that there are many uncertainties, especially around timelines. We just do not know how well Earth's biology will take to this planet. Of one thing you can be certain, though: an Eden of our making will emerge and you will be justly proud of your contribution. The team of specialists will help us through each step of the way."

As the attendees leave, the excitement is palpable as they eagerly talk of what lies ahead.

Our next stop is the Betilla. They greet Julia with enthusiasm, and as with our friends, they too eagerly listen to her account of our trip. Although they are familiar with the rudiments of the accomplishments, there is distinct pride at the achievements to which they contributed and excitement at the extent of the repository that Julia shares with them. She repeats the need for a systematic release of the material into the wild.

After a few days of acclimatization, we are ready to start work.

* * *

Julia's first concern is for the Betilla to clarify the finer details of the incubation method they will employ. Accompanied by the team of specialists, Robin, Dmitri, Jabu and I, and with the Betilla listening, she starts with the format and logic behind the catalog, which is set up as an adjustable database to which they have access, explaining the time dependencies for distribution of the specimens and a rough timeframe for the spread of life across the planet.

My interest is in observing the specialists, for whom this is their first interaction with an alien lifeform of any intellect, let alone one that is equal to them, or superior. They listen intently as the Betilla, mimicking Julia's voice as is their habit, press for details on how an ecological balance will be established and maintained, questioning the interdependencies. It is strange to hear an equivalent sounding voice answer. It seems like a digression, but Julia takes pains to explain the relationships and that there cannot be certainty of complete success; there will be failures that will require corrective measures.

The Betilla plan to set up a quasi-laboratory in the calm waters off the shore-facing side of Pearl Islands. Here they have already begun building their coral structures waiting for the transfer of the first specimens. The first step in their plan is the biological manipulation of the genetics, beginning with a copying process to increase the volume of material for each kind. Then, they will develop ancestral groups by traversing from branches and leaves of the family tree to the apex or trunk to build a historical representation of the family. In doing so they will produce new species or reconstruct missing members. Next, to ensure sustainable diversity within each genus, they will produce male and female varieties and enhance traits for robust survival under the nascent conditions on Hermes.

The logistics for transference to and from the string of islands follows, a subject that has long intrigued Julia. Simplicity being the hallmark of the little ones, she is not surprised when they explain their tactic: they will float a prepared bubble across the waters to the hydroponic farm, which will be converted to serve as the land base for incubation of the embryonic specimens prepared by the Betilla. We then insert microscopic samples into the bubbles along with an aerosol form of liquid taken from the eggs brought from the Earth. This will serve as the starting growth medium and for safeguarding the material. The Betilla will take over the navigation of the bubbles back to the Pearl Islands where gene multiplication and editing will proceed. Bubbles will return the readied material to the land-based laboratory to incubate the ingredients. The gestation will start in test tubes then in tanks, trays or cages appropriate for each specimen, a veritable nursery for plants and animals, until ready for distribution across the planet. This will be the process for flora and fauna, but she must establish the correct sequence in the chronology as needed based on requirements for release into the environment.

To ensure continuity in the event of anything that might sideline Julia, she imparts the structure of her catalog to a recruited group of amateur biologists who will work alongside the specialist. She explains the placement of each specimen in the cold-storage chest for chronological retrieval over a span of many years and the representation in the catalog. Linked to descriptions of the species, she clarifies the documentation methodology of their preferred habitat and climate conditions, the precursors for release of each and instructions on their care and projected time to maturity. For my part, I cover the data backup and recovery procedures that are in place.

A myriad of tasks are assigned to various people, including Dmitri who is to automate as much of the land-based laboratory work as possible. My responsibility lies with general logistics and tracking of activities, including the fieldwork associated with the distribution. Robin tracks statistics of growth patterns, extrapolates these looking for consequences and proposing improvements. Jabu, with his geology expertise, maps out terrain to correspond with Julia's habitat requirements for each lifeform.

As the preparatory work proceeds and the basic facilities are put in place, the first of a steady stream of bubbles begin arriving at the hydroponic farm from the Pearl Islands. Within weeks, various grasses and pollinators are ready for trial distribution to land adjacent to the moss fields. The purpose is to test soil growth conditions and provide natural pollination to the nearby farmland tilled for our food supply. By the end of the week, we are able to stand back and wait for signs of success. In time, the pollinators are first to adapt, the farmlands soon abuzz with bees, wasps, hornets and butterflies going about their business, oblivious to the fact of their displacement from Earth to Hermes. The grasses do not wither and die but after an initial dormancy they too flourish, the hardy traits engineered into their makeup by the Betilla having their effect. The first tentative steps soon become a rigorous routine as we spread farther afield. Vegetation of varying sorts takes root and nonthreatening insects that crawl, jump and fly adopt their new home unchallenged by creatures further up the food chain, until a need for balance dictates their introduction, at which point the plan is to release larger varieties to control their proliferation.

With controlled impatience, the day finally arrives for the release of clones of the field mouse. We see the fruition of the process of the transformation of the blood taken from the feather of the hawk into living replicas of the original and diversified into a brood of males and females, of sufficient genetic diversity to ensure sustainability. With the cage door open, they sniff the air as if in recognition that something is different. Instinctively they scan the skies for the archenemy, the hawk, seeing none. Cautiously they exit the cage and enter the nearby stand of brushes and grasses, disappearing from sight. The thrill of the moment is captured on video as Julia and I share a glance, unnoticed by the others, a reflection of the moment that gave rise to the events before us.

* * *

Two, three, four years pass and the plains of West Riven sway gently with savannah grasslands. Developing trees climb the escarpment of East Riven and a profusion of flowering plants offer up a kaleidoscope of colors. Trout splash in the fresh waters of the Rent and fish of every variety swim alongside the coral castles of the Betilla. Salmon start their first migration up rivers and streams to the spawning grounds where we first introduced them. The mild winds of Hermes blow seeds across the breadth and width of the continent, relieving the labor of human and Betilla, the natural order asserting itself. As if in correspondence, New Greenwich, the name given to the village taking shape at the Podium and the meridian on which we base our time, displays a spread of quaint homesteads of baked mud walls reinforced with stones and with crowns of thatch, a picturesque vista reminiscent of medieval times and also of the Mount Elias of our youth.

22

ELSEWHERE

Earth gradually emerges from its devastation. Somber, it takes stock. A planet recovering from an extinction event. The natural order starts on a new footing, determinedly rebuilding what is broken. The population of humanity, now half its previous size, re-evaluates its habits and with resilience, some move forward on a new foundation. Abandoning the errors of their ways, these few recognize humanity as just one of a multitude of species that inhabit the world and begin to treat the inheritance with care and diffidence. Although well intentioned, these efforts contend with the opposing forces of greed and righteousness, the good and the bad meted out in equal measure. Regretfully, while these noble endeavors alleviate pressures on the environment, exploitation continues unabated. Still well in excess of the ideal carrying capacity of the planet of two billion inhabitants, humankind's invasive tendencies remain untamed. Like weeds, we choke the full expression of life from the ground, the waters and the skies.

Alas, a parallel continues. Two world wars of the twentieth century failed to end wars and squalor persisted after the pestilence of the plague years despite halving the affected population. Here now, true to form, people with power, people who seldom give up what they hold dear unless forced, and those set in their ways, even erroneous ones, remain bent on persisting in their course. Polluters continue to pollute for short-term profit, despite full knowledge of the consequences, trusting that the obligation to clean up will fall to others. A consolation is that nature, now contending with a lower global human population, and aided by those that strive to redress past errors, doggedly struggles on a path to restoration.

Under commands from home, robots on Titan and other moons resume where they left off, revisiting the once great promise of exploiting the riches of space. Woken from sleep, they take up their directive and search for lifeforms before starting their industry. Robots on asteroids once towed to orbit Earth, now aroused from dormancy under new instructions, mine for minerals with the hope of reducing the exploitative practices on the ground. Even Faust and his anti-science activists and climate change skeptics cannot stop the new momentum.

Mars is less fortunate in circumstance. Frigid temperatures discourage all but the most determined from making this their home. It will never be more than an outpost of humanity, barren as it stands lifeless, water only available by dint of onerous labor. Nevertheless, a new realization dawns: this world is an unparalleled treasure-trove of minerals, and it stands ready to deliver. It can be a powerhouse of industry to supply the needs of other planets, with no lifeform to safeguard, no environmental considerations to block its progress, no seas to restrict movement or limit access to the riches.

* * *

While a semblance of order takes form on Mars and Earth, asteroids restlessly shift in the asteroid belt as Mars in its new proximity disturbs their sleep. Stray as they randomly will along the ecliptic plane, ever a threat, they are now a menace, like a disturbed hornet's nest, a wasp seeking where to administer the sting. Mars, the most vulnerable, is nearest on the orbital disk of the solar system. Earth and Venus are next, while Hermes floats at a right angle to the plane, and intersects briefly twice in its revolution, and is therefore least at risk.

* * *

Anuar scans the skies, as is his routine, his investment in the telescope a boon to the unfolding plan. He remains tight-lipped on his purpose as his bunker takes shape deep in the mountainside where his subordinates work unceasing, day and night, shift after shift towards the conclusion. He sneers at the regeneration that is evident in the world at large, certain that the disaster brewing from afar will bring all to naught under a fireball. A repetition of the end of time for so much where only fossils marks their dominance, relics of denizens of a bygone era; Tunguska, similar but a minor foretaste of what is to come.

His loan of the *Destiny* spacecraft to the people of Hermes is of little consequence under the circumstances. More and better craft, requisitioned from those indebted to him and worked on at this very moment, will serve his new plan. Money is not the object.

Casual in his disregard for responsibilities and lost causes, the sociopath smiles at the concerns raised when he abandoned the spacecraft *Destiny* to its own devices in their approach to the Earth.

"Besides," he muses aloud, "that girl, what is her name? She was onboard. A pity the ESA came to the rescue."

"My interest in Hermes is not spent. The creatures the planet harbors present a challenge; one that is entirely surmountable. I will occupy that planet if my strategy here on Earth fails."

Once superficial imagining now take form.

"In fact, it may even be the centerpiece of my plan. Why not?"

"First, I need to complete my simple test. These creatures brought from Hermes and now infesting our world, providence has conveniently placed them on my doorstep. No need to confront them on their home territory – we can do it right here. If I am to dominate

Hermes, I will have to neutralize their magic tricks. I too have a means to an end. It is merely a question of which poison to use. My first attempts failed, but succeed I will; trial and error!"

"Besides, if all fails, Mars is ripe for extortion. So many choices! Ha, ha, ha!"

* * *

Using their planet-wide telescopic aperture, with all objects in the realm under constant view, the Betilla note the passage of Mars and its effect on the asteroids and the movements tracked. Earth-based computational forecasts constantly predict their paths mapped decades into the future. The sheer volume limits the analysis, but those that present a threat receive close attention. Strategies to nudge the threats out of harm's way, the forces needed, reaction time and time-lapse models provide options hitherto not feasible. Potentials become apparent. Asteroids previously locked in the zone of the belt stray close to Earth and Mars, presenting chances to tether them to the gravitational forces of the planets, providing a prospect for mining. Earth and Hermes collaborate to catalog the opportunities, prepare plans for exploitation of promising prospects, fend off those that can be feasibly nudged out of harm's way and prepare for the perilous. To avoid hysteria, distressing news is restricted to certainties; threats veiled in secrecy until confirmed, tactics matured, dates determined, decisions solidified and plans formulated to avert dire consequences and maximize favorable outcomes. Then in suspense, they wait and watch as predictions unfold. When the time is ripe, they will release actions, launch safeguarding missions to intercept, divert or destroy threats, but still they wait to confirm the perils, always measuring required response times and steeling the populace with reassurances that quieten panic.

* * *

Meanwhile Mars, the god of war, tires of its warlike stance, and beckons. The asteroid Eros responds as a mistress to the embrace of love and desire. Loosed from the clutch of the belt, she circles her smitten prey, ever closer, circle after circle, irrevocably closer to fulfill his longings. Deimos, the distant moon, borne of dread, locked in Mars' hostile spell, feels heightened terror at the approaching lover. Phobos, the moon closer to the heart of the warrior, in fear for millennia, escalates dread to panic but cannot lose its chains from Mars. Helpless, it awaits its fate.

Red alert rings out from Hermes and Earth to forewarn Mars of the approaching ruin. They brace for impact. Mere days separate them from doom unless they can vacate the southeast quartile, which predictions point to as the zone likely to be worst affected.

The news, carefully crafted, no longer held in secret, is out. Earth can expect to be next. Reassurances are repeated: time is on its side and plans are afoot. These secure some measure of calm, but yet glued to their sets, they watch the unfolding drama.

Eros tumbles headlong in its rush to satisfy its lover's desires, the arrow poised in her bow dipped in the poison of ardor and ready to administer its potion. Mars waits, arms outstretched, gravity reaching to forge a lasting embrace. The hour draws near. She enters the breath of his atmosphere. Searing white heat envelopes her as she plunges into his depth. Striking at a shallow angle she tears at his mantle and rips open a lesion where the arrow lodges. It is critical but not fatal. She leaves the article of faith, a promise of a future clandestine rendezvous. They part ways as quarreling lovers do. She flees, leaving a glancing wound.

A shudder ripples through the crust. Olympus Mons on the far side rumbles in response, a side of the mountain torn down as the dormant volcano wakes to the provocation. The tectonic crack of Valles Marineris widens and water flows again briefly into the basin of Chryse Planitia before the heat dissipates, leaving a frozen expanse. Dust envelopes the planet in murky darkness for two

Martian years and ejecta escapes, disrupting the regolith of Phobos to form a ring of red around Mars, the knot of fear and panic dissipated into a thousand lesser concerns.

The people, shaken but not injured, need to rebuild or repair homes and industries. Not all is lost, but hardship will deepen under the obscure sun as temperatures drop, heralding a winter of discontent for the inhabitants.

* * *

Anuar wakes from his delusion, the mirage of his secret shattered by the extent of the preparations evident in the communiqués that preceded the events. He was not alone in his observations. Nevertheless, the awakening serves to galvanize his intent. Secure in his belief that disaster will befall the Earth, he expedites the completion of his bunker, assembles an army of spacefarers and prepares a fleet to launch in the direction of Hermes when the time is ripe. He will keep an eye on the recovery of Mars. In its weakened state, timing is everything. Two years under the cloud fits well with arrival plans if this is to be the course of his action.

23

DISILLUSIONMENT

Doctor Levisohn, the intern who arrived with Julia's cohort, approaches Jabu as chairperson for the Management Committee. "Say Jabu, I have something curious for you and your management team. It is about the reproductive health of our settlers."

"Sounds serious, should I be worried?"

"No, but I think they should know about it."

"Okay, we are due to meet next week. I will add it to the agenda. Two thirty, Wednesday. See you there."

At the meeting, Dr. Levisohn speaks. "You may have noticed that there are relatively few children in the village. You may wonder why this is the case. For a young population of adults this is quite unusual. Well, it is not for a lack of trying. But rates of conception are much lower than normal. I have been trying to find an explanation but keep coming up blank. Everyone's in good health – in fact exceptionally so. At first, I assumed it was due to a prolonged hydroponic diet, but we have addressed this with our farming practices. Hormonal conditions are normal, surgical solutions are contra-indicated and IVF will not work, which leaves me without a solution. The odd thing is that tests show them to be fertile and yet, recently, no adults over the age of twenty-eight have conceived, and I suspect that both males and females are afflicted. In other words, it is not due to partner incompatibilities. I thought I should bring this up because I am at a loss to explain it."

Jabu responds, "When we were on Earth, I recall reading about a global decline in fertility, something like fifty percent. Is this an extension of that?"

"It is true that there has been a decline and in the order of magnitude that you mention. However, fertility is the problem there, but I don't think that's the case here. The effect here is also far worse, and the strange thing is the age limitation."

"Have you compared this with trends on Earth?"

"Yes I have, and they too report a continuing trend of infertility. On Earth, there are many reasons for the decline – poor diet, exercise, stress and pollution – but here on Hermes we have none of that. This is why I conclude that this is not a fertility issue. As I say, our people are all very healthy. Good health was one of the selection criteria for coming here, and conditions are almost ideal to support wellbeing. It is for this reason that I feel we need to try to single out a new and different cause. My colleagues on Earth are looking into my contention and will get back to me."

"When will you hear from them?"

"In a month or two. That brings me to my second observation. People here are in better shape than when I first arrived, which seems to contradict their inability to conceive."

"What do you mean, better shape?"

"It is a little subjective. I only see patients if they have a problem. There has been a gradual decrease in the numbers of people coming to me, and those that I see for reasons of injury are in glowing health. It is my opinion that they are better than they were, in fact noticeably so. They report feeling youthful, vigorous – better than they ever have."

Robin interjects, "Now that you say that, I personally feel a general improvement in my condition. 'Youthful vigor,' that about sums it up; I get more things done than previously."

I add, "Yes, I can say the same. I think it is the climate and the active life we lead."

Jabu ends the discussion, "Dr. Levisohn, thank you for bringing this to our attention. I guess all you can do is to continue to monitor the situation and let us know if there is any change or if you find the cause or a solution. Thank you."

When we return to our residence Robin calls Julia over and explains Dr. Levisohn's claims. "What do you think? Could the Betilla be responsible?"

Julia lightheartedly says, "There you go again, ulterior motives. What possible reason could they have for doing this? They are not paranoid like some of us."

"Is it just possible that they have something in mind? It is just weird that this should happen now. There is also that sense of wellbeing. This is not conjecture. I can speak for myself: there is something going on here. Miles feels the same. Do you, Julia?"

"Okay I will admit to feeling great, but that could be for any number of reasons."

Lilian asks, "Do you think I should prepare an article on the subject? People will be interested, although I expect they won't take kindly to the news on lower reproduction."

Robin cautions, "I think we should wait for Dr. Levisohn to get back to us with what is happening on Earth and see whether the problem is happening there. After all, there are Betilla there, and if he comes up negative then we know it is isolated to Hermes. It narrows the problem. At that stage you will have something more concrete to report."

* * *

Two months pass and Dr. Levisohn has no news except that Earth is finding the investigation more complex than first thought; they need more time. A further three months pass before Dr. Levisohn is ready to update the Management Committee.

"The report I have here is from a number of experts in the field on Earth who collaborated on this. Broadly speaking, it corresponds to and elaborates on what I found. Superimposed on the known downward trend in fertility there is another factor at play. They put it down to a genetic abnormality. It is similar to the normal process of aging where there is an accumulation of damage to molecules, cells and tissue over a lifetime; ultimately, genes are also affected. In this case, a chromosome related to reproduction is malfunctioning. The oddity is that genes that you would expect to manifest in aging appear to have healed. It explains the observed infertility but also the improved wellbeing. If this continues, people will live longer but ironically, beyond a certain age, they will not be able to reproduce. A strange combination, wouldn't you say?"

Robin questions, "That is curious. Do they predict the age at which reproduction will stop and on the other side, how long people will live?"

"The observed age limit for reproduction seems to have settled at about twenty-eight, so the window for conception is from the usual early teens to twenty-eight, about twelve to fifteen years. The interesting thing is that, for women, with each child the effect of aging becomes more dominant, along with its healing at the expense of reproduction. Three children during the window is rare. For the longevity, they say it is not easy to determine; it is open to conjecture. The uncertainty is that it depends on whether the genetic healing process will continue. Assuming it does not continue, it will add one normal lifetime on to the person's current age. If the healing in fact continues, well, the sky is the limit; you may find people living to the age of 500. Other factors will begin to impact longevity."

"Do they say what is causing this?"

"No, they are scrambling for answers."

Jabu asks, "What can we do about it?"

Dr. Levisohn shrugs. "Nothing. Nothing from their end, and I am equally baffled."

Dr. Levisohn's update leaves the meeting with little to do but accept the news.

Back in our home, after a few calculations, Robin is quick to assert, "You know what this means? First world countries, where the birth rate is around 1.5, will see their rate drop slightly to 1.0 or 1.2, but initially the longevity will add to the population before it comes down. Third world countries where the rate is around 7.0 will find it dropping to around 1.5 and their population will immediately begin dropping; they will be worst affected. Overall I think the global population will stabilize at around two billion if the longevity reaches 500 years."

Dmitri says, "That is unthinkable. Social changes will have all sorts of effects. People will not just passively accept this. They will be blaming each other and industry; the polluters may take the brunt of it. There could even be riots. Who knows?"

Robin avers, "You are right, and singling out polluters is insightful. It implies that it is caused by an airborne agent which, for me, points to the Betilla with their bubbles. It cannot be a coincidence, them with all their genetic capabilities. It has to be them! They have the means; the only question is motive."

Julia, on the defensive, replies, "Robin, you are always so quick to attack the Betilla. Look at their record; at every turn, they have proven to be trustworthy, even supportive and helpful. Why would they suddenly go behind our backs and do this?"

"Julia, your problem is that you are besotted with them. You are normally so objective. You need to put your scientist's hat on and find an explanation before someone else does."

I say with some irritation, "Okay Robin, please tone it down. This is not personal."

Julia takes a deep breath and says, "Fine, let me talk to them. You will see; they have nothing to do with this."

Wasting no time, Julia and I relay Dr. Levisohn' findings to the Betilla and we wait for a response. A full minute passes before they answer, which does not bode well, and then the admission comes. Yes, they engineered this outcome.

Julia's anger is immediate. "What! How could you possibly do this? For what purpose?"

The response from the Betilla is surreal, listening to them speak across the connection with Julia's inflection and voice. I see that Julia has the presence of mind to record the session, as is her habit when speaking with them. She allows them to speak without interruption.

"Humans are a very successful species. Their body structure lends itself to a variety of functions; walk, run, climb and swim. Their sense of touch, hearing, sight, smell and taste, combined with their intellect and station on land, position them for toolmaking and use of fire to further their aims. They can cope with extremes of climate from equatorial to arctic conditions and consequently occupy every corner of the world. They have subjugated or eliminated all that stood in their way, leaving no natural enemies to oppose or deter them. A truly invasive and pervasive species. The outcome: they have proliferated well beyond the carrying capacity of the planet. To their own detriment, their vice-like grip over the world has subverted the balance of nature, reducing the quality of life for themselves and all living matter. Mass extinction and the rise of monoculture threatens to leave a monochrome world to its descendants; a legacy of only domesticated plants and animals. Some individuals in their midst are well-meaning, but as a group they are exploitative and callous in their disregard for the environment. With time, they have distanced themselves from normality such that they cannot distinguish normal from abnormal."

Alarmed at what we are hearing, they continue, "When we arrived on Earth to help with carbon sequestration, the stench of the excrement of the fossil fuel and chemical industries greeted us; an entire globe bathed in the nauseating fumes of industry. The inhabitants are blissfully unaware of the mess. Having acclimatize to the soiled atmosphere, they know no better. Their numbers have reached proportions where their proximity to each other will be their downfall. Bacteria and viruses, unseen, multiply and mutate continuously. They will inevitably find fertile ground in a virtually limitless supply of hosts at close quarters. A catastrophic collapse of the species will follow as the contagion spreads like wildfire."

"Our solution is to bring the numbers under control, not through death and destruction but through benign control of reproduction, while simultaneously offering longevity in the hope that this will foster wisdom through age.

"Betilla and humans in particular are obligated to bring balance. You have the means to destroy us, but we have the means to subvert such plans. In partnership, we can harness the potential of this solar system for the good of all creatures. This is our appeal to you."

Julia, distraught, responds, "You position yourselves as gods. You have no right to pronounce what is best for us. Suggestions, yes, but unilateral action is outright wrong. You must undo what you have done!"

"This is for the good of all life. Humans took the first step in the destructive cycle. Ours is merely to correct this injustice."

"You can expect riots and bloodshed; people will not take this lightly and your kind will not be immune to attack."

"We stand ready to defend ourselves, and the principle."

Julia relaxes a little. "I understand your motivation, but have to say that you have not gone about this in the correct manner. You needed to consult with us first."

The Betilla say, "Understood. We trust your judgment as a person and will consult with you in future, but in this instance the action taken will not be reversed."

With the connection closed, I can only console her because I can see there will be a lasting effect, "Julia, please don't take this personally. You are not responsible."

Her reply carries the full weight of the consequences. "Do you realize that you, me, our friends: we are all over twenty-eight, and the Betilla have defined our purpose for the next four or five centuries, and that is to mold Hermes to their will. They are in control."

With resignation, we hand the recording to the Management Committee who, through Lilian, release it to the residents and Earth. Predictably, the reaction ranges across the extremes of consequences. Environmentalists praise the action, sociologists draw up new population models, each with widely varying outcomes; they expect a complete upheaval in social structures, especially those over the age of sixty where the working life of individuals will profoundly change industry. Politicians flounder without direction under the competing views. Faust's followers swell, the Earth First demonstrators take to the streets; activists' attempts at destroying the Betilla sites come to naught, repelled by their disorientating pulses. The populace in general, numbed by the catastrophic effects of the recent climate extremes, can only wonder what malevolent forces range against them with this new threat to the populace. Dr. Vespucci raises the issue at a UN forum but the meeting ends in disarray. No single proposal is able to carry the required support for action; the matter flounders unresolved, the status quo persists and each country must fend for itself.

Julia sinks into a somber state. All my attempts to lift her out of the doldrums have little effect as she carries a burden of guilt at her part in bringing about the Betilla's actions. Her relationship with the Betilla, although strained by their differences, continues with the greening of Hermes. In time, she adopts a more pragmatic approach to them, maintaining a distance with an emotional barrier; she is more cautious of them, forgiving without forgetting.

Robin is very attentive to her needs as he rebuilds their fragile relationship while our group coalesces around our commonalities deepening our friendship.

Dmitri, somewhat subdued and introverted since the revelations by Dr. Levisohn, one day surprises us with his thoughts. "I have remained in touch with Noah and Ella on Mars. Ella's condition continues to deteriorate. It occurred to me that if she was here on Hermes, the Betilla's longevity effects could benefit her? I think it is damage to her genes that needs to be repaired."

Robin says, "You know, you may have something there. You should talk to Dr. Levisohn. See what he says."

"Good idea. I will do that."

Dmitri wastes no time and Dr. Levisohn confirms that there is a strong probability of it working and gets back to Robin.

"Robin, Dr. Levisohn more or less confirmed my thinking. When I last spoke to Noah he said that some of the Mars pioneers will be returning to Earth on the next return trip. About a hundred people. As the expert in our group on the orbits of the planets, when do you think Hermes and Mars will be in conjunction again? We should ask them to stop by Hermes on the way to Earth. Ella and the others with her condition could be dropped off here."

"Hmm. Let's see. You are looking at about 18 months."

No second invitation is needed. After checking with Ella and navigating the complexities of getting the authorities to coordinate the return trip around the conjunction, it is finally agreed. Ella is ecstatic. All six of them will be coming to Hermes.

* * *

While we work on the greening of our planet, Ella and her cohort circle the sun in a vast ellipse until the planets finally align with our plans. The orbital mechanics eventually signal an optimum time to depart from Mars and rendezvous with Hermes. Dmitri and Ella show mounting excitement at the prospect of speaking in person with each other rather than contending with the long delays between their exchanges.

The landing of the newcomers off the coast of New Greenwich is uneventful but Ella and Dmitri instantly establish a camaraderie that is a joy to behold.

Julia's disillusionment with the duplicity of the Betilla finds some relief when weeks later Dr. Levisohn confirms the beneficial effects on Ella and her fellow travelers. They are clear of the deleterious consequences of radiation. Although the conditions is rare others on Mars and even on Earth derive hope from the news.

24

TERRAFORM

Hermes increasingly resembles Earth. Grasses, ferns, shrubs and trees cover plains, ravines and slopes; insects that fly and crawl ply their trade, giving and taking, as is their wont. Small mammals, reptiles, amphibians, fish and crab of every sort; omnivorous, carnivorous and vegetarian find their niche. The silence, once so pervasive, is now broken by the rustle of leaves, the chirp, buzz, squeak and croak of creatures, but the skies remain silent, birds the missing element. Julia finds solace in immersing herself in the fieldwork as the terraforming prepares to apply the final brushstroke to the canvas. Thickets of brush, plains of savannah, stands of trees and plants of the aqueous world, the whole biome, expectantly waits for fulfillment.

The incubation of the hawk, the blue waxbill finch and loerie, the first for release into the new world, seemingly know the novelty of the occasion. The fledglings preen and groom each other, like actors about to step onto the stage, and excitement mounts as the audience fidgets in anticipation.

I am cast back to the drama that unfolded in the valley of my youth, reviving emotions that engulfed us as the hawk swept down from the cliff-face, the struggle of the field mouse, the startled finches and the call of the scarlet-feathered loerie echoing across the gorge while the stream continued its unperturbed murmur. We relive the scene here on this distant planet. Around us, West Riven stretches into the distance and to the right, the mountains of the east rise from the Rent. Our selected site for the first release lies north of New Greenwich, in its subtropical character it resembles the ravine from which we drew our immigrants. A cliff rises from the water's edge, not sandstone but of a similar formation, with a ledge two-thirds up the face. Knots of vegetation line the banks of the river; grasses, reeds and brush, selected in resemblance of home.

With us watching from a distance, the blue finches are first in line, unaware of freedom beckoning. Still nervous after transportation to this location, they huddle in corners of the cage, then seeing the opening they cautiously approach, suspicious of a false promise. As a group, with confidence rising they make their way along the launching platform and, seeing no barrier to restrict their exit, first one then all rise to embrace their liberty, heading for a nearby thorn tree. The months that separate the taking of the feathers dislodged during the panic to escape the clutches of the hawk and the release at this time are like naught. The birds immediately begin foraging for insects and seeds, oblivious of this being in a foreign world, fully at home in this new environment.

Next are the scarlet winged birds, who require considerable coaxing to exit the cage. However, once out they delay no further, requiring no second invitation to make for the seclusion of a thicket, where they remain secure in their shyness. We wait and watch until finally they breach the gap to the next brush, flashing the exotic colors to the rise and fall of their call.

Finally the hawk. As I approach the cage to open the door, I note their broad shoulders, sleek wings swept back to the forked tail. Their feathers glisten with health and their talons stand menacingly ready to grasp a victim. With head held erect and beak poised to strike, they are a formidable pair. The intensity of their eyes – the lens a deep black surrounded by perfectly circular irises colored in iridescent shades of ochre and green – give a penetrating glance that speaks of intelligence behind the veil of our differences. My mind casts back to my imaginings of taking flight as a hawk and returning with the experience locked in my subconscious. How strange it is to exchange a silent dialog now, in this place, as we regard each other at close quarters.

Proud in their disdain for their having been caged, the pair strut to the opening. With a steady stare in our direction, a condescending acknowledgment of thanks for the gift of a whole world, as if a right of inheritance, they elegantly rise to accept their freedom, circling, taunting us as they distance themselves from captivity, never to be constrained again.

* * *

There is a freshness in the air as we circle the gathering of humans below. The prison they held us in stands next to the contrivance that transported us to this location. They follow our flight as we ascend; the elation long withheld rises with us, expelling all animosity at the caging for, without understanding, we sense that goodwill pervades their actions. Ever higher, until the lay of the land unfolds in all directions. In one direction, grasslands extend to the horizon over undulating hills, and in the other, an escarpment rises to great heights with snow holding fast at the top of the pinnacle. Cliffs line the edge of a ribbon of lakes linked by streams and cascading falls. The sky, a brilliant blue, with a scattering of clouds deepening to a cumulus bank on the far edge of the hills, presents a picturesque mien as the sun warms the face of the cliffs to a glow of colors marking the striations on the rock formations. There, a short distance from the top, a ledge juts out below an overhang, forming a sheltered space leading into a shallow enclave. My partner and I both see the opportunity at the same time. Retracting our wings to guide our flight thence and reduce buoyance, we drop to the same elevation as the ledge. In flight, we inspect it from a distance, then gently alight on the edge for a closer examination. It is clean, unused and perfect for our purpose; already I feel the urge to collect material to build a nest. Below us, the humans continue to observe us; animatedly they gesticulate to each other, the one hugging the other in a lasting embrace, glee apparent on their faces in clear correspondence to our discovery of the ledge. An unconscious memory stirs as my partner and I look at each other. We and generations to come who inhabit this ledge will bear the names Kite and Aerie.

As the sun sinks below the horizon, sheets of lightning light up the dark underbelly of the distant clouds and a finely veiled rainbow signals the coming of an evening shower to crown our first day in liberty.

* * *

We stash the cage in the vehicle and set up camp for the night. This has been a special day, but only the first of many repetitions in the coming months of bringing life to the skies of Hermes. Seagulls, terns, finches, swallows, frets, sparrows and an assortment of every kind, they spread to all corners of globe. Julia's vision for terraforming this planet is reaching for an end.

25

DARK CLOUDS

The rainbow obscures the ominous clouds. Light and dark, counterpoints like good and evil, chance and design, relentlessly alternating between progress and destruction. What malevolent force conspired to subject us to this? In the end, which will prevail?

While we sow the seeds of progress across Hermes, storm clouds brew to reverse the course; we sense a mounting presence coming to bear, invisible, intangible yet as concrete as its opposite. Now, tomorrow, next week, next year – when? It casts a shadow of unease.

News carries the harbinger of ill, at first innocuous: a report that Betilla along the east coast of Russia are found to be dying, the cause not certain, as investigations continue. Two days later, the analysis reveals traces of pyrethrum present in the waters, indicating probable deliberate poisoning. The entire population in this particular inlet are dead while other localities of Betilla are entirely unaffected.

Under mounting pressure from the public, the launching of an extensive investigation to find the culprits is to no avail. The offender remains at large.

* * *

Anuar is pleased with his efforts. After successive failed attempts, he finally came up trumps with the use of pyrethrum, toxic and rapidly biodegradable. It was not difficult to find a suitable agent to administer after the initial trials. A search revealed a compound extracted from the chrysanthemum flower, which has a natural defense mechanism to protect against insects and pest animals. With glee, he saw that it affects an insect's nervous system through a deadly toxic effect. The insect dies from a form of paralysis almost immediately upon contact. He found that it kills a wide range of insect pests including ants, mosquitoes, moths, flies and fleas and breaks down rapidly, so it does not persist in the environment. Ideal for his nefarious purpose.

Comfortable in his obscurity, the care taken to hide his tracks was worth it; the passion of the public's response was greater than anticipated. Why would they care so much? Unfathomable. As to the disabling capabilities of the Betilla, those too are now under control. It was not difficult to develop a neutralizing mechanism given the detail in the published accounts and the postulated causes. Sometimes a weapon proves to be a countermeasure, turns defense to offense.

The next stage can now proceed.

The ruin brought to Mars, the lengthy recovery process and the likelihood of a recurrence has crystalized Anuar's decision. Earth will surely follow under the nemesis loosed from the asteroid belt. Strike will follow strike, recovery when partially restored, leveled, what use is there in perseverance when greener pastures beckon? Hermes stands insulated from the chaos as it circles the sun in a safe orbit. Perpendicular to the plane of the other planets, this will be his target. His army, small but entirely adequate, stands ready for launch, waiting for his signal.

Not all forces array against the advancement of noble causes. Finely balanced, the principled versus the unscrupulous, ready to tilt this way or that. The diligent hope to steer outcomes, the rash cast their lot to the roulette of chance. Either way, the stakes are high, the prize tantalizing and failure unthinkable, but the dice falls where it will.

News of the poisoning reaches us as our endeavors on Hermes are apparent to see, a planet lush with life. Pride at our accomplishments is somewhat dashed by this wanton act brought on the cousins of our partners. At our distance, we are helpless to intervene. The Betilla are inconsolable in their distress as we reiterate the nature of individuals of our species acting on their own impulses, independent of the body of decency. Incredulous, they listen, struggling to understand the purpose behind the act and at the potential for a recurrence. At their request, we provide them with details of the chemical composition of the poison, but caution that an antidote is useless unless administered directly after the poisoning, and that the toxic effects are immediate.

Days later, the Betilla request samples of chrysanthemum plants. Somehow, they determined pyrethrum to be an extract of this plant. We dutifully provide from the gardens of New Greenwich wondering what their intent is. As calm returns, the subject recedes into the past, not being mentioned further.

* * *

Time moves forward inexorably, the horizon of events lying in a cone of the future, radiating outward from one incident to the next, each a consequence of the former and materializing with the passage of time. As Mars escapes obliteration the cohort accompanying Eros, lesser in size but still a menace, pass silently to their next target. Too numerous for deflection, Earth can only brace for impact. Forewarned is forearmed; they calculate, predict and prepare. No less than seven objects, each with destructive power equivalent to nuclear assaults, stream headlong in close proximity to each other, fragments of a once cohesive object from the asteroid belt.

Faust is a hollow representation of his earlier self without the opium of his follower's adoration, the oxygen of his cause sucked out with Earth seemingly recovering from climate calamities. Having resorted to other prescriptions to sustain his sensibilities, bloated and incoherent, he stands before them preaching hell fire, doom and destruction, throwing scorn on attempts at averting the coming ruin from the sky. His adoring followers return in droves to listen spellbound to his proclamations of heaven's revenge. Some, though, turn away from the shell of his former self. Perplexed and leaderless, they seek other prophets.

Under the disguise of chaos, Anuar watches and waits. At the peak of panic, with attention directed elsewhere, he launches his fleet with him ensconced in *Satyros*, the lead spacecraft. Camouflaged by the noise of events, he speeds on his way armed with a trove of poison and projectiles.

The fragments rain down on Earth, following the rotation of the planet, disbursing the stream from east to west along a line from Australia, across the Indian Ocean, toward southern Africa and on to the South Atlantic Ocean. Australia absorbs the first and smallest of the objects in a central region with no loss of life. Three fall in the Indian Ocean and the rest in the Atlantic. Africa, spared a direct hit, suffers destruction by the resultant tsunamis along both the east and west coastlines as inhabitants watch from higher ground to see their properties swamped and houses swept away. Rebuilding will take time, but life and limb are safe.

We watch events from Hermes. The direct line of site of the Betilla' high-resolution telescopic vision records the fiery entry of the asteroids, the dust cloud over Australia and the radiating waves from each impact point. As the sites rotate out of sight, newscasts are unanimous in expressing relief at the fortuitous location of the strikes and the benefit of the early warnings that enabled people to escape the waves by moving to higher ground ahead of time.

The following day reveals the scene: vegetation swept away up to a kilometer inland depending on the elevation. The coastline of Mauritius and the northern reaches of Namibia are affected. In all likelihood, with the Betilla sites denuded, our little comrades are probably lost to the destruction. On closer inspection, many of the coral structures sustained surface damage with the deeper sections still intact where the majority of the Betilla took refuge. The loss is estimated at twenty percent along coastal Namibia and ten percent of the Mauritius shoreline population. The Betilla on Hermes feel their loss as we would the severing of a limb, the phantom pain and the need for a process analogous to rewiring lost signals, connecting missing clonal parts. A cloud hangs over their behavior, and we note their subdued reactions and withdrawal from conversation; it takes a while to restore normality. Julia restores her relationship with the Betilla. She surmounts the barriers of species differences and their unilateral actions affecting longevity and reproduction, reaching down to a common level of emotions, consoling them through empathy and deepening the bond established over the years. She shares their sufferings with us and other settlers who gather at a local Betilla site to sing songs expressing compassion and identify with their feelings. The community on Hermes, human and Betilla, are as one, forged in times of good and bad, galvanized against future misfortunes.

One event does not dispel a recurrence, ever alert to a repetition; our attention remains focused on Earth. Despite the casualties being still so fresh, we continue to monitor approaching hazards. A lesser grouping of asteroids is en route, requiring detailed observations to predict impact locations and formulate safeguarding measures. The analysis reveals that the majority will burn up in the atmosphere with only two reaching ground level, the Pacific Ocean being the theater of this event. Tsunami concerns relayed to Pacific Rim nations allow coastal areas to prepare. With three days to go, monitoring continues to confirm the locations. If correct, the anticipated effect will be minimal.

As the day draws near, from our vantage point we see an unexpected object crossing the line of sight. Zooming in reveals a fleet of three craft heading away from Earth, in the direction of Hermes.

26

POLES

Stanley stretches to relieve tension and reluctantly pushes aside his bedding, opens the curtains to a dismal day. A fog obscures his view of the inlet. He mutters to himself, "Just how I feel; all fogged up. Another day of board meetings. Curse them, I should resign! Constant demands, explanations, explanations, explanations; like I am supposed to know everything."

Reaching for the phone he dials his office. No reply, just weird noises. Bleary eyed he dresses, eats and robotically drives his usual route to the office, cursing the traffic congestion. Entering the foyer the receptionists stops him and says, "You haven't heard? The magnetic poles have flipped."

It takes a while for him to register what she has said. Then, like a punch to the gut, he recalls the warning of the polar excursions.

The receptionist interrupts, a distant voice barely audible above his thoughts. "All the phones are down."

He makes for his office and once there mumbles sarcastically, "Board meeting. Guess what? 'Hey Stanley! What do we do now? Oh! Don't worry, Stanley has all the answers?' " He slumps into his chair, thankful that no one can call him.

It must be the final straw, surely. How much can a society endure and remain sane? The asteroid impacts coming so soon after the devastation of the climate effects, the silver lining of recovery that held a promise of a new beginning only to be tarnished by the constraint on reproduction. How much can they tolerate? Their endurance now faces a new assault.

Despite all the warnings, few are prepared. The military, and some for whom communications are mission critical, but the majority are ill prepared; trains grind to a halt, ships stand moribund and planes grounded as contingency plans are activated. Haltingly, some services resume thanks to decades of preparation, averting the worst, but many aspects of the communication infrastructure lie in tatters. People long dependent on social media for interaction wander the streets like waifs waiting for a resumption of their rituals as Earth struggles under yet another legacy of the arrival of Hermes. Links with Hermes, already fraught with difficulties, now suffer compounding difficulties.

Stanley, as the last act as coordinator for the sponsors, dispatches a message via the military.

"Hermes: This message is a transcription of the decision by the board. The mining initiative that this venture started out as is no longer viable. We have provisioned a basis for the settlers to be fully self-supporting. Given the state of Earth following the catastrophes that have befallen it, regretfully our continuing role will be limited to providing support as circumstances allow. Local recovery efforts here on Earth, by nature, take precedence. When combined with communication difficulties affecting interplanetary missions, only minimal support can be counted on. When circumstances return to normal we will resume a relationship with Hermes for mutual benefit. Thank you."

* * *

On receipt of Stanley's communiqué Graham springs into action; just what he has been waiting for. He convenes a Management Committee meeting in a concerted bid to advocate for his dream of independence from Earth. Somewhat reluctantly, the group agrees and on polling the residents, they too favor this course of action. Graham formulates principles to guide independence, which after multiple rounds of discussion and with concurrence of the settlers and the Betilla stands for reference. Simple in its outline, it strives to avoid Earth's mistakes and allows for progressive advancement under these parameters:

The planet will be a single borderless self-governing state with no political enclaves.

Only renewable resources may be used, which rules out mining unless the output can be recycled back to its natural state. Off-planet production facilities, on lifeless artifacts such as asteroids, comets and planets and imported to meet Hermes' needs, will substitute for provisioning by industry that is environmentally harmful to the planet.

The human population will be limited to a target of three million individuals. Immigration will encourage diversity but constrained to 1000 individuals per year until the population reaches the three million mark.

An eight-body leaderless Management Committee, with Betilla occupying one seat, elected every four Hermes years, will serve the planet. Humans and Betilla as separate constituents of the committee may veto decisions with consensus the implied requirement. Their mandate is the coordination of activities and conducting decision-making using referenda for contentious issues.

Three members, with Betilla being one of them, will make up a judicial panel to address breaches of behavioral norms, with full integration back into society being the preferred outcome.

This charter applies to the planet and surrounding space to the extent of LaGrange Point #1 in the Hermes / Sun system; a jurisdiction reserved exclusively for peaceful purposes.

Using the guidelines, a snap referendum confirms the charter but to solidify Graham's drive for independence, Earth needs to sign off as well. To that end we decide to again enlist the help of Dr. Vespucci to shepherd the charter through the United Nations bureaucracy. That proves to be more difficult than anticipated; the simple act of transmitting the guidelines to them itself takes a month because of the communication difficulties before Dr. Vespucci confirms receipt. He refers us to the Treaty on Activities of States on the Moon and other Celestial Bodies, indicating that this should apply and therefore our charter cannot stand. We counter that because of the presence of the Betilla, an intelligent species with aboriginal rights, the treaty is not applicable. We emphasize that the charter fully represents the Betilla's input and that they have the ability to enforce its dictates. After further back-and-forth which takes another six months, finally, Graham's dream of independence from Earth, his sole driving force, comes to fruition. Hermes has sovereign status.

At a gathering of the settlers, he proudly proclaims Hermes' first calendar entry, Hermes Day, and joyous celebrations mark the holiday.

27

UPHEAVAL

Uncomfortable in the constrained space, bored at the interminability of the flight in the *Satyros*, the novelty of low gravity long worn off, Anuar takes his frustration out on his personal attendant with short-tempered requests for video entertainment better than the inane subject matter he keeps plying him. Cursing at his lack of foresight for not bringing enough to alleviate the tedium, he is further plagued by the mounting sense of futility in this venture brought on by his declining condition without exercise, exertion being something he does not enjoy. He imagines arriving at his destination on a stretcher, unable to walk under the planet's gravity. How embarrassing will that be?

Obscured by events on the ground, back on Earth, the fleet has progressed further than anticipated without discovery.

He mutters to himself, "Not that it matters much. What can they do about it, anyway? Nothing."

Newscasts have begun speculating on their purpose, now four months into the flight. Radio requests to identify themselves go unanswered.

Why should I give any hint at my intent or who I am? Ha!

The final two months seem longer than the preceding four, but as the planet grows larger in their sights a degree of enthusiasm mounts. Each day he looks out expecting to see more detail but the changes are frustratingly imperceptible. The wait provides time to reconsider his strategy. His original intent was to eliminate the orbiting communication satellites and survey probes then land with guns blazing to take control, but given their deteriorating physical condition that may not be feasible. He knows the settlers will be unarmed since their intent was mining on Mars, nothing remotely like fending off an aggressor.

No, I will need time to adjust to the gravity, rebuild my team's strength and then go on the offensive. I can use the time to check the lay of the land, get accustomed to conditions and see what their strengths and weaknesses are. Besides, they do not have an inkling of my intent.

He instructs the crew on all three craft to remove the cannons and missiles and hide them onboard along with anything with a hostile intent, including the stock of poison and the devices for protection against electromagnetic pulses.

* * *

We track the approach of the three spacecraft, speculating as to what their intent may be. The first impression is of a military nature; they have a martial stance but are seemingly unarmed, reminiscent of the *Destiny* that we used to travel to the Earth and back. Two enter a low orbit while the third peels off to a higher level.

A radio message comes through; they are refugees from the recent devastation on Earth and request permission to land and receive asylum. There are thirty people onboard the three craft and they will abide by any regulations in force.

We cannot but associate them with the backer of the *Destiny* and their failure to provide navigational assistance to us in our approach to the Earth. There is also their dubious reputation as cautioned by the ESA.

With these thoughts in mind, we ask for details of their backer and what association they have to the *Destiny*.

Their response is that they are from the same organization and the backer, Anuar is onboard.

With great trepidation, in a quandary, we vacillate between denying and allowing landing but finally conclude that we cannot turn them away and expect them to undertake the eight-month return trip to the Earth or press on to Mars. Furthermore, the assimilation of the *Destiny* crew into our population in part turned out to be a valuable addition. The hope is that these people will follow suit. Hesitantly, we agree to let them land but decide to be watchful and place them in multiple dwellings, dispersed across New Greenwich, a case of divide and conquer.

The two craft land without incident, hovering to settle on a flat area to the west of the village. The newcomers are not in good shape. They require assistance to exit their craft and support as we take them to their lodgings. En route, they wave at their colleagues from the *Destiny*; clearly some of them are acquainted. A cursory check of the two craft reveals nothing in the cargo to raise concern. We make every effort to welcome them, bringing fresh food and beverages on a daily basis to ensure their wellbeing. As the days pass, they begin moving about, chatting with people in a friendly way, curious about life on this planet as would be normal for anyone transplanted from one world to another. Our concerns begin to fade. Anuar proves to be perplexing: awkwardly affable, excessively amiable one minute and callously indifferent the next with shifting eyes, never making eye contact. When introduced to Julia, a flash of sheer hatred crosses his face, but he quickly regains control and effusively congratulates her on her accomplishments.

His explanation for the failure to provide navigational assistance to us in our approach to Earth is not very convincing. They suffered a three-day power failure at their control center but noted that ESA had the flight under control. On solving the electrical problems, they had no means to reach us because we had landed and proceeded elsewhere.

When asked why the third craft has not landed Anuar says they are repairing a technical problem with the guidance system needed to execute the landing. Nothing serious, but better to have it fixed rather than taking the risk of entry without it. He declines our offer of assistance and further discussions are vague on detail, our assumption being that he does not have the technical knowledge necessary to provide a full explanation of what is wrong.

A mounting intangible unease permeates New Greenwich as the days since their landing stretch on to four or five weeks. Anuar frequently visits the parked spacecraft with his fellow travelers surreptitiously joining him in relays. Our curiosity is aroused but there is nothing concrete enough to question the behavior. A rift seems to be growing between a contingent of the old *Destiny* crew and the new arrivals, while Kostya and his kind obsequiously attend to Anuar's wishes. Life on Hermes has taken a turn, the refreshing cheerfulness so evident before displaced by uncertainty and dispiritedness difficult to identify.

Without explanation, Anuar's team start constructing a transmitter-like device on top of the nearest spacecraft bearing the name *Satyros*. On a particular day, when the apparatus seems complete, it begins emitting a high frequency sound only just audible but sufficiently piercing to become an irritation after a while. They feel obligated to explain; it is part of their communication system with the orbiting craft, and once fully functional it will be used intermittently prior to and during the descent. The clarification is not entirely plausible, but to avoid an argument and since it is a temporary solution, we let matters rest at that.

The newly arrived show little sign of wanting to integrate with the rest of the community, remaining aloof despite being scattered across the village. Some take to walking along the beach in the evenings. They enquire after Betilla sites so they can witness the light-emitting bubbles. We happily oblige, hoping the interest will spark further conversation and, like all the other inhabitants, engender awe and respect for our friendly neighbors, but even this activity leads to no new camaraderie.

* * *

During the sixth week following their arrival, the Betilla report a change in the orbit of the third craft. Rather than dropping to an entry-level, they move higher. Monitoring reveals that the new orbit aligns with the survey probes and the communication satellite. The gap between one of the probes and the third craft narrows to only a few meters then the camera arm disintegrates. The probe loses its bearings and begins tumbling out of control, the flow of survey data ceases.

The event, so contrary to our expectations, takes us by complete surprise. We stand frozen, unable to react to the unfolding drama.

With mounting alarm, we watch as the craft approaches the second probe. It is not far off and the results are the same, it too is lost. The craft veers off to another orbit, its target clear: the communication satellite. The only link we have to Earth is in jeopardy. Will the same fate befall it? The craft nears the satellite but continues to draw nearer until the two are alongside each other. The high-resolution view shows a person exiting the craft, manipulating something on the satellite for about fifteen minutes and in the next instance – radio silence. The craft separates to a lower orbit, positioning for entry.

As if choreographed, events on the ground happen in quick succession, stunning in their audacity and leaving us helpless to react. Dressed in military gear, helmeted soldiers burst out of the two landed craft bearing arms and begin circling the compound. The high-pitched transmission starts up, pervading the entire village with its incessant low-level whine. A drone takes to the air from one of the two craft and heads over the village along the coast. Before the men can fully encircle the compound, Julia reacts. She grabs my arm and dashes out a back door, and obscured by some buildings we make our way in the direction of the drone, eluding the soldiers. Without uttering a word, and knowing her singular concern, we make for the nearest Betilla site. It is apparent that a deep-seated bond between her and the Betilla still exists, one that takes precedence over the gulf of mistrust when faced with the advent of harm.

As we disappear over a ridge, a bullhorn booms out: "This is a coup; remain in your houses and you will come to no harm. Anyone venturing out will be shot." Anuar's voice repeats the warning three times, then silence.

We stumble along the familiar path down to the sea edge, along the beach, keeping a safe distance from the drone in case they have cameras onboard. Before long we crest another rise and in the distance the drone drops to a few feet above the water as it approaches the first of the corals. All we can do is watch in horror as a fine mist sprays from the plane, like a crop-duster. It circles back and repeats the run then heads up the valley, no doubt to the moss field. We cannot follow; the distance too far and its speed too great, we sink back in the sand, distraught at what has happened.

The events all connect: the poisoning on Earth, the callous attitude of the immigrants, especially Anuar, and now this. Out of concern for the Betilla, Julia establishes a link to them on her cell phone. Their response is subdued, and no panic is evident as they calmly explain that we are not to worry, they have developed a vaccine against pyrethrum and so far, they are not experiencing any ill effects. In addition, they also have an antidote in case the vaccine is not effective. We explain that the drone is now en route to the moss fields. Will they be safe? The answer comes back more cautiously than before; the moss itself will be unharmed but the older of the juvenile Betilla may need more time to reach full immunity, it takes about a week to take effect. A supply of the antidote compound, sent in bubbles just a week ago, is available onsite if needed.

Relief is quickly replaced by anger at the wonton harmful intent of our kind. We update the Betilla on events, the coup and threat of physical harm threatened. We are at the mercy of these brutes. Unless we do something, life on Hermes will not be the same.

Before we can broach the subject of a possible solution, the Betilla indicate that their incapacitating abilities will be ineffectual because the occupiers have deployed a broad-spectrum electro-magnetic pulse jamming device rendering the capability useless. It will mean that the plotters cannot stray outside the umbrella of the village to a range with a radius of about a kilometer. If we can turn off the transmitter, the incapacitating pulse will work and they can restore control.

Our immediate problem is that, contrary to instructions, we are not in our house, and if seen risk being shot. We have three choices: re-enter with arms raised in surrender on the pretext of returning from a walk; remain outside the perimeter of the village, from where we can stage a plan to retake control; or simply disappear into the mountains, hoping that matters will resolve themselves with time. First things first, we need to get hold of Jabu, Robin, Dmitri and Lilian to tell them we are safe and update them on the status of the Betilla and the purpose of the transmitter noise pervading the village. We can then allow time to plan our next steps.

A call to our friends goes through without difficulty. How long will it take Anuar to turn off communications? He probably does not yet know that we are outside the village. Robin speaks first. Relief in his voice at learning that we are safe, he explains that the thugs are going house to house conducting a census of who is there. They will probably reach our dwelling in about half an hour, at which point they will realize that we are missing and raise the alarm. We quickly inform them of the attempted poisoning of the Betilla, the transmitter problem and that we are undecided on what to do next. To buy time we suggest that they say that we are on a three-day hike up the valley.

Before we can make further plans the link fails, we are alone.

* * *

Dmitri takes control, immediately scrambling to hide some of our possessions to give the impression that we are on a prolonged absence. He glances out of the window: they still have a few more minutes, time to agree on being as vague as possible about our absence to give the impression that we frequently disappear for lengthy periods. At a loss for what else to do or suggest, anxiety written on their faces, they wait for the intruders.

A beefy soldier barges into the dwelling, heading straight for the sleeping quarters demanding to know who sleeps where. It quickly becomes obvious that two individuals are absent. They take names and somewhat skeptically listen to the explanation of their where-abouts, wanting details of the possible direction taken. The man relays this information to Anuar who angrily instructs them to con-tinue their census; he will dispatch another team to the house for details and launch a search.

As the man exits, a message on his two-way radio system instructs him to hurry. "The third craft will be landing shortly. Stop what you are doing and proceed to the landing site to assist in unloading and installing the newcomers in their designated quarters."

An hour later the craft appears over the horizon and lands heavily under a cloud of dust alongside the village. The undercarriage appears damaged, standing tilted to one side. Ten soldiers spend the better part of the day stabilizing the vehicle, supporting the crew to their rooms and unloading the craft while the other ten patrol the streets or finish their census taking.

Jabu shakes his head and observes, "We just lost an opportunity. While they were distracted by the landing, we should have done something to regain control."

332

Dmitri rejoins, "Da, yes but they still have to acclimatize to the gravity. In a week, they will be at full strength, so we had better do something in that time. There are only twenty to deal with now; later there will be thirty. We have a week; if we lose this chance, it will be more difficult. Any ideas?"

The group is at a loss.

As evening sets, an announcement booms over the loudspeaker: "Everyone must convene in the hub at six o'clock – no exceptions allowed, no exceptions."

With only fifteen minutes to the stated time, assuming they will be laying down the law, the group have no choice but to prepare to go, abandoning ideas to counter the hostility until they have heard what the ground-rules will be. Shepherded into the room crowded to capacity with armed guards standing around the perimeter and at the doors, Anuar stands at the podium. He is brimming with confidence at his maneuver. Things have gone remarkably smoothly from his perspective, contrasting markedly with the gloomy despondency of the residents and the fidgety alertness of the guards. He wastes no time in getting down to business by reading from a list:

- A curfew will be in effect from dust to dawn every day, six pm to six am.
- The guard's instructions are to shoot anyone found outside during the curfew.
- Until further notice, everyone is restricted to the village area during the day.
- The landing craft are out of bounds.
- Adjustments to the communication satellite provide bi-directional backchannel contact with Earth for my personal use only. It is out of bounds to everyone else.
- In case you think rescue from your predicament is possible, forget it. Craft leaving Earth for Hermes or approaching Hermes will not survive the trip. I guarantee that.

As to the future:

- Mining operations will resume when conditions are right.
- Men will carry out these activities on an assigned quota basis.
- Women are there for the pleasure of the guards.
- Women will attend to crops in the fields and prepare food under strict oversight by the guards.
- Children are restricted to the crèche during the day, with two women in attendance.

He waves his list and posts it on the notice board, the message clear.

With an air of supreme control, he adds, "Two residents are missing; anyone withholding information on their whereabouts will suffer consequences."

With a curt thanks to everyone for attending, he exits without taking questions.

Downcast, the residents are marshaled back to the homes. The first curfew comes into effect; the Eden enjoyed stands corrupted.

* * *

Julia and I make for the east side of the Rent, up a rise to overlook the valley and in the distance, New Greenwich. The three newly arrived spacecraft and the one we used on our honeymoon to Earth, tower over the buildings in the village, juxtaposing the modern alongside the olde worlde homesteads. As the sun sets over our homes, the sky takes on a ruddy complexion. The now verdant green pastures surrounding the village and the deep blue ocean shimmering with touches of red belie the turmoil within. Mixed emotions swarm as the view brings to mind our travels from such innocent beginnings. The circumstance of intertwining lives, the intervention of a world from distant parts, our accomplishments laid out before us and now ripped aside. All these thoughts and, most intense, the strange little creatures and their illuminating intelligence with their sound moral compass and touching passions so similar to ours. Yet next to me is Julia. The bond tears at the breast, a pain of union at once profound as it confounds explanation, uplifts and plumbs the depth of internal senses. Bathed in the turbulence of inner conflicts, we watch as darkness creeps over the valley and stillness descends. We huddle for warmth, locked in an emotional embrace wondering what the morrow will bring.

* * *

Dmitri wakes from a fitful sleep. Darkness still draws its curtain, dawn a way off in these elongated days.

What to do? There must be a way. One person cannot hold sway over a whole community. We must strike before they consolidate their hold.

The only protection that the invaders have is the infernal jamming transmitter. Without it, the Betilla would come to our rescue and sabotage their plans. Our focus needs to be on disabling the device.

He looks out the window.

There it is, mounted on top of the nearest rocket with a rotating light that flashes as it circles every few seconds, taunting, daring someone to act.

A guard strolls down the road. Fingering a menacing looking weapon, he mechanically checks between the buildings as he proceeds, but all is quiet. Down the path, a second guard languorously fails to evince any enthusiasm for his duty, yawning at the slow passage of time. The scene is wracked by contradictions, the imposed control and implied threat of violence so alien to the ambience of the peaceful homesteads. Which will consume the other?

Determined to lance the cyst, to reverse injustices imposed, Dmitri weighs the alternatives.

Failure will wreak vengeance on many; deaths a certainty, yet the penalty of inaction is enduring suffering, hardship and subservience. The choices are stark.

As twilight dawns, an outline of a plan takes shape. Jabu and Robin stir from sleep. Contrasting to the brilliance of the rising sun, the bleakness of their circumstance dawns on them, clouding their countenance.

Dmitri animatedly begins, "Listen, we have to do something, and soon. One of the drones housed in an area that we have legitimate access to during the day; if we secret it to our quarters, we could launch it at the transmitter. It should damage it enough for the Betilla to incapacitate the guards before they can fix it."

Continuing, he breathlessly urges as his sentences run into each other, "To do so, we need the precise coordinates of the transmitter on *Satyros* to preprogram the drone to home in on the target. We must do this. To hide the flight path of the drone and the launch point, we would have to launch from outside the village."

In a whisper he goes on, "The return to the quarters would need to be under the cover of darkness and before they can figure out who is responsible. They will probably assume that Miles and Julia did it. From my observations during the night, the guards are not very vigilant, making it easy to remove the drone from the village to an overlooking hill. They would have to repeat a census of the whole village to figure out who is responsible. Also, the distraction of attending to the broadcasting device will allow time for us to return to the quarters unseen while they conduct the census."

Jabu inserts, "I think you a right. We need to do something and urgently. The main drawback to the plan is that if the venture is not successful, Miles and Julia will take the blame and if captured, execution cannot be ruled out."

Robin offers, "The only way around this is for them to remain as refugees until the whole matter is resolved. Depending on how events unfold, we should consider joining them at some point."

Lilian points out, "If we are to escape, an escape at night is quite feasible. Food is the problem though, both now and if we join them. We need to get food to them as soon as possible. They can't live by raiding the vegetable gardens, if that is what they are doing. The guards will probably realize this in the next few days anyway and secure the area."

Robin completes the circle of logic: "The entire plan is contingent on us contacting the Betilla and Miles to coordinate the exercise."

Dmitri's overriding concern is for our safety, driven by stories handed down to him by his father of life under a dictatorial regime and the hardships experienced. The hopelessness of the society and the legacy his country inherited, the intruders sow seeds of a similar discontent; he is adamant, they must not flourish. Anxiety and determination join to stimulate his plan. Conscripting the others, they amplify and expand the strengths, check and recheck to minimize risks and improve the probability of success, but alternatives explored inevitably return to Dmitri's plan. After a final round of ideas, they agree to proceed, but recognize that the execution needs to be flexible. They may have to adjust as circumstances dictate.

* * *

The starting point is to contact the Betilla. They agree that there are two methods; either use the cell phone link at the training laboratory or risk a trip to the field near their coral structures to communicate with them directly. The training laboratory, which has been under lock and key since the occupation, leaves the need for an excursion to the Betilla site to establish contact as the only option. Being restricted to the village effectively means risking a clandestine hike along the shore to the nearest site.

Before reaching a decision, a guard bangs at the door and barges in, summoning Jabu to accompany him to the office. He exits, leaving the group wondering what they want. An hour later, he returns. He is required to present mining options in the vicinity. Their intent is to examine nearby sites to formulate decisions on how to proceed with extraction of rare Earth minerals. Jabu explains that they have everyone's personal records, from which they established his geological engineering expertise. He has one day to provide the information and the trip will take place on the following day, two days hence.

The news provides opportunities. Jabu could say he needs access to the training laboratory on the pretext of looking up his mining records, or during the field trip, he could surreptitiously contact the Betilla if he leads them past one of their sites. Things are looking up.

Food for the fugitives is the next urgent item, but Dmitri is quick to point out, "We don't know where they are. If we knew their location, assuming they are at a distance from the camp, we could use a drone to deliver small quantities every other day. If they are nearby, we can provision them at night in person, but contact with the Betilla is key to this. They will be able to communicate with Julia. After we make contact, we can adjust the plan as needed."

Without further considerations, the plan moves forward.

With computer underarm and cell phone in his pocket, Jabu saunters over to the guard who escorted him to the office and requests access to the training laboratory. Inside the room, he plugs his computer into the network and pretends to access geological survey information. The guard waits a few minutes, decides that his activities are legitimate and exits. He wastes no time in locating the parameters for the Betilla communication address and establishes contact using text messaging. He submits a preloaded description of the plan to the Betilla and directs them to link Julia into the dialog. Patching her in will also provide their geographical location on a continuous basis. Relieved at the immediate acknowledgment from the Betilla and shortly later a confirmation from Julia, with Dmitri online, Jabu explains where he is and what the occupiers have in mind with regard to the mining excursion and his role in it.

Retaining the coordinates of the link for ongoing access, he returns to the residence, ending the first part of the plan with no difficulties.

Information from Julia and the Betilla comes through quickly. She is located about two kilometers from the sea, in the valley of the Rent, and they are in need of food. Their intent was to raid the vegetable gardens at night, but they are open to suggestions. The Betilla intervene, saying they can immobilize fish in the vicinity, in the same way as was done to the humans on Farland, so that they can catch and eat them. After some discussion, it is agreed; a supply of processed food and a means to make fire to cook the fish, left at the far edge of the vegetable garden, will suffice for the next three days, with replenishment by midnight every third day.

To take the offensive, it is best to wait for Jabu and the excursion group to leave for the mining site. This will mean fewer guards at the camp to contend with when Dmitri launches the drone at the transmitter. The Betilla will incapacitate the excursion group at their first overnight camp, while another group of Betilla will relocate to the waters near the village to immobilize the guards in the village after the transmitter is disabled. The Betilla will signal a start to the operations around midnight of the first night of the excursion. Everyone agrees.

Eager to complete preparations ahead of schedule, Dmitri dismantles a drone under the pretext of repairing a robot in need of attention. The workshop is on the seaward edge of the village with an open stretch separating it from the rest of the village. To move the parts making up the complete drone to the sleeping quarters will require three trips. To avoid looking suspicious, small packages of the disassembled craft must fit into a backpack for carrying across the open area.

The first two trips are uneventful but on the third trip, a guard with a slight limp steps nearer and stops him: "Hey mister, open your backpack, I need to see what you have there. You cannot wander around here like that. This is the third trip you have made to the workshop. What are you doing?"

With pulse racing, Dmitri nonchalantly opens the bag and the guard examines the contents. Uncertain what the items are but not wanting to appear to be ignorant, he pulls him over to a building. As they enter, Anuar walks in from a side corridor. Dmitri's anxiety rises another level as Anuar questions the guard, apparently assuming he is in cahoots with Dmitri on some counterrevolutionary activity.

The guard stumbles over his words so Dmitri offers an explanation, "I am preparing the mining survey equipment for the trip you have planned. I have the parts in my backpack to take them to my residence to set them up for Jabulani."

Dmitri continues, hoping to sound legitimate: "I was en route to our hut when the guard rightly stopped me to check on my activities."

Anuar asks, "What is your role here? Why can he not do this himself?"

Dmitri explains: "I have robotic interfacing and reconfiguration expertise. It is my responsibility to do this and I don't think Jabu can do it."

Anuar eyes him suspiciously then seems to accept the explanation: "Okay, since you have robot expertise, I want you to prepare a robot for the mining excursion. You know, to reduce the amount of walking required so that I can join the expedition and travel in the robot as a vehicle."

In a lighter mood, he says, "The long flight, I am still recovering from zero-G. Didn't think it would take this long to adjust. Anyhow, thankfully the gravity is not as bad as on Earth."

Casually slapping the guard on his helmet, he instructs him to keep up the good work and walks out of the room.

The guard, relieved at escaping a reprimand, lets Dmitri go. In parting, Dmitri asks whether he is enjoying the planet. He responds with a long list of grievances regarding his treatment at the hands of Anuar.

The guard rambles on: "We have very little leisure time. We are constantly at Anuar's disposal. Any missteps and he reduces our privileges."

Anxiously, he continues, "My family back on Earth are held hostage; I have to cooperate. Anuar, he has a whole cockroach nest of thugs who look after his interests; he pays them to terrorize my family if I step out of line. I have no way of improving my life or theirs. Any misdemeanors, even the smallest errors, he transmits a message to Earth through the backchannel link, and his cronies there, on Earth, they punish my family."

Suspecting a scenario such as this, Dmitri questions him on whether the other guards are similarly under Anuar's control. It turns out that at least a half of them are, and the balance, the inner circle, are thugs who enforce the controls; there is very little opportunity to extricate himself from the situation. Offering regret, they exchange names, his being Kirill. Dmitri returns to their residence, where on relaying his experience to the others, they agree that they must execute their plan with extreme care. The inner circle are clearly ruthless but there just may be an opportunity for revolt to bring freedom to the rest.

While Dmitri was out, the Betilla provided the precise coordinates of the jamming transmitter, which he enters into the navigation system of the reassembled drone. He charges the battery and finds a hiding place to store it to await moving to the fields under cover of darkness. Lilian has a stash of food packed and ready for placement in the fields as well.

* * *

In the distance, Julia and I hear the six o'clock curfew bell sounding and the village turns quiet, abandoned to the patrolling guards. From our elevated observation post, we watch as darkness envelopes the village. Drawn by our growling stomachs we decide to move closer to the settlement in preparation for collecting the ration of food. Despite our circumstances, the sounds of nocturnal creatures emerging to claim the night enthrall us as we lie in the tall grasses. A swarm of bats zigzags over our hillock, intent on reaching its source of food. The gentle breeze carries the sounds of frogs from the ravine behind us as they serenade their counterparts, strangely rhythmic, superimposed by the irregular hypnotic hoot of an owl from a nearby tree. Spellbound by nature's choir, we have little difficulty in remaining awake. We watch for movement in the orchard and vegetable fields illuminated by the spray of stars in the arc of the Milky Way projecting an ethereal glow as from a magician's wand. As midnight approaches, we see Dmitri fugitively moving from one obscuring shrub to another. All is clear; he is safe as he struggles under the weight of his burden. We move to meet him, hugging each other, overcome with emotions at seeing our dear friend.

After an exchange of news, we return to our promontory, the proposed launch site for the drone. Dmitri surveys the location and the view across the village to the transmitter on the towering rocket, which continues to flash its light every few seconds, and agrees to its suitability. We hide the partly disassembled drone under the undergrowth and prepare to part, agreeing to meet at this spot ahead of the midnight start time two nights hence. No alarms sound as Dmitri makes his way back to the residence.

Ravished, we consume half of the first day's ration of food and wander down to the seclusion of the valley to find a place to rest. Dmitri had the foresight to provide a lightweight canvas for a groundsheet and a tent-like cover. It has been a long day and exhaustion brings sleep in a matter of moments.

A clear day dawns. We feel the need for more sleep, but a warm breakfast soon revives us. It will be a long wait to the following evening with all manner of anxieties flooding in, in the absence of a role to play in the unfolding events. Via our link through to the Betilla, we hear that the mining excursion will go ahead as planned.

Jabu has submitted his mining survey report and met with his counterparts in Anuar's group. After some cajoling, Jabu reached agreement for the first stop, a cliff overlooking the Rent at a point where striations of various deposits may interest them. More importantly, the campsite is within range of the Betilla's incapacitating electronic pulse. Activation of the pulse will coincide with Dmitri launching the drone at the transmitter. The intended route to the campsite will pass the Betilla coral site at the foot of the Rent.

After another night out in the open, day breaks with news from Jabu that the excursion is about to move out of the village. We decide to return to the promontory, which provides a view of the village and the procession along the coast.

As we arrive at our lookout, the expedition winds its way along the edge of the sea, with a single robotic vehicle trundling along in its wake, the helmeted heads bobbing up and down out of step with one another. In approaching the coral site, the vehicle stops at the water's edge and a man wades into the water only to emerge to gesticulate to another person. This individual enters the water, circles a few times then raises his arms in surrender, unable to find what he was looking for. Frustration evident in the posture of the director, he removes his boots and splashes into the water with a determined step only to exit again. He angrily punches the soldier in his midriff and re-enters the vehicle, and the procession moves off in the direction of the Rent. Anuar has just discovered that his poison has had no effect on the Betilla. Amused at the scene, we find it difficult to suppress our laughter. We imagine him glowering, red faced, as they disappear around a bend in the course of the river.

As evening settles over the theater Jabu updates us over the channel in whispers, "Anuar is angry at discovering that the poison sprayed in the area has been ineffectual. It is alarming that he then gave strict instructions to his soldiers to keep their helmets on and activated at all times. It seems that the helmets provide supplementary jamming of the electromagnetic pulse in the event that they are out of range of the transmitter at the village. Since he is not wearing a helmet, I assume there is a portable jamming device inside his robotic vehicle. He, Anuar was probably operating on the assumption that the Betilla in this location died after the poisoning. It leaves him with only the helmets and his vehicle as defense against the Betilla."

After a quick discussion, Robin articulates everyone's agreement over the transmitter, "Okay then. Let's proceed with destroying the transmitter in the village. Even despite the general ineffectiveness of the incapacitating pulse, some guards may not be wearing their helmets. It is better to proceed rather than do nothing. At minimum, some will be affected."

With a significant portion of our strategy in tatters, we despondently wait for the midnight hour on our hillock. As before, we see Dmitri emerge from our residence, glance about and then, crouching, proceed slowly along a low hedge to the perimeter, through the orchard and on to the vegetable garden to join us at the top of the rise. We have an hour. The Betilla and Jabu confirm their readiness on the communication channel and Dmitri prepares the drone for launch. We use a lull in the activity to still our rumbling stomachs with some of the food our friend brought for us.

Taking in the restful state of the village, we watch the dim outline of the guards as they stroll back and forth along the central road, stopping to chat as they pass each other.

Dmitri recognizes one of the guards by the slight limp in his step. "That must be Kirill. I wonder what thoughts he is struggling with at this moment."

As the hour approaches, the drone stirs to life under remote controls as Dmitri tests it for acceleration and lift. Designed for silence, it noiselessly rises and turns in a tight circle. As the allotted hour draws near, the whirr of the propeller increases, the craft rises vertically for a few feet and orientates in the direction of the *Satyros*. Holding its position, he waits. The seconds tick by and moments later, the signal comes through from the Betilla. The time is midnight.

At his command, the drone accelerates to maximum velocity. It covers the distance to the target in mere seconds. Over the village, as deadly in its accuracy as a kamikaze pilot, its only intent is suicide and destruction of its target. On impact, the transmitter erupts in a flash of metal on metal; scrap disburses in a cascade of pieces. The circling light ceases its revolution, the incessant noise stills and for a moment, silence descends on the scene. Then chaos breaks loose.

* * *

Kirill stops in midstride. With a whirr of sound overhead, an object visible only by its obscuring of the background smudge of stars streaks across the sky. Startled, he instinctively ducks then - CRASH; illuminated by a collision at the far end of the street, he sees pieces scattering in all directions. Gathering his senses, his training takes effect and he rapidly moves to conceal himself between two buildings, weapon at the ready, anticipating a foe. His colleague does likewise further up the street. Then guards burst out of their quarters, some incongruously dressed in sleepwear with guns at the ready. They cast about for the disturbance, then realizing its location begin a cautious approach.

Kirill quickly sums up the situation: the settlers have launched an attack hoping to disable the jamming transmitter, not realizing that the Betilla have been poisoned and are therefore not able to incapacitate the guards. As the guards further down the street take up defensive positions, anticipating an attack, villagers peer through windows wandering what the commotion is. In the melee, Kirill realizes an opportunity; Anuar is away and his quarters are unguarded. Cloaked by the deep shadows of the eves of the building, he stealthily makes his way to the section of the village resident to some of the occupiers, passes his bungalow, glances in and sees one or two guards still asleep in their beds. He moves on down the passage to Anuar's room.

It is locked.

With the butt of his rifle and one measured blow to minimize the noise, he enters. The room, his office, leads into a separate room, his bedroom. On a table, two communication devices stand facing the seat; one, turned on and lights blinking, has a pair of headphones plugged in. The other is less sophisticated and stares blankly back at him. Without hesitation, he tests the weight of each, unplugs the live one, places them both in a nearby crate and exits the room.

At best, he can bear the weight for about fifteen minutes. He will have to either hide them temporarily to move them later or destroy them now or abandon them. Undecided, he backs into the office. Time is ticking, what to do? Vacillating between his options, then seeing no advantage in keeping them, he vent his pent-up frustration on them, reducing them to a jumble of wires, bent metal and shards of plastic and glass.

Outside, the fresh breeze brings rationality and certainty that his decision was correct. Moving unnoticed to the opposite side of the village, he relaxes and takes up a position appropriate for the circumstances. Then, hearing voices, he moves closer. The second in charge is speaking to Anuar on the radio, informing him of events. Even at this distance, the anger in his voice is obvious.

The conversation continues as Anuar informs the 2IC, Kostya: "The poison has been ineffectual. The beetles are not dead. Do you hear me? Not dead! Make sure the guards wear their helmets at all times – until after completing the repair or replacement of the jamming transmitter. I will break camp and be back at the village tomorrow." Cursing, he ends the communiqué.

28

CONFRONTATION

From our vantage on the hill, we watch as the transmitter disintegrates in a shower of sparks, followed by a brief pause before a rush of guards take up positions to protect themselves. Nothing further happens for a few moments, then, assuming all is safe, they move closer to the rocket, becoming more relaxed as the event recedes. Up the street, the silhouette of a fugitive figure limps across the street in the darkness looking about for movement. He sees another guard taking up a position down the road and moves to conceal himself in the deep shadow of a building. To better obscure his movements he slinks along the side of a passage, then, surprisingly, heads away from the commotion towards the guard's quarters and disappears inside the building.

Dmitri exclaims, "Kirill, what can he be doing? Look! Strange!"

Later he emerges with a crate, hesitates then re-enters the structure and shortly re-emerges without the crate to return to his post in the main walkway.

With no obvious explanation, Dmitri moves to go. "I had better get back before they check on us. See you later!"

Wasting no further time, with a quick goodbye he steals back to the residence unobserved. After a while, the guards return to their barracks. Suddenly all the lights in their part of the camp turn on and an angry exchange ensues as they vent their anger at one another.

Two prostrate figures on stretchers carried from the dormitory to the infirmary indicate some form of mishap. Moments later Kostya rounds up the guards and wildly gesticulates at the door to an apartment, the same door that Kirill entered earlier. Muffled sounds reach us as they argue with each other inside the building.

Gradually silence returns, but an almost tangible tension permeates the village. All are fearful of what the morning will bring.

We gather up our belongings and the fresh supply of food to move to better concealment where we contact the Betilla, Jabu and Dmitri by text message to provide an update from our perspective. We assume that the two guards taken to the infirmary are immobile due to incapacitation by the Betilla, probably for not wearing helmets while asleep. Jabu reports that the entire excursion team wore helmets and are unharmed. Our plans achieved a measure of success, but the vengeance that Anuar will exact on the village in response will surely be fierce.

* * *

A gray dawn heralds daylight as the residents spend a sullen day under an unarticulated cloud of suspicion waiting for Anuar's return. Even the guards fear the return of their boss. The intrusion into the chief's domain is inexplicable but blame seems to lie within their group. The underlings have motive, but the tie to the destruction of the jamming transmitter would require unlikely collusion.

Startling frayed nerves, the bullhorn blurts out, "Everyone, without exception, you are to attend a meeting at noon tomorrow in the hub. I repeat. No exceptions! Everyone must stay in your bungalows until then."

With mounting tension and an uncertain night, the time finally arrives. Anuar's group march into the village from their excursion with arms at the ready and head straight for the hub.

In the crowded space, filled with the acrid smell of perspiration brought on by fear, Anuar paces back and forth at the lectern, surrounded by his henchmen, his large frame exuding aggression.

Finally, he stands still at the podium, anger writ large across his face: "You dare to contravene my instructions! The curfew has been broken!"

The weight of his words carry undisguised hatred. "Blame for the destruction of the jamming transmitter on the spacecraft falls squarely on the two absent fugitives. Yes, but that is not all. One or more of you conspired with them. Someone in this village acquired the drone. Together with the fugitives, you launched the thing."

Leaning forward he pauses to let the import of his words resonate. "The person or people responsible will come forward before the curfew starts this evening. Failure to do so means that I will personally begin executing people on the hour, every hour, until the culprits come forward."

Without diminishing his threatening tone: "Whoever is responsible for or colluded to damage the contents of my office will likewise need to own up by curfew time, or someone will suffer the same penalty."

With a smirk, he adds, "The two other onsite spacecraft are fitted with a backchannel communication device to communicate with Earth and the transmitter will be repaired. The attack did not accomplish much."

Dull resignation hangs over the crowd as they wait for him to elaborate further, but he merely stands there glaring, in supreme command of the situation.

The silence stretches for what seems like an eternity. With each passing second, the crowd withers by degrees under his glare. None dares move. Frozen under his spell, they hold their breath. Dmitri is on the verge of taking responsibility; the thought of random executions because of his actions is too much to bear.

Then, a movement in a corner of the room. In unison, a gasp spreads through the gathering as the focal point of the drama shifts to the disturbance.

Robin stands up and all faces turn to him.

In a clear and rational voice, without emotion he looks Anuar in the eye. Unnerving in his certainty he declares: "You are in a precarious position; take your helmet off for one second, day or night, and you will be immobilized. You are destined to live under that threat for as long as you are on this planet.

"Go anywhere near the rockets and we will dynamite all three spacecraft, stranding you here permanently.

"The riches you thought you would extract from this world are a false dream; every grain you take will be under the duress of a reluctant workforce, a threat of revolt your constant companion.

"Lift so much as a finger against anyone in this village, guard or resident, and with time, we will banish you and your cronies to an island with nothing but the clothes you wear.

"The threats that you say will take effect at sunset – null and void. With immediate effect, there will be no further curfews.

"We are a peaceful community. You are welcome to be a part of it, but the privilege of belonging requires you to destroy your arms and subscribe to our principles without reservation. The crew that you sent to us on the *Destiny* can attest to a fulfilling life here. Instruct your guards to stand down now."

A duel of wills, a challenge issued. The moment is finely balanced. Robin has gambled on uncertainty. Will they take the bait? A stalemate reigns. Neither party holds the trump card, but it is clear for all to see that Anuar's rule is nearing an end.

A tortured look crosses his face as he struggles to comprehend another failure, this time at the hands of this motley group. Then with certainty, the crowd begins clapping in unison, slowly, a challenge to his autocracy. It continues until he wilts under the force of it, succumbs. Dmitri, Jabu, Kirill and others move forward, standing in front of the guards. Hands outstretched, they wait for them to hand over their weapons. Reluctantly at first, with heads bowed in shame, after the first, the second then all are compelled to do so. Anuar's stature seems to shrivel with each surrender, the pompous bearing replaced by abject resignation.

To everyone's surprise, there is a moment of quiet, as if an omnipresent force is dictating proceedings. One resident embraces a guard, then another and another, forgiveness the message and relief the outcome. It seems as if the standoff is at an end, but in a spasmodic reaction, as if to ward off rigor mortis in the throes of death, Anuar, realizing his predicament, fumbles for the weapon on his belt. Kirill, nearest him, lunges forward to avert the danger but two shots fired in rapid succession shatter the moment and Robin falls to the ground. A struggle ensues on the floor as the weight of Kirill brings the pair to the ground. Each desperate to reach the upper hand, the bulk of Anuar wins control only to be swamped by three or four guards who subdue the man by force of numbers. The crowd stand frozen in alarm. Caught in the act of embracing their foes turned friends, from moments earlier, they stand transfixed by events.

Lilian is first to react. Kneeling over Robin she sobs, "Robin, Robin, please, please stay still. Dear Robin." Turning she shouts, "Is there a doctor? Call the doctor. Dr. Levisohn!"

Dr. Levisohn barges through the crowd, who disperse as he progresses. Without hesitation, he stems the flow of blood from Robin's head with a makeshift bandage then removes his shirt to reveal a wound penetrating his left shoulder. Robin is unconscious. With the help of Dmitri and Jabu, he is carefully moved to Dr. Levisohn's clinic where Lilian stays by his side to assist the doctor as necessary. The prognosis is unclear as they monitor his vital signs.

The guards who came to Kirill's assistance manhandle Anuar to his feet, handcuff him and lead him away to an improvised holding cell. Kostya and Anuar's inner circle, reluctantly at first, submit to the other guards under pressure from the baying crowd. Locked in their bungalow, they await a decision on their complicity in Anuar's scheme.

A thorough search of the village, spacecraft and environs yields an assortment of firearms, from handguns to shoulder propelled grenade launchers. With the exception of a few weapons for the reliable guards, the rest are destroyed, along with the dynamite blast caps. We are determined to be a safe community, nonthreatening and not to be threatened.

For his part, Kirill wastes no time in boarding the two spacecraft to disable the backchannel communication link as insurance for the wellbeing of his family on Earth and those of his fellow travelers who were subservient, their families no longer held hostage to Anuar.

29

AFTERMATH

Graham quickly convenes an emergency meeting of our Management Committee. He issues instructions for the re-establishment of contact with Earth, emphasizing the need for due care in recommissioning the transmitter to avoid giving any hint to Anuar's cronies on Earth of events on Hermes, in case they harm the families of Kirill and others in his situation. The communication technician initiates the link to the satellite via an alternative radio wavelength to avoid activating the currently configured channel to Anuar's contacts, thereby warning them of the failed coup. A hastily prepared transmission is prepared and sent to *Overture*, detailing events including the identity of Anuar as the person probably responsible for poisoning the Betilla on Earth.

Julia and I hear the news over the connection. We are at once relieved, worried and filled with hope, but Robin's state casts a shadow over us as we gather our belongings and make for the clinic. Lilian sits alongside the bed, holding Robin's hand. Worriedly, she whispers encouragement to the unresponsive patient.

Dr. Levisohn updates us. "He took two shots; one entered his left shoulder and exited without damaging vital organs, although the glands under his arm will be affected. The other, more serious wound is just behind his left ear. The bullet partially penetrated the bone without entering the brain, which is a godsend. The shock of the impact has rendered him unconscious. We lack equipment to see the extent of the damage so it is difficult to say what the prognosis is. Right now, he needs constant monitoring, which Lilian is doing and Ella will take turns as needed. Other than that, quiet, a dimly lit room and of course, rest."

"When can we see him again?"

"I suggest that you limit it to two visits per day."

After consoling the distraught Lilian, we return to our residence where Jabu and Dmitri fretfully wait. All we can do is wait.

Two weeks pass and still Robin remains in a coma. Lilian spends each day at his side. When words of encouragement fail her, she resorts to reading from books that she knows he enjoys: records of the chronology of discoveries in mathematics and physics and the emergence of logic that supports the principles. She returns to our bungalow every evening convinced that he can hear her speaking. In the third week, to Lilian's joy, he emerges from his incapacity weak and confused, but he immediately recognizes her, stretches out his hand and grasps her for long moments as tears well up in her eyes. They hug in a lasting embrace, each fulfilling in the other some deeper meaning.

Robin's recovery is steady but sure; in a couple of weeks he is able to walk assisted by a support, which Lilian is ever ready to provide. He greets her arrival at the clinic each morning with obvious delight as they share breakfast and talk about matters both trivial and complex. Finally, the day comes for him to leave the clinic. In celebration, Lilian welcomes him home with food and music and the room decorated with flowers now freely available from the fields. We share in the moment, which marks the end of Anuar's attempt at occupation and a return to normality for Robin – save for the fact that he will need to use a cane as support for walking for the rest of his life and he must wear dark glasses to shield his eyes from the glare of even ordinary light.

It is also special for Dmitri. Feeling accountable for Robin's injury for taking the initiative to counter Anuar, he is at last able to shrug off the burden of guilt. The villagers meanwhile congregate in the hub and at an agreed time we walk Robin to the hall on the pretext of seeing Dr. Levisohn.

As he enters, a shout goes up, "Welcome back – our HERO!"

A long round of applause culminates with Graham addressing the audience, "Robin, we are indebted to you for standing up to Anuar the way you did. Thank you; you will always be special to us."

As I watch the proceedings it strikes me how Robin's insights into the deeper nuances of interactions between the disparate groups galvanized him into action and brought it to bear on Anuar. Acting on everyone's hopes, hidden intensions and ambitions, inarticulate even in their own minds, the bluff called and the obsequiousness that followed – all quite remarkable. The gamble on a stash of dynamite hidden at the hands of the *Destiny* crew, whether existent or not, must have crossed their minds and festered like a thorn in the side of Anuar, gnawing at his certainty. My thoughts cast back to Robin's rationality that opened a route to Hermes as we traveled aboard the *Forerunner* en route to Mars. We stand in admiration at this, his second intervention, the intellect that cleared a path forward for us; we stand humbled in the presence of our treasured professor of mathematics.

Graham continues, "I am pleased to say that shortly after the incident, we re-established contact with our sponsors and advised them of the situation. The police immediately surrounded Anuar's compound on Earth and took the personnel into custody. A security detail was deployed to protect family members of Anuar's guards, who were brought here against their will, by holding their kin on Earth hostage."

Dmitri too receives recognition. His concern for the plight of the villagers, his determination to act and the plan he formulated all stand as evidence of a generous caring individual, one to whom we all owe a great debt of gratitude.

Expressions of appreciation at the small part Julia and I played in the unfolding drama greeted us when we first returned to the village and Graham repeats these, also recognizing the part played by the Betilla. We feel pride in the old cohesiveness now apparent again, heralding a return of contentment to our days.

Robin, as mediator of disputes for the Management Committee, calls an ad hoc meeting of the three-member judicial panel required by the Charter.

With Graham, Robin and the Betilla patched-in, the meeting gets underway.

Robin starts the meeting with a statement. "The purpose of our meeting is to decide on punishment for Anuar and his co-accused. Anuar stands accused of poisoning the Betilla on Earth, armed insurrection on Hermes and injury to me. The only charge against the guards is insurrection. The use of pyrethrum as the agent for the poisoning on Earth and on Hermes connects Anuar to both events and therefore is not in dispute. To guide the decision on punishment, I quote from the Charter: We will address breaches of behavioral norms with full integration back into society being the preferred outcome."

To open the discussion Robin says, "Betilla, please state your position."

With Julia absent they respond with a text message, "We see the poisoning as premeditated murder. In our community, as a clonal species, we do not have a precedent on which to base retribution. We therefore defer to your practice, as adjusted to meet the Charter requirements to decide, but require punishment commensurate with homicide in the first degree."

It does not take long for a decision: House arrest for Anuar for a period of twelve months with one-hour supervised excursions allowed per day. The co-accused are subject to a nightly curfew for a year. A review after six months will decide on relaxing the sentences on the basis of the extent of their integration into the society.

The weeks that follow take on a new appreciation for the re-established peace. The divisions melt and the old order returns. A splinter however remains embedded in the side of Anuar and his inner circle, like a festering sore that cannot heal. They cannot bring themselves to integrate with the settlers. Anuar morosely withdraws from interaction with others, including his inner circle. We fear that he is either plotting a new scheme or cannot deal with the humiliation of the failure. We witness his downward spiral. Will he ultimately succumb to insanity, or lash out violently at those around him?

Kostya increasingly takes on a leadership role within their group, which exacerbates Anuar's condition. At a chance meeting of Anuar and Julia, in one of his infrequent appearances outside his quarters, Anuar stops dead in his tracks and glares at Julia with that expression of hatred that I once witnessed, but on this occasion without desisting. Startled and unnerved by the malevolence in his face, Julia moves away, but the statement is clear: he means to harm her. She retreats and makes for the safety of our home.

Concerned at the effect that is apparent I enquire, "Julia, are you alright? We are going to have to take this up with Robin and Graham. I don't trust him; something must be done."

Julia, recovering, says, "I have never seen such blatant hatred in anyone."

"It is unfathomable! What reason could he have? I think the guards need to be more vigilant; they cannot let him out of their sight. Since Robin is in charge of justice, he needs to double up on the supervision."

"Miles, maybe it is better that we just leave it. There is nothing concrete with which to charge him. I think I will be okay."

"Okay, but I want someone to accompany you whenever you are out."

Despite Julia's apparent recovery from the incident, she is markedly cautious when in public. Combined with the trauma of the demonstrators chanting her name when we prepared to leave Earth, this has left a scar on her. Her usual cheerful and engaging personality only returns when out on excursions into the wild.

* * *

In contrast to the sullenness of Anuar's group, Kirill has endeared himself to everyone in the village, bringing a new zest for life with a cheerful demeanor, greeting others freely and engaging in conversations with jokes and contagious laughter. On weekends, he plays a dombra, a two-stringed lute from his home region, and dances in what we assume to be a Cossack style, encouraging his fellow travelers and novices to join in. Before long, it becomes a much-anticipated weekly occurrence and the town center resembles a medieval market place with people displaying their wares and parading their particular skills and abilities.

We seldom have need to stray into the area adopted by the intruders, building an immunity to the undercurrents. Unless we chance to cross paths with them we are seldom reminded of the force of their discontent by their unfriendly bearing. Except for these disheartening occurrences, a pleasant if uneventful few months pass as we, working with the Betilla, make progress on our self-sufficiency plans and resume ambitions for a rewarding lifestyle.

* * *

News of yet another meteor strike on Earth interrupts our calm. This time multiple events follow in quick succession, one of which inflicts a populated area in Brazil with significant loss of life. Mars too suffers a reign of terror by a cluster of asteroids but is spared severe physical damage and deaths.

Months later, as Hermes transits the ecliptic plane of the solar system, the atmosphere of Hermes absorbs the majority of the shock of an incoming asteroid the size of a bus, with the remainder landing in the Dracon Seas of Oceana and resulting in a tsunami pushing northwards through the Pearl Islands to our coastline. The surge damages houses in the lower reaches of the village but thanks to forewarning by the Betilla, the people are safe. As cleanup operations start, we are surprised to see Anuar's group assisting, even though their quarters are unaffected. Led by Kostya, they quickly restore a semblance of order and help in rebuilding the homesteads. At the weekly gathering at the town center they too arrive and with some reticence join in the dancing. With a little encouragement, however, they are soon fully immersed in the freedom that dance brings. Only Anuar remains aloof of the participation, choosing to remain in his room during his allowed supervised excursions.

30

IRIDESCENCE

Kite and Aerie scan the valley below for threats as junior prepares for his maiden flight. This is the first of their offspring on this adopted planet. Pride fills their breasts as the stout youngster stands ready, feathers shining, bearing erect and eyes startlingly penetrating, the hallmarks of aristocracy in the kingdom of birds.

Dangers abound if junior fails in the first endeavor or brazenly chooses to test his hunting instincts on prey on the land; canine and feline pose certain risk. All is clear and he tilts forward from the ledge, as instructed, to glide faultlessly in the up-current. We, Kite and Aerie, follow in encouragement to a higher elevation, broadening the vision to distant hills then, circling, watch the exhilaration evident in the youngster as we too never fail to enjoy. The lay of the land is strangely familiar beyond memories since birth. A spur of land breaks a valley of a thousand hills, jutting eastward into the path of the river, forcing a U-shaped detour and eroding the side of the mountain to form deeply striated cliffs. Descending from the spur, we see a pair of humans pick their way around boulders and over the rock-strewn ravine, he holding her hand as they negotiate their way.

A generational memory stirs: ancestors in the lineage of Kite and Aerie, forebears with the same namesakes. A subconscious recollection conjures an image of these two humans.

The same determined step marks their passage as they delight in nature around them and with themselves. He points upwards to us, drawing her attention, and they stop to watch as we continue our circles. On impulse we drop to a lower altitude, sure in the safety of the maneuver. We alight on the skeletal branch of a dry tree on the bank of the river. Curiosity draws junior to join us and the three of us and the two of them thrill in the exchange of mutual wonderment of the moment.

The intersection of destiny unspoken yet safe in a tacit bond. The intertwining of lives holds the participants in a mutual embrace for many minutes.

Finally, Julia waves a salute at the avian friends who rise as one, the adults proudly on either side of the young one. Up, up they ascend, and with a cry bid farewell. The event is a reminder of so much that went before.

We wander on and as evening draws near, we stop to prepare a bivouac for the night. As the first stars pierce the velvety sky, we watch the glowing embers of Betilla making their way in their tiny bubbles to the moss fields opposite.

My mind strays to earlier times, my awakening at Windy Hill. The first consciousness of my surroundings as objects took shape and meaning, each building on the other to comprehension, an understanding of the purpose of things and the instinctive acceptance of others without question. Then the juvenile questioning, exploring and probing for answers as the world widened. Mount Elias and the magic of a playground without limit, the excursion to school, work and career. The intersection of individuals with lasting fellowship, and right here the merging of mind and body and of love with Julia. And all the while, Earth continues its relentless circle around the sun and then the fateful intersection with Hermes. In this moment as I lie here thinking, where once my mind writhed under the belief of the indifference of destiny circumscribed by sarcasm and cynicism, now a new consciousness explores the hand of a great design, of purpose, a journey of understanding, a future of opportunity infinite in scope, predestined, trusting in the unfathomable through faith in the unknown and unknowable.

Julia interrupts my reverie. "Look – Earth rising! There above the horizon. Isn't it beautiful?"

My thoughts move with my line of sight to the brightly shining light, the brightest in the sky. The hint of blue is unmistakable, like a dewdrop. My eyes mist over and nostalgia overwhelms me at the recognition of what the singular pale glow represents: family, friends and acquaintances. Old Mkize, what can he be doing? An inexplicable certainty passes over me that he too is looking at the night sky in his blindness and picturing the valley of mists in the evening glow, recalling the firmament in his mind's eye with a dim recollection of seeing a new star.

Turning to look over the valley, we see a cloud of Betilla approaching. A pulsing glow, nearer and nearer they come, and surprisingly they pass over the moss fields to continue their advance until they envelop us in the mist of their presence. A faint exquisite perfume exudes from the tiny bubbles, evoking a strange feeling of expanded clarity of thought, a depth of understanding, of compassion, of insights and broadening of perspectives. They hover over us for ten or fifteen minutes, then, as with a sigh of the wind, disperse down the valley. I close my eyes to fasten the experience in my mind.

Julia turns to me. "Enchanting, just enchanting, the fragrance like the freshest meadow." As tears well in her eyes, she says, "Sorry. I just feel overwhelmed with emotions. They surprise at every turn. I cannot explain it."

I too struggle to contain my emotions, unable to find words to express the sensations that swirl. Covering my eyes with my hands I try to take in the very core of consciousness, of being, the deepest meaning of cognizance. These thoughts struggle for explanation, seemingly precipitated by the event. What evokes this now? Feelings that usually lie dormant without explanation, ever present but subconscious, now they come to the fore and yet the mystery remains. A certain freedom takes hold in me, dissipating any last vestiges of the stress of the demands of life on me. Calm suffuses my being.

Julia summons my attention again, "Look – the rings of Saturn. Yes, and look, its moons!"

Reaching for the binoculars, I take them up but in turning, to my utter surprise, I see that Julia's hands are empty. "Julia, how can you see them? Your binoculars are lying next to you!"

Startled she responds, "What, what, oh! But I can see them. Look. What's happening?" Julia exclaims in confusion, "I can see them without the binoculars?"

As she turns I see a glint in her eyes. Drawing nearer, I cup her face in my hands. Her eyes glisten with radiance. Her irises sparkle with an iridescence not previously there. She too looks into my face and I see the surprise registering on her countenance at the mirror before her, just as I too am astonished. Slowly laying down the binoculars I turn to look up. There it is. Saturn in clear view spins its wheel of fortune, the rings, the symmetry, spellbinding in its magnificence.

To an outside observer it must seem strange; two people staring at each other in silence for long minutes. Then as reason apparently takes hold, he turns to look up and is frozen in place at the sight before him.

Julia is first to exclaim, "The fragrance. The Betilla have transferred the iridescence of their carapaces to us. We see what they see. We are one with them. We are part of their planet-wide telescope."

A shrill cry interrupts our train of thought. In the failing light of evening the hawk turns a final circle as it prepares to descend to the cliff for the night. Like a switch, my thoughts turn to the hawk and to my complete amazement I find myself looking down at two people, Julia and I, at the foot of the cliff. My view is that of the hawk. As I watch the spectacle, I remember: when we released the pair from their cage, there was a certain intelligence in their eyes – an iridescence in the irises.

I am not alone in this as Julia has followed my observation. "They have also received the iridescence from the Betilla."

We follow their flight, as seen through their eyes, as they descend to alight on the ledge. We see the nest of sticks and down at close quarters as the hawk reassures the fledging nestled there.

Darkness closes the chapter for the day.

It is a strange night. For long hours we lie sleeplessly looking up at the darkness. So many questions come to the fore and with each question we explore for answers. Some raise alarming consequences, others excite, and some remain without answer. For comfort we hold hands in the darkness as answers emerge from a haze of the inexplicable to become apparent. Not only do we hold the visionary capability of the Betilla in our gaze, we also find that we can dialog with the Betilla without the use of technology or sound.

It is from this source that the answers come. Like turning the dial of a radio from one wavelength to another we can, as if at will, switch between communication to resolve questions we pose or see what they see. They tell of genes implanted in our eyes as part of the iridescence that emit in a format and frequency that they can detect and interpret. These same genes act as receptors to detect what they have to say or show us. The optical nerve in the eye acts as the sensory organ for frequencies in the range from ultraviolet, through the normal visible range to infrared and radio waves, provided they are in a straight line of sight. They can penetrate barriers such as walls and have a range of about a kilometer. The brain distinguishes between these types of stimuli for integration into our thought processes.

The carapaces of the Betilla operate as receptors, transmitters or transponders to receive, send, relay or boost the signals if degradation has occurred due to distance or disturbance. All communications are via these features of the carapaces. It is this interconnectivity that resulted in the Betilla acting as a single planet-wide sentience; thoughts, memories, auditory and vision stimuli shared instantly and on a continuous basis until independence gave way to the semblance of a unitary mind. For us, we stand to tap into their memory bank, to dialog with them unrestrained by technology, and to see what they and other species imbued with the receptors and transmitters see; the Betilla being the nexus through which all exchange occurs. Birds with iridescent eyes and the Betilla's floating bubbles also act to relay the transmissions, thereby expanding the perspective.

The answers come when solicited through this integration with our neighbors. During the decades since our first encounter with the Betilla, they determined that we, and Julia in particular, are trustworthy. They have imparted to us the inheritance normally reserved for their offspring through multiplication by cell division, albeit limited to access their stored memory and active sights as opposed to thought processes. They recognize that this gift may not be welcomed by us and as such is reversible if that is our wish. Alternatively, they are open to extending this to other humans if in our judgment this is advisable.

Exploring our newfound abilities, we learn and now stand to explore in absolute detail what the Betilla previously patiently shared with us. We are heirs to a full understanding of DNA manipulation, gene editing, quantum mechanics, nanotechnology and the details of photosynthesis. Their knowhow is now freely available to us.

We are also able to recall the memory of their journey through the void, the encounter with Alpha Centauri, even back to the precipitous causes when they were ejected from their solar system. They share their memories of the anxiety of being bound to the rogue planet and the relief of a safe harbor here in our solar system.

The night draws to an end and despite our sleeplessness there is a certain exhilaration in the dawn. New ethereal realms beckon for exploration, promising to elevate our beings to higher levels of understanding. Capabilities for enhanced vision, deep insights and thoughts present themselves to us, not to mention flying with our avian friends the hawks. The scope of what has taken place since last evening is breathtaking in its ramifications for the expansion of our intellect through the symbiotic interplay between us and the Betilla.

An impediment however presents itself. Julia and I will effectively be elevated above our fellow human beings through our access to the vast repository of information stored in the Betilla's memory if left solely to us. We will be placed on a pedestal which separates us from our fellows. With time we will migrate away from our inherent commonality with our friends and society, a prospect that Julia and I find difficult to accept. A decision point has been reached: either we accept this new mantle solely for ourselves, share it in equal measure with all humanity, or turn down the Betilla's gift. The multiplicand of humankind's knowledge with that of the Betilla's will advance our understanding of every aspect of this universe for good or bad. Like all advances, the dichotomy of risk and benefit are stark in their implications, and in this case we dare not adjudicate on this alone. Just as the splitting of the atom offered limitless power, it at the same time threatened destruction on an unprecedented scale. This is a moment for a considered decision.

We decide to linger a day longer, putting off the inevitability of the decision before us, choosing rather to indulge in our newfound abilities for a while. My greatest joy is to join with the avian pair in flight, liberated of all concerns. My mind soars with theirs on effort-less wings to great heights that provide a broad panorama of the land and the greening brought to this planet. Valleys, rivers, lakes, plains, mountains and seascapes enchant the view. At times, joined by Julia, we share the experience, enthralled like children with new toys. For her part, she spends time in dialog with her Betilla hosts as they exchange knowledge, practices and understanding of a range of topics. Julia can barely contain her excitement as she tells me what she finds. The Betilla's advanced understanding in her field of exper-tise is both broad and deep.

She excitedly remarks, "Their memory bank is so meticulously organized compared to ours. They have compartmentalized all their knowledge by category, much like a library. It is fascinating. DNA versus photosynthesis versus quantum mechanics and so on; it is all there and they are happy to explain what I can't understand."

All good things must come to an end. On the third day we can no longer procrastinate without certitude on the way forward. The days have been addictive, causing us to lean in favor of a continuance; we cannot reserve this for us alone, but the mention of this to others will lead to its adoption. What to do? The question vexes us but the absence of an answer is not a solution.

I put it to Julia, "Are there compromises? Is there a middle ground? Things are seldom black or white."

She in turn questions, "I can't think of any. What would Robin, Jabu or Dmitri do? Especially Robin. He is so rational, but is he wise? And there is also Lilian to consider."

I have to concur, "Yes, as a group they would give a balanced view. However, as an option, how about extending this capability to them as a group? Would they accept being thrust onto a pedestal? Because that is the inevitable outcome. If we want guidance, Dmitri is probably the most grounded of the group, more caring. He would give the wisest answer. Even Ella could contribute with her nursing and healing perspective."

Our preferences swirl between these choices but repeatedly gravitate to Dmitri as the best for guidance. He is the most sensible of the group. Finally, still uncertain, we decide to defer to the group as a whole for opinion.

With some reluctance we strike camp and make for the village.

* * *

As we enter our residence and call to the others to meet, they immediately suspect a new revelation from Julia and jokingly ask

367

what the Betilla have been up to – little realizing that that is exactly correct. Julia and I decided to hold off looking them in the eye until they are all gathered. When they are seated, we look up and wait for a response as we turn to each one in the circle. It takes a few moments of silence before curiosity focuses their attention.

A puzzled look crosses Jabu's face. "What have you done to your eyes?"

It takes a supreme effort for me to remain serious. "Oh, that! We are trying out the latest in contact lenses. Do you like them?"

Julia cannot contain herself and bursts out laughing, but that just adds to their confusion. Lilian comes up close to examine our eyes and the others follow suit.

As expected, Robin is first to make the connection. "Iridescence – that's it! It had to be the damn Betilla."

It takes a while to explain the event, the nuances of the capabilities and the dilemma. They understand the predicament; the elevated status Julia and I would have, the knowledge and power that would accrue with time, and ultimately the separation from our friends and colleagues as we grow apart. They recognize that it opens access to a deep reservoir of profound subject matter based on the emerging consensus that, despite their physical limitations, the Betilla are superior in intellect and aspects of technology when compared to humans.

Dmitri has been silent for much of the discussion. It is with interest that I listen when he speaks. "I think it should be all or nothing. If it is limited to the two of you or expanded to our group the pedestal problem would apply. I don't think any of us are cut out to be super-humans. In the end we would not be happy. Rather enjoy the experience for a short while and then have it removed. The same if it is expanded to our group. The period should be very limited to avoid addiction, which you have already mentioned. Of course you could, now and then, ask for a temporary reinstatement, say, to solve a technical problem; it would give us direct input to the Betilla. As you know, we have struggled with a number of explanations from them in the past."

Having explained his view on the "Nothing" part of his opinion, he then explains the "All" part of his argument. "Here is what I think is best; the capability should be made available to everyone here on Hermes without exception. You should approach the Betilla to see whether the features can be disabled in anyone leaving Hermes."

Going on with this theme he explains, "The biggest benefit will be that scientists will come here to gain access to information. They will have to document their findings before leaving because they will lose access to the source information on leaving Hermes. Hermes would become a center of learning."

I offer an opinion, "The Betilla have said that the feature is reversible, so I think you can take it that it can be disabled when people leave Hermes. It is probably just a matter of logistics to have it removed. When they arrive we give it to them and when they leave we take it away."

We discuss these details and other choices but elect to propose Dmitri's Hermes solution to the Management Committee for ratification.

As a parting thought Robin adds, "You may laugh at me if you like, but I think the Betilla have another agenda. They are doing this supposedly in the open; we decide what we want. Well, by now they know humans well enough to bank on the fact that we will not reject the offer. Mark my words, Earth will follow shortly after Hermes adopts this. The Betilla already control our birthrate and longevity. I can't say what they are hiding but, believe me, they are here to advance their own cause, not ours. We are the pawns in their game."

Julia interjects, "There you go again – hidden agenda. What could that be? Please tell."

Robin, adjusting the dark glasses he has worn since the shooting, says, "As before, I don't mean to upset you Julia. You are right, I have no idea what they may be trying to do other than simply sharing with us, but I thought I should just caution against being too hasty. That is all."

Lilian says, "Robin has a legitimate concern and it is better to discuss that now, because the Betilla will be present at the management meeting so it can't be discussed there."

Dmitri says, "It comes down to whether you trust the Betilla or not. I suggest that you go into the meeting and vote on that as the basis. If you trust them then vote to go ahead; if not, vote against it."

Jabu adds, "Remember, our charter states that the Management Committee is supposed to reach consensus on any decision. It also states that contentious decision should be settled by means of a referendum. That means that all we need to vote on at the meeting is whether to have a referendum or not. We can worry about whether to go ahead with the actual thingamajig later. Come to think of it, the Betilla should really recuse themselves from the meeting, because this is a matter for the settlers, not the Betilla. I will check with Graham to see what he thinks."

Previously a decision of this magnitude would be referred to Earth, but under Hermes' newfound autonomy from Earth, decisions can be made locally. On convening the Management Committee on the following day, they recognize that the scope of implications is significant for the residents of Hermes and exceedingly exclusionary for the people of our home planet, Earth. After the shock of the revelations subsides, the decision is referred to a referendum. Graham, having heard some of the details from Jabu, enthusiastically embraces the idea that Hermes will attract visiting scientists and industrialists, making Hermes a center of learning and advancement.

Lilian is tasked with drafting a factual description of what we decide to call 'The Nexus.' Residents are to vote for one of three options:

- Reject Nexus
- Nexus for Hermes only
- Nexus for Hermes and offered to Earth

The second option accepts that visitors will be welcome to Hermes at any time to experience the Nexus for themselves, and that at a future date, consideration will be given to expanding it to Earth if they so wish.

Within a few days Lilian completes the description for the vote. The committee signs off the ballot and the information is distributed to the local populace with a date for the vote set at thirty days in the future.

Pros and cons swirl as the residents eagerly debate the best way forward. Earth too weighs in to tilt the decision in favor of option three, but in the end, much to their dismay, the plebiscite overwhelmingly elects options two; Hermes alone will receive the gift from the Betilla.

* * *

Julia and I watch from our promontory overlooking the rift valley as a slow procession of residents makes its way through the gorge. There is a sense of apprehension mixed with expectancy as they follow the course of the river into a mist of Betilla bubbles. As the leaders enter the haze their reaction is immediate. Exclamations of surprise evident even at our distance, as the sensation dispels trepidation, replaced by delight at the freshness of the fragrance enveloping them. They turn to each other in wonder at the experience of the opening of their minds to new realms of understanding, of sights hitherto not seen. The followers see the change and excitedly jostle for entry until all are consumed by it to emerge with a new sense, Nexus is complete.

Hermes is entering a new dispensation.

As our friends part from the procession we wave to them to join us on the promontory. Jabu and Dmitri are first to arrive. They can barely contain their excitement at the newfound abilities, flying with the ever-present seagulls who also have the Nexus, or delving into the depth of the Betilla's repository of information. Robin, limping along with his cane, and Lilian supporting him arrive a while later.

Lilian gleefully follows the sights from the seagulls as they glide along the shore, ecstatically proclaiming her enjoyment. She turns to Robin, who finds a comfortable resting place and looks about to witness what the others see. A perplexed expression crosses his face and somewhat embarrassed he asks, "Lilian, am I doing something wrong? I don't see anything different. What do you have to do to get it working?"

We gather around as Lilian suggests, "Try taking your glasses off. Maybe they are blocking the process."

He slowly removes them and his face lights up. "Wow, what a sight, looking down from the birds."

I take up the glasses and try them on, "Yep, that's the problem. It's the glasses. I can't see the view from the birds or access the Betilla."

Robin says, "You know, I bet it is the polarization in the lenses; distorting the image."

Jabu jokes, "There's a thing. If ever you want to block the discussions with the Betilla, just borrow Robin's sunglasses."

31

RECOVERY

On Earth, the transposition of the magnetic poles proves to be the final straw that breaks the back of convention. In its wake, following the compounding effects of the preceding cataclysmic events, an inevitable realignment of socio-political allegiances manifests itself. Like all revolutions, as people jostle for power, clashes occur. Violent upheavals ripple through the populace, and death and destruction abates only when exhaustion stems the tide. A new world order emerges for the vastly diminished population. In typical fashion, the pendulum of history swings from one extreme to another. Peace follows pandemonium, calm follows discord, aggression turns to pacifism, intolerance to tolerance. Fortunately, the survivors inherit repairable infrastructure and the bank of knowledge held in unscathed repositories, enabling them to reconstruct the civilization on this foundation. Decades in the making, on a new footing, order gradually takes hold and the wheels of industry haltingly begin turning. Following Hermes' example, they adopt elements of its charter to forge and preserve an Eden for its tenants, human and non-human. Under their newfound optimism, renewed dialog opens up with Hermes with the re-establishment of communication links. Interplanetary travel again finds favor and the isolation of Hermes fades as scientists collaborate with Hermes as an intellectual partner and sovereign state.

* * *

A strange confidence takes hold over the pioneers of Hermes. The youthful vigor brought on by the longevity drives us to scale the heights of endeavor not previously imagined. An entrepreneurial spirit arises, with audacious plans and energy to match, propelling us forward each day to scale heights that previously seemed insurmountable. Our previous attempts at self-sufficiency pale in comparison.

Our relationship with the Betilla deepens; a mutual recognition of the contributions made, respect for the ways of each, a society interdependent on each other and with time the merging of values and of shared aspirations. The old order's obsession with growth are displaced by stability, and a central theme of quality before quantity. Life takes on new meaning; the object is shared enrichment and sustenance rather than greed and concentration of power. Custodianship of nature turns from paternal intrusion under the guise of oversight, to recognition of its sovereignty and equal worth, intervention only for maternal care to nurture self-reliance.

Independence and liberation from the dictates of Earth, in partnership with the Betilla, translate into novel solutions for overcoming challenges. Silicon crystals of suitable quality, identified as a finite resource on Hermes and grown in aseptic conditions on Earth, prove advantageous. Recognizing the semi-conducting features of silicon for temporal memory in computer systems leads the partnership with our neighbors to in-depth exploration of bits and bytes, and / or gates, binary versus hexadecimal, analog versus digital, serial versus parallel, macro versus Nano and quantum versus biological. We explore biocomputers as systems given the inherent biological skills of the Betilla. We examine the use of molecules derived from DNA and other proteins in the performance of computational calculations for storing, retrieving, and processing data. We consider implementations at a Nano-level using re-engineered molecules that interact in a fashion suitable for computing purposes.

To avoid re-inventing the wheel, we build on Earth-based technology. There, ordinary computers use zeros and ones in electrical circuits to represent either a flow or no flow as a binary condition with strings of bits to make up bytes to encode information. Knowing that at a quantum level, zeros, ones or both can exist in the form of electrons and if used can remove the binary constraint in classical computers, we see that quantum computers can work with these particles to provide significantly greater computational powers, as theory has already established on Earth.

Silicon, the fourteenth element on the periodic table, is one of the fundamental constituents of the universe. Jabu confirms that it is the second most abundant element in Hermes' crust after oxygen. We all recognize that it is the basis of all current computer processors as a semi-conductor. With chuckles from the group, I point out that it is supposedly the most likely candidate for the basis for alien, non-carbon-based life, which elicits some speculation about the makeup of the Betilla. The problem with silicon is that it usually comes in the form of a compound highly contaminated with other elements like silica, the primary component of sand. For a transistor in a computer that must be able to switch on and off at will to represent zeros and ones, we too require a semi-conductor, a substance with a resistance somewhere between that of a conductor and an insulator. Silicon is ideal for this when treated to adjust the resistance to the desired level.

The breakthrough comes with the realization that the Betilla's habit of building silicon crystals in their submarine castles can be adapted for this use. Their photosynthetic use of quantum mechanics, and their use of ozone's diamagnetic properties for altering the polarity of electrical current to aid navigation of the bubbles, all form the ingredients to our solution. Before long, our computing capabilities expand significantly, using these features combined with Earth-based theories. We build a vast planet-wide biological network of circuits for storage and processing of complex mathematical reckonings, making it possible to delve into previously unfathomable puzzles. Combined with the telescopic resolution of distant objects, we plumb the depth of the first spark of the original bang, unify theories previously held discreet, confirm models and explore theories beyond elemental fermion and boson particles of the subatomic.

Under these advances, Robin oversees predictive modeling based on the rich data emanating from the computer systems. He steers a course for the development of facilities on the planet. Dmitri extends the robotic capabilities to fashion replacement parts for the robots and an array of tools, using biologically engineered substitutes for plastic in 3D printing technology. Julia works with the Betilla to oversee planetary biodiversity, enriching the environment with a wide spectrum of flora and fauna. My responsibilities are to coordinate the diverse activities with a special interest in the data center, spread out as it is across the planet in an interconnected labyrinth set up by the Betilla.

Jabu, in a moment of inspiration, looks further afield to geological resources from asteroids and comets to harness for onsite use. He is overwhelmed by a singular objective: the construction of a space elevator to facilitate access to space without the use of combustion technology used in rockets. Jabu's dream is for a type of planet-to-space transportation system comprising a cable or tether anchored to the surface and extending into space to permit vehicles to travel along the cable from the planetary surface, directly into space or orbit, without the use of volatile propellants. The cable attached to the surface near the equator will extend into space to and beyond a geo-stationary orbit at an altitude of about 30,000 km. The competing inward force of gravity and outward centrifugal force will hold the cable up under tension in a stationary position over a single point on Hermes.

Specially designed elevator cars would climb the tether to space by mechanical or other means, releasing their cargo to orbit or descend to return freight to the surface from orbit. Hermes' gravity being marginally less than Earth's, the strength requirements for the tether are not as onerous and can be met using composite materials harvested from asteroids and comets. He uses computer models to simulate a geo-stationary position in space from where construction can start in orbit, progressively extending the cable downward from the top until it reaches the surface of Hermes. He wastes no time in presenting his plans. Despite the audaciousness of the venture, he gets overwhelming support as the plan limits environmental damage and meets our charter requirements. Where once he mined for minerals deep in the Earth's crust, now his sights turn to the heavens for these.

Our ambitious plans progress rapidly on the enthusiasm engendered by collaboration and recognition of the worth of each contributor. Our world is a land of promise. Reductive and deductive logic powered by the cross-pollination of ideas between the Betilla and human carries us to heights previously only imagined. The ever-present Betilla prod and prompt progress, steering a bold course that relentlessly challenges us to steadily greater achievements.

32

METEOR

The forewarning of the strike on Hermes came from systematic tracking of stray objects, aside from those approaching Earth and Mars, thereby limiting the toll on the populations. Earth suffered significant loss of life but evacuations from predicted strike points halved the potential death toll. The forecast is that planetary impacts will tail-off as Jupiter weighs in on the orbits of these threats. Proactive missions launched well in advance will nudge the remaining threats that still present a danger out of harm's way.

Close tracking of the meteor that struck Hermes shows a second much larger asteroid in its wake, sufficiently offset to bypass the planet. The trailing asteroid is following a separate elongated orbit, aligned to pass Hermes in a few months' time. Observations show that it is largely carbon based with a fair share of iron, silicon and traces of other elements. Using Earth-based concepts for the capture and towing of asteroids developed prior to Hermes' arrival in our solar system, and using our vastly improved computational and tracking capabilities, we study the velocity and feasibility of harnessing the object to further our plans for self-sufficiency. The assessment shows that we can nudge its orbit to intersect with Hermes in about twenty months. By using the remaining fuel of two of Anuar's spacecraft, with precision burns, we can deflect its course sufficiently as it travels a separate path around the sun to rendezvous with Hermes on a future date.

In approaching Kostya for the use of the spacecraft, he unfortunately believes that he must defer to Anuar for a decision. At our request to act as an intermediary, he takes up the subject with him. Apparently, at the first approach, he declined. After some coaxing Kostya convinced him by emphasizing the importance this contribution will have on the development of Hermes. Appealing to his ego did the trick. Anuar himself comes out to confirm his decision and our appreciative response clearly raises his spirits. We have no further difficulties with Anuar, who seemingly realizes that alternatives to integration into the community have many drawbacks and his prior ambitions, including a take-over of Mars, have little chance of success.

* * *

Planning immediately gets under way and with time to spare, the two craft stand ready for their mission. The missiles stashed by Anuar prior to their landing now have a tether added to the rear, and the explosives are changed to penetrate the asteroid and lodge an anchor in the object. Three projectiles are prepared for each craft. At the designated hour, with everyone standing on our historic hilltop overlooking the event, we witness the roar of the first followed later by the second craft as they take to the sky carrying our dream for the future. The crowd cheers as the contrails mark the path. Glancing over at Kostya and Anuar, their pride in the contribution by their engineers is obvious on their faces, with all malicious intent thankfully dispelled.

Using the communication satellite combined with the Betilla's optical resolution, we watch the rendezvous from our control center. Precision maneuvering positions the first craft to discharge its first tether. The strike is perfect, confirmed by the taut line between object and craft. The second craft maneuvers into position on the far side and it too lodges its line. Of the six tethers, only one fails to take hold and is detached from the craft, languidly disappearing into the void. Under control of the computer, the puff of the guidance systems position the two spacecraft for towing. The target lies a Hermes-year away and the mass, velocity, force and fuel parameters combine to set the operation in motion. The craft will tug at the asteroid, by degrees adjusting its solar orbit to intersect with that of Hermes after a complete revolution around the sun. All we can do now is wait and prepare for the event.

With growing excitement, the year is one of unparalleled intensity. Our plan is to guide the asteroid into a geo-stationary orbit directly above the equator a little distance south of New Greenwich and midway to the string of Pearl Islands. The third spacecraft sent ahead to meet the asteroid in its approach will apply the final adjustments to correctly position the orbit. The finale is the launch of the *Destiny*, our honeymoon vessel, with a precious microscopic cargo onboard for release on the rock: a limited set of multi-purpose Nano-robots constructed from atoms in proportion to the main minerals assessed to be on the asteroid. The design of the Nanobots combines input from Earth and the Betilla, and they were architecturally completed and built by our friends in their submarine castles. Once on the asteroid – which we call "Dais" to represent a platform for the future – the Nanobots will first start replicating themselves by extracting material from the asteroid. At a sign, when the numbers are adequate, they will cease replication and begin producing carbon nanofibers from carbon and silicon to produce a semi-translucent double-piped tube of exceptional strength. Extrusion of the cable will proceed from above, extending downwards from the asteroid to Hermes. The altitude of the captured satellite will undergo continual adjustment by the *Destiny* to maintain the geographically stationary and stable orbit as the Nanobots consume the asteroid. The mass of extruded cabling and the diminishing mass of the rock are balanced to maintain an equilibrium of inward gravitational attraction to Hermes and outward centrifugal force away from the planet while synchronized to the rotation of the planet around its axis. As the cable extends from the asteroid, the end will reach the surface for anchoring in the sea off New Greenwich, forming the basis for a space elevator. Immersed in the technicalities of tensile strength, orbital forces and nanotechnology, complex activities absorb each day as Dais draws nearer.

* * *

Finally, the kilometer-sized asteroid, under adjusted thrust by the two accompanying spacecraft, edges forward to park above our village. Using our newfound telescopic vision, it is visible as a miniature moon at a height of thirty thousand kilometers.

Destiny, with its near weightless load, rises with a roar to reach for Dais. The village, devoid of towering rockets, is left with a more medieval aspect but for the incongruous remnants of the journey from Earth still dotting the landscape, the modernistic pods that sheltered us in transit.

As the *Destiny* draws near, the bulk of Dais looms large, the smooth surface pockmarked with impact craters. Engulfed by the asteroid's sheer size, the diminutive craft anchors to the surface and a robotic arm with a capsule of micro machines extends to the asteroid. The transfer, deceptively miniature in size, gives no hint at the enormity of the task and the realization of its outcome. The capsule opens like the petals of a flower to release its pollen, tenderly. With the gentleness of a feather, the microgravity of the rock draws the invisible workers to its surface where, on contact, a magnetic embrace holds them in place. The *Destiny*, its task accomplished, distances itself from Dais to await instructions from its masters on Hermes, who signal to the Nanobots to begin replicating themselves. The replicants do likewise, creating exponential duplication. At first there is no evidence of the instruction bearing fruit, but as time passes, close observation reveals subtle changes as the numbers grow until the entire surface crawls with the miniature workers, like termites chiseling the asteroid to a perfect octagonal pyramid. Then, with the threshold numbers reached, they cease duplication and like an army on the march, turn to converge at the planet-facing edge, where extrusion of the carbon fiber Nanotubes begins. The *Destiny* maneuvers to the far side. There, locked to the asteroid it stands ready to compensate for the hollowing of the satellite, as it is converted from dust to cable, by adjusting its orbital distance to maintain the state of equilibrium for the geo-stationary position to hold.

The months pass, with bated breath we wait. Will our venture succeed? Our suspense converts to a daily routine of convening at the town center at dawn to gaze skyward, looking for confirmation via direct observation of the snaking tube as it descends to us.

The machines labor without ceasing, day and night, month in and month out, and on the second year a cheer goes up, "There, there," everyone points, at the height of the clouds, "A speck, yes, yes it is coming!"

Each day the buzz of excitement grows as the length extends and finally touches down at the docking port where, like a helium-filled balloon, Dais is moored, our gateway to the stars secured.

The activities of the Nanobots are reconfigured to harvest mineral nutrients from the sea to line the outer edge of the cable with iridescent material, matching the carapace of the Betilla, to provide protection against solar radiation and further enhance the tensile strength of the link to space. The iridescence builds skyward and we now marvel at the shimmering spectacle each day. Again, the days extend to months and in the second year the iridescence is complete.

As the tireless micro machines reach the summit, they again change mandate. A bubble-like hemispherical reservoir is furnished on the flat planet-side of the asteroid. A hole is made through the middle of Dais into the hollow center, and the cable is passed through it to emerge on the far side. Here they construct a spherical shaped bubble reservoir at the pinnacle of the pyramid.

Activity at the docking station off the Pearl Islands now takes center stage. One of the two tubes within the cable extending from the sky is submerged in the ocean and at a radio signal to the Nanobots on Dais, they open the end of the tube at their end. As we watch the meniscus of saltwater in the translucent tube begins to rush upwards. The vacuum of space draws the water upward in a capillary action, flowing to the orbiting asteroid. Three days later the water reaches the top and first fills the lower reservoir before flowing through the provisioned hole with the cable through the center of the rock to the reservoir on the far side. Under controlled pressure the flow is stopped at the optimum level, completing a twenty-centimeter diameter liquid artery to the asteroid. Next, the second tube, with the upper end voided to space and the bottom end dangling above the level of the sea at the Pearl Islands, is opened and the air rushes in until equilibrium with the atmosphere is reached. The Nanobots then move the upper end into the reservoir and open a lock in the tube. The water rushes downward, drawn by gravity in a reverse capillary action. Three days later it gushes out into the ocean and is sealed. As before, the reservoirs are refilled using the other tube. A circular flow of fresh sea water is achieved by a series of controlling locks at each end of the two tubes, completing a bi-directional highway to the reservoirs.

Access for humans then becomes the focus; the iridescent coating over the descending cable acts as an array of photoelectric cells on the same basis that the Betilla use light for metabolism instead of consuming food. The electrical current generated from the cells and salt water power an elevator pod, magnetically levitating from and attracted to the cable without touching, thereby allowing pods to pass each other unhindered en route to their destination whether up or down. A midway station, at an altitude of fifteen thousand kilometers, provides a harbor for upward and downward bound pods before continuing their journeys. A reservoir of seawater at the midpoint services the needs of the Betilla.

The construction of the infrastructure at the top and bottom of the cable as well as the midway harbor take another year. During this time some of the Nanobots are programmed to direct their energies at opening vast windows to space in the hollowed asteroid to provide a weightless environment for people, safe against solar radiation and with a view of the universe. Work also begins on a rotating circular structure radiating out from an extension of the pinnacle of the pyramid. In a carousel format, similar to that used on the *Forerunner* to simulate gravity for prolonged stays in space, access is provisioned by an extension cable linked to the pinnacle and from there to Dais below.

To provide an atmosphere within the hollowed-out asteroid, air is bubbled up through the first of the two conduits within the cable leading from Hermes. The inside of the asteroid will be breathable, but weightless. The water-filled lower reservoir will connect to the atmosphere of the hollowed-out asteroid to provide access to an environment for juvenile Betilla during their amphibious stage. It allows for moss to grow on the floor or ceiling in this weightless world where up and down have no meaning.

Five years after the start of construction the work is completed and our pride stands before us, the labor of each and every person and innumerable Betilla, a spectacle of wonder to behold. Yet we are humbled by the accomplishment, the outcome of a partnership of minds and collaboration of proportions not imagined possible.

* * *

At the anchor off the Pearl Islands, about two hundred adult Betilla assemble at their entrance and Julia, Robin, Lilian, Jabu, Dmitri, Ella and I enter one of our old pods, repurposed for the elevator. Attached to the underside of the pod is a transparent reservoir to accommodate Betilla who enter via a channel and locks leading from the sea. Meanwhile, a steady stream of bubbles are release into the upward bound tube to make their way to the reservoir on Dais. Contained in each double-bubble is air for flotation and the usual algae spore wrapped in Betilla skin particles for release and proliferation in the hollowed-out asteroid. Once mature, the juvenile Betilla will return to Hermes through the downward bound tube within the elevator cable to complete their life cycle on the planet. Adult Betilla may, at any time, optionally travel up to Dais in the aquarium attached under each pod.

We carry with us provisions for ten days and nervously wait for the pod to move. The excitement is palpable as the countdown to our journey starts. Unlike the bone jarring launch of the conventional rockets, we start moving without so much as a jerk. The ferry smoothly shifts from a stationary position to glide slowly upwards, gradually gaining momentum. Under constant thrust the pod accelerates ever faster, seamlessly passing the boundary between the atmosphere and space as gravity loses its grip, faster still until a speed of over 500 kilometers per hour is achieved. Meanwhile Hermes falls away below us, noticeably diminishing in size with every passing hour while the universe opens up before us, greeting us with a limitless array of stars spread across our view. The sun, powering our ascent, seemingly beams at our achievement. The cable stretches out ahead of us, disappearing in the distance as our destination grows, shining as a perfectly shaped octagonal pyramid. A quarter-moon welcoming smile glistens off the hemispherical underbelly.

In our approach, the dark form of Dais hangs threateningly above us, obscuring the stars and sun. Slowing to a crawl, we edge nearer to the transparent reservoir of sea water clinging to the undersurface of the asteroid like a great water droplet. Our passage passes through the middle of the aquarium, where we come to a stop to see the adult Betilla emerge from the transport to float in the water. This our first direct unobstructed view of our friends since landing on the planet.

We marvel at their agility. Tiny webbed feet propel them through the water where they congregate in ever increasing numbers. They too are clearly amazed at the sensation of floating here high above our home, the planet that changed our lives and theirs so irrevocably. We move on through the gap into the yawning mouth of the asteroid. Darkness envelopes us momentarily before we emerge in a great hall, where an atrium of wide windows allow the sun and stars to provide light that sparkles off iridescent walls, magically transformed from granite to a welcoming kaleidoscope. The pod comes to a stop in the middle of the chamber and the door slides open, proffering a welcome to enter. Floating freely in the weightless hall we use aerosol wands, loosely strapped to our arms, to move about, exploring, sailing to the distant walls, roof and floor, where magnetized boots allow for conventional walking. Empty troughs line walkways on the floor, waiting for soil and plants to be introduced to convert the chamber into an arboretum and nursery of vegetation with birds, butterflies and creatures of flight added to complete a living garden in the sky.

As we watch, the first of the bubbles emerge from a turret at the end of the cable, to float in their magical way to a landing of their choice. They glow with sparkling intensity as they flicker their way through the weightless atmosphere. For me, thoughts of Mount Elias and the fireflies' fliting across the lawn in the warm summer evening, now transposed to this distant setting, overwhelm me with delight, bringing my dreams full circle.

33

MOTIVE

We have accomplished much in our extended life, but one dream remains unfulfilled: the distant lands of Hermes remain unexplored. Julia and I resolve to correct this with an adventure along the East Riven coastline to the peninsula that extends down to North Falcate, the crescent land mass facing its counterpart south of the equator, South Falcate. Dmitri, with his newfound abilities of extracting the most from the robotic technology, prepares a vessel powered by wind and solar energy coupled to a propeller to drive it forward at a moderate speed.

We set out on a breezy day with a supply of dried food to last many weeks. The ubiquitous seagulls, themselves imbued with the Nexus, enable us to see what obstacles lie ahead. The delight at seeing the passing landscape now covered with vegetation, the results of Julia's work, thrills her. Each evening we stop and set up camp on the beaches to watch the Betilla rise from their turrets and head inland. The great expanse of the world works its magic on us as we feel the stresses seeping from us, dispelling all concerns and energizing us to explore what lies ahead. Northwards, the coast eventually veers off due east before heading southwards along the peninsula to its extremity. A strait separates the isthmus from the distant Falcate Peninsula, which stretches northwards to us, just visible when viewed from the circling seagulls. We overnight on a rocky ledge to take in the view as the sun sets behind a bank of clouds building behind a brisk westerly wind that looks to be bringing rain.

"Julia, this is about as far as we can go. We have enough food to do the return trip with a little in reserve in case we are delayed."

"I'm so curious to see North Falcate. It is so near. Come on, let's at least cross the strait and camp on the other side for a day or two before returning."

"Well the weather doesn't look too good. If we wait here for it to clear, when it blows over we can decide if the provisions will still last for the trip back."

"We can cut back to half rations and eat berries from the field. I saw some on our way up. Please, please, I couldn't bear going back when we are so close."

"Okay, let's see what the morning brings."

Rain and gusty winds greet us in the morning, and the following day is the same.

As the first rays of the next day wake us, Julia is quick to exclaim, "Yippee! Miles, look, the weather is perfect."

"We are now down to just enough provisions to get back. Look, if we make the crossing, it will have to be just a day or two and back. Agreed?"

"Okay, I'll stock up on berries. Let's go."

Just 200 meters into the strait and the current sweeps us westwards. Our efforts to return to the Riven Peninsula are in vain, leaving us no choice but to tack southwards with the flow in the hope of reaching landfall further down the North Falcate peninsula. By evening, we safely moor on the new continent, somewhat unsure of what to do next.

"Julia, if this planet is anything like Earth, I suspect that the current is a northern hemisphere circular flow within the Salacia Ocean that would take us back to East Riven just north of the equator. I noticed that the current along the coastline of East Riven was flowing in an easterly direction. This here must be the counter flow."

"That sounds logical. I suggest we follow the coastline of North Falcate to its western end and then launch into the return flow. We may even get back home earlier than we need to."

"If we run out of provisions we will have to ask Dmitri to use a drone to dispatch more. Actually, I think I will send him a message now. He can send provisions to the westerly end of Falcate. We can meet the drone there."

That done and a confirming message is enough to set us on our way. The topography is quite different along this stretch as we hug the coast, but Julia is quick to point out that there are no Betilla along the way to dialog with. Interestingly, the seagulls lack the Nexus, so we are limited to negotiating the coastline without the aid of seeing ahead. After a week, we arrive at the westerly extremity of Falcate only half a day ahead of the drone, which followed the same route we traversed. Unsurprisingly, Julia agitates for an excursion into the Middle Sea. The calm waters of the sea beckon enticingly and I can only offer weak resistance since we now have enough provisions for the return trip assuming we can follow the easterly current along the equator all the way back home. The Middle Sea has an alluring azure color and the shore shows signs of forces released on the planet from the meteor impact that the Betilla mentioned; sheer cliffs and tumbling rock-strewn mountainsides line the way.

There is something mysterious about Iris Island, which I know is Julia's unspoken destination wish. The island has long intrigued her, not least since it marks ground-zero of the meteor impact. To save time I decide to head straight for the island.

In our approach, the tip of the island shimmers like a mirage above the brilliant blue, mirror-flat sea. Not a breath of wind disturbs the view as our vessel plows through the stillness. Julia is first to notice the iridescent effects from Betilla as the shoreline meets our line of sight. Unexpectedly, there is a population of Betilla here.

She startles me with a shout. "Stop! Can you go back a little?"

Without hesitation, I reverse a stretch and we wallow in the calm.

"What is it?"

"Something is different. Let me think… Yes! I think I know what it is. Remember when we first got access to their mind. It was compartmentalized; sort of by subject matter, so organized. It immediately struck me as unusual. This is different. I tuned into what they are actually thinking. Go forward again, just slowly."

I inch the vessel forward until the island is again partially visible.

"Yes, I see what you mean. They blocked us from this part of their mind. It was previously like a library of facts; a memory bank as opposed to active thought processes. What can it mean?"

"Okay! Just retreat again. I need to think about this."

Back out of sight, we ponder the strangeness of what we witnessed.

"Julia, it seems like they are unaware of our presence here. Remember, we never intended to come this far. In fact, we thought the southern tip of the East Riven Peninsula was as far as we would go."

"Yes, and the seagulls along the North Falcate coast didn't have the Nexus. I suspect they have just recently arrived on the Falcate Continent. Our drone survey found no Betilla here but that was years ago. My guess is that they are just now starting out on Iris Island."

"You are probably right. They cannot know that we are here. If they intercepted my message to Dmitri, they would think we are on the westerly edge of North Falcate. Thinking we are elsewhere, they dropped their guard and the parts of their mind that were blocked are now open for us to see."

"I'm intrigued to know what they are thinking. If we edge closer we may be able to listen in."

What we glean is both alarming and fascinating.

Julia's alarm is evident as she learns that she features prominently in their thought patterns. Disconcertedly she proclaims, "Look, they know about the oak tree in the center of Lillington which marks the center of England. I have never mentioned this to them. The only way they could know is if they have access to my mind. There is nothing they don't know about what I think and experience."

"I can see our meeting with Old Mkize and his accidental blinding. How can that be?"

"See there, they can even manipulate our thoughts. This is just not right!"

"They have all sorts of grandiose plans that could never be accomplished without us as vassals in their hands. They are using us. With hindsight, it explains Jabu's elaborate plans for a space elevator, all the computer development we did using quantum computers, 3D printing using biological ingredients, on and on; we alone never really had the intelligence or drive to do these things ourselves."

Gradually the alarming truth becomes evident; the iridescence now functioning in all humans on Hermes is a first step before broadening it to Earth. Their intent is complete control. The Nexus is not only what we assumed it to be – a means to access the Betilla library, extend their view of the skies to us and allow us to see what other creatures see, such as hawks and seagulls. It is actually bi-directional. It provides them with access to our minds where they insert ideas and motivations disguised as our own. Combined with the longevity and the focused energy we all now enjoy, they have effectively harnessed us to single-mindedly work on their agenda. The seagulls and hawks with Nexus are the means to extend their range, and for surveillance. When combined with the bubbles, they have coverage of most of the planet to gain access to our thoughts and influence our decisions and actions.

Iris Island is the focal point for remembering the Betilla who succumbed under the meteor strike back when Falcate was a single landmass. They plan to use the island as a launch platform for ambitious plans to expand into other parts of the solar system.

Angered by what we learn, Julia in particular feels deeply injured by the dishonesty of their actions. Understandably, her resolve is to confront them for an explanation and, if correct in our assessment, to demand a reversal of the Nexus. The consequence of this would be to slow progress to a trickle, progress that has benefited the population of Hermes. The second realization is that humans are no longer at the top of the food chain, for the first time in many millennia.

I sense Julia spiraling down a vortex of depression, as she feels responsible for what has transpired. In the hope of finding some rational explanation for what we surmise to be the truth, I encourage Julia to confront the Betilla.

As we venture into plain sight of the island, their surprise at our presence confirms our assumption that they did not expect us here. The immediate closure of access to their thought processes is the second indication that their motives are questionable. They have no alternative but to admit to the intent of complete control over the human population. We are second-rate citizens. Their belief is that they had no alternative. Inquisitiveness led them to a cursory exploration of what humans think, and their findings were so alarming that the only course of action that seemed reasonable to them was to take full control.

The fallibility knitted into human nature stood as a threat to the very existence of all life, and theirs in particular. The depth of greed, avarice, envy, wrath, gluttony, sloth, anger, hatred, discontent and other deadly sins imbedded in individuals and compounded as a group assured a future fraught with uncertainty, save for certain destruction. The counterbalance of compassion, tolerance and respect for all else will not prevail, leaving the Betilla no alternative but to take control.

With the sun setting, we come away drained and despondently turn our vessel for the return trip. Once out of sight of the island we turn the motor off and allow the craft to drift in the stillness.

With their intentions laid bare, in an act of apparent contrition – perhaps to cement their belief – they provide Julia and me with the ability to read each other's thoughts as the Betilla do with their own kind, an extension of the iridescence and the Nexus effects. They say we may extend this to others if we so choose. There is the rub. Have they committed to one final act of malevolence to secure a footing in their path to full control? Although couched, as usual, in an apparent gesture of goodwill, does it come with a deeply embedded statement of intent, destruction of humankind?

As husband and wife, the sharing of thoughts, emotions, hopes and desires indisputably offers to bring a deepening bond, but it also exposes selfish intentions, absurdities and convictions that are the reserve of the individual. Is it fair to share these? In the hands of all people, this will surely bring all manner of strife: disloyalties between individuals, groups and nations. It will provoke dysfunction at every level even nations pitted against each other. No, this is an invitation to end civilization by the quickest means possible.

In the past, I have often looked at Julia, wondering what she is thinking. Usually I look for the rationality behind decisions and experiences, look for conclusions and how these form from disparate sets of information. Expecting a calculator of sorts, one that can eliminate the superfluous and stitch together the relevant. Clarity of thought is her strength compared to the emotional jumble that circles in my brain always clutching at straws before stepping forward on uncertain ground.

To enter the mind of another person, unimpeded by externalities, to occupy the space as though it were one's own is daunting. Stepping in is at once a breach of confidentialities as it is an imposition on secrets held dear. What to expect? Is the mind a kaleidoscope of colors, pictures in abstract or is it in clear outline? Is it a set of mathematical equations where one concept leads logically to the next without form or pictorial representation? Will I be able to objectively view the contents or will I be subjectively included in the turmoil of emotions? These are the thoughts that I struggle with before entry.

Inside. I see a vast network, layer on layer, stretching from the forefront to the distance like a hall of parallel mirrors. Swirling emotions mixed with logic as hopes, ambitions, fears, feelings, memories and ideas float back and forth, each presented in abstract shades of colour and strains of music, but also a maelstrom slowly mingling. Sound, touch, sight, taste and smell pierce the mix momentarily then subside as other concepts take precedence in the kaleidoscope. In the mixture of irrationality combinations emerge, solidify and prepare for articulation.

Delving deeper, I search for the one thing that matters to me. I do not need long; there I see it. It stands separate and in firm outline; the unconditional love that Julia has for me. Thoughts seamlessly return to my own consciousness, an exit from the bidirectional conduit, and I feel the relief of having found the answer I longed for in my world that always lacked confidence.

Returning to explore Julia's repository of memory, I travel from the present to the past, where I find the shared experiences that echo those in my memory. Interspersed with my experiences I see her determination to explain the Betilla. Reaching back to a mirage of Lillington, Julia's place of birth, I see the formative years; playfully innocent under the great oak in the center of the village in the middle of England. I see the sadness at finding the fallen tree, the decision to emigrate to Canada and the matching evolution of her art and music. The discovery of Hermes is etched in bold as are her findings related to the Betilla; pride in these accomplishments is clear but she attaches an equal share of the acknowledgments to our group.

As we return from our excursions into each other's private world an unspoken deepening of our relationship is evident. We hold each other in an embrace that surpasses previous intimacies. There is a silent question of the Betilla's intended purpose, a rare gift, to be treasured, or some new form of control of us as a pair even if we do not share it with others?

"Julia, we have decisions to make. Do we keep this or share it and what do we tell the others when we get back?"

"Can you imagine the chaos if we tell the others. Some will want the Nexus removed despite all the advances we have made and others will want to continue with it."

"Can we agree that this mind sharing thing stops here?"

"Yes, that is definitely a no-no. What about keeping it between us?"

"I suggest that we continue for a while longer and if it is problematic we can ask for its removal."

"Okay, that sounds reasonable but we should not tell the others about it."

"As for telling the others about the Betilla's control over us. I suppose we have no alternative but to be open with them and tell them. Let the chips fall where they must."

"Yes, I agree."

Dawn comes with a fresh breeze behind our backs which quickly brings us to the gateway out of the Middle Sea where North and South Falcate reach down to cliffs on either side of the exit. As expected a westerly current sweeps along parallel to the equator and with days to spare before our rations are used up we make landfall on East Riven. We idle along the coast to New Greenwich to delay the inevitable meeting with our friends, carrying our disquieting news.

The usual welcoming return greets us, postponing the need to explain but as the excitement of relaying the path of the journey, the sites seen and the spread of flora, fauna, fish and birds, we inevitably reach Dmitri's provision drop at the entrance to Middle Sea in our narrative of the trip. There is an air of expectancy for, just as I knew that the Middle Sea held a special intrigue for Julia, so too do the others. We hesitate.

Jabu questions, "So, tell us about the Middle Sea. You can't tell me you didn't go there, surely."

Robin joins in, "Why the hesitation? Come on, were there dragons or sea monsters?"

Julia and I turn to each other. Inexplicably we feel a mental block that intrudes in our minds. I can see her struggling to articulate the news but nothing comes, like someone who has experienced a traumatic incident and subconsciously suppresses the event in their memory. I decide to take the lead but cannot find the words to explain what happened. Only moments pass for us to realize the impasse.

Dmitri however notices the flicker of confusion in our eyes and with concern asks, "Is something worrying you? Did something happen there? You know you can tell us."

Before we can dispel his concerns, Robin interjects, "Have you had another experience with the Betilla?"

I decide that we need to quash this in no uncertain terms otherwise it will be a lingering problem. Julia and I need to discuss our reticence before we provide an explanation.

"Oh no, it is nothing really. Stranded as we were, we were unable to return on the journey along the same route that we came on. It was quite nerve racking. Initially, we had no idea whether you would be able to send supplies before we ran out."

Julia adds, "The provisions arrive later in the day that we arrived. It was quite a relief."

"Yes and we then took a short trip into Middle Sea. The water was as flat as a mirror."

They accept the explanation but I can see skepticism on Robin's face and echoed on Lilian's but they say nothing further. Robin was so right about the Betilla having some alternative agenda.

Once alone Julia's agitation is clear, she says, "They, the damn Betilla, have blocked us from relating what happened. Look, I will prove it to you."

She takes the computer and begins typing a description of what transpired at Middle Sea. Her hands begin shaking and meaningless words appear on the screen. Continuing she then enters the words, 'It has been a nice day', and these words flow unrestricted. My attempts produce the same pattern. The Betilla are effectively preventing us from carrying a warning in any form to humanity.

"Julia, it seems like there is nothing we can do about it. People will go on believing they are accomplishing great things in collaboration with the Betilla whereas the work is largely at the Betilla's behest."

"It is a difficult pill to swallow. I have spent so much time cultivating a relationship with them only to find that they think they are so superior, that they can dictate what happens here. I realize that they are, even now, listening in to this conversation and following what we think but they may as well know it, I will work to undermine their plans."

"Yes. I think that would be a better use of your time and energy. You could very easily sink into depression if you dwell on their callous disregard for you and all you have done."

"Thanks Miles. I do appreciate your understanding. On a slightly different matter but related; I think we should persist with this ability to read each other's thoughts. It is a comfort."

"I agree, I also need it for now."

34

JUSTICE

The weeks and months that follow are a hollow image of former times. An inner vibrancy is scoured from our beings by the duplicity. We cannot shake the sense of helplessness at what to do. At every turn, we grasp at straws. Solutions that offer hope inevitably come to naught and we again languish in denial as a temporary reprieve. Both Julia and I withdraw into cocoons, regurgitating options only to return empty-handed. Efforts by our friends to revive us only increase their perplexity at a lack of explanation. Finally, we decide to separate ourselves by moving to temporary accommodation built at short notice beyond the promontory from which we witnessed so much. Here, somewhat out of reach of the Betilla unless Nexus hawks or seagulls are overhead, we shelter to think.

With the resumption of interplanetary travel, visiting scientists frequent our shores and Julia is a sought-after person as the pre-eminent expert on the Betilla. We sometimes host them in our accommodation to answer questions and exchange information. This offers Julia some solace, by downplaying the virtues of the Betilla, but we are constrained to be explicit on our reasons. It nevertheless allows us to sow a seed of doubt in the visitors, a minor chink in the armor undermining the Betilla's control plans.

Robin, shielded for much of the time from the Betilla by wearing his polarized glasses, retains a sense of objectivity not common among the others. He and Lilian, who also takes to wearing glasses, piece together a semblance of what we are experiencing at the hands of the Betilla. Robin dwells on this as a potential explanation of what he continues to see as the questionable motives of the Betilla, but is not able to pinpoint the extent of it.

At one of the Management Committee meetings, the Betilla obliquely initiate a discussion on the possibility of Earth too receiving the Nexus. When the group takes it up for serious consideration, alerted, I find myself silenced to comment on their subversive intent. Fortunately, Robin vacillates, prompting a deferment of a decision to a future meeting. I decide to invite Robin and Lilian to our residence on the pretext of socializing.

In seclusion from the probing presence of the Betilla, I broach the awkward exchange. I can only hint at what concerns us, "Robin, do you have any news of the Betilla on Earth. Are they flourishing?"

Robin answers from behind his protective glasses, "Not much, but as you know there are only small pockets of them where you established them."

Julia lets me proceed as she follows my thought pattern.

"Yes, they are nowhere nearly as widespread as here on Hermes."

Robin takes the bait and elaborates on the discussion at the meeting. "If they were to spread the Nexus there it would be a major logistical exercise with people funneled through to each site for the fragrance. Quite an undertaking."

Lilian adds, "Robin and I are against spreading the Nexus there. As Robin has said on many occasions, they must have ulterior motives. We still don't know what that may be, so we need more time to think about it before proceeding with it."

I reply, "We have quite a number of scientists visiting us to learn more about the Betilla and their methods."

Robin immediately latches on to this. "Good point! It attracts them to Hermes to exchange knowledge on a wide range of subject matter. They would have no reason to come here if they had the Nexus there on Earth."

At the Management meeting, the matter comes up again and this time Robin directs the conversation, reiterating our discussion.

I watch Graham, who we all know has been fixated on making Hermes a destination for specialists. He squirms undecided, clearly under the spell of the Betilla, who must be internally prompting him to deviate from his usual stand.

The Betilla interject, "As per our constitution, should this be referred to a referendum?"

They know that they can steer the outcome to their liking through a referendum, just as they have me under a spell that prevents me from taking a contrary stand.

Robin, however, is up to the challenge. "It is not really a question that we on Hermes can answer. The people on Earth should make the call. It is after all their lives that are impacted."

Jabu rejoins, "Yes, true. The problem with that is that it would be impossible to conduct a worldwide referendum. The range of literacy is extensive and political lines will prevent cross-border coordination. No, that would simply not work."

Robin adds, "Yes, and add to that the catastrophes they have suffered. No, it just will not fly. Even the UN could not carry off such a project."

Jabu ends the conversation. "Okay, let's move on to other matters."

My relief must have been apparent, but I manage to contain myself until later to share our small victory with Julia. She is clearly pleased but undeterred in finding other means to undermine their control of the very essence of us as a species, our minds.

Hermes is an island of control and in the context of aboriginal rights, which should arguably fall to the Betilla. Some consolation comes with knowing that humankind is indispensable to their plans here on Hermes, but Earth should remain firmly the preserve of humankind. Where Julia took a more pragmatic approach to her relationship with the Betilla following the imposition of longevity on the populace, she now fatalistically studies them as objects for learning, devoid of an emotional bond. Withdrawn in to a reclusive shell, she is impassive to all but our closest associates. She keenly observes every move of the Betilla, looking for an opportunity to correct the injustices for which she still feels partly responsible.

35

EARTH

Climate, disease and asteroid catastrophes reduced Earth's population to two billion people, a fifth the number at its peak. The longevity brought by the Betilla contains the population at this number, with people experiencing the improved living conditions that smaller families bring.

The climate remains stable under arrested global warming conditions. The Betilla continue to play an important role in this regard and in maintaining clean oceans, free of the pollution of plastics.

A new appreciation for the diversity of life on Earth has taken root, with large areas of the land and oceans dedicated to nature and out of bounds to humans.

Environmentally harmful industries operate exclusively from space, where Earth dominates the technology for harvesting materials from asteroids, comets and the moons of Jupiter and Saturn. To facilitate this, propulsion technology has shortened trip durations and artificial intelligence combined with automation forms the backbone of industry. Modeled on the space elevator on Hermes, Earth too began work on an elevator bringing the riches of space to Earth without the harmful effects on the environment.

Political and religious differences, once so malignant, now function productively, having matured under the effects of sufferings that knew no such boundaries.

36

MARS

Mars remains locked in the embrace of cold and after decades of searches, living forms of life continue to elude investigations. Instead, evidence is found of the presence of bacteria in a watery past at least three billion years ago.

The planet specializes in extraction and export of minerals to Earth and Hermes. Three space elevators centered on mineral rich areas along the equator, constructed under contract to Hermes' elevator specialists, reduce the cost of taking cargo to space.

A small hardy community of multi-national employees direct automated mining technologies that help the colony sustain itself using local resources. Volcanoes and impact craters hold significant deposits of nickel, copper, iron, titanium, cobalt, platinum and clay-like minerals common in the surface soils to facilitate the production of ceramics for pottery. Silicon dioxide, a common and basic constituent of glass, enables the production of fiberglass to build various structures. Five of the ten most expensive minerals on Earth are found in abundance on Mars.

Mars supports thirty thousand people in domed cities near each of the elevators. Three space mirrors, one for each elevator, focus sunlight to heat land adjoining the settlements to provide subterranean melt water, thereby alleviating the need to mine for ice to meet the one essential requirement to support life. The poles hold ice lakes near the surface. A facility established at the North Pole uses the water in combination with atmospheric carbon dioxide to provide some of the raw materials to produce oxygen, plastics, hydrogen fuels and methane. Automated mining operations load the output onto conveyor systems for transport over land to populated areas for use on Mars or for export.

37

BETILLA

The march of progress continued unabated on Hermes. Men and women slavishly followed the Betilla's dream and with time, two more space elevators, modeled on the first, added to the compliment; one anchored at Iris Island and the other off the Farland continent. On completing each of the elevators, the adult Betilla immediately began constructing a labyrinth of castles within the reservoirs over-looking the planet below and in the pinnacles of each elevator with a view of space.

As their numbers increased, the resolution of their images of space improved. The space elevators extended the habitable area of humans and Betilla beyond the confines of the planet. For the Betilla, the telescopic base from which they view the universe widened from the diameter of the planet to the extent of the reservoirs on Dais 1, 2 and 3; and the light-gathering aperture widened by fifty to sixty thousand kilometers.

With the enhanced optics, their gaze turned to the inner reaches of Orion's Arm of the Milky Way galaxy. Here, their origin, half a billion years ago when their two home stars combined in a cata-strophic supernova and flung Hermes into the void of interstellar space, stands changed, no longer the binary star system with its coterie of planets. Now a sole star burns, spewing lethal radiation as it spins on its axis, one thousand times in a second, a clear signature of a Standard Candle with its characteristic high rotation rate. Like all such objects, they provide the Betilla with a known luminosity or absolute magnitude, enabling them to determine the distance to the object with a great degree of accuracy. As in this case, this class of object is formed when two stars in a binary system orbit in close proximity to each other and one of the two stars siphons enough material from its partner and ultimately explodes and is incinerated. How strange it is that the Betilla can vouch for this theory based on their own experience. In the following formula, the distance D (in cm) is calculated from the apparent magnitude:

$m = M - 97.5 + 5xlog(D)$.

The calculation provides a precise measure of its distance at 40.43 light years away, a testament to their long journey through the void.

A second curiosity intrigues them: what is the fate of life, if any remains, on the fragments of their planet, remnants from the bombardment they suffered while in their home system? To find out the Betilla conduct a test of Schrodinger's paradox. They use deeply entangled elemental particles created at the same time but now separated by the distance from the home star and our solar system. Since the mathematics implies that a measurement on one immediately influences the other, regardless of the distance between them, if successful, they could strike up a rudimentary conversation with them.

By toggling a local particle between an off and on state, they hope to elicit a corresponding response from the other location. If successful, it will imply intelligent activity at the other end. The test reveals no activity despite trying multiple particles using entangled pairs from their distant past. Repetition using other particles also produces no response. Undaunted, they decide to use particles from the Middle Sea area of Hermes at the foot of the Iris Elevation.

Systematically working through the material they try, and try again; still no response. Then, just when they are about to abandon the effort, thinking they are the sole survivors, they detect a response on one particle. With rising interest, they listen, repeating the effort from other locales on Hermes. Triangulating to find the source, they narrow the range closer and closer to a pinpoint. Then using optics, they see an object tumbling headlong in the void beyond the outer reaches of our solar system, moving away at a significant speed. Focusing their sights, they resolve an object, blackened white 230 X 35 meters in extent. Trapped within the ice, their brethren survived the catastrophe cocooned in a form of hibernation with limited mobility on a splinter of Hermes. Thrust into the void on a parallel path, but as chance would have it, the splinter was not captured by the gravity of our sun and has no chance of retrieval. They listen but without hope, offering encouragement to endure and to await their fate.

A second signal penetrates the discussion using a different particle, this from closer quarters judging by the triangular displacement. Tracking the source, they narrow the search until, with optical resolution they see the splinter, three kilometers in diameter and circling Jupiter in retrograde orbit.

Julia wastes no time to make the connection. In her mind, she asks the Betilla whether these two interstellar objects are the ones detected years earlier, Nuntius 4I/2047 U1 and 3I/2045 BZ1. They confirm this. The splinters are from the final reign of terror while in the frozen outer wasteland of their home system. They suffered impacts that must have stripped these two from the Middle Sea impact zone. Julia silently recalls the dearth of Betilla activity on land adjoining the Middle Sea. Here stands evidence of the horror the Betilla endured in that distant time. It explains the crater-shaped impact area, the two sickle-shaped continents of North and South Falcate facing each other and, strikingly, Iris Island formed by the rebounding center of the crater, in the middle of the sea.

News of the subset of Betilla circling Jupiter receives immediate interest from a group of Betilla watchers on Earth. Endeared by these seemingly remarkable creatures and taken to following their habits, they propose towing the object to safety and uniting them with their fellows either on Earth or on Hermes. A more audacious counter-proposition comes from the Betilla themselves. They suggest towing the fragment to Mars and anchoring it in geo-stationary orbit near one of the elevators. Because of the size of the object, it holds a significant amount of water. From its anchored position, with the ice thawed using a plutonium heat source, a conveyance can be provisioned down the tubes in the elevator cable to a domed pond at the foot of the elevator with a reservoir at the top. The space mirrors will maintain the liquid state for the water at the base of the elevator, enabling the Betilla to work their transformational magic, a start to the greening of Mars.

The Mars community wasted no time in pursuing this endeavor and within ten years, the first stream of Betilla arrived in the pond at the base and the terra-formation of Mars begins. In a parallel project, comets harnessed for the other two elevators, provided a water source to the settlements below and additional Betilla habitats.

Initial attempts at terraforming Mars failed and the plans relegated to the distant future on the hope that technology would evolve to the point of feasibility. When the Betilla established a presence on the surface, these plans were revived and actioned posthaste. Repeating the lessons in the greening of Hermes, planetary temperatures are rising and pockets of cold-tolerant desert vegetation are evident across warmer reaches near the equator. Lakes established from comets, with frozen surfaces but liquid underneath, dot this area and contribute to supply the needs of the habitants.

Julia and I watch these events with interest, wondering whether this is an opportunistic extension of their intensions at domination.

38

RESOLUTION

Over the years that follow, Julia continues to observe their ways and notes a subtle change in their behavior. Where once they struggled to understand love between human partners or enmity between individuals, now, with three separate populations of Betilla, one on Hermes, one on Earth and another on Mars, divergent and independent norms begin to arise in each population. There are even minor differences between Hermes groups at Riven, Falcate and Farland. They argued about the Iris Island site, whether it should be preserved untouched as a memorial to the deaths that followed the meteor strike in bygone eons, or developed as the anchor for the space elevator that was later built.

The Betilla on Earth and Mars, where they are in the minority in relation to humans, begin to understand the rich fabric that makes up the human psyche. Their resilience and fortitude under dire conditions, inventiveness in striving to overcome obstacles, compassion for those less fortunate, capacity to forgive and forget those that wrong them and a yearning for a brighter future stand as evidence of their remarkable nature. By contrast, the Betilla on Hermes, who only have a distant view of life on Earth and see the stark global effects of humans on the planet, from which they extrapolate a dystopian future degenerating into self-destruction, take a more paternalistic approach, wanting to control outcomes.

Eventually, they share these disparate viewpoints with Julia and for the first time acknowledge and embrace the value in compromise and trust, the transcendental power of love and forgiveness. Julia takes the opportunity to challenge them on the need to delve into the consciousness of people and the stunting consequences of not trusting people to resolve differences through trial and error.

Subsequently, they lift the intrusive elements of Nexus, quietly and unostentatiously. Julia and I alone know the extent of their infringement on our privacy and find relief in their recognition of wrongs now rectified. To savor the moment, we sit on a rocky outcrop on our promontory to relish the new calm, after the inner turmoil that plagued us for so long.

Lying in the warm grass, gazing upwards, we see the immense glowing crystalline octagonal pyramid overhead. Suspended in space, a chandelier inconceivable in its proportions back in the days of Windy Hill, it performs a leisurely pirouette in its majestic dance. Dais has expanded and is reaching high above the founding platform. From its zenith the towering pillar rises, the center of a carousel radiating outwards. Below Dais a steady stream of lights mark the passage of pods on the cable, ascending or descending as people and Betilla come and go. Then looking eastwards, the Betilla emerge from their turrets at sea and circle us in a pattern reminiscent of the first engagement when they displayed the solar system to our intrigue. This time we see the missing planet Hermes in the display of the constellation and understand the unity in our love for this corner of the universe. When the light fades, we wander the well-trodden path to the village and there Jabu, Robin, Lilian, Dmitri and Ella, our dear forbearing friends, notice the change in us and like long lost friends welcome our return to normality in unspoken understanding of the lifting of a barrier.

Age has finally caught up with us. We are graying. The effects of longevity having run their course, we are content with our friends each so special to us. With over 400 years passed, aging resumes its natural course and our end is in sight.

39

EPILOGUE

The events of the past century transformed the solar system beyond recognition. Stemming from millions of years and many, many light years away, Destiny contrived to intervene in our corner of the universe. Humbled at the certainty of the pervasiveness of life in the universe, intelligent or not, the anthropic throne as center no longer belongs to us. Sharing it with the Betilla comes with the realization that even this is likely a manifestation of the tip of the iceberg in which teaming hordes are out there to challenge for the crown. Fermi may no longer ask, "Where are they?"

Distance, at least for now, insulates us from intervention by other beings, and on this basis, we can but make the best of what we have. We have taken one small step up the rung of maturity as Hermes, Mars and Earth stand more cohesive than before, casting aside differences. The Betilla are now truly partners in all we do.

39.1

HERMES

Our pristine world, declared a nature preserve, supports three settlements along the equator, each serviced by a space elevator.

The original, called the Pearl Elevation, is named after the Pearl Islands where it is anchored, which is off the coast of Riven at the village of New Greenwich representing longitude zero, the meridian on which the planet bases its time.

The second is named Iris Elevation after its base at the Iris Island, in the center of the Middle Sea separating the continents of North and South Falcate, with the village of Crescent nearby on North Falcate.

The third, Summation Elevation, is named after the Summation Peninsula, a sigma shaped southward extension of the continent of Farland with the town of Sigma on the mainland.

The three elevators reach up to Dais platforms One, Two and Three. These are connected to each other by the Tripartite Bridge, an iridescent double tubed cable, similar to the elevation cables. This globe-spanning structure circles the entire planet at an elevation of thirty thousand kilometers to transport people and Betilla in ferries between the platforms. It took fifty years to complete.

The three daises each support layers within them that alternate between Betilla aquariums and platforms for humans. They form crystalline octagonal shaped pyramids extending upwards, each to a pinnacle at the top where a rotating carousel radiates outwards to simulate gravity for people who live, work and play at the extremities. They support complete communities of residents and visitors to Hermes. Arms of docking stations extend outwards from the base of each pyramid to welcome flights from Earth and Mars. From here visitors enter the labyrinth above to proceed to quarters in the carousel or descend to the surface of the planet.

Hermes now supports a population of three hundred thousand people, equally shared across the three settlements.

At the foot of each elevator an adjoining lounge welcomes guests and residents, who can opt to receive the genetic receptors and transmitters. One hundred percent of the residents have elected to acquire the capability of the Nexus. Visitors leaving Hermes have the feature removed on exiting the departure area.

Hermes is an interplanetary destination for an array of disciplines, a leader in astronomy, space elevation, solar energy, quantum mechanics, biological computing, genetic engineering and music. Scientists, tourists and the simply curious visit to learn more and explore or participate.

39.1.1

HERMES SPACE ELEVATORS

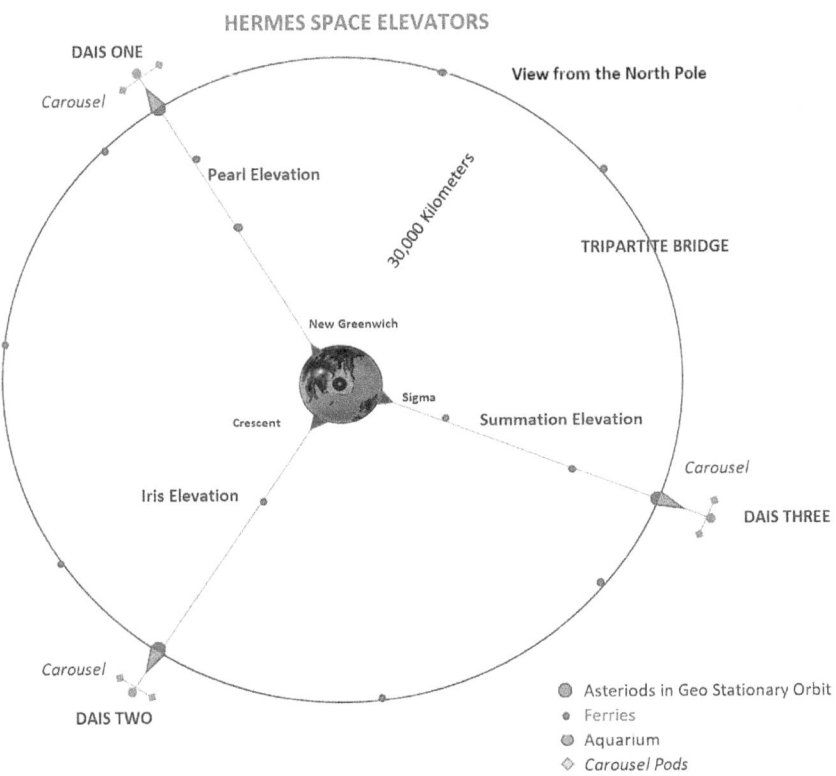

39.1.2

CENTRAL HEMISPHERE

North Pole

- West Riven
- East Riven
- The Rent
- New Greenwich and the Podium
- The Pearl Islands and the foot of The Pearl Elevation
- Dracon Peninsula and Islands
- Oceana
- Salacia Ocean

South Pole

39.1.3

WESTERN HEMISPHERE

North Pole

South Pole

- Farland
- West Farland
- Sigma City
- Foot of Summation Elevation and Summation Peninsula
- Hadean Ocean
- Salacia Ocean

39.1.4

EASTERN HEMISPHERE

North Pole

- Priscoan Ocean
- North Falcate
- Crescent City
- Foot of Iris Elevation and Iris Island
- Middle Sea
- South Falcate

South Pole

39.2

VENUS

On hearing about the bacteria and archaic life forms that survive at the superheated hydrothermal vents in the mid-Atlantic, the Betilla, supported by scientists, acquired samples. Held in specialized containers, they re-engineered them to sequestrate sulfuric acid and carbon dioxide from the atmosphere of Venus. This work is ongoing and surface temperatures have begun falling from the mean of 462 degrees Celsius in the twenty-five years since their release into the atmosphere. The reversal of the runaway greenhouse effect holds the promise of one day enabling the terraforming of the surface.

The Betilla, who adapted to withstand the harsh extremes of binary suns in their home solar system, are preparing a giant reservoir above Dais 2 to transport many of their kind to inhabit the planet when it is ready.

39.3

ENCELADUS

Even Enceladus, the sixth largest moon of Saturn, which holds a globe-spanning liquid ocean below a frozen surface, offers the prospect of establishing a colony of Betilla. The complex macromolecular organics in the ocean will provide food for their partners the algae and moss. An atmosphere of air, trapped in a bubble underneath the ice cap, will sustain the moss and juvenile Betilla on the ceiling of the space during this stage of their lifecycle.

The internal heat of the rocky core sustains the warmth of the ocean at a temperature that is well above the required metabolism level that the Betilla endured during their torpor through the cold of the void. As such, they are well adapted for the expected climate.

A plutonium heat source will secure a molten exit through the frozen surface to provide access to a docking area and harbor for visiting spacecraft.

This will establish an outpost to the farther reaches of the solar system for research and as a staging area for exploratory missions.

40

DIMENSIONS

The following dimensions apply to each of the planets:

	Mars	Earth	Hermes
Year (Pre-Hermes)	687 Days	365 Days	
Year (Post-Hermes)	756 Days	328 Days	567 Days
% + -	10.0%	-10.0%	
Earth Year	1.88	1.00	1.41
Trip Duration from Earth	261 Days	-	151 Days
Pre-Hermes Trip Duration from Earth	200 Days	-	-

Every 3 to 4 years Hermes and Earth are nearest opposition.
One day = 24 Hours on Earth (Used in the above stated periods)
One day = 26 Hours on Hermes

41

ABOUT THE AUTHOR

The background described in this book reaches back to Maurice's early life and in many respects depicts real experiences around which the futuristic story of tranquility and chaos are woven.

At university, the study of Business Economics, Information Systems and Marketing Management prepared him for a career as project manager. He developed extensive experience in proposing corporate computer systems and the installation and support of them.

In this fast-changing environment it was always necessary to stay abreast of the latest trends and apply these in a pragmatic way that ensured a return on investments for the stakeholders.

For Maurice, with the demands of a career in the corporate world addressed, a standout subject at university was astronomy. There to test the practical application of computer science, quantitative methods and statistics, it led to an interest in astronomy.

Inherent in the drive to understand what technology held for the future, a parallel was found in the incredible advances in astronomy and our understanding of the universe. This enticed Maurice into this, his first excursion into fiction, and plausible science fiction in particular.

Email Address: maurice.schmidt@telus.net

Website: https://storylinebooks.com

42

REVIEW

Please take time to review the book on your supplier's website and drop me a line in an email. It helps fledging authors establish a footing in this competitive field. Your support is appreciated.

Be assured that I will read your review.

Thank you.

Maurice Schmidt